I0663294

Leatherface

A Tale of Old Flanders

Baroness Emmuska Orczy

Leatherface: A Tale of Old Flanders

Copyright © 2020 Bibliotech Press
All rights reserved

ISBN: 978-1-64799-115-9

CONTENTS

PROLOGUE

MONS: SEPTEMBER, 1572

It lacked two hours before the dawn on this sultry night early in September. The crescent moon had long ago sunk behind a bank of clouds in the west, and not a sound stirred the low-lying land around the besieged city.

To the south the bivouac fires of Alva's camp had died out one by one, and here the measured tread of the sentinels on their beat alone broke the silence of the night. To the north, where valorous Orange with a handful of men–undisciplined, unpaid and rebellious–vainly tried to provoke his powerful foe into a pitched battle, relying on God for the result, there was greater silence still. The sentinels–wearied and indifferent–had dropped to sleep at their post: the troops, already mutinous, only held to their duty by the powerful personality of the Prince, slept as soundly as total indifference to the cause for which they were paid to fight could possibly allow.

In his tent even Orange–tired out with ceaseless watching–had gone to rest. His guards were in a profound sleep.

Then it was that from the south there came a stir, and from Alva's entrenchments waves of something alive that breathed in the darkness of the night were set in motion, like when the sea rolls inwards to the shore.

Whispered words set this living mass on its way, and anon it was crawling along–swiftly and silently–more silently than incoming waves on a flat shore–on and on, always northwards in the direction of the Prince of Orange's camp, like some gigantic snake that creeps with belly close to the ground.

"Don Ramon," whispered a voice in the darkness, "let Captain Romero deal with the sentinels and lead the surprise attack, whilst you yourself make straight for the Prince's tent; overpower his guard first, then seize his person. Two hundred ducats will be your reward, remember, if you bring Orange back here–a prisoner–and a ducat for each of your men."

These were the orders and don Ramon de Linea sped forward with six hundred arquebusiers–all picked men–they wore their shirts over their armour, so that in the mêlée which was to come they might recognise one another in the gloom.

Less than a league of flat pasture land lay between Alva's entrenchments at St. Florian near the gates of beleaguered Mons, and Orange's camp at Hermigny. But at St. Florian men stirred and planned and threatened, whilst at Hermigny even the sentinels slept. Noble-hearted Orange had raised the standard of revolt against the most execrable oppression of an entire people which the world has ever known–and he could not get more than a handful of patriots to fight for their own freedom against the tyranny and the might of Spain, whilst mercenary troops were left to guard the precious life of the indomitable champion of religious and civil liberties.

The moving mass of de Linea's arquebusiers had covered half a league of the intervening ground; their white shirts only just distinguishable in the gloom made them look like ghosts; only another half-league–less perhaps–separated them from their goal, and still no one stirred in Orange's camp. Then it was that something roused the sentinels from their sleep. A rough hand shook first one then the others by the shoulder, and out of the gloom a peremptory voice whispered hurriedly:

"Quick! awake! sound the alarm! An encamisada is upon you. You will all be murdered in your sleep."

And even before the drowsy sentinels had time to rouse themselves or to rub their eyes, the same rough hand had shaken the Prince's guard, the same peremptory voice had called: "Awake! the Spaniards are upon you!"

In the Prince's tent a faint light was glimmering. He himself was lying fully dressed and armed upon a couch. At sound of the voice, of his guards stirring, of the noise and bustle of a wakening camp, he sat up just in time to see a tall figure in the entrance of his tent.

The feeble light threw but into a dim relief this tall figure of a man, clad in dark, shapeless woollen clothes wearing a hood of the same dark stuff over his head and a leather mask over his face.

"Leatherface!" exclaimed the Prince as he jumped to his feet. "What is it?"

"A night attack," replied a muffled voice behind the mask. "Six hundred arquebusiers–they are but half a league away!–I would have been here sooner only the night is so infernally dark, I caught my foot in a rabbit-hole and nearly broke my ankle–I am as lame as a Jew's horse ... but still in time," he added as he hastily helped the Prince to adjust his armour and straighten out his clothes.

The camp was alive now with call to arms and rattle of steel, horses snorting and words of command flying to and fro. Don Ramon de Linea, a quarter of a league away, heard these signs of troops well on the alert and he knew that the surprise attack had failed. Six hundred arquebusiers–though they be picked men–were not sufficient for a formal attack on the Prince of Orange's entire cavalry. Even mercenary and undisciplined troops will fight valiantly when their lives depend upon their valour. De Linea thought it best to give the order to return to camp.

And the waves of living men which had been set in motion an hour ago, now swiftly and silently went back the way they came. Don Ramon when he came once more in the camp at St. Florian and in the presence of Alva's captain-in-chief, had to report the failure of the night attack which had been so admirably planned.

"The whole camp at Hermigny was astir," he said as he chawed the ends of his heavy moustache, for he was sorely disappointed. "I could not risk an attack under those conditions. Our only chance of winning was by surprise."

"Who gave the alarm?" queried don Frederic de Toledo, who took no pains to smother the curses that rose to his lips.

"The devil, I suppose," growled don Ramon de Linea savagely.

And out at Hermigny—in Orange's tent—the man who was called Leatherface was preparing to go as quietly and mysteriously as he had come.

"They won't be on you, Monseigneur," he said, "now that they know your troops are astir. But if I were you," he added grimly, "I would have every one of those sentinels shot at dawn. They were all of them fast asleep when I arrived."

He gave the military salute and would have turned to go without another word but that the Prince caught him peremptorily by the arm:

"In the meanwhile, Messire, how shall I thank you again?" he asked.

"By guarding your precious life, Monseigneur," replied the man simply. "The cause of freedom in the Low Countries would never survive your loss."

"Well!" retorted the Prince of Orange with a winning smile, "if that be so, then the cause of our freedom owes as much to you as it does to me. Is it the tenth time—or the twelfth—that you have saved my life?"

"Since you will not let me fight with you..."

"I'll let you do anything you wish, Messire, for you would be as fine a soldier as you are a loyal friend. But are you not content with the splendid services which you are rendering to us now? Putting aside mine own life—which mayhap is not worthless—how many times has your warning saved mine and my brother's troops from surprise attacks? How many times have Noircarmes' or don Frederic's urgent appeals for reinforcements failed, through your intervention, to reach the Duke of Alva until our own troops were able to rally? Ah, Messire, believe me! God Himself has chosen you for this work!"

"The work of a spy, Monseigneur," said the other not without a touch of bitterness.

"Nay! if you call yourself a spy, Messire, then shall the name of 'spy' be henceforth a name of glory to its wearer, synonymous with the loftiest patriotism and noblest self-sacrifice."

He held out his hand to the man with the mask, who bent his tall figure over it in dutiful respect.

"You see how well I keep to my share of the compact, Messire.

Never once–even whilst we were alone–hath your name escaped my lips."

"For which act of graciousness, Monseigneur, I do offer you my humble thanks. May God guard your Highness through every peril! The cause of justice and of liberty rests in your hands."

After another deeply respectful bow he finally turned to go. He had reached the entrance of the tent when once more the Prince spoke to him.

"When shall I see you again–Leatherface?" he asked cheerily.

"When your Highness' precious life or the safety of your army are in danger," replied the man.

"God reward you!" murmured Orange fervently as the man with the mask disappeared into the night.

BOOK ONE

BRUSSELS

CHAPTER I

THE BLOOD COUNCIL

I

Less than a month later, and tyranny is once more triumphant. Mons has capitulated, Orange has withdrawn his handful of mutinous troops into Holland, Valenciennes has been destroyed and Mechlin—beautiful, gracious, august Mechlin—with her cathedrals and her trade-halls, her ancient monuments of art and civilisation has been given over for three days to the lust and rapine of Spanish soldiery!

Three whole days! E'en now we think on those days and shudder—shudder at what we know, at what the chroniclers have told us, the sacking of churches, the pillaging of monasteries, the massacre of peaceful, harmless citizens!

Three whole days during which the worst demons that infest hell itself, the worst demons that inspire the hideous passions of men—greed, revenge and cruelty—were let loose upon the stately city whose sole offence had been that she had for twenty-four hours harboured Orange and his troops within her gates and closed them against the tyrant's soldiery!

Less than a month and Orange is a fugitive, and all the bright hopes for the cause of religious and civil freedom are once more dashed to the ground. It seems as if God Himself hath set His face against the holy cause! Mons has fallen and Mechlin is reduced to ashes, and over across the borders the King of France has caused ten thousand of his subjects to be massacred—one holy day, the feast of St. Bartholomew—ten thousand of them!—just because their religious beliefs did not coincide with his own. The appalling news drove Orange and his small army to flight—he had reckoned on help from the King of France—instead of that promised help the news of the massacre of ten thousand Protestants! Catholic Europe was horror-stricken at the crime committed in the name of religion; but in the Low Countries, Spanish

1

tyranny had scored a victory—the ignoble Duke of Alva triumphed and the cause of freedom in Flanders and Hainault and Brabant received a blow from which it did not again recover for over three hundred years!

II

Outwardly the house where the Duke of Alva lodged in Brussels was not different to many of the same size in the city. It was built of red brick with stone base and finely-carved cornice, and had a high slate roof with picturesque dormer windows therein. The windows on the street level were solidly grilled and were ornamented with richly-carved pediments, as was the massive doorway too. The door itself was of heavy oak, and above it there was a beautifully wrought niche which held a statue of the Virgin.

On the whole it looked a well-constructed, solid and roomy house, and Mme. de Jassy, its owner, had placed it at the disposal of the Lieutenant-Governor when first he arrived in Brussels, and he had occupied it ever since. The idler as he strolled past the house would hardly pause to look at it, if he did not happen to know that behind those brick walls and grilled windows a work of oppression more heinous than this world had ever known before, was being planned and carried on by a set of cruel and execrable tyrants against an independent country and a freedom-loving people.

Here in the dining-hall the Duke of Alva would preside at the meetings of the Grand Council—the Council of Blood—sitting in a high-backed chair which had the arms of Spain emblazoned upon it. Juan de Vargas and Alberic del Rio usually sat to right and left of him. Del Rio—indolent and yielding—a mere tool for the carrying out of every outrage, every infamy which the fiendish brain of those tyrants could devise wherewith to crush the indomitable spirit of a proud nation jealous of its honour and of its liberties: and de Vargas—Alva's double and worthy lieutenant—no tool he, but a terrible reality, active and resourceful in the invention of new forms of tyranny, new fetters for the curbing of stiff-necked Flemish and Dutch burghers, new methods for wringing rivers of gold out of a living stream of tears and blood.

De Vargas!—the very name stinks in the nostrils of honest men even after the lapse of centuries!—It conjures up the hideous image of a human bloodhound—lean and sallow of visage, with drooping, heavy-lidded eyes and flaccid mouth, a mouth that sneered and jested when men, women and children were tortured and butchered, eyes that gloated at sight of stake and scaffold and gibbet—and within the inner man, a mind intent on the science of murder and rapine and bloodshed.

2

Alva the will that commanded! Vargas the brain that devised! Del Rio the hand that accomplished!

Men sent by Philip II. of Spain, the most fanatical tyrant the world has ever known, to establish the abhorrent methods of the Spanish Inquisition in the Low Countries in order to consolidate Spanish rule there and wrest from prosperous Flanders and Brabant and Hainault, from Holland and the Dutch provinces enough gold to irrigate the thirsty soil of Spain. "The river of gold which will flow from the Netherlands to Madrid shall be a yard deep!" so had Alva boasted when his infamous master sent him to quell the revolt which had noble-hearted Orange for its leader–a revolt born of righteous indignation and an unconquerable love of freedom and of justice.

To mould the Netherlands into abject vassals of Spain, to break their independence of spirit by terrorism and by outrage, to force Spanish ideas, Spanish culture, Spanish manners, Spanish religion upon these people of the North who loathed tyranny and worshipped their ancient charters and privileges, that was the task which the Duke of Alva set himself to do–a task for which he needed the help of men as tyrannical and unscrupulous as himself.

Granvelle had begun the work, Alva was completing it! The stake, the scaffold, the gibbet for all who had one thought of justice, one desire for freedom. Mons razed to the ground, Valenciennes a heap of ruins and ashes, Mechlin a hecatomb. Men, women and children outraged and murdered! Whole families put to the torture to wring gold from unwilling givers! churches destroyed! monasteries ransacked!

That was the work of the Grand Council–the odious Council of Blood, the members of which have put to shame the very name of religion, for they dared to pretend that they acted in its name.

Alva! de Vargas! del Rio! A trinity of fiends whose deeds would shame the demons in hell! But there were others too, and, O ye gods! were they not infinitely more vile, since their hands reeked with the blood of their own kith and kin? Alva and his two bloodhounds were strangers in a strange land, owing allegiance to Spain alone–but Councillor Hessels sat on this same infamous board, and he was a patrician of Brabant. And there was Pierre Arsens, president of Artois, there was de Berlaymont and Viglius and Hopper–gentlemen (save the mark!) and burghers of Flanders or Hainault or the Dutch provinces!– and who can name such creatures without a shudder of loathing?

III

As for don Ramon de Linea, he was just the usual type of Spanish soldier–a grandee of Spain, direct descendant of the Cid, so he averred,

3

yet disdained to prove it. For in him there was no sense of chivalry—just personal bravery and no more—the same kind of bravery you would meet in a tiger or a jaguar. In truth there was much in common between don Ramon and the wild feline tribes that devastate the deserts: he had the sinuous movements, the languorous gestures of those creatures, and his eyes—dark and velvety at times, at others almost of an orange tint—had all the cruel glitter which comes into the eyes of the leopard when he is out to kill. Otherwise don Ramon was a fine-looking man, dark-skinned and dark-eyed, a son of the South, with all those cajoling ways about him which please and so often deceive the women.

He it was who had been in command at Mechlin—entrusted by General de Noircarmes with the hideous task of destroying the stately city—and he had done it with a will. Overproud of his achievements he had obtained leave to make personal report of them to the Lieutenant-Governor, and thus it was that on this 2nd day of October, 1572, he was present at the council board, talking with easy grace and no little satisfaction of all that he had done: of the churches which he had razed to the ground, the houses which he had sacked, of the men, women and children whom he had turned out naked and starving into the streets.

"We laboured hard for three days," he said, "and the troops worked with a will, for there were heavy arrears of pay due to them and we told them to make up those arrears in Mechlin, since they wouldn't get any money from headquarters. Oh! Mechlin got all that she deserved! Her accursed citizens can now repent at leisure of their haste in harbouring Orange and his rebel troops!"

His voice was deep and mellow and even the guttural Spanish consonants sounded quite soft when he spoke them. Through half-closed lids his glance swept from time to time over the eager faces around the board, and his slender hands emphasised the hideous narrative with a few graceful gestures. He looked just the true type of grand seigneur telling a tale of mild adventure and of sport, and now and then he laughed displaying his teeth, sharp and white like the fangs of a leopard's cub.

No one interrupted him, and Councillor Hessels fell gradually—as was his wont—into a gentle doze from which he roused himself now and again in order to murmur drowsily: "To the gallows with them all!"

Viglius and Hopper and de Berlaymont tried hard to repress a shudder. They were slaves of Spain, these gentlemen of the Low Countries, but not Spanish born, and were not accustomed from earliest childhood to listen—not only unmoved but with a certain measure of delight—to these tales of horror. But there was nothing in what don Ramon said of which they disapproved. They were—all of them—loyal subjects of the King, and the very thought of rebellion was abhorrent to them.

But it was passing strange that the Duke of Alva made no

4

comment on the young captain's report. There he sat, at the head of the table, silent and moody, with one bony fist clenched above a letter which lay open beneath his hand, and which bore a large red seal with the royal arms of Spain impressed upon it. Not a word of praise or blame did he speak. His heavy brows were contracted in a sullen frown, and his protruding eyes were veiled beneath the drooping lids.

De Vargas, too, was silent—de Vargas who loved to gloat over such tales as don Ramon had to tell, de Vargas who believed that these rebellious Low Countries could only be brought into subjection by such acts of demoniacal outrage as the Spanish soldiery had just perpetrated in Mons and in Mechlin. He, too, appeared moody to-day, and the story of sick women and young children being dragged out of their beds and driven out to perish in the streets while their homes were being pillaged and devastated, left him taciturn and unmoved.

Don Ramon made vain pretence not to notice the Lieutenant-Governor's moodiness, nor yet de Vargas' silence, but those who knew him best—and de Vargas was among these—plainly saw that irritation had seized upon his nerves. He was talking more volubly, and his voice had lost its smoothness, whilst the languor of his gestures had given place to sharp, febrile movements of hands and shoulders which he tried vainly to disguise.

"Our soldiers," he was saying loudly, "did not leave a loaf of bread in the bakeries, or a bushel of wheat in the stores of Mechlin. The rich citizens we hanged at the rate of twenty a day, and I drew orders for the confiscation of their estates to the benefit of our Most Gracious King and suzerain Lord. I tell you we made quick work of all the rebels: stone no longer stands on stone in Mechlin to-day: its patricians are beggars, its citizens are scattered. We have put to the torture and burned at the stake those who refused to give us their all. A month ago Mechlin was a prosperous city: she gave of her wealth and of her hospitality to the rebel troops of Orange. To-day she and her children have ceased to be. Are you not satisfied?"

He brought his clenched fist crashing down upon the table: surely a very unusual loss of restraint in a grandee of Spain: but obviously he found it more and more difficult to keep his temper under control, and those dark eyes of his were now fixed with a kind of fierce resentment upon the impassive face of the Duke.

Councillor Hessels, only half awake, reiterated with drowsy emphasis: "To the gallows with them! Send them all to the gallows!"

Still the Duke of Alva was silent and de Vargas did not speak. Yet it was the Duke himself who had given the order for the destruction of Mechlin: "as a warning to other cities," he had said. And now he sat at the head of the table sullen, moody and frowning, and don Ramon felt an icy pang of fear gripping him by the throat: the thought that censure of his conduct was brewing in the Lieutenant-Governor's mind caused him to lose the last vestige of self-control, for he knew that censure could have but one sequel—quick judgment and the headman's axe.

5

"Are you not satisfied?" he cried hoarsely. "What more did you expect? What more ought we to have done? What other proof of zeal does King Philip ask of me?"

Thus directly challenged the Duke raised his head and looked the young man sternly in the face.

"What you have done, Messire," he said slowly—and the cold glitter in his steely eyes held in it more real and calculating cruelty than the feline savagery of the other man, "what you have done is good, but it is not enough. What use is there in laying low an entire city, when the one man whose personality holds the whole of this abominable rebellion together still remains unscathed? You hanged twenty noted citizens a day in Mechlin, you say," he added with a cynical shrug of the shoulders, "I would gladly see every one of them spared, so long as Orange's head fell on the scaffold."

"Orange has disbanded his army and has fled almost alone into Holland," said don Ramon sullenly. "My orders were to punish Mechlin and not to run after the Prince of Orange."

"The order to bring the Prince of Orange alive or dead to Brussels and to me takes precedence of every other order, as you well know, Messire," retorted Alva roughly. "We decided on that unanimously at the meeting of the Grand Council on the day that I sent Egmont and Horn to the scaffold and Orange refused to walk into the trap which I had set for him."

"He always escapes from the traps which are set for him," now broke in de Vargas in his calm, even, expressionless voice. "During the siege of Mons, according to don Frederic's report, no fewer than six surprise night-attacks—all admirably planned—failed, because Orange appeared to have received timely warning."

"Who should know that better than I, señor?" queried don Ramon hotly, "seeing that I led most of those attacks myself—they were splendidly planned, our men as silent as ghosts, the night darker than hell. Not a word of the plan was breathed until I gave the order to start. Yet someone gave the alarm. We found Orange's camp astir—every time we had to retire. Who but the devil could have given the warning?"

"A spy more astute than yourselves," quoth Alva dryly.

"Nay!" here interposed del Rio blandly, "I am of the same opinion as don Ramon de Linea; there is a subtle agency at work which appears to guard the life of the Prince of Orange. I myself was foiled many a time when I was on his track—with Ribeiras who wields a dagger in the dark more deftly than any man I know. I also employed Loronzo, who graduated in Venice in the art of poisons, but invariably the Prince slipped through our fingers just as if he had been put on his guard by some mysterious emissary."

"The loyalists in Flanders," quoth President Viglius under his breath, "declare that the agency which works for the safety of the Prince of Orange is a supernatural one. They speak of a tall, manlike figure whose face is hidden by a mask, and who invariably appears whenever the Prince of Orange's life is in danger. Some people call this mysterious being 'Leatherface,' but no one seems actually to have seen him. It sounds as if he were truly an emissary of the devil."

And as the President spoke, a strange silence fell around the council board: every cheek had become pale, every lip quivered. De Vargas made a quick sign of the Cross over his chest: Alva drew a small medal from the inside of his doublet and kissed it devoutly. These men who talked airily of rapine and of violence perpetrated against innocent people, who gloated over torture and misery which they loved to inflict, were held in the cold grip of superstitious fear, and their trembling lips uttered abject prayers for mercy to the God whom they outraged by every act of their infamous lives.

IV

When the Duke of Alva spoke again, his voice was still unsteady: "Devil or no devil," he said with an attempt at dignified composure, "His majesty's latest orders are quite peremptory. He desires the death of Orange. He will have no more cities destroyed, no more wholesale massacres until that great object is attained. Pressure has been brought to bear upon him: the Emperor, it seems, has spoken authoritatively, and with no uncertain voice. It seems that the destruction of Flemish cities is abhorrent to the rest of Europe."

"Rebel cities!" ejaculated de Berlaymont hotly.

"Aye! we know well enough that they are rebel cities," quoth Alva fiercely, "but what can we do, when a milk-livered weakling wears the Imperial crown? Our gracious King himself dares not disregard the Emperor's protests—and in his last letter to me he commands that we should hold our hand and neither massacre a population nor destroy a town unless we have proof positive that both are seething with rebellion."

"Seething with rebellion!" exclaimed don Ramon, "then what of Ghent—which is a very nest of rebels?"

"Ah!" retorted Alva, "Ghent by the Mass! Seigniors, all of you who know that accursed city, bring me proof that she harbours Orange or his troops! Bring me proof that she gives him money! Bring me proof that plots against our Government are hatched within her walls! I have moral proofs that Orange has been in Ghent lately, that he is levying troops within her very walls—I know that he has received promises of support from some of her most influential citizens..."

"Nay, then, let your Highness but give the order," broke in don Ramon once more, "my soldiers would spend three fruitful days in Ghent."

"As I pointed out to His Highness yesterday," rejoined de Vargas in mellifluous tones, "we should reduce Ghent to ashes before she hatches further mischief against us. Once a city hath ceased to be, it can no longer be a source of danger to the State ... and," he added blandly, "there is more money in Ghent than in any other city of Flanders."

"And more rebellion in one family there than in the whole of the population of Brabant," assented Councillor Arsens. "I have lived in that accursed city all my life," he continued savagely, "and I say that Ghent ought not to be allowed to exist a day longer than is necessary for massing together two or three regiments of unpaid soldiery and turning them loose into the town—just as we did in Mechlin!"

The others nodded approval

"And by the Mass..." resumed don Ramon.

"Enough, Messire," broke in the Duke peremptorily, "who are you, I pray, who are you all to be thus discussing the orders of His Majesty the King? I have transmitted to you His Majesty's orders just as I received them from Madrid yesterday. It is for you—for us all—to show our zeal and devotion at this critical moment in our nation's history, by obeying blindly, whole-heartedly, those gracious commands. Do we want our King to be further embarrassed by a quarrel with the Emperor? And what are those orders, I ask you? Wise and Christianlike as usual. His Majesty doth not forbid the punishment of rebel cities—No!—all that he asks is that we deliver Orange unto him—Orange, the arch-traitor—and that in future we prove conclusively to Europe and to Maximilian that when we punish a Flemish city we do so with unquestioned justice."

He paused, and his prominent, heavy-lidded eyes wandered somewhat contemptuously on the sullen faces around the board.

"Proofs, seigniors," he said with a light shrug of the shoulders, "proofs are not difficult to obtain. All you want is a good friend inside a city to keep you well informed. The paid spy is not sufficient—oft-times he is clumsy and himself an object of suspicion. Orange has been in Ghent, seigniors; he will go again! He has disbanded his army, but at his call another will spring up ... in Ghent mayhap ... where he has so many friends ... where money is plentiful and rebellion rife.... We must strike at Ghent before she becomes an open menace..."

"You'll never strike at Orange," broke in Councillor Arsens obstinately, "while that creature Leatherface is at large."

"He is said to hail from Ghent," added Viglius with conviction.

"Then by the Mass, seigniors," interposed Alva fiercely, "the matter is even more simple than I had supposed, and all this talk and these murmurings savour of treason, meseems. Are you fools and dolts to imagine that when His Majesty's orders were known to me, I did not at once set to work to fulfil them? We want to strike at Ghent, seigniors, and want proofs of her rebellion—His Majesty wants those proofs and he wants the death of Orange. We all desire to raze Ghent to the

8

ground! Then will you give me your close attention, and I will e'en tell you my plans for attaining all these objects and earning the approval of our gracious King and recognition from the rest of Europe."

"Then should not don Ramon de Linea retire?" queried President Viglius, "surely His Highness's decision can only be disclosed to members of his council."

"Let don Ramon stay," interposed de Vargas with unanswerable authority, even as the young man was preparing to take his leave. "The matter is one that in a measure will concern him, seeing that it involves the destinies of the city of Ghent and that His Highness is pleased to give him the command of our troops stationed in that city."

V

Don Ramon de Linea glanced up at de Vargas with a look of agreeable surprise. The command of the troops in Ghent! Of a truth this was news to him, and happy news indeed. Rumour was current that the Duke of Alva—Lieutenant-Governor of the Low Countries and Captain-General of the forces—was about to visit Ghent, and the captain in command there would thus be in a position of doing useful work, mayhap of rendering valuable services, and in any case, of being well before the eyes of the Captain-General.

All the young man's elegant, languid manner had come back to him. He had had a fright, but nothing more, and commendation—in the shape of this important promotion—had allayed all his fears: his being allowed to be present at a deliberation of the Grand Council was also a signal mark of favour granted to him, no doubt in recognition of his zeal and loyalty whilst destroying the noble city of Mechlin for the glory of King Philip of Spain.

He now resumed his seat at the board, selecting with becoming modesty a place at the bottom of the table and feeling not the least disconcerted by the wrathful, envious looks which President Viglius and one or two other Netherlanders directed against him.

"The plan, seigniors, which I have in my mind," resumed the Duke after a slight pause, "could never have come to maturity but for the loyal co-operation of señor Juan de Vargas and of his equally loyal daughter. Let me explain," he continued, seeing the look of astonishment which spread over most of the faces around the board. "It is necessary, in view of all that we said just now, that I should have a means—a tool I might say—for the working out of a project which has both the death of Orange and the punishment of Ghent for its aim. I have told you that I am morally certain that Orange is operating in Ghent at the present moment. Is it likely that he would leave such a storehouse of wealth and rebellion untouched?—heresy is rampant in

9

Ghent and treachery goes hand in hand with it. Our spies unfortunately have been unable to obtain very reliable information: the inhabitants are astute and wary—they hatch their plots with devilish cunning and secrecy. Obviously, therefore, what we want is a loyal worker, an efficient and devoted servant of the King in the very heart of the civic life of the town: if only we can get to know what goes on in the intimate family circles of those townsfolk, I feel sure that we shall get all the proofs that the King desires of the treachery of Ghent."

He paused a moment in order to draw breath; absolute silence—the silence of tense expectation—hung around the council-board. The Netherlanders hung obsequiously on the tyrant's lips, del Rio leaned back in his chair—seemingly indifferent—and de Vargas was closely watching don Ramon de Linea; the young man was trying to appear calmly interested, but the restless look in his eyes and a slight tremor of his hand betrayed inward agitation.

"Some of you reverend seigniors," continued the Duke of Alva after awhile, in powerful, compelling tones, "will perhaps have guessed by now, what connection there is in my mind between that vast project which I have just put before you and the daughter of my loyal coadjutor don Juan de Vargas. I have arranged that she shall marry a man of influence and position in Ghent, so that she can not only keep me informed of all the intrigues which are brewing in that city against the Government of our gracious King, but also become the means whereby we can lure Orange to his doom, capture that mysterious Leatherface, and then deliver Ghent over to don Ramon's soldiery."

He struck the table repeatedly with his fist as he spoke: there was no doubting the power of the man to accomplish what he wanted, as well as the cruelty and vindictiveness wherewith he would pursue anyone who dared to attempt to thwart him in his projects. No one thought of interrupting him. Don Ramon kept his agitation under control as best he could, for he felt that de Vargas's eyes still watched him closely.

"A very admirable idea," now murmured Viglius obsequiously.

As usual on these occasions, it was obvious that he and the other Netherlanders were mere figureheads at the council-board. Alva was directing, planning, commanding, de Vargas had been the confidant, and del Rio would always be the ready tool when needed: but Viglius, de Berlaymont, Hessels, and the others, were mere servile listeners, ready to give the approbation which was expected of them and withholding every word of criticism.

VI

"And doth donna Lenora de Vargas enter into all these far-

10

reaching schemes?" now asked don Ramon coldly. "Meseems, they are above a woman's comprehension."

De Vargas' persistent glance was irritating his nerves; he threw a challenging look—wholly defiant—across the table at the older man.

"My daughter, Messire," said the latter loftily, "is above all a true Spaniard. She has been brought up to obey and not to discuss. She is old enough now to forget all past youthful follies," he added, answering don Ramon's defiant glance with one that conveyed a threat. "Her devotion to her Church, her King and her country, and her hatred of Orange and all rebels will influence her actions in the way the Lieutenant-Governor desires."

Don Ramon was silent. He had understood the threat which de Vargas' glance had expressed, and he knew what the other meant when he spoke of "past youthful follies"—it meant the breaking off of a pleasing romance, a farewell to many an ambitious dream. Don Ramon suppressed a sigh of anger and of disappointment: donna Lenora de Vargas was beautiful and wealthy, but it were not wise to let her father see how hard he—Ramon—had been hit. He took no further part in the discussion, and after awhile he succeeded in appearing wholly indifferent to its sentimental side; but he listened attentively to all that was said, and when he met de Vargas' glance, which now and then was fixed mockingly upon him, he answered it with a careless shrug of the shoulders.

"And," now rejoined Pierre Arsens, who was president of Artois and a patrician of Hainault, "may we ask if His Highness has already chosen the happy man who is to become the husband of such a pattern of womanhood?"

"My choice has naturally fallen on the son of Mynheer Charles van Rycke, the High-Bailiff of Ghent," replied Alva curtly.

"A family of traitors if ever there was one," growled Alberic del Rio savagely. "I know them. The father is all right, so is the younger son Mark—younger, I believe, by only a couple of hours—a wastrel and something of a drunkard, so I understand; but the mother and the other son are impudent adherents of Orange: they have more than once drawn the attention of the Chief Inquisitor on themselves, and if I had my way with such cattle, I would have had the men hanged and the woman burned long before this."

"Van Rycke," said Alva coldly, "is High-Bailiff of Ghent. He is a good Catholic and so is his wife: he is a man of great consideration in the city and his sons are popular. It has not been thought expedient to interfere with them up to now. But—bearing my schemes in mind—I have caused the man to be severely warned once or twice. These warnings have reduced him to a state of panic, and lately when my scheme had matured I told him that my desire was that one of his sons should wed don Juan de Vargas' daughter. He had no thought of refusal. In fact his acceptance was positively abject."

"And on what grounds was the marriage suggested to him?" questioned President Arsens.

"Grounds, Messire?" retorted the Duke; "we give no grounds or reasons for our commands to our Flemish subjects. We give an order and they obey. I told Mynheer van Rycke that I desired the marriage and that was enough."

"Then," interposed President Viglius with an attempt at jocularity, "we shall soon be able to congratulate two young people on a happy event!"

"You will be able to do that to-morrow, Messire," quoth the Duke. "Señor de Vargas goes to Ghent for the purpose of affiancing the two young people together; the marriage ceremony will take place within the week. His Majesty hath approved of my scheme: he desires that we should expedite the marriage. Señor de Vargas is willing, Messire van Rycke would not think of objecting, donna Lenora is heart free. Why should we delay?"

"Why, indeed?" murmured don Ramon under his breath.

"Donna Lenora," resumed Alva sententiously, "is indeed lucky in that—unlike most women—she will be able to work personally for the glory of her King and country. If through her instrumentality we can bring Orange to the block and Ghent to her knees, there is no favour which her father could not ask of us."

As he said this, he turned to de Vargas and stretched out his hand to him. De Vargas took the hand respectfully and bent over it in dutiful obedience.

"Now, seigniors," resumed the Duke more gaily, and once more addressing the full council-board, "you know the full reason of my projected journey to Ghent. I go ostensibly in order to inaugurate the statue of our Sovereign King erected by my orders in the market place, but also in order to ascertain how our loyal worker will have progressed in the time. Donna Lenora de Vargas will have been the wife of Messire van Rycke for over a sennight by then: she will—and I mistake not—have much to tell us. In the meanwhile señor de Vargas will take up his residence in the city as vicarius criminalis: he will begin his functions to-morrow by presiding over the engagement of his daughter to the son of the High-Bailiff: there will be much public rejoicing and many entertainments during the week and on the day of the wedding ceremony: to these, seigniors, ye are graciously bidden. I pray you go and mingle as far as you can with that crowd of uncouth and vulgar burghers whose treachery seems to pierce even through their ill-fitting doublets. I pray you also to keep your eyes and ears open ... an my conjectures are correct, much goes on in Ghent of which the Holy Inquisition should have cognisance. We are out on a special campaign against cunning traitors, and Ghent is our first objective. When we turn our soldiery loose into the city, yours, seigniors, will be the first spoils.... Ghent is rich in treasure and money ... those first spoils will be worth the winning. Until that happy day, I bid you au revoir, gentle Sirs, and let your toast be at every banquet: 'To the destruction of Ghent, and to the death of Orange!'"

After which long peroration the Lieutenant-Governor intimated with a casual wave of his be-ringed hand that the sitting of the Grand Council was at an end. The illustrious councillors rose with alacrity: they were now in rare good humour. The parting speech of His Highness tickled their cupidity. The first spoils at the sacking of Ghent should mean a fortune for every member of the board. General de Noircarmes had made a huge one at the sacking of Mons, and even younger officers like don Ramon de Linea had vastly enriched themselves when Mechlin was given over to the soldiers.

One by one now the grave seigniors withdrew, having taken respectful leave of His Highness. To the salute of the Netherlanders—of Viglius and Hessels, of Berlaymont and the others, the Duke responded with a curt bow—to de Vargas and del Rio, and also to don Ramon, he nodded with easy familiarity. However obsequious the Netherlanders might be—however proven their zeal, their Spanish masters never allowed them to forget that there was a world of social distinction between a grandee of Spain and the uncouth burghers and even patricians of this semi-civilised land.

VII

Having made his last obeisance before the Duke of Alva and taken leave of the grave seigniors of the Grand Council, don Ramon de Linea bowed himself out of the room with all the ceremony which Spanish etiquette prescribed. As he did so he noticed that at a significant sign from Alva, de Vargas and Alberic del Rio remained behind in the council-chamber, even while all the Netherlanders were being dismissed. He watched these latter gentlemen as one by one they filed quickly out of the house—loath even to exchange a few friendly words with one another on the doorstep in this place where every wall had ears and every nook and cranny concealed a spy. He watched them with an air of supercilious contempt, oblivious of the fact that he himself had been not a little scared by the black looks cast on him by the all-powerful tyrant and merciless autocrat.

The scare had been unpleasant, but it was all over now: Fate—that ever fickle jade—seemed inclined to smile on him. The penniless scion of a noble race, he seemed at last on the high road to fortune—the command of the troops in Ghent was an unexpected gift of the goddess, whilst the sacking and looting of Mechlin had amply filled his pockets.

But it was a pity about donna Lenora!

Don Ramon paused in the vast panelled hall and instinctively his

13

eyes wandered to the mirror, framed in rich Flemish carved wood, which hung upon the wall. By our Lady! he had well-nigh lost his self-control just now under de Vargas' mocking gaze, and also that air of high-breeding and sang-froid which became him so well: the thought of donna Lenora even in connection with her approaching marriage caused him to readjust the set of his doublet and the stiff folds of his ruffle, and his well-shaped hand wandered lovingly up to his silky moustache.

A sound immediately behind him caused him to start and to turn. An elderly woman wrapped in a dark shawl and wearing a black veil right over her face and head was standing close to his elbow.

"Inez?" he exclaimed, "what is it?"

"Hist! I beg of you, señor," whispered the woman, "I am well-nigh dead with terror at thought that I might be seen. The señorita knew that you would be here to-day: she saw you from the gallery above, and sent me down to ask you to come to her at once."

"The señorita?" broke in don Ramon impatiently, and with a puzzled frown, "is she here?"

"Señor de Vargas won't let her out of his sight now. When he hath audience of the Lieutenant-Governor or business with the council he makes the señorita come with him. The Duke of Alva hath given her a room in this house, where she can sit while her father is at the Council."

"But Heavens above, why all this mystery?"

"The señorita will tell your Graciousness," said the woman, "I beg of you to come at once. If I stay longer down here I shall die of fright."

And like a scared hen, old Inez trotted across the hall, without waiting to see if don Ramon followed her. The young man seemed to hesitate for a moment: the call was a peremptory one, coming as it did from a beautiful woman whom he loved: at the same time all that he had heard in the council-chamber was a warning to him to keep out of de Vargas' way; the latter—if Inez spoke the truth—was keeping his daughter almost a prisoner, and it was never good at any time to run counter to señor de Vargas.

The house was very still. The Netherlanders had all gone: two serving men appeared to be asleep in the porch, otherwise there came no sign of life from any part of the building: the heavy oak doors which gave on the anteroom of the council-chamber effectually deadened every sound which might have come from there.

Don Ramon smiled to himself and shrugged his shoulders. After all he was a fool to be so easily scared: a beautiful woman beckoned, and he had not been forbidden to see her—so—after that one brief moment of hesitation he turned to follow Inez up the stairs.

The woman led the way round the gallery, then up another flight of stairs and along a narrow corridor, till she came to a low door, beside which she stopped.

14

"Go in, I pray you, señor," she said, "the señorita expects you."

The young man walked unannounced into the small room beyond.

There came a little cry of happy surprise out of the recess of a wide dormer window, and the next moment don Ramon held Lenora de Vargas in his arms.

VIII

Lenora with the golden hair and the dark velvety eyes! Thus do the chroniclers of the time speak of her (notably the Sieur de Vaernewyck who knew her intimately), thus too did Velasquez paint her, a few years after these notable events–all in white, for she seldom wore coloured gowns–very stately, with the small head slightly thrown back, the fringe of dark lashes veiling the lustre of her luminous eyes.

But just at this moment there was no stateliness about donna Lenora: she clung to don Ramon, just like a loving child that has been rather scared and knows where to find protection; and he accepted her caress with an easy, somewhat supercilious air of condescension–the child was so pretty and so very much in love! He patted her hair with gentle, soothing gesture and thanked kind Fate for this pleasing gift of a beautiful woman's love.

"I did not know that you were in Brussels," he said after awhile, and when he had led her to a seat in the window, and sat down beside her. "All this while I thought you still in Segovia."

His glance was searching hers and his vanity was pleasantly stirred by the fact that she was pale and thin, and that those wonderful, luminous eyes of hers looked as if they had shed many tears of late.

"Ramon," she whispered, "you know?"

"The Duke of Alva," he replied dryly, "gave me official information."

Then seeing that she remained silent and dejected he added peremptorily: "Lenora! how long is it since you have known of this proposed marriage?"

"Only three days," she replied tonelessly. "My father sent for me about a month ago. The Duchess of Medina Coeli was coming over to the Netherlands on a visit to her lord, and I was told that I must accompany her. We started from Laredo in the Esperansa on the 10th of last month and we landed at Flushing a week ago. Oh! at first I was so happy to come ... it is nine months and more since you left Spain and my heart was aching for a sight of you."

"Then ... when did you first hear?"

"Three days since, when we arrived in Brussels. The Duchess herself took me to my father's house, and then he told me ... that he had

15

bade me come because the Lieutenant-Governor had arranged a marriage for me ... with a Netherlander."

Don Ramon muttered an angry oath.

"Did he—your father I mean—never hint at it before?" he asked.

"Never. A month ago he still spoke of you in his letters to me. Had you no suspicions, Ramon?"

"None," he replied.

"It was he of course who obtained for you that command under don Frederic, which took you out of Spain."

"It was a fine position and I accepted it gladly ... and unsuspectingly."

"It must have been the beginning: he wanted you out of my way already then, though he went on pretending all this while that he favoured your attentions to me. He thought that I would soon forget you. How little he knows me! And now he has forbidden me to think of you again. Since I am in Brussels he hardly lets me out of his sight. He only leaves the house in order to attend on the Duke, and when he does, he brings me here with him. Inez and I are sent up to this room and I am virtually a prisoner."

"It all seems like an ugly dream, Lenora," he murmured sullenly.

"Aye! an ugly dream," she sighed. "Ofttimes, since my father told me this awful thing, I have thought that it could not be true. God could not allow anything so monstrous and so wicked. I thought that I must be dreaming and must presently wake up and find myself in the dear old convent at Segovia with your farewell letter to me under my pillow."

She was gazing straight out before her—not at him, for she felt that if she looked on him, all her fortitude would give way and she would cry like a child. This she would not do, for her woman's instinct had already told her that all the courage in this terrible emergency must come from her.

He sat there, moody and taciturn, all the while that she longed for him to take her in his arms and to swear to her that never would he give her up, never would he allow reasons of State to come between him and his love.

"There are political reasons it seems," she continued, and the utter wretchedness and hopelessness with which she spoke were a pathetic contrast to his own mere sullen resentment. "My father has not condescended to say much. He sent for me and I came. As soon as I arrived in Brussels he told me that I must no longer think of you: that childish folly, he said, must now come to an end. Then he advised me that the Lieutenant-Governor had arranged a marriage for me with the son of Messire van Rycke, High-Bailiff of Ghent ... that we are to be affianced to-morrow and married within the week. I cried—I implored— I knelt to my father and begged him not to break my heart, my life.... I told him that to part me from you was to condemn me to worse than death...."

"Well? and–?" he queried.

"You know my father, Ramon," she said with a slight shudder, "almost as well as I do. Do you believe that any tears would move him?"

He made no reply. Indeed, what could he say? He did know Juan de Vargas, knew that such a man would sacrifice without pity or remorse everything that stood in the way of his schemes or of his ambition.

"I was not even told that you would be in Brussels to-day–Inez only heard of it through the Duke of Alva's serving man–then she and I watched for you, because I felt that I must at least be the first to tell you the awful–awful news! Oh!" she exclaimed with sudden vehemence, "the misery of it all! ... Ramon, cannot you think of something?–cannot you think? Are we going to be parted like this? as if our love had never been, as if our love were not sweet and sacred and holy, the blessing of God which no man should have the power to take away from us!"

She was on the point of breaking down, and don Ramon with one ear alert to every sound outside had much ado to soothe and calm her. This he tried to do, for selfish as he was, he loved this beautiful woman with that passionate if shallow ardour which is characteristic in men of his temperament.

"Lenora," he said after awhile, "it is impossible for me to say anything for the moment. Fate and your father's cruelty have dealt me a blow which has half-stunned me. As you say, I must think–I am not going to give up hope quite as readily as your father seems to think. By our Lady! I am not just an old glove that can so lightly be cast aside. I must think ... I must devise.... But in the meanwhile...."

He paused and something of that same look of fear came into his eyes which had been there when in the Council Chamber he had dreaded the Duke of Alva'a censure.

"In the meanwhile, my sweet," he added hastily, "you must pretend to obey. You cannot openly defy your father! ... nor yet the Duke of Alva. You know them both! They are men who know neither pity nor mercy! Your father would punish you if you disobeyed him ... he has the means of compelling you to obey. But the Duke's wrath would fall with deathly violence upon me. You know as well as I do that he would sacrifice me ruthlessly if he felt that I was likely to interfere with any of his projects: and your marriage with the Netherlander is part of one of his vast schemes."

The look of terror became more marked upon his face, his dark skin had become almost livid in hue: and Lenora clung to him, trembling, for she knew that everything he said was true. They were like two birds caught in the net of a remorseless fowler: to struggle for freedom were worse than useless. De Vargas was a man who had attained supreme power beside the most absolute tyrant the world had ever known. Every human being around him–even his only child–was a mere pawn in his hands for the great political game in which the Duke of Alva was the chief player—a mere tool for the fashioning of that monstrous chain which was destined to bind the Low Countries to the chariot-wheels of Spain. A useless tool, a superfluous pawn he would throw away without a pang of remorse: this don Ramon knew and so did Lenora—but in Ramon that knowledge reigned supreme and went hand in hand with terror, whilst in the young girl there was all the desire to defy that knowledge and to make a supreme fight for love and happiness.

"I must not stay any longer now, my sweet," he said after awhile, "if your father has so absolutely forbidden you to see me, then I have tarried here too long already."

He rose and gently disengaged himself from the tender hands which clung so pathetically to him.

"I can't let you go, Ramon," she implored, "it seems as if you were going right out of my life—and that my life would go with you if you went."

"Sweetheart," he said a little impatiently, "it is dangerous for me to stay a moment longer. Try and be brave—I'll not say farewell—We'll meet again...."

"How?"

"Let Inez be at the corner of the Broodhuis this evening. I'll give her a letter for you. In the meanwhile I shall have seen your father. Who knows his decision may not be irrevocable—after all you are the one being in the world he has to love and to care for; he cannot wilfully break your heart and destroy your happiness."

She shook her head dejectedly. But the next moment she looked up trying to seem hopeful. She believed that he suffered just as acutely as she did, and, womanlike, did not want to add to his sorrow by letting him guess too much of her own. She contrived to keep back her tears; she had shed so many of late that their well-spring had mayhap run dry: he folded her in his arms, for she was exquisitely beautiful and he really loved her. Marriage with her would have been both blissful and advantageous, and his pride was sorely wounded at the casual treatment meted out to him by de Vargas: at the same time the thought of defiance never once entered his head—for defiance could only end in death, and don Ramon felt quite sure that even if he lost his beautiful fiancée, life still held many compensations for him in the future.

Therefore he was able to part from Lenora with a light heart, whilst hers was overweighted with sorrow. He kissed her eyes, her hair, her lips, and murmured protestations of deathless love which only enhanced her grief and enflamed all that selfless ardour of which her passionate nature was capable. Never had she loved don Ramon de Linea as she loved him at this hour of parting—never perhaps would she love as fondly again.

And he with a last, tender kiss, airily bade her to be brave and trustful, and finally waved her a cheery farewell.

CHAPTER II

THE SUBJECT RACE

I

"I cannot do it, mother, I cannot! The very shame of it would kill me!"

Laurence van Rycke sat on a low chair in front of the fire, his elbow propped on his knee, his chin buried in his hand. His mother gave a little shiver, and drew her woollen shawl closer round her shoulders.

"You cannot go against your father's will," she said tonelessly, like one who has even lost the power to suffer acutely. "God alone knows what would become of us all if you did."

"He can only kill me," retorted Laurence, with fierce, passionate resentment.

"And how should I survive if he did?"

"Would you not rather see me dead, mother dear, than wedded to a woman whose every thought, every aspiration must tend toward the further destruction of our country—she the daughter of the most hideous tyrant that has ever defamed this earth—more hideous even than that execrable Alva himself..."

He paused abruptly in the midst of this passionate outburst, for the old house—which had been so solemn and silent awhile ago, suddenly echoed from end to end with loud and hilarious sounds, laughter and shouts, heavy footsteps, jingle of spurs and snatches of song, immediately followed by one or two piteous cries uttered in a woman's piercing voice. Laurence van Rycke jumped to his feet.

"What was that?" he cried, and made a dash for the door. His mother's imploring cry called him back.

"No, no, Laurence! don't go!" she begged. "It is only the soldiers! They tease Jeanne, and she gets very cross! ... We have six men and a sergeant quartered here now, besides the commandant..."

"Eight Spanish soldiers in the house of the High-Bailiff of Ghent!" exclaimed Laurence, and a prolonged laugh of intense bitterness came from his overburdened heart. "Oh God!" he added, as he stretched out his arms with a gesture of miserable longing and impotence, "to endure all this outrage and all this infamy!—to know as we do, what has happened in Mons and Mechlin and to be powerless to do anything—anything against such hideous, appalling, detestable tyranny—to feel every wrong and every injustice against the country one loves, against one's own kith and kin, eating like the plague into one's very bones and to remain powerless, inert, an insentient log in the face

19

of it all. And all the while to be fawning—always fawning and cringing, kissing the master's hand that wields the flail.... Ugh! And now this new tyranny, this abominable marriage.... Ye Heavens above me! but mine own cowardice in accepting it would fill me with unspeakable loathing!"

"Laurence, for pity's sake!" implored the mother.

At her call he ran to her and knelt at her feet: then burying his head in his hands he sobbed like a child.

"I cannot do it, mother!" he reiterated piteously, "I cannot do it. I would far rather die!"

With gentle, mechanical touch she stroked his unruly fair hair, and heavy tears rolled down her wan cheeks upon her thin, white hands.

"Just think of it, mother dear," resumed Laurence a little more calmly after a while, "would it not be introducing a spy into our very home? ... and just now ... at the time when we all have so much at stake ... the Prince..."

"Hush, Laurence!" implored the mother; and this time she placed an authoritative hand upon his arm and gave it a warning pressure; but her wan cheeks had become a shade paler than before, and the look of terror became more marked in her sunken eyes.

"Even these walls have ears these days," she added feebly.

"There is no danger here, mother darling ... nobody can hear," he said reassuringly. But nevertheless he, too, cast a quick look of terror into the remote corners of the room and dropped his voice to a whisper when he spoke again.

"Juan de Vargas' daughter," he said with passionate earnestness, "what hath she in common with us? She hates every Netherlander; she despises us all, as every Spaniard does: she would wish to see our beautiful country devastated, our cities destroyed, our liberties and ancient privileges wrested from us, and every one of us made into an abject vassal of her beloved Spain. Every moment of my life I should feel that she was watching me, spying on me, making plans for the undoing of our cause, and betraying our secrets to her abominable father. Mother dear, such a life would be hell upon earth. I could not do it. I would far rather die."

"But what can you do, Laurence?" asked Clémence van Rycke, with a sigh of infinite misery.

Laurence rose and dried his tears. He felt that they had been unmanly, and was half ashamed of them. Fortunately it was only his mother who had seen them, and ... how well she understood!

"I must think it all over, mother dear," he said calmly. "It is early yet. Father will not want me to be at the Town-house before eight o'clock. Oh! how could he ever have been so mean, so obsequious as to agree to this selling of his son in such a shameful market."

"How could he help it?" retorted the mother with a fretful little

20

sigh. "The Duke of Alva commanded in the name of the King, and threatened us all with the Inquisition if we disobeyed. You know what that means," she added, whilst that pitiable look of horror and fear once more crept into her eyes.

"Sometimes I think," said Laurence sombrely–he was standing in front of the fire and staring into the crackling logs with a deep frown right across his brow–"sometimes I think that the worst tortures which those devils could inflict on us would be more endurable than this life of constant misery and humiliation."

The mother made no reply. Her wan cheeks had become the colour of ashes, her thin hands which were resting in her lap were seized with a nervous tremour. From below came still the sound of loud laughter intermixed now with a bibulous song. A smothered cry of rage escaped Laurence's lips: it seemed as if he could not stay still, as if he must run and stop this insult in his mother's house, silence those brawling soldiers, force their own obscene songs down their throats, regardless of the terrible reprisals which might ensue. Only his mother's thin, trembling hand upon his arm forced him to remain, and to swallow his resentment as best he could.

"It is no use, Laurence," she murmured, "and I would be the first to suffer."

This argument had the effect of forcing Laurence van Rycke to control his raging temper. Common sense came momentarily to the rescue and told him that his mother was right. He started pacing up and down the narrow room with a view to calming his nerves.

II

"Have you seen Mark this morning?" asked Clémence van Rycke suddenly.

"No," he replied, "have you?"

"Only for a moment."

"What had he to say?"

"Oh! you know Mark's way," she replied evasively. "It seems that he caught sight of donna Lenora de Vargas when she passed through the Waalpoort yesterday. He made a flippant joke or two about your good luck and the girl's beauty."

Laurence suppressed an angry oath.

"Don't blame Mark," interposed Clémence van Rycke gently, "he is as God made him–shallow, careless..."

"Not careless where his own pleasures are concerned," said Laurence, with a laugh of bitter contempt. "Last night at the 'Three Weavers' a lot of Spanish officers held carouse. Mark was with them till far into the night. There was heavy drinking and high play, and Mark..."

21

"I know, I know," broke in the mother fretfully, "do not let us speak of Mark. He is his father's son ... and you are mine," she added, as with a wistful little gesture she stretched out her arms to the son whom she loved. Once more he was at her feet kissing her hands.

"Do not fret, mother dear," he said, "I'll think things out quietly, and then do what I think is right."

"You'll do nothing rash, Laurence," she pleaded, "nothing without consulting me?"

"I must consult my conscience first, dear," he said firmly, "and then I must speak with the Prince.... Yes! yes! I know," he added somewhat impatiently, as once again he felt that warning pressure on his arm. "Next to God my every thought is for him; nor did he think of himself when he refused to acknowledge the autocracy of Alva. Our time is at hand, mother dear, I feel it in my bones. The last response has been splendid: we have promises of close on two thousand ducats already, and two hundred men are ready to take up arms in the city at any moment. Yes! yes! I know! and I am careful—I am as wary as the fox! But how can I at such a moment think of matrimony? How can I think of bending the knee to such abominable tyranny? I bend the knee only to the Prince of Orange, and by him I swear that I will not wed the daughter of Juan de Vargas! I will not bring to this hearth and to my home one of that gang of execrable tyrants who have ravaged our country and crushed the spirit of our people. I have work to do for Orange and for my country. I will not be hindered by bonds which are abhorrent to me."

He gave his mother a final kiss and then hurried out of the room. She would have detained him if she could, for she was terrified of what he might do; but she called after him in vain, and when presently she went to his room to look for him, he was not there. But on his desk there was a letter addressed to his father; Clémence van Rycke took it up: it was not sealed, only rolled, and tied with ribbon: this she undid and read the letter. There were only a few words, and when the unfortunate woman had grasped their full meaning she uttered a moan of pain and sank half-fainting on her knees. Here Jeanne found her half an hour later, sobbing and praying. The faithful creature comforted her mistress as best she could, then she half carried, half led her back to her room. The letter written to his father by Laurence van Rycke contained the following brief communication:

"Find fomeone elfe, My Father, to help you lick our Spanifh tyrants' boots. I cannot do it. I refufe to wed the Daughter of that Bloodhound de Vargas, but as I cannot live under Your roof and difobey You, I will not return until You bid Me come."

22

III

This had occurred early this morning; it was now late in the afternoon, and Laurence had not returned. The levie at the Town Hall was timed for eight o'clock, and the High-Bailiff had just come home in order to don his robes for the solemn occasion.

Clémence van Rycke had made an excuse not to see him yet: like all weak, indecisive natures she was hoping against hope that something would occur even now to break Laurence's obstinacy and induce him to bow to that will against which it was so useless to rebel.

But the minutes sped on, and Laurence did not return, and from a room close by came the sound of Messire van Rycke's heavy footstep and his gruff voice giving orders to the serving man who was helping him with his clothes. Another hour, or perhaps two at most, and she would have to tell her husband what had happened—and the awful catastrophe would have to be faced. As she sat in the high-backed chair, Clémence van Rycke felt as if an icy chill had crept into her bones.

"Put another log on the fire, Jeanne," she said, "this autumn weather hath chilled me to the marrow."

Jeanne, capable, buxom and busy, did as she was bid. She did more. She ran nimbly out of the room and in a trice had returned with Madame's chaufferette—well filled with glowing charcoal—and had put it to her mistress' feet: then she lit the candles in the tall candelabra which stood on a heavy sideboard at the further end of the room, and drew the heavy curtains across the window. The room certainly looked more cosy now: Madame only gave one slight, final shiver, and drew her shawl closer round her shoulders.

"Is Messire Mark dressed yet, Jeanne?" she asked wistfully.

"Messire came in about ten minutes ago," replied the woman.

"Let him know that I wish to speak with him as soon as he can come to me.'

"Yes, Madame."

"You have seen to the soldiers' supper?"

"They have had one supper, Madame. They are on duty at the Town Hall till eleven o'clock; then they are coming home for a second supper."

"Then will don Ramon de Linea sup with us, think you?"

"He didn't say."

"In any case lay his place ready in case he wants to sup. He'll be on duty quite late too, and it will anger him if his supper is not to his taste."

"Whatever I do will never be to the commandant's taste: he didn't like his room and he didn't like the dinner I had cooked for him. When he heard in whose house he was he swore and blasphemed, as I never heard any one blaspheme before. I worked my fingers to the bone

23

last night and this morning to mend his linen and starch his ruff, but even then he was not satisfied."

There was a tone of bitter wrath in Jeanne's voice as she spoke. Madame drew a fretful little sigh, but she made no comment. What was the use? The Spanish soldiers and officers quartered in the houses of Flemish burghers had an unpleasant way of enforcing their wishes with regard to food and drink which it was not wise to combat these days. So Clémence van Rycke dismissed Jeanne, and remained brooding alone, staring into the fire, repeating in her mind all that Laurence had said, looking into the future with that same shiver of horror which was habitual to her, and into all the awful possibilities which must inevitably follow Laurence's hot-headed act of rebellion.

IV

And as she sat there huddled up in the high-backed chair it would be difficult to realise that Clémence van Rycke was still on the right side of fifty.

She had married when she had only just emerged out of childhood, and had been in her day one of the brightest, prettiest, gayest of all the maidens in the city of Ghent. But now her eyes had lost their sparkle, and her mouth its smile. Her shoulders were bent as if under a perpetual load of care and anxiety, and in her once so comely face there was a settled look of anxiety and of fear. Even now, when a firm footstep resounded along the tiled corridor, she lost nothing of that attitude of dejection which seemed to have become habitual to her.

In answer to a timid knock at the door, she called a fretful "Enter!" but she did not turn her head, as Mark—her younger son—came close up to her chair. He stooped to kiss the smooth white forehead which was not even lifted for his caress.

"Any news?" were the first words which Clémence van Rycke uttered, and this time she looked up more eagerly and a swift glimmer of hope shot through her tear-dimmed eyes.

"Nothing definite," replied Mark van Rycke. "He had food and drink at the hostelry of St. John just before midday, and at the tavern of 'The Silver Bell' later in the afternoon. Apparently he has not left the city as no one saw him pass through any of the gates—but if Laurence does not mean to be found, mother dear," he added with a light shrug of the shoulders, "I might as well look for a needle in a haystack as to seek him in the streets of Ghent."

The mother sighed dejectedly, and Mark threw himself into a chair and stretched his long legs out to the blaze: he felt his mother's eyes scanning his face and gradually a faint smile, half ironical, half impatient, played round the corners of his mouth.

24

To a superficial observer there was a great likeness between the two brothers, although Mark was the taller and more robust of the two. Most close observers would, however, assert that Laurence was the better-looking; Mark had not the same unruly fair hair, nor look of boyish enthusiasm; his face was more dour and furrowed, despite the merry twinkle which now and then lit up his grey eyes, and there were lines around his brow and mouth which in an older man would have suggested the cares and anxieties of an arduous life, but which to the mother's searching gaze at this moment only seemed to indicate traces of dissipation, of nights spent in taverns, and days frittered away in the pursuit of pleasure.

Clémence van Rycke sighed as she read these signs and a bitter word of reproach hovered on her lips; but this she checked and merely sighed–sighing and weeping were so habitual to her, poor soul!

"Have you seen your father?" she asked after a while.

"Not yet," he replied.

"You will have to tell him, Mark. I couldn't. I haven't the courage. He has always loved you better than Laurence or me–the blow would come best from you."

"Have you told him nothing, then?"

"Nothing."

"Good God!" he exclaimed, "and he has to meet señor de Vargas within the next two hours!"

"Oh! I hadn't the courage to tell him, Mark!" she moaned piteously, "I was always hoping that Laurence would think better of it all. I so dread even to think what he will say ... what he will do...."

"Laurence should have thought of that," rejoined Mark dryly, "before he embarked on this mad escapade."

"Escapade!" she exclaimed with sudden vehemence. "You can talk of escapade, when..."

"Easy, easy, mother dear," broke in Mark good-humouredly, "I know I deserve all your reproaches for taking this adventure so lightly. But you must confess, dear, that there is a comic side to the tragedy–there always is. Laurence, the happy bridegroom-elect, takes to his heels without even a glimpse at the bride offered to him, whilst her beauty, according to rumour, sets every masculine heart ablaze."

The mother gave a little sigh of weariness and resignation.

"You never will understand your brother, Mark," she said with deep earnestness, "not as long as you live. You never will understand your mother either. You are your father's son–Laurence is more wholly mine. You can look on with indifference–God help you! even with levity–on the awful tyranny which has well-nigh annihilated our beautiful land of Flanders. On you the weight of Spanish oppression sits over lightly.... Sometimes I think I ought to thank God that He has given you a shallow nature, and that I am not doomed to see both my sons suffer as Laurence–my eldest–does. To him, Mark, his country and her downtrodden liberties are almost a religion: every act of tyranny perpetrated by that odious Alva is a wrong which he swears to avenge. What he suffers in the innermost fibre of his being every time that your father lends a hand in the abominable work of persecution nobody but I–his mother–will ever know. Your father's abject submission to Alva has eaten into his very soul. From a gay, light-hearted lad he has become a stern and silent man. What schemes for the overthrow of tyrants go on within his mind, I dare not even think. That awful bloodhound de Vargas–murderer, desecrator, thief–he loathes with deadly abomination. When the order came forth from your father that he should forthwith prepare for his early marriage to the daughter of that execrable man, he even thought of death as preferable to a union against which his innermost soul rose in revolt."

She had spoken thus lengthily, very slowly but with calm and dignified firmness. Mark was silent. There was a grandeur about the mother's defence of her beloved son which checked the word of levity upon his lips. Now Clémence van Rycke sank back in her chair exhausted by her sustained effort. She closed her eyes for a while, and Mark could not help but note how much his mother had aged in the past two years, how wearied she looked and how pathetic and above all how timid, like one on whom fear is a constant attendant. When he spoke again, it was more seriously and with great gentleness.

"I had no thought, mother dear," he said, "of belittling Laurence's earnestness, nor yet his devotion. I'll even admit, an you wish, that the present situation is tragic. It is now past six o'clock. Father must be at the Town Hall within the next two hours.... He must be told, and at once.... The question is, what can we tell him to ... to..."

"To soften the blow and to appease his fury," broke in Clémence van Rycke, and once more the look of terror crept into her eyes–a look which made her stooping figure look still more wizened and forlorn. "Mark," she added under her breath, "your father is frightened to death of the Duke of Alva. I believe that he would sacrifice Laurence and even me to save himself from the vengeance of those people."

"Hush, mother dear! now you are talking wildly. Father is perhaps a little weak. Most of us, I fear me, now are weak. We have been cowed and brow-beaten and threatened till we have lost all sense of our own manhood and our own dignity."

"You perhaps," protested the mother almost roughly, "but not Laurence. You and your father are ready to lick the dust before all these Spaniards–but I tell you that what you choose to call loyalty they call servility; they despise you for your fawning–men like Orange and Laurence they hate, but they give them grudging respect..."

"And hang them to the nearest gibbet when they get a chance," broke in Mark with a dry laugh.

V

Before Clémence van Rycke could say another word, the heavy footstep of the High-Bailiff was heard in the hall below. The poor woman felt as if her heart stood still with apprehension.

"Your father has finished dressing: go down to him, Mark," she implored. "I cannot bear to meet him with the news."

And Mark without another word went down to meet his father.

Charles van Rycke—a fine man of dignified presence and somewhat pompous of manner—was standing in the hall, arrayed ready for the reception, in the magnificent robes of his office. His first word on seeing Mark was to ask for Laurence, the bridegroom-elect and hero of the coming feast.

"He is a fine-looking lad," said the father complacently, "he cannot fail to find favour in donna Lenora's sight."

The news had to be told: Mark drew his father into the dining-hall and served him with wine.

"This marriage will mean a splendid future for us all, Mark," continued the High-Bailiff, as he pledged his son in a tankard of wine: "here's to the happy young people and to the coming prosperity of our house. No more humiliations, Mark; no more fears of that awful Inquisition. We shall belong to the ruling class now, tyranny can touch us no longer."

And the news had to be told. Clémence van Rycke had said nothing to her husband about Laurence's letter—so it all had to be told, quietly and without preambles.

"Laurence has gone out of the house, father, vowing that he would never marry donna Lenora de Vargas."

It took some time before the High-Bailiff realised that Mark was not jesting; the fact had to be dwelt upon, repeated over and over again, explained and insisted on before the father was made to understand that his son had played him false and had placed the family fortunes and the lives of its members in deadly jeopardy thereby.

"He has gone!" reiterated Mark for the tenth time, "gone with the intention not to return. At the reception to-night the bride will be waiting, and the bridegroom will not be there. The Duke of Alva will ask where is the bride-groom whom he hath chosen for the great honour, and echo will only answer 'Where?'"

Charles van Rycke was silent. He pushed away from him the tankard and bottle of wine. His face was the colour of lead.

"This means ruin for us all, Mark," he murmured, "black, hideous ruin; Alva will never forgive; de Vargas will hate us with the hatred born of humiliation.... A public affront to his daughter! ... O Holy Virgin protect us!" he continued half-incoherently, "it will mean the scaffold for me, the stake for your mother..."

He rose and said curtly, "I must speak with your mother."

27

He went to the door but his step was unsteady. Mark forestalled him and placed himself against the door with his hand on the latch.

"It means black ruin for us all, Mark," reiterated the High-Bailiff with sombre despair, "I must go and speak of it with your mother."

"My mother is sick and anxious," said Mark quietly, "she cannot help what Laurence has done—you and I, father, can talk things over quietly without her."

"There is nothing that you can say, Mark ... there is nothing we can do ... save, perhaps, pack up a few belongings and clear out of the country as quickly as we can ... that is, if there is time!"

"Your imagination does not carry you very far, meseems," quoth Mark dryly. "Laurence's default is not irreparable."

"What do you mean?"

"Am I not here to put it right?"

"What?—you?"

"By your leave."

"You, Mark!"

VI

The transition from black despair to this sudden ray of hope was too much for the old man: he tottered and nearly measured his length on the floor. Mark had barely the time to save him from the fall. Now he passed his trembling hand across his eyes and forehead: his knees were shaking under him.

"You, Mark," he murmured again.

He managed to pour himself out a fresh mug of wine and drank it greedily: then he sat down, for his knees still refused him service.

"It would be salvation indeed," he said, somewhat more steadily.

Mark shrugged his shoulders with an air of complete indifference.

"Well! frankly, father dear," he said, "I think that there is not much salvation for us in introducing a Spaniard into our home. Mother—and Laurence when he comes back—will have to be very careful in their talk. But you seem to think the present danger imminent...."

"Imminent, ye gods!" exclaimed the High-Bailiff, unable to repress a shudder of terror at the thought. "I tell you, Mark, that de Vargas would never forgive what he would call a public insult—nor would Alva forgive what he would call open disobedience. Those two men—who are all-powerful and as cruel and cunning as fiends—would track us and hunt us down till they had brought you and me to the scaffold and your mother to the stake."

"I know that, father," interposed Mark with some impatience,

28

"else I would not dream of standing in Laurence's shoes: the bride is very beautiful, but I have no liking for matrimony. The question is, will de Vargas guess the truth; he hath eyes like a lynx."

"No! no! he will not guess. He only saw Laurence twice—a fortnight ago when I took him up to Brussels and presented him to señor de Vargas and to the Duke: and then again the next evening: both times the lights were dim. No! no! I have no fear of that! de Vargas will not guess! You and your brother are at times so much alike, and donna Lenora hath not seen Laurence yet."

"And you did not speak of Laurence by name? I shouldn't care to change mine."

"No, I don't think so. I presented my son to the Duke and to señor de Vargas. It was at His Highness' lodgings: the room was small and dark; and señor de Vargas paid but little heed to us."

"We Netherlanders are of so little account in the sight of these grandees of Spain," quoth Mark with a light laugh, "and in any case, father, we must take some risk. So will you go and see my mother and calm her fears, whilst I go and don my best doublet and hose. Poor little mother! she hath put one foot into her grave through terror and anxiety on Laurence's account."

"As for Laurence..." exclaimed the High-Bailiff wrathfully.

"Don't worry about Laurence, father," broke in Mark quietly. "His marriage with a Spaniard would have been disastrous. He would have fallen violently in love with his beautiful wife, and she would have dragged sufficient information out of him to denounce us all to the Inquisition. Perhaps," he added with good-humoured indifference, "it is all for the best."

The High-Bailiff rose and placed a hand upon his son's shoulder.

"You are a true son to me, Mark," he said earnestly, "never shall I forget it. I am a wealthy man—more wealthy than many suppose. In virtue of your marriage with that Spanish wench you will be more free from taxation than we Netherlanders are: I'll make over the bulk of my fortune to you. You shall not regret what you have done for me and for your mother."

"It is time I went up to dress," was Mark's only comment on his father's kindly speech, and he quietly removed the paternal hand from off his shoulder.

"Hurry on," said the High-Bailiff cheerfully, "I'll wait until you are ready. I must just run up to your mother and tell her the good news. Nay! but I do believe if that hot-headed young rascal were to turn up now, I would forgive him his senseless escapade. As you say, my dear son, it is all for the best!"

CHAPTER III

THE RULING CASTE

I

Donna Lenora de Vargas stood beside her father whilst he–as representing the Lieutenant-Governor–was receiving the homage of the burghers and patricians of Ghent. This was a great honour for so young a girl, but every one–even the women–declared that donna Lenora was worthy of the honour, and many a man–both young and old–after he had made obeisance before señor de Vargas paused awhile before moving away, in order to gaze on the perfect picture which she presented.

She was dressed all in white and with extreme simplicity, but the formal mode of the time, the stiff corselet and stomacher, the rigid folds of the brocade and high starched collar set off to perfection the stateliness of her finely proportioned figure, whilst the masses of her soft fair hair crowned her as with a casque of gold.

When the brilliant throng of Flemish notabilities and their wives had all filed past the Duke of Alva's representative and had all had the honour–men and women alike–proud patricians of this ancient city, of kissing his hand, the High-Bailiff respectfully asked for leave to formally present his son to the high officers of state.

All necks were immediately craned to see this presentation, for already the rumour had spread abroad of the coming interesting engagement, and there were many whispers of astonishment when Mark's tall figure–dressed in sombre purple silk with fine, starched ruff of priceless Mechlin lace–came forward out of the crowd. Every one had expected to see Laurence van Rycke as the happy bridegroom-elect, and it seemed passing strange that it should be Mark–happy-go-lucky, easy-going Mark, the wastrel of the family, the ne'er-do-well–who had been selected for the honour of this alliance with the daughter of all-powerful de Vargas.

Well! perhaps Laurence never would have stooped before a Spaniard as Mark had done quite naturally; perhaps Laurence was too avowedly a partisan of the Prince of Orange to have found favour in beautiful donna Lenora's sight. She certainly looked on Mark van Rycke with cool indifference; those who stood close by vowed that she flashed a glance of contempt upon him, as he bowed low before señor de Vargas and the other officers of state.

"Your eldest son, Messire?" asked one of these seigniors graciously.

"My sons are twins," replied the High-Bailiff, "and this is my son Mark."

"Señor del Rio," said de Vargas turning to his colleague, "I have the honour to present to you Messire Mark van Rycke, son of a loyal subject of our King, the High-Bailiff of Ghent."

After which he turned to speak again with the High-Bailiff, and don Alberic del Rio drew Mark into a brief conversation. Excitement in the gaily-dressed throng was then at its height: the vague feeling that something unusual and even mysterious was occurring caused every one's nerves to be on tenterhooks. All this while donna Lenora had been quite silent, which was vastly becoming in a young girl, and now her father came up to her and he was closely followed by Mark van Rycke.

The momentous presentation was about to take place: a man and a woman—of different race, of different upbringing, of the same religion but of widely different train of thought—were on the point of taking a solemn engagement to live their future life together.

Those who stood near declared that at that moment donna Lenora looked up at her father with those large, dark eyes of hers that had been veiled by the soft, sweeping lashes up to now, and that they looked wonderfully beautiful, and were shining with unshed tears and with unspoken passion. They also say that she was on the point of speaking, that her lips were parted, and that the word "Father!" came from them as an appealing murmur.

But the next moment she had encountered Vargas' stern glance which swiftly and suddenly shot out on her from beneath his drooping lids—that cruel, evil glance of his which dying men and women were wont to encounter when their bodies were racked by torture and which gave them a last shudder of horror ere they closed their eyes in death. Donna Lenora too shivered as she turned her head away. Her cheeks were whiter than her gown, neither had her lips any colour in them, and the kindly Flemish women who stood by felt that their motherly heart ached for this beautiful young girl who seemed so forlorn in the midst of all this pomp.

II

The curious formalities demanded by ancient Flemish custom had now to be complied with, before Messire van Rycke and donna Lenora de Vargas could be publicly announced as affianced to one another.

Mark having his father on his right and Messire Jean van Migrode, chief-sheriff of the Keure, on his left, advanced toward his future bride. Young Count Mansfeld and Philip de Lannoy seigneur de Beauvoir walked immediately behind him, and with them were a number of gentlemen and ladies—relatives and friends of the High-Bailiff of Ghent.

In like manner a cortège had been formed round the bride-elect: she was supported on either side by her father and by don Alberic del Rio, his most intimate friend, and around her were many Spanish seigniors of high rank, amongst whom the Archbishop of Sorrento, who was on a visit to Brussels, and don Gonzalo de Bracamonte, commanding the Governor's bodyguard, were the most noteworthy.

A tense silence hung over the large and brilliant assembly, only the frou-frou of brocaded gowns, the flutter of fans, and up above in the vaulted roof the waving of banners in the breeze broke that impressive hush which invariably precedes the accomplishment of something momentous and irrevocable.

And now the High Bailiff began to speak in accordance with the time-honoured tradition of his people—wilfully oblivious of the sneers, the sarcastic smiles, the supercilious glances which were so conspicuous in the swarthy faces of the Spanish grandees opposite to him.

"It is my purpose, señor," he began solemnly, and speaking directly to don Juan de Vargas, "to ask that you do give your daughter in wedlock to my son."

And don Juan de Vargas gave answer with equal solemnity:

"Before acceding to your request, Messire," he said, "I demand to know whether your son is an honourable man and possessed of goods sufficient to ensure that my daughter continue to live as she hath done hitherto, in a manner befitting her rank."

"My son Mark, señor," thereupon rejoined the High-Bailiff, "is possessed of ten thousand ducats in gold, of twelve horses and of one half-share in the fleet of trading vessels belonging to me, which carry the produce of Flemish farms and of Flemish silk-looms to the ports of France, of Italy and of England. Moreover, six months after my son's marriage I will buy him a house in the St. Bavon quarter of this city, and some furniture to put into it so that he may live independently therein and in a manner befitting his rank."

"My daughter, Messire," resumed de Vargas still with the same grave solemnity, "is possessed of five thousand ducats and of the prestige attached to her name, which next to that of the Lieutenant-Governor himself hath more power than any other name in this land."

The chief sheriff now spoke:

"And on the day of the marriage of Messire van Rycke," he said, "with the bride whom he hath chosen, I will give him sixteen goblets of silver and four silver tankards."

"And on the day of the marriage of donna Lenora de Vargas with the bridegroom chosen for her by her father," said don Alberic del Rio, "I will give her a girdle of gold, a necklace of pearls and three rings set with diamonds and rubies."

"I will give the bridegroom two silver dishes and four gold salt cellars," came in solemn fashion from young Count Mansfeld.

"To the bride I will give two gold bracelets and a rosary specially blessed by His Holiness," announced the Archbishop of Sorrento.

"To the bridegroom I will give two gold dishes and four silver spoons," said the seigneur de Beauvoir.

"To the bride I will give a statue of Our Lady wrought in ivory, and two silken carpets from Persia," said don Gonzalo de Bracamonte.

Whereupon the High-Bailiff spoke once more:

"My son Mark hath two hundred and twenty friends and kindred each of whom will present him with a suitable wedding gift."

"My daughter will have a gift from our Sovereign Lord the King, from the Governor of the Provinces and from the Lieutenant-Governor, and from fifteen Spanish grandees, three of whom are Knights of the Golden Fleece."

"Wherefore, O noble seignior," continued the High-Bailiff, "I do ask you to give your daughter to my son for wife."

"Which request I do grant you, Messire," said de Vargas, "and herewith make acceptance on my daughter's behalf, of your son Mark to be her husband and guardian."

Don Gonzalo de Bracamonte now handed him a drawn sword, a hat, a ring and a mantle: de Vargas holding the sword upright, placed the hat on the tip of the blade and hung the ring upon a projecting ornament of the hilt. This together with the mantle and a piece of silver he then handed over to Mark, saying:

"With these emblems I hereby hand over to you the custody of my daughter, and as I have been her faithful custodian in the past, so do I desire you to become her guardian and protector henceforth, taking charge of her worldly possessions and duly administering them honourably and loyally."

In the meanwhile the chief sheriff had in similar manner given Mark seven gloves: these the young man now handed to señor de Vargas in exchange for the emblems of his own marital authority, and saying the while:

"I accept the trust and guardianship of your daughter Lenora which you have imposed upon me, and herewith I plight you my troth that I will henceforth administer her worldly possessions both honourably and loyally."

With this the quaint ceremonial came to an end. The Spanish seigniors very obviously drew deep sighs of relief. The Archbishop and don Gonzalo as well as de Vargas himself had studied their parts carefully, for the Lieutenant-Governor had expressly desired that the betrothal should be done with all the formalities and ceremonies which the custom of the Netherlands demanded. All three seigniors had chafed at this irksome task—they found torrents of ridicule to pour upon the loutish Netherlanders and their vulgar and unseemly habits;

but the Duke was firm, and obedience was obligatory. Lenora had, of course, not been consulted on the subject; she was just the sad little bundle of goods which was being bargained for, for the furtherance of political intrigues, together with her five thousand ducats, her golden girdle and rosary specially blessed by the Pope. She stood by while the solemn bargaining was going on, the centre of the group–a pathetic young figure in her white gown, a curious flush–maybe of shame–upon her cheeks. But at last it was over and de Vargas now turned to his daughter.

"Lenora," he said, "this is Mark, the son of the High-Bailiff of Ghent; the alliance which you are about to contract with him is a source of great satisfaction to me."

Mark in the meanwhile had stood by–quite impassive and seemingly indifferent–while the ceremony of betrothal was taking place. There was nothing new to him in the solemn speeches delivered by his father and his friends, nor in those which the Spanish seigniors had learned so glibly by heart; he had more than once been present at the betrothal of one or other of his friends, and these customs and ceremonials were as familiar, as sacred to him, perhaps, as the divine service of his Church. Now at de Vargas' last words he advanced, with back bent, nearer to his beautiful fiancée. He had refrained from looking on her while his worldly goods and hers were being thus proclaimed in loud tones by their respective friends, because he felt that she–being a total stranger–must find his country's custom either ridiculous or irksome.

But now when he straightened out his tall figure, he suddenly sought her eyes, and seemed to compel her glance by the very intentness of his own.

"Give Messire van Rycke your hand, Lenora," commanded de Vargas.

And the girl–obediently and mechanically–stretched out her small, white hand and Mark van Rycke touched her finger tips with his lips.

Every one noticed how closely señor de Vargas had watched his daughter all the while that the formal ceremony of betrothal was taking place, and that, as soon as donna Lenora had extended her hand to Messire van Rycke a smile of intense satisfaction became apparent round the corners of his mouth.

"And now, Messire," he said solemnly, and turning once more to the bridegroom-elect, "it is my pleasant duty to apprise you that our Sovereign Lord and King hath himself desired that I should be his mouthpiece in wishing you lasting happiness.

"I thank you, Messire," said Mark van Rycke quietly.

"As you know," continued de Vargas speaking with paternal benevolence, "it is the Lieutenant-Governor's earnest wish that we should hasten the wedding. He himself hath graciously fixed this day

34

sennight for the religious ceremony—the festival day of Our Lady of Victory—a great and solemn occasion, Messire," he continued unctuously, "which will sanctify your union with my daughter and confer on it an additional blessing."

"As His Highness commands," rejoined Mark somewhat impatiently.

He had made several efforts to meet his beautiful bride's glance again, but she kept her eyes steadily averted from his now.

Truly so cold and unemotional a bride was enough to put any bridegroom out of patience. No doubt had Laurence van Rycke stood there instead of Mark there might have been enacted a little scene of ill-temper which would have disturbed don Juan de Vargas' unctuous manner. But Mark took it all as a matter of course: he looked supremely indifferent and more than a little bored whilst his prospective father-in-law delivered himself of all these urbane speeches. He had obviously been deeply struck at first by donna Lenora's exquisite beauty, but now the effect of this pleasing surprise had worn off, he looked down on her with cool indifference, whilst a little smile of irony became more and more accentuated round his lips. But the High-Bailiff appeared overjoyed; his flat, Flemish face gradually broadened into a huge, complacent smile, he leaned on the arm of his son with easy familiarity and every one felt that—had señor de Vargas demanded such a token of gratitude and loyalty—Mynheer Charles van Rycke would have laid down on the floor and licked the dust from Monseigneur's slashed shoes.

III

At last the interminable ceremony of betrothal was over and donna Lenora was given a little breathing time from the formal etiquette which surrounded her father whenever he represented the Lieutenant-Governor, and which oppressed this poor young girl physically like the stiff corslet which she wore.

She looked around her a little wistfully: her father was busy conversing with the High-Bailiff, no doubt on matters connected with the respective marriage-jointures: all around in the magnificent hall, under the high roof emblazoned and decorated with the arms of the city and the banners of the city guilds, a noisy throng, gaily dressed, pressed, jostled and chattered. The ladies of Ghent—somewhat unwieldy of figure and with none of the highly-trained æsthetic taste of Spanish civilisation—had decked themselves out in finery which was more remarkable for its gorgeousness than for harmony of colour.

The lateness of the season had proved an excuse for wearing the rich velvets and brocades imported from Italy, cloth of gold heavily embroidered, stomachers wrought in tinsel threads and pearls, hooped petticoats and monster farthingales moved before donna Lenora's pensive eyes like a kaleidoscope of many colours, brilliant and dazzling. The deep window embrasures each held a living picture grouped against the rich background of heavy velvet curtains or exquisite carved panelling; men and women in bright crimson, or yellow or green, the gorgeous liveries of one or other of the civic corporations, the uniforms of the guild-militia, the robes of the sheriffs and the wardmasters, all looked like a crowd of gaily plumaged birds, with here and there the rich trenchant note of a black velvet tunic worn by a member of one of the learned bodies, or the purple satin doublet of a Spanish grandee. The Flemish bourgeoisie and patriciate kept very much to itself—the women eyeing with some disfavour the stiff demeanour and sombre clothes of the Spaniards who remained grouped around the person of don Juan de Vargas. There was also the element of fear, never far distant when the Spanish officers of State were present. They personified to all these people the tyranny of Spain—the yoke of slavery which would never again be lifted from the land. The Netherlanders feared their masters, and many cringed and fawned before them, but they never mixed with them; they held themselves entirely aloof.

There were no Spanish ladies here. The Duchess of Alva was not in Flanders, the grandees and officers of Alva's army had left their wives and daughters at home in Arragon or Castile; the stay in these dour and unsympathetic Low Countries was always something of a punishment to these sons and daughters of the South, who hated the grey skies, the north-easterly winds and perpetual rains.

Thus donna Lenora found herself strangely isolated. The Flemish ladies banded themselves in groups, they chatted together, whispered and made merry, but the Spanish girl who had stood in high honour beside the Lieutenant-Governor's representative was not one of themselves. She was slim and tall and graceful, she was dressed in simple white; above all, she belonged to the ruling caste, and though many a kind-hearted Flemish vrouw pitied her in her loneliness, not one of them thought of going to speak to her.

Donna Lenora sighed and her eyes filled with tears—with tears not altogether of sorrow, but also of self-pity mingled with bitter resentment. Even the company of her future husband might have been acceptable at this moment, when she felt so very lonely.

But Mark van Rycke was no longer nigh.

IV

Then suddenly her face lit up with joy, the colour rushed to her cheeks, and her lips parted in a smile.

She had just espied in the brilliant throng, one no less brilliant figure which was slowly pushing its way through the crowd in her direction.

"Ramon," she whispered, as soon as the young man was quite close to her, "I didn't know you were here."

"His Highness," he replied, "has given me command of the garrison here; I arrived last night with my regiment."

"But where are your lodgings?"

"At the house of those thrice accursed van Ryckes," he muttered with an oath. "The billeting was arranged without my knowledge, and of course I and my men leave those quarters to-morrow. Every morsel I eat in that house seems to choke me."

"Poor Ramon!" she whispered with tender pity. "I too have been unutterably wretched since I saw you in Brussels."

"I couldn't communicate with you again, sweetheart—and this to my great grief—but I was bundled out of Brussels like a bale of goods, and here I am! Imagine my joy when I realised that I should see you to-night."

"Hush!" she murmured quickly, for with a quick impulse he had seized her hand and was pressing it to his lips. "My father can see us."

"What matter if he do," retorted don Ramon. "He has taken you from me, but he cannot kill my love ... our love, Lenora," he added with passionate ardour—an ardour in which he himself believed for the moment, since he loved Lenora and she was so exquisite, in her stateliness, her white gown and that casque of golden hair upon her head.

"You must not say that, Ramon," she said with earnestness that was far more real than his, "you must try and help me ... and not make my sacrifice altogether unbearable. It has been terrible," she added, and a curious, haunted look came into her eyes.

"It has been the most damnable thing that has ever been done on this earth, Lenora. When I arrived in this accursed city last night and quartered myself and some of my men in the house of the High-Bailiff, I would gladly have put the whole accursed family to the sword. There is no limit to my hatred of them—and of all those who stand between me and your love. I have hated your father, Lenora, ever since he parted us.... I have hated Alva! God help me! I have hated even the King!"

Ramon spoke in a low, hoarse murmur, inaudible to every one save to the shell-like ear for which it was intended. With irresistible force he had drawn Lenora's arm through his own, and had led her—much against her will—into one of the deep window embrasures, where heavy curtains of Utrecht velvet masked them both from view. He pressed her to sit on one of the low window seats, and through the soft-toned stained glass the dim light of the moon came peeping in and threw ghostlike glimmers upon the tendrils of her hair, even whilst the ruddy lights of the candles played upon her face and her white gown. For the first time to-night the young man realised all that he had lost and how infinitely desirable was the woman whom he had so airily given up without a fight. He cursed himself for his cowardice, even though he knew that he never would have the courage to dare defiance for her sake.

"Lenora," he said, with passionate intensity, "ever since your father and the Duke of Alva made me understand that they were taking you away from me, I have been wondering if it was humanly possible for any man who has known you as I have done, who has loved you as I love you still, to give you up to another."

"It has to be, Ramon," she said gently. "Oh! you must not think that I have not thought and fought—thought of what was my duty—fought for my happiness. Now," she added with a little sigh of weariness, "I cannot fight any more. My father, the Duke of Alva, the King himself in a personal letter to me, have told me where my duty lies. My confessor would withhold absolution from me if I refused to obey. My King and country and the Church have need of me it seems: what is my happiness worth if weighed in the balance of my country's service?"

"You are so unfitted for that sort of work," he murmured sullenly, "they will make of you something a little better than a spy in the house of the High-Bailiff of Ghent."

"That is the only thing which troubles me," she said. "I feel as if I were doing something mean and underhand. I shall marry a man whom I can never love, who belongs to a race that has always been inimical to Spain. My husband will hate all those whom I love. He will hate everything that I have always honoured and cherished—my King, my country, the glory and grandeur of Spain. He will rebel against her laws which I know to be beneficent even though they seem harsh and even cruel at times. A Netherlander can never have anything in common with a Spaniard...."

"Oh! they'd murder us if they could," the young man rejoined with a careless shrug of the shoulders, "but only in the dark streets or from behind a hedge."

"The King is very angry with them, I know; he declared that he would not come to the Netherlands until there is not a single rebel or heretic within its shores."

"The terms are synonymous," he retorted lightly, "and I fear that His Majesty will never grace this abominable country with his presence, if his resolution holds good. They are a stiff-necked crowd, these Netherlanders—Catholics and heretics, they are all rebels—but the heretics are the worst."

Then, as she said nothing, but stared straight out before her at this crowd of people amongst whom she was doomed to live in the future, he continued with a tone of sullen wrath:

"We have burnt a goodly number of these rebels, but still they swarm."

"It is horrible!" exclaimed the young girl with a shudder.

"Horrible, my dear love?" he said with a cynical laugh, "it is the only way to deal with these people. Their arrogance passes belief; their treachery knows no bounds. The King's sacred person would not be safe here among them; the Duke's life has often been threatened; the heretics have pillaged and ransacked the churches! No! you must not waste your sympathy on the people here. They are rebellious and treacherous to the core. As for me, I hate them tenfold, for it is one of them who will take you from me."

"He cannot take my heart from you, Ramon, for that will be yours always."

"Lenora!" he whispered once more with that fierce earnestness which he seemed unable to control, "you know what is in my mind?— what I have thought and planned ever since I realised that you were being taken from me?"

"What is it, Ramon?"

"The Duke of Alva—the King himself—want you to work for them—to be their tool. Well! so be it! You have not the strength to resist—I have not the power to rebel! If we did we should both be crushed like miserable worms by the powers which know how to force obedience. Often have I thought in the past two miserable days that I would kill you, Lenora, and myself afterwards, but..."

The words died on his lips, his olive skin became almost livid in hue. Hastily he drew a tiny image from inside his doublet: with it in his hand he made the sign of the Cross, then kissed it reverently.

"You would die unabsolved, my Lenora," he whispered, and the girl's cheeks became very white, too, as he spoke, "and I should be committing a crime for which there is no pardon ... and I could not do that," he added more firmly, "I would sooner face the fires of the Inquisition than those of hell."

Superstitious fear held them both in its grip, and that fanatical enthusiasm which in these times saw in the horrible excesses of that execrable Inquisition—in its torture-chambers and scaffolds and stakes—merely the means of killing bodies that were worthless and saving immortal souls from everlasting torture and fire. Lenora was trembling from head to foot, and tears of horror and of dread gathered in her eyes. Don Ramon made a violent effort to regain his composure and at the same time to comfort her.

"You must not be afraid, Lenora," he said quietly, "those demons of blind fury, of homicide and of suicide have been laid low. I fought with them and conquered them. Their cruel temptations no longer assail me, and the Holy Saints themselves have shown me the way to be patient—to wait in silence until you have fulfilled your destiny—until you have accomplished the work which the King and the Church will demand of you. After that, I know that the man who now will claim what I would give my life to possess—you, Lenora—will be removed from your path. How it will be done, I do not know ... but he will die, Lenora, of that I am sure. He will die before a year has gone by, and I will then come back to you and claim you for my wife. You will be free then, and will no longer owe obedience to your father. I will claim you, Lenora! and even now, here and at this hour, I do solemnly plight you my troth, in the very teeth of the man whose wife you are about to be."

"And of a truth," here broke in a pleasant and good-humoured voice with a short laugh, "it is lucky that I happened to be present here and now and at this hour to register this exceedingly amiable vow."

V

Don Ramon de Linea had jumped to his feet; his hand was upon his sword-hilt; instinctively he had placed himself in front of donna Lenora and facing the intruder who was standing beside the velvet curtain, with one hand holding back its heavy folds.

"Messire van Rycke?" he exclaimed, whilst he strove to put into his attitude all the haughtiness and dignity of which the present situation had undoubtedly robbed him.

"At your service, señor," replied Mark.

"You were spying on donna Lenora and on me, I see."

"Indeed not, señor. I only happened upon the scene—quite accidentally, I assure you—at the moment when you were prophesying my early demise and arranging to be present at my funeral."

"Are you trying to be insolent, sirrah?" quoth don Ramon roughly.

"Not I, señor," rejoined Mark, good-humouredly, "I should succeed so ill. My intention was when I saw señor de Vargas' angry glance persistently directed against my future wife to save her from the consequences of his wrath, and incidentally to bear her company for awhile: a proceeding for which—I think you will admit, señor—I have the fullest right."

"You have no rights over this gracious lady, fellow," retorted the Spaniard with characteristic arrogance.

"None, I own, save those which she deigns to confer upon me. And if she bid me begone, I will go."

"Begone then, you impudent varlet!" cried don Ramon, whose temper was not proof against the other's calm insolence, "ere I run my sword through your miserable body...."

"Hush, Ramon," here interposed donna Lenora with cool authority, "you forget your own dignity and mine in this unseemly quarrel. Messire van Rycke is in the right. An he desires to speak with me I am at his disposal."

"Not before he has arranged to meet me at the back of his father's house at daybreak to-morrow. Bring your witnesses, sirrah! I'll condescend to fight you fairly."

"You could not do that, señor," replied Mark van Rycke with perfect equanimity, "I am such a poor swordsman and you so cunning a fighter. I am good with my fists, but it would be beneath the dignity of a grandee of Spain to measure fists with a Flemish burgher. Still—if it is your pleasure..."

Although this altercation had been carried on within the depth of a vast window embrasure and with heavy curtains to right and left to deaden the sound of angry voices, the fact that two men were quarrelling in the presence of donna Lenora de Vargas had become apparent to not a few.

De Vargas himself, who for the past quarter of an hour had viewed with growing wrath his daughter's intimate conversation with don Ramon de Linea, saw what was happening, and realised that within the next few moments an exceedingly unpleasant scandal would occur which would place don Ramon de Linea—a Spanish officer of high rank, commanding the garrison in Ghent—in a false and humiliating position.

In these days, however, and with the perfect organisation of which de Vargas himself was a most conspicuous member, such matters were very easily put right. A scandal under the present circumstances would be prejudicial to Spanish prestige, therefore no scandal must occur: a fight between a Spanish officer and the future husband of donna Lenora de Vargas might have unpleasant consequences for the latter, therefore even a provocation must be avoided.

And it was done quite simply: don Juan de Vargas whispered to a man who stood not far from him and who was dressed very quietly in a kind of livery of sombre purple and black—the livery worn by servants of the Inquisition. The man, without a word, left de Vargas' side and edged his way along the panelled walls of the great hall till he reached the window embrasure where the little scene was taking place. He had shoes with soles of felt and made no noise as he glided unobtrusively along the polished floor. Neither Mark van Rycke nor don Ramon de Linea saw him approach, but just as the latter, now wholly beside himself with rage, was fingering his glove with a view to flinging it in the other's face, the man in the purple and black livery touched him lightly on the shoulder and whispered something in his ear. Then he walked away as silently, as unobtrusively as he had come.

But don Ramon de Linea's rage fell away from him like a mantle; the glove fell from his nerveless hand to the floor. He bit his lip till a tiny drop of blood appeared upon it; then he hastily turned on his heel,

41

and after a deep bow to donna Lenora but without another word to Mark van Rycke he walked away, and soon disappeared among the crowd.

VI

Donna Lenora was leaning back against the cushioned window-sill, her hands lay in her lap, slightly quivering and twisting a tiny lace handkerchief between the fingers: in her eyes, which obviously followed for some time the movements of don Ramon's retreating figure, there was a pathetic look as that of a frightened child. She seemed quite unaware of Mark's presence, and he remained leaning back against the angle of the embrasure, watching the girl for awhile, then, as she remained quite silent and apparently desirous of ignoring him altogether, he turned to look with indifferent gaze on the ever-changing and moving picture before him.

One or two of the high officers of State had retired, and the departure of these pompous Spanish officials was the signal for greater freedom and merriment among the guests of the High-Bailiff and of the Sheriffs of the city of Ghent. The orchestra in the gallery up above had struck up the measure of a lively galliarde the centre of the hall had been cleared, and the young people were dancing whilst the graver folk made circle around them, in order to watch the dance.

As was usual, the moment that dancing began and hilarity held sway, most of the guests slipped on a velvet mask, which partly hid the face and was supposed—owing to the certain air of mystery which it conveyed—to confer greater freedom of speech upon the wearer and greater ease of manner. There were but few of the rich Spanish doublets to be seen now: the more garish colours beloved of the worthy burghers of Flanders held undisputed sway. But here and there a dark figure or two—clad in purple and black of a severe cut—were seen gliding in and out among the crowd, and wherever they appeared they seemed to leave a trail of silence behind them.

Mark was just about to make a serious effort at conversing with his fiancée, and racking his brain as to what subject of gossip would interest her most, when a man in sombre attire, and wearing a mask, came close up to his elbow. Mark looked him quietly up and down.

"Laurence!" he said without the slightest show of surprise, and turning well away from donna Lenora so that she should not hear.

"Hush!" said the other. "I don't want father to knew that I am here ... but I couldn't keep away."

"How did you get through?"

"Oh! I disclosed myself to the men-at-arms. No one seemed astonished."

42

"Why should they be? Your escapade is not known."

"Has everything gone off well?" queried Laurence.

"Admirably," replied the other dryly. "I was just about to make myself agreeable to my fiancée when you interrupted me."

"I'll not hinder you."

"Have you been home at all?"

"Yes. My heart ached for our dear mother, and though my resolution was just as firm, I wanted to comfort her. I slipped into the house, just after you had left. I saw our mother, and she told me what you had done. I am very grateful."

"And did you speak to father?"

"Only for a moment. He came up to say 'good-night' to mother when I was leaving her room. She had told me the news, so I no longer tried to avoid him. Of course he is full of wrath against me for the fright I gave him, but, on the whole, meseemed as if his anger was mostly pretence and he right glad that things turned out as they have done. I am truly grateful to you, Mark," reiterated Laurence earnestly.

"Have I not said that all is for the best?" rejoined Mark dryly. "Now stand aside, man, and let me speak to my bride."

"She is very beautiful, Mark!"

"Nay! it is too late to think of that, man!" quoth Mark with his habitual good-humour; "we cannot play shuttlecock with the lovely Lenora, and she is no longer for you."

"I'll not interfere, never fear. It was only curiosity that got the better of me and the longing to get a glimpse of her."

VII

This rapid colloquy between the two brothers had been carried on in whispers, and both had drawn well away from the window embrasure, leaving the velvet curtain between them and donna Lenora so as to deaden the sound of their voices and screen them from her view.

But now Mark turned back to his fiancée, ready for that tête-à-tête with her which he felt would be expected of him; he found her still sitting solitary and silent on the low window seat, with the cold glint of moonlight on her hair and the red glow of the candles in the ballroom throwing weird patches of vivid light and blue shadows upon her white silk gown.

"Do I intrude upon your meditations, señorita?" he asked, "do you wish me to go?"

"I am entirely at your service, Messire," she replied coldly, "as you so justly remarked to don Ramon de Linea, you have every right to my company an you so desire."

43

"I expressed myself clumsily, I own," he retorted a little impatiently, "nothing was further from my thoughts than to force my company upon you. But," he added whimsically, "meseems that—since we are destined to spend so much of our future together—we might make an early start at mutual understanding."

"And you thought that conversation in a ballroom would be a good start for the desirable purpose?" she asked.

"Why not?"

"As you say: why not?" she replied lightly, "there is so little that we can say to one another that it can just as well be said in a ballroom. We know so little of one another at present—and so long as my looks have not displeased you..."

"Your beauty, señorita, has no doubt been vaunted by more able lips than mine: I acknowledge it gratefully and without stint as an additional gift of God."

"Additional?" she asked with a slight raising of her brows.

"Aye! additional!" he replied, "because my first glance of you told me plainly that you are endowed with all the most perfect attributes of womanhood. Good women," he added quaintly, "are so often plain and beautiful women so often unpleasant, that to find in one's future wife goodness allied to beauty is proof that one of singularly blessed."

"Which compliment, Messire, would be more acceptable if I felt that it was sincere. Your praise of my looks is flattering; as to my goodness, you have no proof of it."

"Nay! there you wrong yourself, señorita. Are you not marrying me entirely against your will, and because you desire to be obedient to your father and to the Duke of Alva? Are you not marrying me out of loyalty to your King, to your country, and to your church? A woman who is as loyal and submissive as that, will be loyal to her husband too."

"This will I strive to be, Messire," rejoined Lenora, who either did not or would not perceive the slight tone of good-humoured mockery which lurked in Mark van Rycke's amiable speech. "I will strive to be loyal to you, since my father and the King himself, it seems, have desired that I should be your wife."

"But, by the Mass," he retorted gaily, "I shall expect something more than loyalty and submission from so beautiful a wife, you know."

"Next to the King and to my faith," she replied coldly, "you will always be first in my thoughts."

"And in your heart, I trust, señorita," he said.

"We are not masters of our heart, Messire."

"Well, so long as that precious guerdon is not bestowed on another man," said Mark with a sigh, "I suppose that I shall have to be satisfied."

"Aye, satisfied," broke in the girl with sudden vehemence. "Satisfied, did you say, Messire? You are satisfied to take a wife whom

44

till to-day you had not even seen—who was bargained for on your behalf by your father because it suited some political scheme of which you have not even cognizance. Satisfied!" she reiterated bitterly; "more satisfied apparently with this bargaining than if you were buying a horse, for there, at least, you would have wished to see the animal ere you closed with the deal, and know something of its temper.... But a wife! ... What matters what she thinks and feels? if she be cold or loving, gentle or shrewish, sensitive to a kind word or callous to cruelty? A wife! ... Well! so long as no other man hath ever kissed her lips—for that would hurt masculine vanity and wound the pride of possession! I am only a woman, made to obey my father first, and my husband afterwards.... But you, a man! ... Who forced you to obey? ... No one! And you did not care.... This marriage was spoken of a month ago, and Segovia is not at the end of the world—did you even take the trouble to go a-courting me there? Did you even care to see me, though I have been close on a week in this country? ... You spoke of my heart just now ... how do you hope to win it? ... Well! let me tell you this, Messire, that though I must abide by the bargain which my father and yours have entered into for my body, my heart and my soul belong to my cousin, Ramon de Linea!"

She had thus poured forth the torrent of bitterness and resentment which had oppressed her heart all this while: she spoke with intense vehemence, but with it all retained just a sufficiency of presence of mind not to raise her voice—it came like a hoarse murmur choked at times with sobs, but never loud enough to be heard above the mingled sound of music and gaiety which echoed from wall to wall of the magnificent room. So, too, was she careful of gesture; she kept her hands pressed close against her heart, save when from time to time she brushed away impatiently an obtrusive tear, or pushed back the tendrils of her fair hair from her moist forehead.

Mark had listened quite quietly to her impassioned tirade: there was no suspicion now in his grave face of that good-humoured irony and indifference which sat there so habitually. Of course he could say nothing to justify himself: he could not explain to this beautiful, eminently desirable and sensitive woman, whose self-respect had already been gravely wounded, that he was not to blame for not going to woo her before; that she had originally been intended for his brother, and that all the reproaches which she was pouring upon his innocent head were really well deserved by Laurence but not by him. He felt that he was cutting a sorry figure at this moment, and the sensation that was uppermost in him was a strong desire to give his elder brother a kick.

He did his best with the help of the curtain and his own tall figure, to screen donna Lenora from the gaze of the crowd. He knew that señor de Vargas was still somewhere in the room, and on no account did he want a father's interference at this moment. Whether he was really very sorry for the girl he could not say; she certainly had given him a moral slap on the face when she avowed her love for don Ramon, and he did not feel altogether inclined at this precise moment to soothe and comfort her, or even to speak perfunctory words of love, which he was far from feeling, and which, no doubt, she would reject with scorn.

Thus now, when she appeared more calm, tired, no doubt, by the great emotional effort, he only spoke quite quietly, but with as much gentleness as he could:

"For both our sakes, donna Lenora," he said, "I could wish that you had not named Ramon de Linea. It grieves me sorely that the bonds which your father's will are imposing upon you, should prove to be so irksome; but I should be doing you an ill-turn if I were to offer you at this moment that freedom for which you so obviously crave. Not only your father's wrath, but that of the Duke of Alva would fall on you with far greater weight than it would on me, and your own country hath instituted methods for dealing with disobedience which I would not like to see used against you. That being the case, señorita," he continued, with a return to his usual good-tempered carelessness, "would it not be wiser, think you, to make the best of this bad bargain, and to try and live, if not in amity, at least not in open enmity one toward the other?"

"There is no enmity in my heart against you, Messire," she rejoined calmly, "and I crave your pardon that I did so far forget myself as to speak of don Ramon to you. I'll not transgress in that way in future, that I promise you. You have no love for me—you never can have any, meseems: you are a Netherlander, I a Spaniard: our every thoughts lie as asunder as the poles. You obey your father, and I mine; our hands will be clasped, but our hearts can never meet. Had you not been so callous, it might have been different: I might have looked upon you as a friend, and not a mere tool for the accomplishment of my country's destiny.... And now may I beg of you not to prolong this interview.... Would we had not tried to understand one another, for meseems we have fallen into graver misunderstandings than before."

"When may I see you again?" asked Mark van Rycke, with coolness now quite equal to hers.

"Every day until our wedding, Messire, in the presence of my aunt, donna Inez de Salgado, as the custom of my country allows."

"I shall look forward to the wild excitement of these daily meetings," he said, quite unable to suppress the laughter which danced in his grey eyes.

She took no notice of the gentle raillery, but dismissed him with a gracious nod.

"Shall I tell señor de Vargas," he asked, "that you are alone?"

"No, no," she replied hastily. "I prefer to be alone for a little while. I pray you to leave me."

He bowed before her with all the stiffness and formality which Spanish etiquette demanded, then he turned away from her, and soon she lost sight of his broad shoulders in the midst of the gayest groups in the crowd.

VIII

The interview with her future husband had not left donna Lenora any happier or more contented with her lot. The callousness which he had shown in accepting a fiancée like a bale of valueless goods was equally apparent in his attitude after this first introduction to her. The poor girl's heart was heavy. She had had so little experience of the world, and none at all of men. Already at an early age she had become motherless; all the care and the tenderness which she had ever known was from the father whose pride in her beauty was far greater than his love for his child. A rigid convent education had restrained the development of her ideals and of her aspirations; at nineteen years of age the dominating thought in her was service to her King and country, loyalty and obedience to her father and to the Church.

In the crowded ballroom she saw young girls moving freely and gaily, talking and laughing without apparently a care or sorrow; yet they belonged to a subject and rebel race; the laws of a powerful alien government dominated their lives; fear of the Inquisition restrained the very freedom of their thoughts. They were all of them rebels in the eyes of their King: the comprehensive death-warrant issued by the Duke of Alva against every Netherlander—man, woman, and child, irrespective of rank, irrespective of creed, irrespective of political convictions—hung over every life here present like the real sword of Damocles: even this day all these people were dancing in the very presence of death. The thought of the torture-chamber, the gibbet, or the stake could never be wholly absent from their minds. And yet they seemed happy, whilst she, donna Lenora de Vargas, who should have been envied of them all, was sitting solitary and sad; her lace handkerchief was soaked through with her tears.

A sudden movement of the curtain on her left roused her from her gloomy meditations. The next moment, a young man—with fair unruly hair, eyes glowing through the holes of the velvet mask which he wore, and sensitive mouth quivering with emotion—was kneeling beside her: he had captured one of her hands, and was kissing it with passionate fervour. Not a little frightened, she could hardly speak, but she did not feel indignant for she had been very lonely, and this mute adoration of her on the part of this unknown man acted like soothing balm on her wounded pride.

"I pray you, sir," she murmured timorously, "I pray you to leave me...."

He looked up into her face, and, through the holes of the mask, she could see that his eyes were—like hers—full of tears.

"Not," he whispered with soulful earnestness, "till I have told you that your sorrow and your beauty have made an indelible impression on my heart, and that I desire to be your humble servitor."

"But who are you?" she asked.

"One who anon will stand very near to you—as a brother...."

"A brother? Then you are...?"

"Laurence van Rycke," he replied, "henceforth your faithful servant until death."

Then as she looked very perplexed and puzzled, he continued more quietly: "I stood there—behind the curtain—quite close—whilst my brother spoke with you. I heard every word that you said, and my heart became filled with admiration and pity for you. I came here to-night only because I wished to see you. I looked upon you—without knowing you—as an enemy, perhaps a spy; now that I have seen you I feel as if my whole life must atone for the immense wrong which I had done you in my thoughts. You cannot guess—you will never know how infinite that wrong has been. But there is one thing I would wish you to know: and that is that I am a man to whom happiness in her most fulsome beauty stretched out her hands, and who in his blindness turned his back on her; if you can find it in your heart to pity and to trust me you will always find beside you a champion to defend you, a friend to protect you, a man prepared to atone with his life for the desperate wrong which he hath unwittingly done to you."

He paused, and she—still a little bewildered—rejoined gently: "Sir, I thank you for those kind words; the kindest I have heard since I landed in the Low Countries. I hope that I shall not need a champion, for surely my husband—your brother, Messire—will know how to protect me when necessary. But who is there who hath no need of a friend? and it is a great joy to me in the midst of many disappointments, that in my husband's brother I shall have a true friend. Still, methinks, that you speak somewhat wildly. I am not conscious of any wrong that you or your family have done to me, and if your mother is as kind as you are, why, Messire, mine own happiness in her house is assured."

"Heaven reward you for those gentle words, Señorita," said Laurence van Rycke fervently, as he once more took her hand and kissed it; she withdrew it quietly, and he had perforce to let it go. It might have been his for always—her tiny hand and her exquisite person: but for his hot-headed action he might have stood now boldly beside her—the happy bridegroom beside this lovely bride. The feeling of gratitude which he had felt for Mark when the latter chose to unravel the skein of their family's destiny, which he—Laurence—had hopelessly embroiled, was now changed to unreasoning bitterness. What Mark had accepted with a careless shrug of the shoulders he—Laurence—

48

would now give his life to possess. Fate had indeed made of her threads a tangle, and in this tangle he knew that his own happiness had become inextricably involved.

He could not even remain beside donna Lenora now: he was here unbeknown to his father, a looker-on at the feast, whereat he might have presided. Even at this moment, señor de Vargas, having espied his daughter in conversation with an unknown man, was making his way toward the window embrasure.

"Señorita," whispered Laurence hurriedly, "that ring upon your middle finger ... if at any time you require help or protection will you send it to me? Wherever I may be I would come at once ... whatever you told me to do I hereby swear that I would accomplish ... will you promise that if you need me, you will send me that ring?"

And she, who was lonely, and had no one to love her devotedly, gave the promise which he asked.

CHAPTER IV

JUSTICE

I

Don Ramon de Linea was one of the last to leave the Town House. He was on duty until all the Spanish officers of State had left the building, and it was long past midnight before he wended his way through the narrow streets of the city till he reached the house of the High-Bailiff in the Nieuwstraate not far from the new bridge.

The outward appearance of the house suggested that most of its occupants were abed, although there was a light in one of the windows on the ground floor, and through the uncurtained casement don Ramon caught sight of the High-Bailiff and his two sons sitting together over a final cup of wine.

All the pent-up wrath against Mark van Rycke, which Ramon had been forced to keep in check under the eye of señor de Vargas, gave itself vent now in a comprehensive curse, and forgetting every code of decency toward his host and hostess he went up to the front door and gave the heavy oak panels a series of violent kicks with his boot.

"Hey there!" he shouted roughly, "open, you confounded louts! What manners are these to close your doors against the soldiers of the King?"

He had not finished swearing when the serving man's shuffling footsteps were heard crossing the tiled hall. The next moment there was a great rattle of bolts being drawn and chains being unhung, whereupon don Ramon—still impatient and wrathful—gave a final kick to the door, and since Pierre had already lifted the latch, it flew open and nearly knocked the poor man down with its weight.

"Curse you all for a set of lazy louts," shouted don Ramon at the top of his voice. "Here, fellow," he added flinging himself into a chair, "take off my boots and cloak."

He held out his leg, and Pierre, dutiful and obedient, took off the long boots of untanned leather which protected the slashed shoes and silk trunk-hose beneath, against the mud of the streets.

"Where is your master?" queried the Spaniard roughly.

"In the dining hall, so please you, señor," replied the man.

"And my men?"

"They went to the tavern over the way about an hour ago, after they had their supper—and they have not yet returned. They are making merry there, señor," added old Pierre somewhat wistfully.

And—as if in direct confirmation of the man's words—there came from the tavern on the opposite side of the street a deafening noise of wild hilarity. The peace of the night was broken and made hideous by hoarse shouts and laughter, a deafening crash as of broken glass, all intermixed with a bibulous song, sung out of tune in a chorus of male voices, and the clapping of empty mugs against wooden tables.

Don Ramon cursed again, but this time under his breath. The order had gone forth recently from the Lieutenant-Governor himself that the Spanish troops quartered in Flemish cities were to behave themselves in a sober and becoming manner. The tavern of the "Three Weavers" being situated just opposite the house of the High-Bailiff, it was more than likely that the latter would take it upon himself to complain of the ribaldry and uproar which was disturbing his rest, and as the High-Bailiff was in high favour just now a severe reprimand for don Ramon might ensue, which prospect did not appeal to him in the least.

For a moment he hesitated whether he would not go back across the road and order the men to be silent; but as luck or fate would have it, at that very moment the High-Bailiff opened the door of the dining-room and stepped out into the hall. Seeing the young Spaniard standing there, sullen and irresolute, he bade him courteously to come and join him and his two sons in a tankard of wine.

Don Ramon accepted the invitation. The spirit of quarrelsome fury still brooded within him, and it was that spirit which made him wish to meet Mark van Rycke again and either provoke him into that quarrel which señor de Vargas' timely intervention had prevented before, or, at any rate, to annoy and humiliate him with those airs of masterfulness and superiority which the Spaniards knew so well how to wield.

II

Mark and Laurence greeted their father's guest with utmost politeness. The former offered him a tankard of wine which don Ramon pushed away so roughly that the wine was spilled over the floor and over Mark van Rycke's clothes, whereupon the Spaniard swore as was his wont and murmured something about "a clumsy lout!"

Laurence sitting at the opposite side of the table clenched his fists till the knuckles shone like ivory and the skin was so taut that it threatened to crack; the blood rushed up to his cheeks and his eyes glowed with the fire of bitter resentment and of indignation not easily kept under control. But Mark ignored the insult, his face expressed nothing but good-humoured indifference, and a careless indulgence for the vagaries of a guest, like one would feel for those of an irresponsible child. As for the High-Bailiff, he still beamed with amiability and the determination to please his Spanish masters in every way that lay in his power.

"We would ask you, señor," said Laurence after a slight pause during which he had made almost superhuman efforts to regain his self-control, "kindly to admonish the soldiery in the tavern yonder. My mother is an invalid, the noise that the men make is robbing her of sleep."

"The men will not stay at the tavern much longer," said don Ramon haughtily, "they are entitled to a little amusement after their arduous watch at the Town Hall. An Madame van Rycke will exercise a little patience, she will get to sleep within the hour and can lie abed a little longer to-morrow."

"It is not so much the lateness of the hour, señor," here interposed the High-Bailiff urbanely, noting with horror that his son was about to lose his temper, "neither I nor my sons would wish to interfere with the innocent pleasures of these brave men, but..."

"Then what is the pother about, sirrah?" queried the Spaniard with well-studied insolence.

"Only that..." murmured the unfortunate High-Bailiff diffidently, "only that..."

"There are only two women in charge of the tavern at this hour," broke in Mark quietly, "two young girls, whose father was arrested this morning for attending a camp-meeting outside the city. The girls are timid and unprotected, therefore we entreat that you, señor, do put a stop to the soldiers' brawling and allow the tavern to be closed at this late hour of the night."

Don Ramon threw back his head and burst into loud and affected laughter.

"By the Mass, Messire!" he said, "I find you vastly amusing to be thus pleading for a pair of heretics. Did you perchance not know that to attend camp meetings is punishable by death? If people want to hear a

51

sermon they should go to church where the true doctrine is preached. Nothing but rebellion and high-treason are preached at those meetings."

"We were pleading for two defenceless girls," rejoined Laurence, whose voice shook with suppressed passion. Even he dared not say anything more on the dangerous subject of religious controversy which Don Ramon had obviously brought forward with the wish to provoke a discussion—lest an unguarded word brought disaster upon his house.

"Pshaw!" retorted don Ramon roughly, "surely you would not begrudge those fine soldiers a little sport? Two pretty girls—did you not say they were pretty?—are not to be found in every street of this confounded city: and by the Mass! I feel the desire to go and have a look at the wenches myself."

He rose, yawned and stretched. Laurence was white with passion: there was a glow of deadly hate in his eyes—of fury that was almost maniacal: with a mechanical gesture he tore at the ruff at his throat. Don Ramon looked on him with contempt in his eyes and a malicious smile round his full lips. He shrugged his shoulders and laughed softly—ironically to himself. The next moment Laurence, unable to control himself, had sprung to his feet: he would have been at the other's throat, but that Mark who had been quietly watching him was just in time to seize him round the shoulders and thus to prevent murder from being done.

Don Ramon had not failed to notice Laurence's unreasoning rage, nor the gesture which for one instant had threatened his own life, but he showed not the slightest sign of fear. The sarcastic laugh did not wholly die down on his lips, nor did the look of contempt fade out of his eyes. He looked on—quite unmoved—whilst Mark succeeded, if not in pacifying his brother, at least in forcing him back to his seat and regaining some semblance of control over himself. The High-Bailiff, white as a sheet, was holding out his hands in a pathetic and futile appeal to his son and to the Spaniard. Then as Laurence overcome with the shame of his own impotence threw himself half across the table and buried his face in his hands, don Ramon said coldly:

"Your senseless rage has done you no good, my friend. After half a century, you Netherlanders have, it seems, yet to learn that it is not wise to threaten a Spanish gentleman either by word or gesture. Perhaps I would have protected the two females in the tavern yonder from the brutality of my soldiery—perhaps I wouldn't—I don't know! But now, since you chose to raise an insolent hand against me I certainly will not raise a finger to save them from any outrage—I'll even countenance my men's behaviour by my presence in the tavern. Understand? That is what you have gained by your impudence—both you and your brother—for with him too I have a score to settle for impudence that literally passes belief. If your father were not so well-accredited as a good Catholic and a loyal subject of the King, I would ...

52

But enough of this. Let the lesson be a fruitful one: and you Messire High-Bailiff–an you are wise–will inculcate into your sons a clearer notion of respect, duty and obedience toward their superiors."

He nodded curtly to the High-Bailiff, took no further notice of Mark and Laurence, but turned on his heel and went out of the room slamming the door behind him.

After he had gone, the three men remained silent for a while: the High-Bailiff feeling deeply resentful against his son, would not trust himself to speak. Mark was leaning against the window sill and staring moodily out into the darkness. Laurence still held his head buried in his hands.

The Spaniard's loud voice was heard giving orders to Pierre, then there came the sound of bolts being pushed back, of the heavy oaken door groaning on its hinges, then the reclosing of the door and Pierre's shuffling footsteps crossing the hall.

Laurence rose and passed the back of his hand once or twice across his eyes: "And to think," he murmured dully, "that brutes such as that are allowed to live. Has God turned the light of His countenance quite away from us?" He remained standing for a while gazing out blankly before him, and with trembling fingers he traced intricate patterns upon the table-top. Then with a heavy sigh he bade father and brother "good-night" and quietly went out of the room.

"Mark!" said the High-Bailiff quickly, "keep an eye on that hot-headed young ruffian. In his present state of mind there's no knowing what he might do."

Whereupon Mark, in his usual good-tempered, indolent way also bade his father good-night, and followed his brother out of the room.

III

The scene which met don Ramon's eyes when he entered the tavern of the "Three Weavers"–which was situate, be it remembered, almost opposite the house of the High-Bailiff of Ghent–was, alas! not an unusual one these days.

For five years now–ever since the arrival of the Duke of Alva in the Low Countries as Lieutenant-Governor and Captain-General of the Forces–the Netherlander had protested with all the strength and the insistence at their command against the quartering of Spanish troops upon the inhabitants of their free cities. The practice was a flagrant violation of all the promises made to them by the King himself, and an outrage against their charters and liberties which the King had sworn to respect. But it also was a form of petty tyranny which commended itself specially to Alva, and to the Spanish ministers and councillors of State who liked above all to humiliate these Dutch and Flemish free men and cow them into complete submission and silent acquiescence by every means which their cruel and tortuous minds could invent.

Don Ramon knew quite well that he could offer no greater insult to the High-Bailiff of Ghent and to his sons—or, for the matter of that, to the whole city—than to allow his soldiery to behave in a scandalous and ribald manner in one of the well-accredited and well-conducted taverns of the town. And to him this knowledge gave but additional zest to what otherwise would have been a tame adventure—two women to bully and eight men to do it was not nearly as exciting as he could wish. But that fool Laurence van Rycke had to be punished—and incidentally don Ramon hoped that Mark would feel that the punishment was meted out to him more than to his brother.

On the whole don Ramon de Linea felt, as he entered the tap-room of the "Three Weavers," that the presence of the two van Ryckes was all that he needed to make his enjoyment complete.

That the Spanish provost and the six men under his command were already drunk there was no doubt: some of them were sitting at a long trestle table, sprawling across it, lolling up against one another, some singing scraps of bibulous songs, others throwing coarse, obscene jests across the table. Two men seemed to be on guard at the door, whilst one and all were clamouring for more wine.

"Curse you, you..." the provost was shouting at the top of his voice when don Ramon entered the tap-room, "why don't you bring another bottle of wine?"

Two women were standing at the further end of the long low room, close to the hearth: they stood hand in hand as if in an endeavour to inculcate moral strength to one another. The eldest of the two women might have been twenty-five years of age, the other some few years younger: their white faces and round, dilated eyes showed the deathly fear which held them both in its grip. Obviously the girls would have fled out of the tap-room long before this, and equally obviously the two men had been posted at the door in order to cut off their retreat.

At sight of their captain, the men staggered to their feet; the provost passed the word of command, fearful lest the ribald attitude of his men brought severe censure—and worse—upon himself. He stood up, as steadily, as uprightly as he could; but don Ramon took little notice of him; he called peremptorily to the two girls—who more frightened than ever now, still clung desperately to one another.

"Here, wench!" he said roughly, "I want wine, the best you have, and a private room in which to sit."

"At your service, señor!" murmured the elder of the two girls almost inaudibly.

"What's your name?" he asked.

"Katrine, so please your Magnificence."

"And yours?"

"Grete, at your service, Magnificence," whispered the girls one after the other, clinging one to the other, like two miserable atoms of humanity tossed about by the hard hand of Fate.

"At my service then, and quickly too," retorted don Ramon curtly, "go down into the cellar, Katrine, and get me a fresh bottle of Rhine wine—the best your heretical father hath left behind. And you, Grete, show me to another room, and when presently I order you to kiss me, see that you do not do it with such a sour mouth, or by Our Lady I'll remember that your father must hang on the morrow, and that you are nothing better than a pair of heretics too. Now then," he added harshly, "must I repeat the order?"

He had undone the buckle of his sword-belt, and was carrying his sheathed sword in his hand: he found it a splendid weapon for striking further terror into the hearts of the two girls, whose shrieks of pain and fear caused great hilarity amongst the soldiers. Don Ramon felt that if only Mark van Rycke could have been there, all the wounds which that young malapert had dared to inflict upon the pride of a Spanish grandee would forthwith be healed. Indeed, don Ramon enjoyed every incident of this exhilarating spectacle; for instance, when buxom Katrine had at last toddled down the steps into the cellar, the soldiers closed the trap-door upon her; whereupon the provost, who had become very hilarious, shouted lustily:

"What ho! what are you louts doing there? His Magnificence will be wanting the wine which he has ordered. If you lock the cellarer into her cellar, she'll come out presently as drunk as a Spanish lord."

"All right, provost," retorted one of the men, "we'll let her out presently. His Magnificence won't have to wait for long. But we can levy a toll on her—do you understand?—whenever the wench is ready to come out of prison."

"Oh! I understand!" quoth the provost with a laugh.

And don Ramon laughed too. He was enjoying himself even more than he had hoped. He saw the other girl—Grete—turn almost grey with terror, and he felt that he was punishing Mark van Rycke for every insolent word which he had uttered at the Town Hall and Laurence for every threatening gesture. He gave Grete a sharp prodding with the hilt of his sword:

"Now then, you Flemish slut," he said harshly, "show me to your best parlour, and don't stand there gaping."

Perforce she had to show him the way out of the public tapperij to the private room reserved for noble guests.

"Send one of your men to fetch the wench away in about half an hour, provost," called don Ramon loudly over his shoulder, "I shall have got tired of her by then."

Loud laughter greeted this sally and a general clapping of mugs against the table. Grete more dead than alive nearly fell over the threshold.

IV

The private room was on the opposite side of the narrow tiled hall and was dimly lighted by a small iron lamp that hung from a beam of the ceiling above. The door was half open and Grete pushed it open still further and then stood aside to allow the señor captain to pass.

"Will your Magnificence be pleased to walk in," she whispered.

Great tears were in her eyes; don Ramon paused under the lintel of the door, and with a rough gesture pinched her cheek and ear.

"Not ugly for a Flemish heifer," he said with a laugh. "Come along, girl! Let's see if your heretical father hath taught you how to pay due respect to your superiors."

"My humblest respect I do offer your Magnificence," said Grete, who was bravely trying to suppress her tears.

"Come! that's better," he retorted, as he pushed the girl into the room and swaggered in behind her, closing the door after him. "Now, Grete," he added, as he threw himself into a chair and stretched his legs out before him, "come and sit on my knee, and if I like the way you kiss me, why, my girl, there's no knowing what I might not do to please you. Come here, Grete!" he reiterated more peremptorily, for the girl had retreated to a dark corner of the room and was cowering there just like a frightened dog.

"Come here, Grete," he called loudly for the third time. But Grete was much too frightened to move.

With a savage oath don Ramon jumped to his feet, and kicked the chair on which he had been sitting so that it flew with a loud clatter half way across the room. Grete fell on her knees.

"Good Lord deliver me!" she murmured.

Don Ramon seized her by her two hands that were clasped together in prayer, he dragged her up from her knees, and toward the table which stood in the centre of the small, square room. Then he let her fall backwards against the table, and laughed because she continued to pray to God to help her.

"As if God would take any notice of heretics and rebels and Netherlanders generally," he said with a sneer. "Stand up, girl, and go back to my men. I have had enough of you already. Ye gods! what a vile crowd these Netherlanders are! Go back into the tap-room, do you hear, girl? and see that you and your ugly sister entertain my men as you should. For if you don't, and I hear of any psalm-singing or simpering nonsense I'll hand you over to the Inquisition as avowed heretics to-morrow."

But truly Grete was by now almost paralysed with fear; she was no brave heroine of romance who could stand up before a tyrant and browbeat him by the very force of her character and personality, she was but a mere wreckage of humanity whom any rough hand could send hopelessly adrift upon the sea of life. Her one refuge was her tears, her only armour of defence her own utter helplessness.

But this helplessness which would appeal to the most elementary sense of chivalry, had not the power to stir a single kind instinct in don Ramon de Linea. It must be admitted that it would not have appealed to a single Spaniard these days. They were all bred in the one school which taught them from infancy an utter contempt for this subject race and a deadly hatred against the heretics and rebels of the Low Countries. They were taught to look upon these people as little better than cattle, without any truth, honesty or loyalty in them, as being false and treacherous, murderous and dishonest. Don Ramon, who at this moment was behaving as scurrilously as any man, not absolutely born in the gutter, could possibly do, was only following the traditions of his race, of his country and its tyrannical government.

Therefore when Grete wept he laughed, when she murmured the little prayers which her father had taught her, he felt nothing but irritation and unmeasured contempt. He tried to silence the girl by loud shouts and peremptory commands, when these were of no avail he threatened, to call for assistance from his sergeant. Still the girl made no attempt either to move or to stem the flood of tears. Then don Ramon called aloud: "Hallo there, sergeant!" and receiving no answer, he went to the door, in order to reiterate his call from there.

V

His hand was on the latch, when the door was suddenly opened from without; so violently that don Ramon was nearly thrown off his balance, and would probably have measured his length on the floor, but that he fell up against the table and remained there, leaning against it with one hand in order to steady himself, and turning a wrathful glance on the intruder.

"By the Mass!" he said peremptorily, "who is this malapert who..."

But the words died on his lips; the look of wrath in his eyes gave way to one of sudden terror. He stared straight out before him at the sombre figure which had just crossed the threshold. It was the tall figure of a man dressed in dark tightly-fitting clothes, wearing high boots to the top of his thighs, a hood over his head and a mask of untanned leather on his face. He was unarmed.

Don Ramon, already a prey to that superstitious fear of the unknown and of the mysterious which characterised even the boldest of his country and of his race, felt all his arrogance giving way in the presence of this extraordinary apparition, which by the dim and

57

flickering light of the lamp appeared to him to be preternaturally tall and strangely menacing in its grim attitude of silence. Thus a moment or two went by. The stranger now turned and carefully closed and locked the door behind him. Key in hand he went up to the girl–Grete– who, no less terrified than her tormentor, was cowering in a corner of the room.

"Where is Katrine," he asked quickly; then, as the girl almost paralysed by fear seemed quite unable to speak, he added more peremptorily:

"Pull yourself together, wench; your life and Katrine's depend on your courage now. Where is she?"

"In ... in ... the cellar ... I think," stammered Grete almost inaudibly and making a brave effort to conquer her terror.

"Can you reach her without crossing the tap-room?"

The girl nodded.

"Well, then, run to her at once. Don't stop to collect any of your belongings, except what money you have; then go ... go at once.... Have you a friend or relative in this city to whom you could go at this late hour?"

Again the girl nodded, and looked up more boldly this time: "My father's sister..." she whispered.

"Where does she live?"

"At the sign of the 'Merry Beggars' in Dendermonde."

"Then go to her at once–you and Katrine. You will be safe there for awhile. If any further danger threatens you or your kinsfolk, you shall be advised ... in that case you would have to leave the country."

"I shouldn't be afraid," murmured the girl.

"That's good!" he concluded. "Come, Grete!"

He turned back to the door, unlocked it, and let the girl slip out of the room. Then he relocked the door.

VI

While this brief colloquy had been going on, don Ramon was making great efforts to recover his scattered wits and to steady his overstrung nerves. The superstitious fear which had gripped him by the throat, yielded at first to another equally terrifying thought: the hood and mask suggested an emissary of the Inquisition, one of those silent, nameless beings who seemed to have the power of omnipresence, who glided through closed doors and barred windows, appeared suddenly in tavern, church or street corner, and were invariably the precursors of arrest, torture-chamber and death. No man or woman–however high-born, however highly placed, however influential or however poor and humble, was immune from the watchful eye of the Inquisition; a thoughtless word, a careless jest–or the mere denunciation of an enemy–and the accusation of treason, heresy or rebellion was trumped up and gibbet or fire claimed yet another victim. Don Ramon–a Spanish grandee–could not of course be denounced as a heretic, but he knew that the eyes of de Vargas were upon him, that he might he thought importune or in the way now that other projects had been formed for donna Lenora–and he also knew that de Vargas would as ruthlessly sweep him out of the way as he would a troublesome fly.

Thus fear of real, concrete danger had succeeded that of the supernatural; but now that the stranger moved and spoke kindly with Grete–the daughter of an heretic–it was evident that he was no spy of the Inquisition: he was either an avowed enemy who chose this theatrical manner of accomplishing a petty vengeance, or in actual fact that extraordinary creature who professed to be the special protector of the Prince of Orange and whom popular superstition among the soldiery had nicknamed Leatherface.

The latter was by far the most likely, and as the stranger whoever he was, was unarmed, don Ramon felt that he had no longer any cause for fear. Though his sword–in its scabbard–was lying on the table, his dagger was in his belt. With a quick movement he unsheathed it, and at the precise moment when the masked man had his back to him in order to relock the door, don Ramon–dagger in hand–made a swift and sudden dash for him. But the stranger had felt rather than seen or heard the danger which threatened him. As quick as any feline creature he turned on his assailant and gripped his upraised hand by the wrist with such a vice-like grip that don Ramon uttered a cry of rage and pain: his fingers opened out nervelessly and the dagger fell with a clatter to the ground.

Then the two men closed with one another. It was a fight, each for the other's throat–a savage, primitive fight–man against man–with no weapon save sinewy hands, hatred and the primeval instinct to kill. The masked man was by far the more powerful and the more cool. Within a very few moments he had don Ramon down on his knees, his own strong hands gripping the other's throat. The Spaniard felt that he was doomed: he–of that race which was sending thousands of innocent and defenceless creatures to a hideous death–he, who had so often and so mercilessly lent a hand to outrage, to pillage and to murder, who but a few moments ago was condemning two helpless girls to insults and outrage worse than death, was in his turn a defenceless atom in the hands of a justiciary. The breath was being squeezed out of his body, his limbs felt inert and stiff, his mind became clouded over as by a crimson mist. He tried to call for help, but the cry died in his throat. And through the mist which gradually obscured his vision he could still see the silhouette of that closely-hooded head and a pair of eyes shining down on him through the holes of the leather mask.

"Let me go, miscreant," he gasped as for one moment the grip on his throat seemed to relax. "By heaven you shall suffer for this outrage."

"'Tis you will suffer," said the other coldly, "even as you would have made two helpless and innocent women suffer."

"They shall suffer yet!" cried don Ramon with a blasphemous oath, "they and their kith and kin—aye! and this accursed city which hath given you shelter! Assassin!"

"And it is because you are such an abominable cur," came a voice relentlessly from behind the leather mask, "because you would hunt two unfortunates down, them and their kith and kin and the city that gave them shelter, that you are too vile to live, and that I mean to kill you, like I would any pestilential beast that befouled God's earth. So make your peace with your Creator now, for you are about to meet Him face to face laden with the heavy burden of your infamies."

In don Ramon now only one instinct remained paramount—the instinct of a final effort for self-defence. When he fell, his knee came in contact with the dagger which he had dropped. It cost him a terrible effort, but nevertheless he succeeded in groping for it with his right hand and in seizing it: another moment of violent struggle for freedom, another convulsive movement and he had lifted the dagger. He struck with ferocious vigour at his powerful opponent and inflicted a gashing wound upon his left arm—the dagger penetrated to the bone, cutting flesh and muscle through from wrist to elbow.

But even as he struck he knew that it was too late; he had not even the strength to renew the effort. The next moment the vice-like grip tightened round his throat with merciless power. He could neither cry for help nor yet for mercy, nor were his struggles heard beyond these four narrow walls.

The soldiers whom he himself had bidden to be merry and to carouse, were singing and shouting at the top of their voice, and heard neither his struggles nor his cries. The dagger had long since slipped out of his hand, and at last he fell backwards striking his head against the leg of the table as he fell.

VII

In the tap-room the soldiers had soon got tired of waiting for Katrine. At first some of them amused themselves by reopening the trap-door, then sitting on the top step of the ladder that led to the cellar and thence shouting ribald oaths, coarse jests and blasphemies for the benefit of the unfortunate girl down below.

But after a time this entertainment also palled, and a council was held as to who should go down and fetch the girl. The cellar was vastly tempting in itself—with no one to guard it save a couple of wenches—

and the captain more than half-inclined to be lenient toward a real bout of drunkenness. It was an opportunity not to be missed; strange that the idea had not occurred to seven thirsty men before.

Now the provost declared that he would go down first, others could follow him in turn, but two must always remain in the tap-room in case the captain called, their comrades would supply them with wine from below. The provost descended–candle in hand–so did four of the men, but Katrine was no longer in the cellar. They hunted for her for awhile, and discovered a window, the shaft of which sloped upwards to a yard at the back of the house. The window was open and there was a ladder resting against the wall of the shaft.

The men swore a little, then went back to investigate the casks of wine. With what happened in the cellar after that this chronicle hath no concern, but those soldiers who remained up in the tap-room had a curious experience which their fuddled brains did not at first take in altogether. What happened was this: the door which gave on the passage was opened, and a man appeared under the lintel. He was dressed in sombre, tight-fitting doublet and hose, with high boots reaching well above his knees; he had a hood over his head and a mask on his face. The soldiers stared at him with wide-open, somewhat dimmed eyes.

The masked man only spoke a few words:

"Tell your provost," he said, "that señor captain don Ramon de Linea lies dead in the room yonder."

Then he disappeared, as quietly as he had come.

CHAPTER V

VENGEANCE

I

"Satan! Satan! Assassin!"

Donna Lenora had stood beside the dead body of her lover and kinsman wide-eyed and pale with rigid, set mouth and trembling knees while her father explained to her how don Ramon de Linea had been murdered in the tavern of the "Three Weavers" by an unknown man who wore a leather mask. She had listened to the whole garbled version of the sordid affair, never thinking to doubt a single one of her father's words: don Ramon de Linea, according to the account given to his daughter by Juan de Vargas, had—while in the execution of his duty—been attacked in a dark passage by a mysterious assassin, who had fled directly his nefarious work had been accomplished.

The murderer, however, was seen by the provost in command and by two of the soldiers, and was accurately described by them as wearing doublet and high-boots of a dark-brown colour, a hood over his head and a mask of untanned leather on his face. The man had rapidly disappeared in the darkness, evading all pursuit.

And donna Lenora—thus face to face for the first time in her sheltered life with crime, with horror and with grief—had, in the first moment of despairing misery, not even a prayer to God in her heart, for it was filled with bitter thoughts of resentment and of possible revenge.

She had loved her cousin don Ramon de Linea with all the ardour of her youth, of her warm temperament and of a heart thirsting for the self-sacrifice which women were so ready to offer these days on the altar of their Love. She had never thought him shallow or cruel: to her he had always been just the playmate of childhood's days, the handsome, masterful boy whom she had looked up to as the embodiment of all that was strong and noble and chivalrous, the first man who had ever whispered the magic word "love" in her ear.

Now an unknown enemy had killed him: not in fair fight, not in the open, on the field of honour, but—as her father said—in a tavern, in the dark, surreptitiously, treacherously; and donna Lenora in an agony of passionate resentment had at last broken the silence which had almost frightened her father and had suddenly called out with fierce intensity: "Satan! Satan! Assassin!" Her father had given her an account of the horrible incident, which was nothing but a tissue of falsehoods from beginning to end, and Lenora had listened and believed. How could she doubt her own father? She hardly knew him—and he was all she had in the world on whom to pour out the wealth of her affection and of her faith.

II

Truth to tell, de Vargas had received the news of don Ramon's death with unbounded satisfaction.

Lenora had obeyed him and had been this night publicly affianced to Mark van Rycke; but between her consent to the marriage and her willingness to become Alva's tool as a spy among her husband's people there was the immeasurable abyss of a woman's temperament and a woman's natural pity for the oppressed.

But the outrage to-night—the murder of the man whom she still loved despite paternal prohibitions—was bound to react on the girl's warm and passionate nature—and react in the manner which her father desired. He trusted to his own powers of lying, to place the case before his daughter in its most lurid light. He had at once spoken of "spies" and "assassins" and his words had been well chosen. Within a few moments after he had told Lenora the news, he felt that he could play like a skilled musician upon every string of her overwrought sensibilities. Her heart had already been very sore at being forced to part from her first lover; now that the parting had suddenly become irrevocable in this horrible way, all the pent up passion, fierce resentment and wrath which she had felt against her future husband and his people could by clever manipulation be easily merged into an equally fierce desire for revenge.

It was a cruel game to play with a young girl who by blood and race was made to feel every emotion with super-acuteness: but de Vargas was not the man who would ever allow pity or chivalry to interfere with his schemes: he saw in his daughter's mental suffering, in the shattering of her nerves and the horror which had well-nigh paralysed her, nothing but a guarantee of success for that comprehensive project which had the death of the Prince of Orange for its ultimate aim.

"It is strange," murmured the girl after awhile, "that when Ramon talked with me in the Town House last night, he said that these Netherlanders had a habit of striking at an enemy in the dark."

"A presentiment, no doubt," rejoined de Vargas with well-feigned gentleness. "Now, my child, you begin to understand—do you not?—why it is that we Spaniards hate these treacherous Netherlanders. They are vile and corrupt to the heart, every single man, woman or child of them. They fear us and have not the pluck to fight us in the open. Orange and his contemptible little army have sought shelter in Holland—they dare not face the valour and enthusiasm of our troops. But mark you, what Orange hath done! He hath sown the entire country with a crop of spies! They are here, there, everywhere—not very cunning and certainly not brave—their orders are to strike in the dark when and how they can. They waylay our Spanish officers in the ill-lighted, and intricate streets of their abominable cities, they dog their footsteps until they meet them in some lowly tavern or a tenebrous archway: then out comes their dagger, swift and sure, and they strike in the gloom—and a gallant Spanish officer's blood stains the cobblestones of one of their towns. It was don Ramon to-day—it will be Julian Romero perhaps to-morrow—or don Juan de Vargas—who knows? or mayhap the duke of Alva one day. Orange and his crowd are out on a campaign of assassination—an army of assassins has been let loose—and their captain-general wears a mask of leather and our soldiery have dubbed him 'Leatherface'!"

"I have heard of this man 'Leatherface,'" said Lenora slowly. "It is he, you think, who murdered Ramon?"

"Have we not the soldiers' testimony?" he rejoined blandly, "two

63

men and the provost saw him quite clearly. As for me, I am not surprised: more than once our spies have reported that the man undoubtedly hailed from Ghent, and once he was traced to the very gates of this city. But," he added insinuatingly, "here he is surrounded by friends: every burgher in Ghent, no doubt, opens wide his hospitable door to the murderer of Spanish officers."

"Think you it is likely that the High-Bailiff of Ghent or ... or ... my future husband would harbour such an assassin?" she asked.

"Well!" he replied evasively, "all Netherlanders are treacherous. The High-Bailiff himself and his son Mark are said to be loyal ... but there's another son ... and the mother ... one never knows. It would be strange," he continued unctuously, "if at some future time the murderer of Ramon should find shelter in your house."

"I shall pray to the saints," she rejoined with passionate intensity, "that he and I may meet face to face one day."

Indeed de Vargas had no cause to fear that henceforth his daughter would fail in her vigilance. The assassination of her lover had stirred her soul to its inmost depths. Indifference and light-hearted girlishness had suddenly given place to all the violent passions of her ardent nature. For the moment desire for vengeance—for justice she called it—and hatred of the assassin and his mates had swept every other thought, every soft aspiration away: all her world—the world as seen through the rose-coloured windows of a convent window—had tottered and opened beneath her feet, and through the yawning chasm she now saw evil and lust and cruelty dancing a triumphant saraband over Ramon's dead body.

"There is a means," resumed de Vargas after a slight pause, during which through half-closed lids he studied the play of every varying emotion upon his daughter's beautiful face, "there is a means, my child, whereby you or any faithful servant of our King can henceforth recognise at a glance the man who killed your cousin Ramon."

"A means?"

"Yes. He carries upon his arm the brand of his own infamy."

"Will you tell me more clearly what you mean?" she asked.

"Ramon had not breathed his last when the provost found him and ultimately brought him here to my lodgings. He was able to speak and to give a fragmentary account of what had taken place: how he was set upon in the dark and stabbed to death ere he could utter a cry. But at the last moment he made a supreme effort and wrenching his dagger from his belt he struck with it at his assailant. It seems that he inflicted a very severe wound upon the miscreant: the dagger penetrated into the left forearm close to the elbow and gashed the flesh and muscle as far as the wrist and right through to the bone. It is not likely that at this moment there is more than one man in Ghent who hath such a wound in the left forearm: the wound was deep too, and will take some time to heal, and even when it is healed it will leave a tell-tale scar which will last for years.

"I think," rejoined Lenora coldly, "that I should know the man who killed Ramon, even if he bore no brand of Cain upon his person."

Father and daughter looked at one another and for the space of a few seconds their souls—so different in every ideal, every feeling, every aspiration—met in one common resolve. He could hardly repress a sigh of satisfaction. He knew that he held her, closely, firmly, indissolubly at last. He held her by all the romance which her girlish imagination had woven round the personality of a worthless man, and by all the deep sense of injury which she felt as well as all the horror and the indignation at the dastardly deed. And his own warped and gloomy soul was at one with her pure and childlike one—pure because even the desire for revenge which she felt, she ascribed to God, and called it justice. The Moorish blood in her which mingles even with the bluest Castilian claimed with savage, primeval instinct that "eye for an eye" and "tooth for a tooth" which alone can satisfy a hot-headed and passionate race.

Lenora's eyes as she met those of her father lost their look of dull despair: something of the fanatical hatred which he felt for the whole of the despised race communicated itself to her, now that she too had so much cause for hatred.

"We understand one another, Lenora," he said. And like a feline creature sure of its prey, he drew quite close to her and took her hand, and began gently to stroke it.

"You will have to teach me what to do, father," she rejoined.

"Your heart and wits will tell you that. In a few days you will have entered the van Rycke household. Keep your eyes and ears open, and win the confidence and love of all those around you. Let not a word, a sign, a gesture escape you, and come and tell me at once all that you see and hear. Will you promise to do that, my Lenora?" he added, forcing his harsh voice to tones of gentleness.

"I promise," she replied fervently.

"The Lieutenant-Governor believes that Orange himself has been visiting Ghent lately! Keep your eyes and ears open, Lenora, you may be the means of bringing that arch-traitor to his just punishment. Promise me that you will listen," he urged.

"I promise," she reiterated firmly.

"The Lieutenant-Governor comes to Ghent in a few days' time. Wherever he goes there is always fear for his precious life. If Orange has been in Ghent then he hath hatched a plot against the Duke—on this I would stake my life—promise me that you will be on the watch, Lenora!"

"I promise."

"Upon your soul, my child?"

"Upon my soul!"

"And next to Orange himself, I'd sooner see that masked assassin Leatherface hang than any man in Europe; remember that, little one!"

"I'll not forget."

"The outrage on don Ramon de Linea must not remain unavenged, remember that."

"I'll not forget."

"Then let Orange and his rebels look to themselves!" ejaculated de Vargas with a note of triumph.

He took from the breast pocket of his doublet a piece of silk ribbon to which was attached a flat, yet curiously fashioned and shaped piece of steel.

"Take this, my child," he said significantly, as he held the trinket out to her. "This little bit of metal hath already done more service to our Lord the King, to our country, and to our faith than a whole army of spies."

"What is it, dear?" she asked.

"It is a little talisman," he replied, "that will turn any lock and open any secret drawer by whomsoever lock and drawer have been manufactured. It was made for me by the finest metal-cutter of Toledo—one in fact whose skill was so paramount that we had reluctantly to ... to put him out of harm's way. He was getting dangerous. This pass-key was his masterpiece. I have tested it on the most perfect specimens of the locksmith's art both in Toledo and in Florence. It hath never failed me yet. Take it, my child, and guard it carefully. An I mistake not, you will find use for it in your new home."

Before she could protest he had thrown the ribbon over her head, and she—mechanically but with unaccountable reluctance withal—slipped the trinket into the bosom of her gown.

"Remember, my dear," concluded de Vargas, "that the day after your marriage I must return to Brussels. But if you see or hear anything that may concern the welfare of our Sovereign Lord the King, or of his government, you must come to me at once—do not hesitate—invent a pretext—come away in secret—do anything rather than delay. And remember also that anything you may tell me, I will treat in absolute confidence. Your name will never appear in connection with any denunciation ... I mean," he interrupted himself hastily, "with any service which you may render to the State. Will you remember that also, my child?"

"I will remember," she replied.

It seemed almost as if she were under the potent spell of some wizard. She spoke and acted just as her father directed—and yet he looked so evil at this moment, hypocrisy and lust were so apparent in his jaundiced face, that even Lenora felt a sudden pang of doubt and of fear—doubt as to the purity of her own motives and fear at the terrible companionship which would henceforth exist between herself and her father's friends, men who—like him—were bent on the destruction of a nation and were actuated by blind hatred to oppress an entire people.

66

De Vargas–vaguely guessing what went on in the girl's mind–made an effort to regain his former bland manner: he strove by gentleness and soft words to lull her suspicions. After all, he was her father and she–a motherless child–had no one now in the world to whom she could cling, on whom she could pour out that wealth of love and tenderness which filled her young heart to overflowing. So now–very soon–she was kneeling close beside him, her head resting against his bosom–the dove nestling near the hawk; and the tears which would not come all the while that her soul was consumed with bitterness, flowed beneficently at last and eased her overburdened heart.

"You will not fail me, little one?" asked de Vargas even in the midst of tender, endearing words.

"Never!" she murmured, "if you turned against me, father dear, whither could I go? I have no one in the world but you."

As her head was bent and her eyes downcast, she could not see the cold and cruel glitter that shone in his face as he heard this simple profession of whole-hearted devotion and faith.

"Tell me what to do and I'll do it," she whispered again.

"Then will God Himself reward you," he rejoined unctuously, "for you will be serving Him and His Church, His anointed and the country of His chosen people."

After which he rose, kissed her and finally with a sigh of intense satisfaction left her to meditate alone, to dream and to pray.

BOOK TWO

DENDERMONDE

CHAPTER VI

A STRANGER IN A STRANGE LAND

I

A week later was the marriage solemnised between donna Lenora de Vargas and Mark van Rycke, son of the High-Bailiff of Ghent.

The religious ceremony took place in the abbey church of St. Bavon in the presence of several members of the Grand Council and of all the high functionaries of the city. Nothing had been spared to make the occasion a magnificent and imposing one. The union between the two young people was known to have the warm approval of the King himself: His Holiness the Pope had sent a special blessing to the bride and bridegroom, whilst the Captain-General had granted the use of a number of picked troops to render the display more gorgeous. Seven hundred and fifty arquebusiers, spearmen and halberdiers lined the route of the bridal procession between the town-house and the church: they were dressed in the heraldic colours of the city of Ghent, one leg blue and the other yellow, and wore enormous hats with huge feathers dyed in the two colours.

The Regent too had graciously lent his court musicians for the occasion and they headed the procession with full orchestra playing the newest motets. The church itself had been magnificently decorated with tapestries, and a huge concourse of people lined the streets in order to view all this pomp and magnificence.

After the religious ceremony a grand banquet was held in the great hall of the Town House at which eighty-four privileged guests were bidden. It was served at separate tables each laid for a dozen guests, and consisted of twenty-five courses—which were both varied and succulent. There were fowls stewed in milk and dressed with sweetmeats and spices, there were pickled partridges and pastries, sausages and omelettes of every kind, whilst huge flagons of iced beer and Rhenish wines added to the conviviality of the entertainment.

Señor de Vargas presided at the chief table, and he had the bride on his right and the bridegroom on his left. The High-Bailiff also sat at this table as did Madame his wife and Messire Laurence van Rycke, and every one remarked that señor de Vargas was in high good-humour and that he bestowed marked evidences of his favour both upon the High-Bailiff and upon the bridegroom.

During the banquet the court musicians discoursed sweet music; in fact everything was done not only with decorum but with liberality: this was the first union between a noted and highly placed Spanish family and an equally distinguished patrician house of Flanders, and in a brief toast, tankard in hand, señor de Vargas expressed the hope that it might prove the precursor of a great many more.

Those present at the feast remarked moreover that the bride was beautiful beyond powers of description, that the bridegroom looked as usual, as if he had been spending half his nights in the taverns, and that Messire Laurence van Rycke looked pale and sick.

But nothing of any grave moment occurred during the length of this exciting and strenuous day. After the banquet the tables were cleared and many more guests arrived to take part in a grand reunion and ball which lasted well into the night. But neither the bride or bridegroom nor any of the grand Spanish seigniors stayed for that: a small procession was formed soon after the conclusion of the banquet, consisting of the parents of bride and bridegroom flanked by a guard of honour, which conducted the young couple from the Town House to the residence of the High-Bailiff, which was to remain their home until such time as a more fitting permanent abode could be provided for them.

II

And now the escort had taken leave of the young people: don Juan de Vargas and the High-Bailiff had to return to their guests at the Town House and Clémence van Rycke had gone to rest. The arquebusiers had gone and the serving men and women—with the exception of Pierre and Jeanne—had gone to watch the illuminations and to listen to the strains of the orchestra which could be heard quite plainly through the open windows of the Town House.

Clémence van Rycke had conducted the bride upstairs to the nuptial-chamber. With her own hands she had drawn a high-backed chair close to the fire and made the young girl sit down. Mark then placed a footstool to her feet and a down cushion to her back.

Lenora accepted all these little attentions without a word, but with a grateful smile. She was far too tired to speak, and when Clémence finally kissed her on the forehead and whispered a motherly:

"God bless you, my child!" she could hardly murmur a feeble "Goodnight!" in reply.

Then Madame van Rycke went away, and the house seemed suddenly to become very still. Lenora was still in her bridal gown, which was of stiff white brocade, with very high starched collar and hard stomacher that cramped her movements and made her sides ache. Her hair had been combed away from her forehead and only a few unruly curls lay moist against her brow: her delicate skin rebelled against the conventional white and pink unguents which the careful fingers of a highly-trained waiting woman had laid upon her cheeks and lips, and the dark lines of a black pencil round her lashes could not add lustre to her luminous dark eyes which, despite fatigue, shone with marvellous brilliancy.

She sat with hands folded before her, staring into the fire, and the flames in wanton frolic threw a golden glow upon her face and her gown and deep blue shadows all around her. Mark van Rycke—unseen by her—stood at the other end of the monumental hearth, one arm resting against the ledge, his head against his hand, so that his face was completely in shadow and she could not know that he was watching her.

"You are tired, Madonna?" he asked after a little while, and she replied, pathetically, like a child about to cry:

"Very tired, Messire."

"It has been a long and trying day for you," he continued lightly. "I confess to being very tired myself, and as soon as Jeanne comes to wait on you, I would beg of you that I might take my leave."

Then as she said nothing, but continued to stare into the fire in a listless manner, he added a little impatiently:

"Jeanne will not be long; she attends upon my mother every night, but will be at your service directly. Can you put up with my company, Madonna, till she come?"

"I am at your service, Messire," she rejoined stiffly, "if there is aught you wish to say to me."

"How cold you are, sweetheart," he said good-humouredly. "It would seem as if we were still in the presence of that awe-inspiring duenna of yours: what was her name?—I forget—but by the Mass! I tell you, sweet, that she froze the very marrow in my bones ... and you were so formal in her presence too—brrrr!—it makes me shiver to think of those half-hours spent during the past week in such a freezing atmosphere!"

He laughed—a quaint little laugh—half merry and half shy, and after an instant's hesitation, he drew a low chair forward and sat down in front of the fire, close to her. Even then she did not turn to look at him.

"Had it not been for your eyes, Madonna," he said softly, "I would have sworn that you were fashioned of marble."

70

Now he was leaning a little forward, his elbow resting on his knee, his hand shading his face from the light of the fire. He was studying her face closely, and thought that he had never seen any woman quite so beautiful. "Laurence was a fool!" he was saying to himself as he took in every detail of the perfect face, the delicate contour of the cheeks, the pearly whiteness of the skin, the exquisite line of chin and throat, and above all those dark, glowing, unfathomable eyes which betrayed all the latent fire and passion which coldness of demeanour strove vainly to conceal. "Laurence was a fool! He would have fallen madly in love with this beautiful creature, and would have made her happy and contented with her lot, whilst the bonds of matrimony would have sat more lightly on him than on me."

He sighed, feeling a little sorry for himself, but nevertheless he stretched out his hand and captured hers—an exquisitely fashioned little hand it was, delicate to the touch and pulsating with life, like a prisoned bird. Mark was a young man—and one who had already got out of life most of the joys which it holds, but just for a moment he felt a curious thrill of unaccustomed pleasure, in holding this perfect thing—donna Lenora's hand. His own hands were strong, yet slender, finely shaped and warm to the touch, but it must be supposed that as he held hers, he must—quite unconsciously—have hurt her, for suddenly he saw that she turned even whiter than she had been before, her eyes closed and quite abruptly she withdrew her hand.

"Do I anger you, Madonna?" he asked.

"Nay, Messire," she replied coldly.

"May I not then hold your hand—for a very little while in mine?"

"If you wish."

But she did not voluntarily put her hand out to him, and he made no second attempt to capture it.

"We do not seem to be getting along very fast," he said quaintly.

She smiled. "Seeing how we came to be together, Messire," she said, "we were not like to have much in common."

"Yet, we shall have to pass our lives together, Madonna."

"Alas!" she sighed.

"I own that the prospect cannot be very alluring for you—it doth not seem to suggest an interminable vista of happiness...."

"Oh!" she murmured as if involuntarily, "I was not thinking of happiness."

"How strange," he retorted gently, "now, whenever I look at you, Madonna, I invariably think of happiness."

"Happiness? With me?"

"With you, sweetheart, if you will but allow me to work for that object. After all, my dear," he added with that whimsical smile of his, "we are both young, you and I; life lies all before us. I own that we have made a sorry beginning, that the first chapter of our book of life hath been ill-writ and by clumsy hands. But suppose we turn over a few

71

pages, do you not think that we might happen on a more romantic passage?"

He drew nearer still to her, so near that as he bent toward her his knee touched the ground and his arm instinctively stretched out behind her, so that at the least movement on her part it would close around her and hold her—as indeed he longed that it should do. She was so very beautiful, and that air of settled melancholy, of childlike helplessness and pathos in her made an irresistible appeal to him.

"Madonna," he whispered, "an you would let me, I should like to make love to you now."

But she, with a quick, impatient jerk suddenly sat bolt upright and freed herself almost roughly from that arm which was nearly encircling her shoulders.

"Love!" she said with cold sarcasm. "You?"

He bit his lip and in his turn drew back: the dour look in his face became more marked and the merry twinkle died out of his eyes: his knee no longer touched the ground, but he remained quite self-possessed and said, still quite good-humouredly:

"Yes, I—your husband as it happens, Madonna. Would love from me be so very distasteful to you then?"

"I have no love for you, Messire, as you well know," she said coldly. "I told you what my feelings were toward yon, the first time that we met—at the Town House, the night of our betrothal."

"Yes," he owned, "you spoke very plainly then."

"And since then I have had no cause to change."

"I am as distasteful to you as I ever was?" he asked with droll consternation.

"Oh!—not distasteful, Messire."

"Come! that's something."

"Enough, methinks."

"Not by a long way, but it is a beginning. To-day I am not altogether distasteful—to-morrow I might e'en be tolerated ... in a week toleration might turn to liking ... and after that, liking to..."

"Never," she broke in firmly, "I should have to forget that which is indelibly writ upon my memory."

"And what is that?"

"That you married me without love and without wooing—bought me like a bundle of goods just because my father is powerful and yours ambitious. A week ago we were betrothed, Messire. Since then how hath your time been passed?"

"In wild, ecstatic half-hours spent in the presence of your duenna and sitting opposite to the chilliest bride in Christendom," he said whimsically.

"And the rest of the time in the taverns of Ghent," she retorted hotly, "and places of ill-repute."

"Who told you that?" he asked quietly.

72

"Oh! your reputation is well known: how could it fail to reach mine ears."

"Evil tongues always make themselves heard, Madonna," he said, still speaking very quietly, although now he sat quite apart from her, with his long legs stretched out before him and his hands clasped between his knees. "I would you had not listened."

"I would I had not heard," she assented, "for then I should not have added one more humiliation to all those which I have had to endure."

"And I another regret," he said with a short sigh. "But even if evil tongues spoke true, Madonna," he continued more lightly, "the shame of my conduct would sit on me and not on you. They call me a ne'er-do-well in the city—and have it seems done so in your hearing! Well! let me plead guilty for the past and lay my contrition at your feet."

Once more the more gentle mood overcame him. The house was so still and there was something quite unaccountably sweet in this sentimental dalliance with this exquisitely beautiful woman who was his wife—sentimental indeed, for though she appeared cold and even cruelly sarcastic, he felt the strength of a fine nature in her. Here was no mere doll, mere puppet and slave of man content to take her lot as her family or her husband chose to shape it—content to endure or accept a husband's love without more return than passive obedience and meaningless kisses. At the back of his mind he still thought Laurence a fool, and felt how well suited two such warm natures would have been to one another, but for the moment a strange desire seized him, to win a kind look from this beautiful woman on his own account, to see her smile on him, willingly and confidingly, to win her friendship and her trust, even though no warmer feeling should ever crop up between him and her.

"Madonna," he said, and once again he dropped his knee to the ground and leaned toward her so that her warm breath touched his hand, which he placed upon hers, "there are many men in the world who ne'er do well because they have been left to the companionship of those who do equally badly. Will you deign to believe that all the evil that is in me lies very much on the surface? They call me wild and extravagant—even my mother calls me careless and shallow—but if you smiled on me, Madonna, methinks that something which lies buried deep down in my heart would stir me to an effort to become worthy of you."

His voice—habitually somewhat rough and always slightly ironical—was wonderfully gentle now. Instinctively, perhaps even against her will, Lenora turned her head slowly round and looked at him. He had never before looked so straight and closely into her eyes; and, as she bore his scrutinising glance, the warm blood slowly mounted to her cheeks. Her face was partly in shadow, only the outline of her small head was outlined by the ruddy glow of the fire, and the tiny ear shone, transparent and crimson, like a shell, with the golden tendrils of her fair hair gently stirring in the draught from the wide, open hearth.

As she was excited and perhaps a little frightened, her breath came and went rapidly, and her lips were slightly parted showing a faint glimmer of pearly teeth beyond. Mark felt a sudden rush of blood to his head; to be alone with this adorable woman so close to him, to feel her panting like a young creature full of life and passion, slightly leaning against his arm, to look into those wonderful, dark eyes and know that she was his, was indeed more than man could endure in cold blood.

The next moment he had caught her with irresistible masterfulness in both his arms and drawn her down to him as he knelt, whilst his eager lips sought hers with a mad longing for a kiss. But with an agonised cry of horror, she pushed him away with all her feeble might. For a moment she struggled in his arms like a wild creature panting for liberty and murmuring mad, incoherent words: "Let me go! Let me go! I hate you!"—the next, she was already free, and he had struggled to his feet. Now he stood at some little distance from her, looking down on her with a scared gaze and passing his hand mechanically backwards and forwards across his brow.

"Your pardon, Madonna," he murmured, "I did not understand that you could hate me so."

The fire was burning low, and the two candles in tall sconces at the further end of the room threw but a fitful light upon that hunched up young figure in the big, high-backed chair, cowering there half frightened at her own violence, tired out with emotion, her nerves quivering after the final, tense moment which had left her exhausted and almost unconscious.

Mark could only see her dimly; the stiff folds of her wedding gown and the high starched collar were alone visible in the gloom; she had hidden her face in the cushion of the chair. Presently a sob rose to her throat, and then another, and soon she was crying just like a tired child. Mark felt that he had been a brute and was seized with an infinite pity for her.

"Madonna," he said gently, "I think I can hear Jeanne's footstep in the corridor. May I call to her to come and attend on you?"

"I thank you, Messire," murmured Lenora, who was making a great effort to swallow her tears.

"Then I pray you dry your eyes," he pleaded, "I would be so ashamed if Jeanne saw that I had made you cry."

She looked up and even in the gloom he thought that he could see a swift smile pass across her face.

"To-morrow an you desire," he continued more lightly, "your old dragon Inez shall be here to wait on you, until then I trust that you will not feel too lonely, away from those you care for. My mother is an

74

angel. You will love her, I think, and my brother Laurence is learned and well-read ... my father too is kind. We will all strive, Madonna, to make you somewhat more contented with your lot."

"You mistake, Messire," she stammered, "I..."

But already he had bowed before her and bidden her a formal good-night. She had meant to give him her hand and to ask his forgiveness, for indeed she had behaved like an ill-tempered child—a bad beginning for the role which she had sworn to play—but he had gone, and before she could call him back he was speeding down the corridor and anon she heard him loudly calling to Jeanne.

III

Lenora did not see her husband during the whole of the next day, and on the one occasion when she ventured to ask after him—with well-feigned indifference lest any one guessed that all was not well between them—Clémence van Rycke sighed, Messire the High-Bailiff gave a forced laugh and Laurence van Rycke frowned with obvious anger. And in the evening—when she retired to her room and felt strangely irritable and hurt at being left in such solitude—she questioned Inez, who had been allowed to come and wait on her and who had a marvellous faculty for gleaning all the gossip that was going about the town.

"They do say, my angel," said the old woman with that complacency which characterises your true gossip, "that Messire Mark van Rycke hath spent his whole day in the tavern opposite. It is known as the 'Three Weavers,' and many Spanish officers are quartered in there now."

"Heaven protect us!" ejaculated Lenora involuntarily, "I trust they did not quarrel."

"Quarrel, my saint?" retorted Inez with a spiteful little laugh, for she had no liking for these Netherlanders. "Nay! Messire van Rycke would not dare quarrel with a Spanish officer. No! no! it seems that the tapperij of the 'Three Weavers' was most convivial all the day. It is always frequented by Spanish officers, although the inn-keeper is said to be an abominable heretic: there was much gambling and heavy drinking there, so they say, and even now..."

And as if to confirm the old woman's say, there came from the house opposite and through the open windows loud noise of gay laughter and hilarious song. A deep flush rose to Lenora's face.

"Close that window, Inez," she said peremptorily, "the night hath turned chilly."

She went to sit by the fire, and curtly dismissed the gossiping old woman. She knew all that she had wanted to know, and the flush of shame deepened on her cheek. There had been times during the past week when a vague hope had stirred in her heart that mayhap life did hold a small measure of happiness for her. There were times when she did not altogether dislike Mark van Rycke, when that winning merriment and good-humour which always lurked in his eyes provoked a response in her own ... and others, when certain notes of gentleness in his voice caused a strange thrill in her heart and brought tears into her eyes, which were not altogether tears of sorrow. She had also felt deeply remorseful at her conduct last night at the cruel words: "I hate you!" which she had flung so roughly in his face: indeed she could scarcely sleep all night, for she was persistently haunted by the dazed look in those merry, grey eyes of his which had just for one brief moment flashed tender reproach on her.

But now she felt nothing but shame—shame that she should ever have thought tenderly of a man who could so wrong her, who had so little thought of her that he could spend his whole day in a tavern whilst his young girl-bride was left to loneliness and boredom in a house where she was a total stranger. She thought him vindictive and cruel: already she had thought so last night when he went away hurriedly without waiting for the apology which was hovering on her lips. Now she was quite sure that she hated him, and the next time she told him so, she certainly would not regret it.

But somehow she felt more forlorn than she had been before that dotard Inez had filled her ears with gossip. The house as usual was very still, but Lenora knew that the family had not yet gone to rest. Awhile ago she thought that she had heard footsteps and a murmur of voices in the hall below. A desire for company seized the young girl, and she racked her brain for an excuse to go down to her mother-in-law, who she knew was kind and who perhaps would cheer and comfort her a little and give her kind pity in her loneliness.

CHAPTER VII

THE REBELS

I

At this same hour in the small withdrawing-room which adjoined the dining-hall in Messire van Rycke's house, five men were sitting round the gate-legged table in the centre of the room. At the top of the table sat Clémence van Rycke, in a tall chair covered with crimson velvet; opposite to her sat a man who was dressed in rough clothes of dark-coloured buffle, and whose ruff was of plain, coarse linen; he wore a leather belt to which was fastened a heavy wallet, and high, tough boots that reached above his knee. His black hat and mantle lay on a chair close by. In fact, his clothes—more than ordinarily sombre and plain—were such as the serving man of a poor burgher might wear; nevertheless this man had round his neck a crimson ribbon to which was attached a gold pendant in the shape of a dead wether—which is the badge worn by the Knights of the Golden Fleece.

When this man spoke the others listened to him with marked deference, and Laurence van Rycke stood all the time beside his chair and served him with wine. In appearance he was spare of build and tall, he wore full beard and moustache and hair brushed away from an unusually high forehead. His eyes were prominent and very keen and astute as well as frank and kindly in expression, and his eyebrows were fully and markedly arched.

Clémence van Rycke was the only woman present. The other three men were all dressed in dark clothes, and their black mantles hung over the backs of their chairs. The room in which these half-dozen people were assembled was narrow and oak-panelled; at the end of it there was a low and very wide window recess, across which heavy curtains of crimson velvet had been drawn; at the side a door gave on the dining-hall; this door was open and the hall beyond was in complete darkness.

The whole room was only dimly lighted by one thick wax candle which burned in a tall sconce that stood on a bracket in an angle of the room, and threw a fitful light on the grave faces of the men sitting around the table.

"The High-Bailiff hath business at the Town House," Clémence van Rycke was saying in reply to the stranger who sat opposite to her. "He will not be home until midnight. My son Mark, too, is from home," she added more curtly. "Your Highness can discuss your plans with these gentlemen in all security. And if you wish me to retire..."

She half rose as if she meant to go, but a word from the stranger kept her in her place.

"I entreat you to stay with us, mevrouw," he said; "we would wish you to hear all that we have to say. Of a truth we have no more loyal adherents than mevrouw van Rycke and her son, and what we should have done in this city without their help I do not know."

He turned at the same time to Laurence and stretched out his hand to him. The young man at once bent the knee and kissed the gracious hand.

"The little that we have done, Monseigneur," said Clémence softly, "hath been done with great gladness seeing that it was in your service."

"Not only mine, mevrouw," rejoined the stranger. "I am but the instrument of God's will, an humble follower of His cause. What you have done was done for Him and for the cause of liberty, of justice and of right."

"May God's blessing rest upon your Highness' enterprise," murmured Clémence fervently. "For God and William of Orange is our cry. Your cause is the cause of God."

"Alas!" said the Prince, with a sigh of utter weariness and dejection, "you know how little success I have had in this city ... promises! promises! promises I have in plenty, and a couple of thousand young men from the town have rallied to my standard. A poor result indeed after all my efforts! So much tyranny!" he exclaimed bitterly, "such wanton oppression! the dastardly outrages at Mons and at Mechlin! and only two thousand men among thirty, willing to take up arms to defend their liberty, their ancient privileges, their very homes!"

He leaned his elbows on the table and buried his head in his hands. Clémence van Rycke was silent as were the men; their hearts echoed all the bitterness which had surged up in William of Orange's heart.

"Yet your Highness refuses to take me with you," said Laurence with gentle reproach.

"Only for the moment, Messire," rejoined the Prince, "only for the moment. Never fear but I will send for you as soon as I have need of you. Can I afford to reject so devoted a champion? But for the moment you can do so much more for me by staying quietly at home than if you followed me on my recruiting campaign. I have not yet exhausted the resources and enthusiasm of this city—of that I feel confident, I shall try again—for another week. There are still several likely houses that I have not visited, and whose cordial invitation I have received..."

"Beware of treachery, your Highness!" broke in Clémence van Rycke suddenly.

"Nay, Madonna," he said, whilst that same winning smile lit up the sombre dejection of his face, "but have I not told you that my dragon is on the watch? Not a step am I allowed to take in this city without his permission. He allowed me to come to this house to-night, because he knew that I desired to express my gratitude to you personally. But I can assure you," he added, laughing softly to himself, "I had to fight for the permission."

"Is that not insolence?" exclaimed one of the others hotly. "Were we not to be trusted with the care of your sacred person?"

"You all, seigniors, and Messire van Rycke and his mother," rejoined the Prince; "but there are others in this house. Do not blame my devoted Leatherface," he continued earnestly; "but for him I should not be here now. No man could be more watchful, no man more brave or more resourceful. Countless times did he save me from the assassin's dagger and the poisoner's cup. If my life is necessary for the cause of freedom and justice, then have freedom and justice in Leatherface their truest and most efficient champion."

"Amen to that," rejoined Clémence van Rycke with fervour. "I only wish I knew who he was, that I might pray more personally for him."

"Ah! we none of us know who he is, Madonna," said William of Orange more lightly. "He is Leatherface, and that is enough for us. And this reminds me that he begged me to be back at my lodgings by ten o'clock, so I have not much time to spend in this pleasing gossip. Shall we to serious business now?"

"At your Highness' service," replied Laurence, and the others also murmured a quick assent.

II

"Well then, seigniors, having decided on our coup we have only the details to consider. You have all assured me that the Duke of Alva will come to Ghent within the next few days, and that our two thousand recruits are ready to carry out the orders which we have framed for them."

"The numbers will be doubled within the next few days," interposed one of the grave seigniors with conviction. "Your Highness' presence in the town–though only known to a very few loyalists–hath wrought miracles already."

"The wave of enthusiasm is spreading," asserted another.

"Well! if we had more men," quoth the Prince cheerily, "our plan would, of a surety, be more certain of success. I cannot say that I altogether approve of the plan–for as you know, I am a soldier and have no great mind for plots and conspiracies; but those on whose judgment I place infinite confidence–men such as Messire Paul Buys, pensionary of Leyden, Marnix of Tholouse, Marnix of St. Aldegonde and others, all approve of it, and I have therefore given it mine assent."

He sank his voice yet lower to a whisper, and he leaned right across the table as did the other men so that their ears were quite close to his mouth.

"The Duke of Alva comes to Ghent in about a week's time," he continued. "The idea is to seize his person and hold him a prisoner here and an hostage whilst we demand the withdrawal of all the Spanish troops from the Netherlands and the abolition of the Spanish Inquisition."

"To seize the person of the Duke of Alva!" murmured Clémence van Rycke, and so great was the terror which the tyrant inspired in every Flemish heart, that even those who already knew of this daring plot were appalled at the magnitude of such an outrage.

79

"Why not?" quoth William of Orange earnestly. "Less than a hundred years ago the town of Brüges held the Archduke Maximilian King of the Romans a prisoner within her walls, until he swore to dismiss all foreign troops from the Netherlands within four days, and gave hostages for his fidelity. What Brüges did then, cannot Ghent do now? With Alva a prisoner in our hands, we can dictate our terms to the King. It is a bold coup, seigniors, I own, but it hath every chance of success."

A murmur of approval went round the table. Clémence alone was silent. She was old and feeble, perhaps she had seen more than one bold coup fail, and terrible reprisals follow such failures; but Laurence was full of eagerness and enthusiasm.

"It cannot fail," he asserted vehemently. "Are there not two thousand men in the city who are devoted to your Highness heart and soul, and who are ready to give their lives for your cause? Two thousand, and within three days there will be five! more than enough for such a bold coup. It will and must succeed! One lucky hazard, and we may win all that we have fought for, lived for, died for, for over a century."

"It cannot fail!" came with fervent conviction from every one of the others.

"Ghent can do what Brüges hath done!" they affirmed.

"With the tyrant a prisoner in our hands, we can dictate terms as Brüges did an hundred years ago."

"Well said, seigniors," rejoined William of Orange, "and your approval—you who know this city so much better than I do—hath given me further encouragement. And now," he added with serious earnestness, "you will want to know why I convened this meeting, which by Mevrouw van Rycke's graciousness I have been able to do, and you will wish to hear what role hath been assigned to each of you in the great event which we are preparing."

"Let me but offer my life..." interposed Laurence eagerly.

"Nay! not your life, I hope, Messire," quoth the Prince with a smile, "your forethought and prudence and your united co-operation are what we want. Ye are risking your lives, seigniors, in this enterprise, that I'll not deny—but ye are men and know which you value most, your life or the very existence of your nation which is threatened with complete destruction."

"For Orange, for faith and for liberty!" said one of the men simply, and the others merely murmured: "Tell us what we must do."

"You must be wary and alert above all things, seigniors, for I have chosen you for a very arduous task in connection with this enterprise, and you must recognise that however carefully we organise it, there will always be one weak link in the chain which we are forging for the capture of that abominable tyrant, the Duke of Alva."

"One weak link?"

"Yes. We do not and cannot know for certain on which date Alva proposes to come to Ghent. The dates of his visits to Flemish towns are always kept a secret until the very moment of departure."

"He dreads assassination," interposed one man with a sneer.

"On the last occasion of the Duke's visit to Ghent," said Clémence van Rycke, "my husband was only apprised of it by courier two hours before his arrival. The courier had started from Brussels a bare half-hour before the Lieutenant-Governor and his cortège left the city."

"Precisely, and even then the High-Bailiff was in advance of every one else with the news," nodded the Prince, "and that is where our difficulty lies. How to collect together a couple of thousand men at perhaps an hour's notice—men who are scattered in different portions of this city and probably engaged in their usual avocations."

"Where will their leaders be?"

"Each at the different points where our secret stores of arms are kept. There are four of these points and four captains whom I have appointed to command five hundred men each. Having distributed the arms, the captains will lead their respective companies to the Waalpoort, where a crowd is sure to collect as soon as the rumour has spread to the town that the Lieutenant-Governor is coming. Our men will mix with the crowd, and at a given signal—when the Duke's cortège crosses the bridge—they will rush the bodyguard, scatter confusion among the escort, and in the mêlée seize the person of Alva. During the inevitable tumult that will ensue among the soldiers and the populace, our valuable hostage shall be conveyed in absolute secrecy to Het Spanjaard's Kasteel, where of course we can easily keep him a close prisoner whilst we negotiate with the King. But this of course is for the future, seigniors," he added, "and my concern now is to explain to you the method which I and my councillors have devised for the calling together of our stalwarts as soon as the Duke's coming visit is announced. Have I your close attention, seigniors?"

He had indeed. The four men round the table bent forward more eagerly still so as not to lose one word of their noble chief's commands. But before they could formulate the words of loyalty and of enthusiasm which hovered on their lips, a soft sound like the beating of a bird's wing against the window-pane froze those whispered words upon their lips.

Every head was immediately turned to the window, every face became rigid and pale, every brow was contracted with the effort to strain the faculty of hearing to its tensest point. It seemed as if six pairs of glowing eyes would pierce the folds of the velvet curtain which hung before the window.

81

III

The Prince was the first to recover himself.

"It is Leatherface," he whispered, "come to give me warning."

He rose and would have gone to the window, but Clémence van Rycke caught him by the arm and clung convulsively to him. "Not you, Monseigneur," she entreated, "not you—it might be a traitor."

Then the tapping was repeated and Laurence went cautiously up to the window, and after an instant's hesitation, he suddenly drew the curtains aside with a resolute gesture. Then he unfastened the tall casement and threw it open.

The night was of an inky blackness, and as the lattice flew open a gust of wind and heavy driving rain nearly extinguished the light of the candle, but in the framework of the window a man's head and shoulders detached themselves from out the gloom. The head and shoulders were closely enveloped in a hood and cape, and the face was hidden by a mask, and all were dripping with wet.

"Leatherface!" murmured the Prince, and Clémence van Rycke gave a sigh of relief.

"There is a light in the window above," whispered the man with the mask, "and a shadow has crossed behind the windows of the corridor. Someone is astir overhead—and the civic business at the Town House is drawing to an end."

"We have nearly finished," murmured the Prince in reply. "And I'll come away at once. Is the street clear?"

"Quite—and will be for another ten minutes till the night-watchman comes round. I saw him just now, he is very drunk and might make trouble."

"I come, friend," rejoined the Prince, "and as soon as may be."

The hooded head disappeared in the gloom; Laurence closed the window and drew the curtains together again.

"I envy that man," he said, and Clémence murmured a fervent: "God bless him!"

IV

Then the Prince turned once more to his friends.

"You see," he said with his grave smile, "how carefully my dragon guards me. There is evidently no time for lengthy explanations, and I must be as brief as I can."

He now opened the wallet at his belt and took out from it a small packet of papers.

"I am going to entrust these papers to Messire Laurence van

Rycke," he said, "they contain the names and places of abode and of business of every one of those two thousand men who have actually tendered me their oath of allegiance, and have sworn to give me unconditional support. I propose that Messire van Rycke keep these lists, because it will undoubtedly be his father, the High-Bailiff, who will learn sooner than any one else in the town the day and hour of the Duke of Alva's visit to Ghent. As soon as this is known to him, Messire van Rycke will then go to each of you, seigniors, and give you each a list of five hundred names, at the head of which will be noted the rallying point where these men will have to meet their captain and receive their arms. You in your turn will then each go and beat up the five hundred men whose names will have been given you, and order them to go to their respective rallying points. All this plan," added the Prince, "has been very carefully thought out, and it seems to me simple and easy of execution. But if any of you, seigniors, can think of a better one, I am, of course, always ready to take advice. You know your own city, better than I do—you might devise something still more practical than what I propose."

"Nay!" interposed one of the men, "meseems that nothing could be more simple, and I for one do vote unconditionally for the acceptance of His Highness' plan."

The others all gave their assent—hastily now, for again that gentle tapping was heard against the window-pane, only rather more firmly, more urgently this time. But no one went to the window to see what the tapping meant; obviously the faithful watcher outside scented some still hidden danger. The Prince at once by rising gave the signal that the conference was at an end. As he did so he handed the packet of papers to Laurence van Rycke who received it on bended knee.

"It is a treasure, Messire," said William of Orange earnestly, "which involves the lives of many and even, perhaps, the whole existence of this city. Where will you keep it?"

It was Clémence van Rycke who replied:

"This room," she said, "is mine own private withdrawing-room; that bureau there hath a wonderful lock which defies the cleverest thief; it contains my most valuable jewels. The papers will be safer there than anywhere."

"Let me see you lock them up in there, mevrouw," rejoined the Prince graciously, "I entrust them to you and to Laurence with utmost confidence."

Clémence then handed a key to her son and he locked the packet up in the tall bureau of carved and inlaid mahogany and satin-wood which stood in an angle of the narrow room close to the window and opposite to the door.

"I am meeting some friends and adherents to-morrow," said William of Orange finally, "at the house of Messire the Procurator-

General whom of a truth God will bless for his loyalty–and I pray you, seigniors, as many of you as can do so to meet me there at this same hour. But should we not meet again, do you understand all that you have to do?"

The men nodded in silence, whereupon the Prince took formal leave of them and of his host and hostess. He said kind and grateful words to Clémence van Rycke, who, with tears in her eyes, kissed the gracious hand which was held out to her. She then escorted her noble guest out of the room and across the dining-hall, the others following closely behind. All were treading as noiselessly as they could. The door which gave from the dining-room on the hall and staircase beyond was wide open: the room itself was in absolute darkness, and only a tiny light flickered in the hall, which made the shadows round corners and in recesses appear all the more dense.

"Will your Highness grope your way to the front door," whispered Clémence van Rycke, "or shall my son bring a lanthorn to guide you?"

"No, no," said William of Orange hurriedly, "that small light yonder is quite sufficient. I can see my way, and we must try not to wake your hall-porter."

"Oh! nothing will rouse him save a very severe shaking, and the bolts and bars have been left undone, as my husband will be coming home late to-night."

"And, if I am not mistaken," quoth the Prince, "my devoted friend Leatherface is waiting for me outside to see me safely to my lodgings. He is always mistrustful of hidden traps or hired assassins for me. Farewell, seigniors!" he added lightly, "remember my instructions in case we do not meet again."

"But to-morrow..." interposed Laurence van Rycke.

"Aye! to-morrow," said William of Orange, "at this hour at the house of Messire Deynoot, the Procurator-General: those of you, seigniors, who care to come will be welcome."

"Not one of us would care to stay away," rejoined Laurence with earnest conviction.

CHAPTER VIII

THE WATCHER IN THE NIGHT

I

Lenora, thinking that Mevrouw van Rycke was still astir, and pining for motherly comfort and companionship, had crept softly down the stairs candle in hand, when all of a sudden she paused in the vast hall. Everything was so still and so weird that any noise, even that of a mouse skimming over a carpet, would have made itself felt in the absolute silence which lay over the house, and Lenora's ear had most certainly heard—or rather felt, a noise—the sound of people moving and speaking somewhere, not very far from where she stood ... listening ... every sense on the alert.

With a sudden instinct, half of fear and half of caution, she blew out the candle and then groped her way, with hands outstretched, hardly daring to breathe. The tiny, flickering light which came from an iron lamp fixed to a bracket at the foot of the stairs made the hall seem yet more vast and strange; but one small, elvish ray caught the polished brass handle of the dining-room door, and this glimmer of metal seemed to attract Lenora toward it. After awhile her eyes became a little more accustomed to the gloom, she tip-toed up to that door-handle which so attracted her, and placing both her hands upon it, she crouched there—beside the door—listening.

In effect there were people moving and talking not far from where she crouched—no doubt that they were in the small withdrawing-room beyond, and that the door of communication between the two rooms was open. Lenora—motionless, palpitating, her heart beating so that it nearly choked her, felt that all her faculties must now be merged into those of hearing, and, if possible, seeing what was going on in this house, and at this hour of the night when the High-Bailiff was from home.

Whether any thought of conspiracy or of State secrets had at this time entered her head it were impossible to say, whether she thought of Ramon's murderer or of her oath to her father just then, who can tell? Certainly not the girl herself—she only listened—listened with all her might, and anon she heard the scraping of a chair against the tiled floor, then the iron rings of a curtain sliding along the rod, finally the whistling sound of a gust of wind rushing through an open window. This moment she chose as her opportunity. She turned the handle of the door very gently, and quite noiselessly it responded to her touch. Then she pushed the door wide open and waited—listening.

The door into the withdrawing-room was wide open just as she had conjectured, the wind was blowing the feeble light about which flickered in that room, and there were men in there who moved stealthily and spoke in whispers. Lenora crept forward—furtive as a mouse. The darkness in the dining-hall was impenetrable, and she in her house-dress of dark woollen stuff made no noise as she glided along, keeping well within the gloom, her hands stretched out before her to feel the objects that might be in her way.

At last she came within range of the open door and had a view of the little room beyond. She saw the table in the centre, the men sitting around it, and Clémence van Rycke in a high-back chair at its further end. Just now they all had their faces turned toward the window, where in the open casement the head and shoulders of a man were dimly visible to Lenora for one instant and then disappeared.

After that she heard the men talking together and heard what they said: she saw that one man appeared to be the recipient of great marks of respect, and that the others called him "Your Highness." She was now listening as if her very life depended on what she heard—crouching in the angle of the dining-room as closely as her unwieldy farthingale would allow. She heard the man whom the others called "Your Highness," and who could be none other than the Prince of Orange, explain to the others a plan for massing together two thousand men in connection with a forthcoming visit of the Duke of Alva to Ghent, she heard the word "Leatherface" and a great deal about a packet of papers. She heard the Prince speak about a meeting to-morrow in the house of the Procurator-General, and finally she saw Laurence van Rycke take a packet of papers from the Prince's hand and lock it up in the bureau that stood close to the window.

Indeed she could not for a moment be in doubt as to the meaning of what she saw and heard.

Here was a living proof of that treachery, that underhand conspiracy of which her father had so often spoken to her of late! Here were these Netherlanders, living under the beneficent and just laws of their Sovereign Lord and Master King Philip of Spain—the man who in every born Spaniard's eyes was greater, nobler, more just and more merciful than any other monarch alive, who next to His Holiness himself was surely anointed by God Himself and placed upon the mightiest throne on earth so that he might administer God's will upon all his subjects—and here were these traitors plotting and planning against the Government of that high and noble monarch, plotting against his representative, the Lieutenant-Governor whom he had himself put in authority over them.

To a girl born and bred in the atmosphere of quasi-worship which surrounded Philip's throne, the revolt of these Netherlanders was the most heinous outrage any people could commit. She understood now the hatred and loathing which her father had for them–she hated them too, since one of these vile conspirators had foully murdered her cousin Ramon in the dark.

"Leatherface!"–the man in the room below whom the others called "Your Highness" spoke of Leatherface as his friend!

A Prince consorting with a hired assassin! and Lenora felt that her whole soul was filled with loathing for all these people. Was not the man who had killed Ramon–foully, surreptitiously and in the dark–was he not even now just outside this very house–the house which was to be her home for life–waiting mayhap for some other unsuspecting Spanish officer whom he could murder in the same cowardly and treacherous way?–and were not all these people in that room yonder, execrable assassins too?–had she not heard them speaking of armed conspirators?–and could she not see even now in her mind's eye the unsuspecting Duke of Alva falling into their abominable trap?

But horror-struck as she was, she never stirred. Truth to tell, a sudden fear held her now–the fear that she might be detected ere she had done her best to save the Duke from this infamous plot. What she would do presently, she did not know as yet–for the moment all that she needed was safety from discovery and the privacy of her own room where she could pray and think.

After Laurence had locked the papers in the bureau it was obvious that the meeting was at an end. She had only just time to flit like a dark ghost through the dining-hall and to reach the stairs, before she heard unmistakable signs that the Prince and his friends were taking leave of their host and hostess. Gathering her wide gown together in her hands, she crept up the stairs as fast as she could. Fortunately she was well out of the range of the small light at the foot of the stairs, before the five men and Clémence van Rycke came out into the hall. She heard their few words of farewell and heard the Prince arranging for the meeting the next evening at the house of Messire Deynoot.

After that she felt that further delay would inevitably spell detection. Even now someone must have opened the front door, for a gust of wind and heavy rain driving into the house told the listener quite clearly that the Prince and his friends were leaving the house: anon Clémence and Laurence would be going up to their own apartments.

As swiftly, as furtively as a mouse, Lenora made her way up the stairs: and now there she sat once more in the vast bedchamber, quivering with excitement and with horror, listening for footsteps outside her door. She heard Clémence van Rycke's shuffling footsteps passing down the corridor, and Laurence's more firm ones following closely in their wake: a few whispered words were spoken by mother and son, then doors were closed and all was still once more.

II

The fire had burnt low, only the last dying embers of the charred pine logs threw a wide glowing band across the centre of the room. Lenora sitting by the fire had scarcely moved for a quarter of an hour or even more. Anon she heard the opening and shutting of the front door.

It was the High-Bailiff returning home—not knowing, of a truth, that his house had just been used as a meeting-place for conspirators. The hall-porter slept between two doors in the outer lobby. Lenora heard him scrambling out of bed, and the High-Bailiff's voice bidding him close everything up for the night. Then came the pushing home of bars and bolts and the rattle of chains, and finally the sound of the High-Bailiff's heavy footsteps across the hall and up the stairs.

After that silence once more.

Lenora, however, still sat on for awhile staring into the glow. Vaguely she wondered if Mark would be staying out all night, or whether he had been home all along, knowing perhaps, and perhaps not caring about, what was going on in his father's house; keeping aloof from it all: or like Laurence, up to his neck in all this treachery and abominable rebellion!

Another quarter-of-an-hour went by: the clock of St. Bavon had chimed the half after eleven, and now the quarter before midnight. Lenora felt that at last she might slip downstairs with safety.

Quickly now she took off her stuff gown and heavy farthingale which had so impeded her movements awhile ago, and groped in the press for a clinging robe which would envelop her closely and glide noiselessly upon the tiled floors.

There is absolutely no doubt that all through this time Lenora acted almost unconsciously. She never for one moment paused to think: she was impelled by a force which she herself could not have defined—a force which can best be described as a blind instinct. Obedience! She had been born and bred in obedience and a sense of sacred duty to her King as Sovereign Lord, to her faith and to her father.

In the convent at Segovia she had learned the lesson of obedience so absolutely that it never entered her mind to question the decrees of those three all-potent arbiters of her destiny. And when—as now—the hour came when the most sacred oath she had ever spoken had to be fulfilled, she would have thought it a deadly sin to search her own heart, to study her feelings, to argue with herself about it. She would as soon have thought of arguing with God.

On Ramon's death-bed she had sworn to her father that she would act and work for her country and for her King in the way that her father would direct.

The time had come, and she did what she believed to be her duty without question and without false shame.

She knew that the knowledge which she already possessed was of paramount importance to the Government: the Prince of Orange was in Ghent—who but he would be called "your Highness"?—and moving about among his friends surreptitiously and at dead of night? Who but he would speak of the mysterious Leatherface as being on the watch for him? The Prince of Orange was in Ghent and was conspiring against the State. There had been talk of the Duke of Alva's visit to Ghent and of two thousand men being secretly armed. What other purpose save that of murder and bloodshed could be served by such secret plottings and the levying of troops in this illegal manner? The Prince of Orange was in Ghent and would on the morrow continue his underhand and treasonable machinations in the house of Messire Deynoot, Procurator-General of Ghent.

That was the extent of Lenora's knowledge, and what could she do with such a secret in her possession—she, a helpless girl, a stranger in the midst of all these enemies of her people and of her race? Could she, having gleaned so much information, quietly go to bed and sleep and let events shape their course?—and detach herself, as it were, from the destinies of her own country which her father had in a measure entrusted to her stewardship? Could she above all be false to her oath at the very moment when God gave her an opportunity of fulfilling it and of working for her country and her King in a manner which was given to very few women to do? Indeed she did not pause to think. Any thought save that of obedience would be treason to the King and sinful before God. The hour for thought would come later, and with it mayhap regret. Then so be it. Whatever suffering she would have to endure in the future, in her sentiment and in her feelings, she was ready to accept unquestioningly, just as she was prepared to fulfil her duty unquestioningly now. She knew a good deal, but surely not enough. She had seen Laurence van Rycke lock up a packet of papers in the bureau, and she had in her possession tied with a ribbon around her neck, the precious pass-key which her father had given her on the very morning when he told her how Ramon had come by his death—the curiously-fashioned piece of steel made by the metal-worker of Toledo—who had been put out of the way, because his skill had made him dangerous—and which would turn any lock or open any secret drawer.

She had no light now and did not know how to use the tinder, but in the wall of the corridor outside her door there was a little niche wherein stood a statue of the Virgin, and in front of the statute a tiny light was kept burning day and night: this would do in lieu of a candle. She would take it, she thought, and carry it into the withdrawing-room with her: it would help to guide her to the bureau where the papers were.

Yes! she was quite prepared for what she had to do, and there was no reason to wait any longer. And yet for some unaccountable reason she suddenly felt strangely inert: there were still a few dying embers in the grate, and she could see quite distinctly the high-backed chair in which she had sat last night, and the low one wherein Mark had half sat, half kneeled close beside her: the memory of that brief interview which she had had with him came upon her with a rush. It had been the only interview between them since the blessing of the Church had made them man and wife. It had ended disastrously it is true. Her words: "I hate you!" had been cruel and untrue, and overwhelming regret suddenly held her in its grip once again—as it had done all the day.

Closing her eyes for a moment—for they felt hot and heavy—she could almost believe that Mark was still there—his merry grey eyes looking deeply earnest, trying to read her innermost thoughts. His personality—so strange, so baffling even—seemed still to linger in this dimly-lighted room, and she almost could hear his voice—rugged, yet at times so sweet and tender—echoing softly along the rafters.

And all of a sudden she realised the full horror of what she was doing—of what she must do now or else become false and perjured—a traitor to her race and to her King. No longer was she a blind and unconscious tool of Fate—she was she herself—a woman who lived and thought and suffered: and before her at this moment there was nothing but an interminable vista of sorrow and suffering and regret.

Whether duty ruled her or sentiment, she—the innocent handmaid of Fate—could reap nothing but remorse in the future; her heart, her very youth, must inevitably be crushed between those two potent factors which were struggling even now for mastery over her soul.

Indeed was there ever a woman—a mere girl—confronted with so appalling, so intricate a puzzle? The lives of men were in her hands—the Prince of Orange, the High-Bailiff, Mark, Laurence, Clémence on the one side, on the other the Duke of Alva, her own father, her kindred, all those whom she had clung to and loved throughout her life.

And knowing that she never could solve such an awful problem by herself Lenora fell on her knees and prayed: she prayed with all the fervour, but also with all the simplicity of primitive faith—the faith that is willing and eager to leave everything in God's hands, to trust to guidance and help from above when life has become a hopeless and inextricable tangle—the faith which hath for its principle loyalty and obedience and which accepts suffering in its cause, and glories in it like in a martyr's crown.

III

After a few minutes Lenora felt more calm. Her deep and fervent religious sentiment had risen triumphant over every doubt. While she prayed so earnestly, so unquestioningly, it had been made clear to her that the issue of the mighty problem which was putting her very soul on the rack must remain in mightier hands than hers. She could not be the arbiter of men's lives and of the destinies of the State; all that she could do was to obey her father and fulfil her oath; beyond that, God must decide; He had shown her the way how to obtain the knowledge which she now possessed, and since her father was now back in Brussels, she must find a means of placing that knowledge in his hands. Her father of a surety was kind and just and God would Himself punish whom He willed.

With this calmer state of mind her resolution became more firm. She felt the pass-key safely in her bosom, then stealthily she slipped out of her room: the tiny light was flickering dimly at the foot of the Virgin's statue; Lenora lifted it carefully and with it in her hand prepared to go downstairs.

Scarce a sound broke the silence of the night: only the patter of the rain against the leaded panes of the windows and an occasional gust of wind that came roaring down the huge chimneys and shook the frames of windows and doors. Before descending the stairs Lenora paused once more to listen. Down the corridor she could hear Clémence van Rycke in her bedchamber still moving about, and Laurence's footstep on the tiled floor of his room.

And then the girl—shading the tiny light with her hand—began to descend.

She paused for a moment upon the landing and peeped into the vast hall below. It was fortunate that she had the tiny light, as the small lamp at the foot of the stairs had since been extinguished; but the little wick she held only threw out a faint glimmer a yard or two in front of her, and beyond this small circle there was nothing but impenetrable darkness.

The house was very still, and Lenora was absolutely without fear. From the church towers of the city, both near and far, there came the sound of bells striking the midnight hour. She waited till the last echo of the chimes had died away, then she continued her way down.

IV

Lenora now entered the dining-hall and carefully closed the door behind her. Light in hand she stood for a moment in the very angle of the room from whence she had watched the plotters an hour ago. Nothing had been deranged.

Then she went into the withdrawing-room, and placed the light upon the centre table. She looked around her mutely challenging the dumb objects–the chairs that stood about in disorder, the curtains which were not closely drawn, the bureau that was in the corner–to tell her all that she had failed to hear. In this spot a vile conspiracy had been hatched against the Duke of Alva–two thousand men were implicated in it–but in what way it threatened the Duke's life she did not know–nor yet who were all these men who had sat around this table and hatched treason against the King and State.

The tiny wick only shed a very feeble glimmer of light on the top of the table: it made the shadows on the ceiling dance a weird rigadoon and grow to fantastic proportions. But Lenora's eyes were growing well-accustomed to the gloom. Quickly now she drew the pass-key from between the folds of her kerchief and went up to the bureau. The ribbon round her neck was in the way so she took it off; with trembling, unerring fingers she groped for the lock and having found it she inserted the pass-key into it. After a little adjustment, a little tugging and pulling, she found that the lock yielded quite smoothly to the pressure. The flap came down and displayed the interior of the bureau, consisting of a number of wide pigeon-holes, in each of which there was a small iron box such as the rich matrons of Flanders used for putting away their pearls and other pieces of jewellery. On the top of one of these boxes there was a packet of papers, tied round with a piece of orange-coloured ribbon. Without a moment's hesitation Lenora took it. She unfolded one of the papers and laid it out flat upon the table, smoothing it out with her hand. She drew the light a little nearer and examined the writing carefully: it was just a list of names–fifty in all– with places of abode all set out in a double column, and at the bottom was written in a bold hand:

"All the above to Afsemble without any delay in the Barn which is fituated in the North-Weft angle of the Cemetery at the back of the Chapel of St. Jan ten Dullen."

Having satisfied herself that the other papers in the packet also contained lists of names and brief orders as to place of assembly, she tied them all up together again with the orange-coloured ribbon. Then she closed the bureau, turned the pass-key in the lock and slipped it, together with the packet, into the bosom of her gown.

Then she turned to go.

V

Light in hand she went tip-toeing across the dining-room; but close to the threshold she paused. She had distinctly heard a furtive footstep in the hall. At once she extinguished the light. Then she waited. Her thoughts had flown to Laurence van Rycke. Perhaps he felt anxious about the papers, and was coming down in order to transfer them to some other place of safety. The supposition was terrifying. Lenora felt as if an icy hand had suddenly gripped her heart and was squeezing her very life out of it. In this deathlike agony a few seconds went by—indeed they seemed to the unfortunate girl like an eternity of torment. She had slipped close to the wall right against the door, so that the moment it was opened from the outside, and someone entered the room, she could contrive to slip out. All might yet be well, if whoever entered did not happen to carry a light.

Then suddenly she heard the steps again, and this time they approached the dining-room door. Lenora's heart almost ceased to beat: the next moment the door was opened and someone stood upon the threshold—just for a second or two ... without moving, whilst Lenora with senses as alert as those of some feline creature in defence of its life—waited and watched for her opportunity.

But that opportunity never came, for the newcomer—whoever he was—suddenly stepped into the room and immediately closed the door behind him and turned the key in the lock. Lenora was a prisoner, at the mercy of a man whose secrets she had stolen, and whose life hung upon all that she had seen and heard this night.

The intruder now groped his way across the room and anon Lenora heard him first draw aside the curtains from before the window, and then proceed to open two of the casements. The window gave on the Nieuwstraate, almost opposite the tavern of the "Three Weavers," at the entrance of which there hung an iron street-lamp. The light of this came slanting in through the open casements and Lenora suddenly saw that it was Mark who was standing there.

Even at this instant he turned and faced her. He showed no sign however of surprise, but exclaimed quite pleasantly: "By the stars, Madonna! and who would have thought of meeting you here?"

The tension on Lenora's nerves had been so acute that her self-control almost gave way with the intensity of her relief when she recognised Mark and heard the sound of his voice. Her hands began to shake so violently that the tiny lamp nearly dropped out of them.

She had been so startled that she could not as yet either speak or move, but just stood there close to the wall, like a pale, slim ghost only faintly illumined by the slanting light of the street-lamp, her soft, white gown clinging round her trembling limbs. Her face, bosom and arms were scarce less white than her gown, and in the dim, mysterious light her luminous, dark eyes shone with a glow of excitement still vaguely tinged with dread.

He thought that never in life had he seen anything quite so beautiful, so pure, so desirable, and yet so pathetic as this young girl, whom but forty hours ago he had sworn to love, to protect and to cherish. Just now she looked sadly helpless, despite the fact that gradually a little air of haughtiness replaced her first look of fear.

"Madonna," he said gently, "are you indeed yourself, or are you your own wraith? If not, why are you wandering about alone at this hour of the night?"

"I came to fetch my prayer-book," she said, trying to speak lightly and with a steady voice. "I thought that I had left it here to-day and missed it when I went to rest."

"You found the book, I hope," he said, without the slightest trace of irony.

"No," she replied coldly. "Inez must have put it away. Will you be so good as to unlock that door."

"I will with pleasure, Madonna. I locked it when I came in, because I didn't want old Pierre to come shuffling in after me, as he so often does when I go late to bed. But," he added, putting out his hand, "may I take this lamp from you. Your hand does not appear to be oversteady and if the oil were to drip it would spoil your gown."

"The draught blew it out," she retorted, "and I would be glad if you would relight it. I am going back to my room."

"Precisely," he rejoined dryly as he took the lamp from her and put it on the table, "and with your leave I would escort you thither."

"I thank you," she rejoined coldly, "I can find my way alone."

"As you please," he said with perfect indifference.

Now that her eyes were more accustomed to the semi-darkness she could see him more distinctly, and she stared at him in amazement. His appearance was certainly very different to what it habitually was— for he usually dressed himself with great care: but now he had on dark clothes, made of thick woollen stuff, which clung closely to his tall figure: he wore no ruff, and had on very high boots which reached high above his knees. Both his clothes and boots were bespattered with mud, and strangely enough looked also wet through. Somehow the appearance appeared unreal. It was Mark—and yet it was not. His face, too, looked flushed, and the lines round his eyes were more deeply marked than they had ever seemed to be before.

The recollection of all the abominable gossip retailed about him by Inez and others took possession of her mind. She had been told by all and sundry that Mark van Rycke had spent most of his day at the "Three Weavers," and now the flush on his face, the curious dilation of the pupils of his eyes, seemed to bear mute testimony to all that she had heard.

Here, then, she already saw the hand of God guiding her future–and showing her the small glimmer of comfort which He vouchsafed her in the midst of her perplexities. Life in this house and with this man–who cared less than nothing for her–would anyhow be intolerable–then obviously the way was clear for her to go back to her father. She wished no harm to these people–none to this poor, drunken wretch, who probably had no thought of rebellion or of heresy, none to Laurence, who loved her, or to Clémence, who had been kind to her. But she despised them–aye! and loathed them, and was grateful to God for allowing her to keep her promise to her father within the first few hours of her married life.

How terrible would have been the long and weary watching! the irresolution, the temptation, mayhap, to be false to her oath through sheer indolence or superacute sentiment!

So now all that she had to do was to go straight back to her father, tell him all that she knew and then go–go back to the dear old convent at Segovia–having done more than a woman's share in the service of her country–and then to rest after that–to spend her life in peace and in prayer–away from all political intrigues–forgetting that she had ever been young and felt a vague yearning for happiness.

VI

Mark had made no sign or movement while Lenora stood there before him, gathering her strength together for what she felt might prove a struggle. In some unaccountable way she felt a little afraid of him–not physically of course, but, despite the fact that she had so impulsively judged him just now–afraid of that searching glance of his which seemed to lay her innermost thoughts like an open book before his eyes. She put this strange timidity of hers down to the knowledge that he had certain lawful rights over her as her lord and husband and that she would have to obtain his consent before she could think of going to Brussels on the morrow.

"Messire," she said abruptly, "during this day which you have seen fit to spend among your habitual boon companions, making merry no doubt, I have been a great deal alone. Solitude begets sober reason–and I have come to the conclusion that life under present conditions would be a perpetual martyrdom to me."

She paused and he rejoined quietly: "I don't think I quite understand, Madonna. Under what conditions would your life become a martyrdom?"

"Under those of a neglected wife, Messire," she said. "I have no

95

mind to sit at home—an object of suspicion to your kinsfolk and of derision to your servants, while the whole town is alive with the gossip that Messire Mark van Rycke spent the first day of his marriage in the taverns of Ghent and left his bride to pine in solitude."

"But methought, Madonna," he retorted, "that it was solitude that you craved for. Both last night and even a moment ago you told me very plainly that you had no desire for my company."

"Last night I was overwrought and would have made amends to you for my thoughtlessness at once, only that you left me incontinently without a further word. As for now, Messire, surely you cannot wonder that I have no mind for your society after a day's carouse has clouded your brain and made your glance unsteady."

She thought herself very brave in saying this, and more than half expected an angry retort from him. Instead of which he suddenly threw back his head and burst into an immoderate and merry laughter. She gazed at him horrified and not a little frightened—thinking indeed that his brain was overclouded—but he, as soon as he had recovered his composure, asked her with grave attempt at seriousness: "You think that I am drunk, Madonna? Ye gods!" he exclaimed not without a touch of bitterness, "hath such a farce ever been enacted before?"

"A farce to you perhaps," she said earnestly, "but a tragedy to me. I have been rendered wretched and unhappy, Messire, and this despite your protestations of chivalry. I did not seek you, Messire. This marriage was forced upon me. It is ungenerous and cowardly to make me suffer because of it."

"Dastardly and abominable," he assented gravely. "Indeed, Madonna, you do me far too much honour even to deign to speak with me. I am not worthy that you should waste a thought on me—but since you have been so kind thus far, will you extend your generosity to me by allowing me to give you my most solemn word—to swear to you if need be that I am not the drunken wretch whom evil tongues have thus described to you. There," he added more lightly, "will you not deign to sit here a moment? You are tired and overwrought; let me get you a cup of wine, and see if some less strenuous talk will chase all those black thoughts from your mind."

He took her hand and then with gentle yet forceful pressure led her to the wide hearth and made her sit in the big chair close beside it.

"Alas! there are not even embers in the grate," he said, "I fear me, you must be cold."

From somewhere out of the darkness—she could not see from where—he brought a footstool for her feet; then he pulled a low chair forward for himself and sat down at some little distance from her, in his favourite attitude, with one elbow on his knee and his face shaded by his hand. She remained silent for a moment or two, for she suddenly felt an extraordinary sense of well-being; just the same as she had felt

96

last night, and once or twice before in his presence. And she felt deeply sorry for him too. After all, perhaps he had no more desired this marriage than she had—and no doubt the furrows on his face came from anxiety and care, and she marvelled what it was that troubled him.

"There," he asked gaily, "are you better now, Madonna?"

"Better, I thank you," she replied.

"Then shall I interpret the thoughts which were coursing behind that smooth brow of yours, when first I startled you by my presence here?"

"If you will."

He waited a moment, then said dryly: "You desired to convey to me your wish to return to your father.... Oh! only for a little while," he added hastily, seeing that she had made a quick, protesting gesture, "but that was in your mind, was it not?"

She could not deny it, and murmured: "Yes."

"Such a wish, Madonna," he rejoined, gravely, "is as a command to me. In the late morning the horses will be at your disposal. I will have the honour to accompany you to Brussels."

"You, Messire!" she exclaimed, "you would..."

"I would do anything to further your wishes, Madonna; this I would have you believe. And a journey to Brussels is such a small matter...."

"As you say," she murmured. For such are the contradictions of a woman's heart that all of a sudden she did not wish to go away. All thoughts of rebellion and conspiracies were unaccountably thrust into the background of her mind, and ... she did not wish to go away....

"There is no hurry," she continued timidly. "I would not like to put you to inconvenience."

"Oh!" he rejoined airily, "there is no inconvenience which I would not gladly bear in order to gratify your wish."

"I shall have to pack my effects...."

"Jeanne will help Inez, and a few things are easily packed. Your effects shall follow in an ox-wagon; they will be two days on the way; so I pray you take what is required for your immediate needs and is easily stowed in your saddle-bow. We shall have to make an early start, if you desire to be in Brussels by nightfall."

"Oh! there is no hurry," she protested.

"Ah? Then in that case I could escort you as far as Alost, and send a courier thence to your father, to meet you there the next day."

She bit her lip and could have cried with vexation. At the present moment she hated him for so obviously wishing to be rid of her. She had quite forgotten that she had ever wanted to go.

"I shall be too tired to make an early start in the morning," she said quite piteously. "Why it is close on early morning now."

She leaned a little forward in order to listen, for just then the chimes of St. Bavon rang the half-hour after midnight. She still looked a small, pale, slim ghost with one side of her exquisite face in shadow, the other but faintly illumined by the light from without. Her vexation, her indecision, were so plainly expressed in her eyes, that he must indeed have been vastly dull or vastly indifferent not to have read her thoughts. Nevertheless, he said with the same calm airiness as before:

"A few hours' rest will revive you, Madonna. And if we only go as far as Alost to-morrow, we need not start before midday."

At this her pride was aroused. His indifference now amounted to insolence. With a vigorous effort she swallowed her tears, for they were very near the surface, and then she rose abruptly, with the air and manners of a queen, looking down in her turn with haughty indifference on that abominable Netherlander whom she had never hated so thoroughly as she did at this moment.

"I thank you, Messire," she said coldly, "I pray you then to see that all arrangements be complete for my journey as early as may be. I would wish to be in Brussels by nightfall, and half a dozen leagues or so does not frighten me."

She rose with all that stateliness which was a part of herself and suited her tall, graceful figure so admirably; as she did so she gave him a curt nod such as she would have bestowed on a serving man. He too rose to his feet but he made no attempt to detain her. On the contrary, he at once busied himself with his tinder box, and relighted the little lamp. Then he went to the door, unlocked it and held it open for her to pass through.

As she did so she took the lamp from him, and for one moment their hands met. His were burning hot and hers quite cold—his fingers lingered upon the satiny softness of hers.

But she sailed past him without bestowing another glance upon him, with little head erect and eyes looking straight out before her. In one hand she held the lamp, with the other she was holding up the heavy folds of her trailing gown, her tiny feet in velvet shoes made no sound as she glided across the hall. Soon she was a mere silhouette with the light just playing faintly with the loose curls round her head and touching the lines of her shoulders and arms and one or two folds of her gown. She mounted the stairs slowly as if she was infinitely weary; Mark watched the graceful, ghostlike form gliding upwards until the gloom had swallowed it up.

Then he turned back into the room.

98

VII

The first thing that Mark did when he was alone was to close the door; then he struck a light and lit a candle. With it in his hand he went into the withdrawing-room and—having peered closely into the four corners of the room, as if he half-expected to see some night-prowler there—he placed the candle on the table, drew a bunch of keys from the inner pocket of his doublet, and going up to the bureau proceeded to unlock it just as Lenora had done.

He gave one quick glance at the interior of the bureau, then he put up the flap and once more turned the key in the lock.

Having done this he stood for awhile quite still, his chin buried in his hand, his broad shoulders bent, a deep, double furrow between his brows. From time to time a deep sigh escaped his lips, and his merry grey eyes almost disappeared beneath the heavy frown. Then he seemed to shake himself free from his obsession, he straightened out his tall figure and threw back his head with a movement of pride and of defiance.

He took up the candle and started to go out of the room, but on the threshold he paused again and looked behind him. The table, the chairs, the bureau seemed in a strange weird way to be mocking him—they looked so placid and so immovable—so stolid in the face of the terrible calamity which had just fallen on this house.

And suddenly Mark with a violent gesture threw the heavy candlestick to the ground. The flame flickered as it fell and the taper rolled about gently for a while from side to side until it landed close to his feet. He smothered a curse and put his heel upon the taper, crushing the wax into a shapeless mass; then with a curious groan, half of pain half of bitter irony, he passed his hand once or twice across his brow.

Slowly the glow of wrath faded from his eyes, a look of wonderful tenderness, coupled with gentle good-humour and kindliness softened the rugged lines of his face. A whimsical smile played round the corners of his lips.

"She must be wooed and she must be won," he murmured. "Mark, you lumbering fool, can you do it? You have less than twenty-four hours in which..."

He sighed again and laughed softly to himself, shaking his head dubiously the while. Then he went out of the room and closed the door softly behind him.

CHAPTER IX

A DIVIDED DUTY

I

Strange and conflicting were the feelings which ran riot through Lenora's soul when she once more found herself alone in her own room. Mortification held for a time undisputed sway–a sense of injury– of having gone half-way to meet she knew not what and having been repulsed. She was quite sure that she hated her husband now, far more bitterly than she had ever hated any one before–at the same time she felt relieved that he at any rate had no part in the treachery which was being hatched under his father's roof.

One thing, however, gave her an infinite sense of relief. She was going back to her father on the morrow. She would leave this house where she had known nothing but sorrow and humiliation since first she entered it; above all she would never see those people again on whom she had been spying!

Yes! Spying!

There was no other word for it; hideous as it was it expressed what Lenora had done. Oh! there was no sophistry about the girl. She was too proud, too pure to try and palliate what she had done, by shirking to call it by its name. She had done a task which had been imposed on her by her King, her country, and her father. She had sworn to do it–sworn it on the deathbed of the only man who had ever loved her, the only man whose voice and touch had thrilled her, the companion of her childhood, her accepted lover and her kinsman.

She had done it because God Himself through her father's and her King's own mouth had ordered her to do it; and it was not for her– ignorant, unsophisticated, sinful mayhap–to question God's decrees. But when she thought back on the events of the past hour, she felt a shudder of horror slowly creeping along her spine.

And she thanked God that He would allow her to leave this house for ever, and for ever to turn her back on those whom she–so unwillingly–had betrayed.

But she would not allow her mind to dwell on such morbid fancies. There was a great deal to be done ere the morning broke. Her task–if it was to be fruitful–was not completed yet.

She began by taking down a pair of metal candlesticks which stood on a shelf above the hearth and lighting the candles at a small lamp which she had brought up with her. These she placed upon the table; then she went to the press where only a few hours ago Inez had ranged all her clothes and effects, her new gowns and linen. From among these things, she took a flat wallet in which were some sheets of paper, a quill and small inkhorn, also some wax for sealing letters down.

She went to her task slowly and methodically, for she was unaccustomed to writing letters. In the convent they had taught her how to do it, and twice a year she had written to her father—once on New Year's Day, and once on the feast of San Juan—but the task before her was a far more laborious one than she had ever undertaken with pen and paper.

But she sat down, courageously, to write.

She wrote an account of everything that she had seen, heard and experienced in this house, from the moment when first she left her room in the evening in order to seek companionship, until the moment when, having secured the packet of papers, she had relocked the bureau with her pass-key and started to go back to her room. What she did not set down in writing was her subsequent meeting with her husband, for that had no connection with the Prince of Orange or with conspiracies, and was merely a humiliating episode in the life of a neglected bride.

The grey dawn slowly creeping in through the leaded glass of her window still found her at her task. The candles had burned down low in their sockets, their light—of a dim yellow colour—fought feebly against the incoming dawn. But Lenora felt no fatigue.

She wrote in a small, cramped hand and covered four sheets of paper with close writing. When she had finished, she read all that she had written down carefully through, made several corrections in the text and folded the sheets neatly together. Then she took from the bosom of her gown the packet of papers which she had found in the bureau, put it together with her own writing and enclosed everything in a clean sheet of paper carefully folded over. Round this she tied a piece of white ribbon, such as she used for doing up her hair, and sealed it all down with wax.

Finally, on the outside of this packet she wrote with a clear hand:

"To don Juan de Vargas at his refidence in Brufsels. To be given unto Him with the Seal unbroken in the eyent of My death."

II

Lenora tired out with emotion and bodily exertion slept soundly for a few hours. When Inez came in, in the late morning to wait on her, she ordered the old woman to put up a few necessary effects in a small leather valise, and to pack up all her things and all her clothes.

"My father hath need of me for a few days," she said in response

101

to Inez' exclamation of astonishment. "We start this morning for Brussels."

"For which the Lord be praised," ejaculated Inez piously, "for of all the dull, miserable, uncomfortable houses that I ever was in in my life..."

"Hold your tongue, woman," broke in Lenora sharply, "and see to your work. You will never be done, if you talk so much."

And Inez—more than ever astonished at this display of temper on the part of a young mistress who had always been kind and gentle—had perforce to continue her mutterings and her grumblings under her breath.

Whilst the old woman laid out carefully upon the bed all the pretty things which she had stowed away in the presses only twenty-four hours ago, Lenora busied herself with yet another task which she had set herself, but which she had been too tired to accomplish in the night.

She wrote a short letter to Laurence.

"My DEVOTED FRIEND," she wrote, "You promifed Me a very little while ago that if ever I wanted You to do fomething for Me, I was only to fend You this ring and You would do whatever I afked. Now, in the name of Our Lady, I adjure You to leave Ghent at once taking Your Mother with You. A grave danger threatens You both. I know that You have relatives in Haarlem. I entreat You—nay! I afk it of You as a fulfilment of Your promife to go to them at once with Your Mother. Your Father is in no danger, and Mark will be efcorting Me to Brufsels, and I fhall try and keep Him there until all danger is paft...."

Having written thus far, she paused a moment, pen in hand, a frown of deep puzzlement and of indecision upon her brow. Then she continued in a firm hand:

"It is Your Mother's and Your own complicity in the plot which is being hatched in Ghent again ft the Duke of Alva which has brought Your lives in danger."

She strewed the sand over her writing, then read the letter carefully through. After which she took a ring from off her finger, enclosed it in the letter and sealed the latter down.

"Inez!" she said.

"Yes, my saint."

"I shall be starting for Brussels within the hour."

"Holy Virgin!" exclaimed the old woman. "I shall not be ready with the packing. Why this hurry, my angel?"

"Your not being ready, Inez, is of no consequence. I shall start with Messire van Rycke. You will follow on in the wagon."

"But, my saint..."

"Now do not talk so much, Inez," broke in Lenora impatiently; "if you add to my anxieties by being quarrelsome and disobedient I shall surely fall sick and die."

Evidently the young girl knew exactly how to work on her faithful old servant's temperament. Inez reduced to abject contrition by the thought that she was rendering her darling anxious and sick, swore by every saint in the calendar that she would bite off her tongue, toil like a slave and be as obedient as a cur, if only her darling angel would keep well and cheerful and tell her what to do.

"You must not fret about me, Inez," resumed Lenora as soon as the old woman's voluble apologies and protestations had somewhat subsided. "My husband will escort me as far as Brussels, and in my father's house little Pepita will wait on me till you come."

"And if that flighty wench doesn't look after you properly..." began Inez menacingly.

"You will make her suffer, I've no doubt," quoth Lenora dryly. "In the meanwhile, listen carefully, Inez, for there is something that I want you to do for me, which no one else but you can do."

"For which the Lord be thanked!" said Inez fervently. "What is it, my dear?"

"This letter," she said.

"Yes?"

"I want Messire Laurence van Rycke to have it, after I have gone."

"He shall have it, my saint."

"He may be from home."

"I shall find him."

"He must have it before midday."

"He shall have it."

"Promise!"

"I'll swear it."

The old woman took the letter with the ring which her mistress held out to her, and then only did Lenora feel that she had done all that lay in her power to reconcile her duty to her King with her sentiment for those who had been kind to her.

III

How Lenora spent the rest of the long, wearisome, interminable morning she never afterwards could have told you. The very atmosphere around her oppressed her well-nigh unbearably. There were the farewells to be said to the family—to the High-Bailiff who was apologetic and obsequious, to Clémence who cried, and to Laurence who looked sadly enquiring and reproachful.

Fortunately Mark had paved the way for these farewells in his usual airy and irresponsible manner. It was the Spanish custom—so he had assured his mother—that brides, after spending twenty-four hours under their husband's roof, returned to their parents or guardians for a few weeks. Clémence had smiled incredulously when she had heard this—but had allowed herself anon to be persuaded. There were such queer marriage customs in different parts of the world these days. (Why! in many parts of Germany the bridegroom was, according to tradition, soundly thrashed by his friends directly after the religious ceremony—it was in order that he should be prepared for the many vicissitudes of connubial life. And there were other equally strange customs in foreign lands.) Spain was a curious country—Clémence was prepared to admit, and ... ah, well! perhaps it was all for the best! She had been attracted by the beautiful girl whom indeed a cruel fate seemed to have tossed into the very midst of a family with whom she had absolutely nothing in common. Clémence had been sorry for her in her gentle, motherly way but she had mistrusted her ... and just now all Clémence's thoughts were centred on her country's wrongs, on the great fight for political and religious liberty which had received so severe a blow, and which the noble Prince of Orange was still determined to carry on with the help of God.

And so—though Clémence cried a little, and though her kind heart ached for the young girl who looked so pathetic and so forlorn when she bade her good-bye—she nevertheless felt a sense of relief when she remembered all that had been talked of and planned in this house last night, and thought of the packet of papers which were locked away with her most precious jewels. She kissed the girl tenderly, and spoke of the happy day when she would come back to her new home never to leave it again. Lenora, pale, like a young ghost, with dark rings under her eyes, and lips that quivered with the sobs she was vainly trying to suppress, made an effort to respond, and then hurried out of the room. But when she saw Laurence he was alone in the hall and she contrived to whisper to him: "You remember the ring?"

He nodded eagerly.

"I shall soon send it you," she said, "and ask you to do something for my sake."

"Command me," he implored, "and it shall be done."

IV

Then at last the farewells were all spoken and Lenora and her husband started on their way. It had rained in torrents all the morning—therefore departure was delayed until long past midday. The wagons for the effects were to be round almost immediately, but their progress would be very slow owing to the bad state of the roads.

The road between Ghent and Brussels runs parallel with the Schelde for the first two or three leagues. The river had overflowed its banks, and in places the road was so deep under water that the horses sank in it almost up to their bellies. Everywhere it was fetlock-deep in mud, and more like a ploughed field than a chaussée owing to the continual passage recently of cavalry and artillery.

Mark and Lenora were travelling alone, which was distinctly unseemly in a lady of her rank, but the distance was not great, and Inez had to be left behind to finish up the packing, whilst Mark refused to take a serving man with him, declaring that the roads were perfectly safe now and free from footpads, and that they would surely be in Brussels before nightfall. Lenora, who was an absolute stranger in the country and did not know one Flemish town from another—and who moreover had done the journey from Brussels to Ghent ten days ago in a covered coach drawn by four horses—was ready to accept any suggestion or any itinerary with the blindness of ignorance.

She hardly noticed that they seemed to be making very slow progress, nor that the sky which had cleared up brilliantly in the early part of the afternoon was once more heavily overcast. Mark at first had made one or two attempts at cheerful conversation, but since Lenora only answered in monosyllables he too relapsed into silence after awhile.

The flat, monotonous country—sodden with rain—looked unspeakably dreary to the girl accustomed to the snow-clad vistas of the Sierras and the blue skies of Castille. As they left Ghent further and further behind them, the country bore traces of the terrible ravages of Alva's relentless occupation. Poverty and wretchedness were writ largely upon every tiny village or hamlet which they passed: everywhere the houses bore a miserable and forlorn aspect, with broken chimneys and shattered roofs, trees cut down to make way for the passage of cavalry or merely for the supplying of firewood for Alva's army. In the little town of Wetteren through which they passed, the houses looked deserted and dilapidated: the people looked ill-clad and sullen, and as they crossed the market-place a crowd of beggars—men, women and children in miserable rags—flocked around their horses' heels begging for alms.

So much had Spanish occupation done for this proud country which only a very few years ago had boasted that not one of its children ever lacked clothing or food. Tears of pity gathered in Lenora's eyes: she, of course, did not know that the misery which she witnessed was due to her people, to her country and to her King ... and in no small measure to her father. She gave the poor folk money and said kindly words of compassion to them. Then she turned to Mark.

"It is dreadful," she said naïvely, "to see so much misery in the land, when our Sovereign Lord the King does so much for its welfare. It is these wretched internal dissensions, I suppose, that are ruining the country. Surely all those abominable rebels must see that their obstinacy and treachery redounds upon their own kith and kin."

105

"They ought to see that, oughtn't they?" was Mark's dry and curt comment. And Lenora, chilled by such strange indifference, once more relapsed into her former silence.

V

When they neared the walls of Dendermonde, Mark announced that his horse had cast a shoe. He dismounted, and leading his horse by the bridle he advanced to the city gate. Here, however, both he and Lenora were summarily stopped by a young provost who demanded to see their papers of identification, their travelling permits, and their permit to enter this fortified city.

To Lenora's astonishment Mark, who was always so good-humoured and placid, became violent and abusive at this formality imposed upon him. It was in no way different to those which the municipality of Ghent would have enjoined on any stranger who desired to enter the city. These had been rendered necessary by the many stringent edicts formulated by the Lieutenant-Governor against the harbouring of rebels in fortified towns, and all law-abiding citizens were in consequence obliged to provide themselves with the necessary passes and permits whenever they desired to travel.

Lenora—whose ignorance of every law, every formality, every duty imposed upon this once free and proud country by its Spanish masters was unbounded—could not quite understand why her husband, who was the son of a high civic dignitary, had not taken care that all his papers were in order, before he embarked upon this journey. It surely had been his duty to do that, in order to save himself and his wife from the humiliation of being thus held up at a city gate by an insolent provost, who had the power to make his authority felt, and was not sparing of abuse of loutish Netherlanders who were wilfully ignorant of the law, or else impudent enough to flout it. An unpleasant quarrel between the two men would undoubtedly have ensued and would inevitably have ended in disaster for Mark, but for the intervention of Lenora who spoke to the provost in Spanish.

"I am this noble gentleman's wife," she said haughtily in response to an insolent look from the young soldier, "and the daughter of señor Juan de Vargas, who will make you responsible, sirrah, for any inconvenience you may cause me."

At mention of the all-powerful and dreaded name, the provost's manner immediately underwent a change. At the same time he was not prepared to accept the statement quite so unconditionally as Lenora had supposed.

"This noble gentleman," he retorted half-sullenly, "hath no papers whereby I can verify the truth of what he asserts. He has none

106

whereby he can prove to me that he is the son of the High-Bailiff of Ghent, and that you are his wife and the daughter of don Juan de Vargas."

"You have my word for both these assertions, you accursed fool," exclaimed Mark hotly.

"And I'll make you rue your insolence, you dog of a Netherlander," retorted the provost, "and teach you how to treat a soldier of the King...."

"Mark, I entreat you, not in my presence," broke in Lenora hastily, for she saw that her husband–apparently beside himself with rage–was about to commit one of those foolish and purposeless acts of violence which would have resulted for them both in a veritable chaplet of unpleasantness: imprisonment in a guard-room, bringing up before a sheriff, interrogations, abuse and insults, until the High-Bailiff or her father could be communicated with–a matter probably of two or three days, dependent on the good will of the very sheriff before whom they would appear.

It was positively unthinkable. Lenora could not understand how Mark could be so foolish as to lose his temper, when he was so obviously in the wrong, nor how he could have been so thoughtless in the matter of the papers.

She managed by dint of tactful speech and the power of her beautiful personality to pacify the wrath of the provost, and to half-persuade him to believe her assertion that she was indeed the daughter of don Juan de Vargas. At any rate the young soldier was by now sufficiently impressed by the sound of that dreaded name to decline any further responsibility in this difficult matter.

He allowed the travellers to pass through the city gates: "And to remain within the city for two hours," he added significantly; "if you wish to stay the night, you must obtain permission from the Schout."

Mark eased his temper by muttering a few more imprecations under his breath, then he seemed content and somewhat pacified, and finally led Lenora's horse and his own quietly through the inner fortifications, and thence across the Flax Market to the Grand' Place.

VI

Mark established his young wife in the ingle-nook of the tapperij in the highly-respectable tavern of the "Merry Beggars," opposite the Cloth Hall.

He enjoined the host and hostess to take every care of the noble lady, and then he went off himself in search of a farrier.

Fortunately at this hour–it was just three o'clock in the afternoon–the tapperij was practically deserted. In one corner by the window, two middle-aged burghers were playing hazard, in another a soldier was fast asleep. Mine host was passing kind; he brought a roomy armchair up to the hearth for the pretty lady, threw a fresh log upon the fire, kicked it into a blaze and placed a footstool at Lenora's feet. His wife—a buxom though sad-eyed Flemish vrouw—brought her some warm milk and a piece of wheaten bread. Lenora ate and drank with relish for she was both hungry and tired, and when she had finished eating, she leaned back in the big armchair and soon fell comfortably asleep. She had had practically no rest the night before: her nerves were overstrung, and her eyes hot with weeping. There was also a heavy load on her heart—a load chiefly weighted by the packet which was destined for her father and which she still carried carefully hidden in the bosom of her gown.

So strange are the contradictions of the human heart—of a woman's heart above all—that ofttimes to-day as her horse ambled slowly along beside Mark's she had caught herself wishing—hoping—that something unforeseen would occur which would make it impossible for her to go to Brussels—something which would force her to go back to Ghent with the contents of that packet still a close secret within her heart. In the morning she had watched the skies anxiously, hardly aware that within her innermost soul she was hoping that the continuous rains had made the roads impassable—broken down a bridge—that some sign in fact would come to her from God that she was absolved from that awful oath, the fulfilment of which seemed indeed an impossible task.

Then would come a terrible revulsion of feeling: she would remember that the Prince of Orange was even now in Ghent, with two thousand men who were to be armed by him so that they might fight against their King and threaten the life of the Lieutenant-Governor, the King's own chosen representative. And she would hate and despise herself for her cowardly irresolution—her very prayer to God appeared like blasphemy—and she wanted to urge the horses forward, she fretted at every delay, for delay might mean the murder of the Duke of Alva, and the standard of rebellion hoisted up in triumph above the Town House of Ghent.

Women will understand and pity her—those at least who once in their life have been torn 'twixt duty and sentiment. Lenora was not one of the strong-minded of her sex: she was very young—a mere girl reared in the tranquillity of convent life, and then suddenly thrown into the vortex of political intrigue, of cruel reprisals and bitter revolt; and heart and mind within her fought a terrible battle which threatened to ruin her entire life.

But in the meanwhile she was sorely in need of rest. The tapperij was so quiet and the ingle-nook was rendered quite private by a tall screen between it and the rest of the room. The soldier in the corner was snoring with insistent monotony, a big blue-bottle droned against

108

the window, and a pleasing glow and cheerful crackling came from the fire in the hearth.

Lenora slept peacefully.

CHAPTER X

ENEMIES

I

When she woke, Mark was sitting as he was so fond of doing on a low stool close to the hearth, with one long leg stretched out to the blaze, his elbow resting on his knee, his face overshadowed by his hand. Lenora—even as she first opened her eyes—saw that he was looking at her. A quick blush rose to her cheeks.

"Is it time to go?" she asked quickly.

"Not yet," he replied.

She was a little startled and looked around her, puzzled and anxious. The room had looked so light and cheerful when she had entered it—two large bow windows gave on the Grand' Place—and the weather had remained clear and bright. But now it seemed so dark, almost as if twilight was fading fast.

"What hour is it?" she questioned, and looked about her anxiously for a clock.

"I do not know," he replied airily.

"But your horse?"

"Still at the farrier's: he was busy and could not shoe her at once."

"But I am sure that it must be getting late," she said with a sudden note of anxiety in her voice.

"Very late, I am afraid," he said lightly.

"Then should we not be starting for Brussels?"

"We cannot. I have no horse."

"You can hire one, surely?"

"Not in this town."

"But I must be in Brussels by nightfall," she urged.

"I am afraid that this is impossible in any case. The powers that reign supreme in this town would not—if you remember—allow us into it, and now they will not allow us out."

"But that is impossible," she exclaimed, "monstrous!..."

109

"Monstrous, as you say, Madonna," he rejoined with a smile. "But do you feel equal to scaling the city walls?"

"Oh!"

"I fear me that that would be the only thing to do, if indeed you desire to be in Brussels this night ... and even then, I doubt but that they would bring us back."

"Then, Messire," she asked, trying to appear as calm, as detached, as he seemed to be, "do you mean to tell me that we must spend the night—here?"

"It is a pretty city..." he suggested.

"That we cannot now start for Brussels?"

"Impossible. The Schout of Dendermonde hath refused to allow us out of this city until we have proved to his satisfaction that we are neither spies of the Prince of Orange, nor emissaries of the Queen of England."

"You should have seen to it, Messire," she said haughtily, "that all our papers were in order. This is an exceedingly mortifying and unpleasant contretemps."

"I did not know the French word for it, Madonna," he rejoined with exasperating good-humour, "but I know that it must be somewhat unpleasant ... for you."

She tried to meet his glance, without that tell-tale blush spreading immediately over her cheeks: and she could have cried with vexation when she saw that the merry twinkle was more apparent in his grey eyes than it had been since their wedding day.

"I believe," she said slowly, "that you, Messire, have devised this scheme from beginning to end. You neglected your papers purposely—purposely you quarrelled with the provost at the gate—purposely you have caused me to be detained in this miserable city...."

"A pretty city, Madonna," he interposed imperturbably, "the church was built three hundred years ago ... the Cloth Hall..."

"And now you are impertinent," she declared hotly.

"Impertinent," he said quietly, even though the merry, gently mocking glance still lingered in his eyes, "impertinent because I decline to look on the present situation as a tragedy? How can I do that, Madonna, since it gives me the opportunity of spending an evening alone with you?"

"You might have done that yesterday and saved me much humiliation," she retorted.

"Yesterday I was a fool, Madonna," he said. "To-day I have become a wise man."

"What hath changed you?"

"Ten minutes of your company in the dining-hall last night."

She made no reply, glad enough that at this moment twilight was already fading into dusk. In the ingle-nook where they sat, there was hardly any light now save the glow of the fire. Anon the buxom, sad-

110

eyed hostess came in carrying a lamp which she placed on one of the tables in the tapperij. She seemed to know—by that subtle instinct which pertains to every woman's heart—that the seignior and his noble lady did not wish to be disturbed. This was not the busy hour at the hostel: in about an hour's time, the soldiers off duty would be coming in, and the shopkeepers from their shops after their day's work; but just now there was no one, so the kindly old soul having so placed the lamp that a beneficent shadow still enveloped the ingle-nook, quietly tip-toed out of the room.

II

Several minutes went by before Lenora was able to shake off the curious torpor which had fallen over her senses: nor could she in any way account for the sweet feeling of well-being which accompanied it. She had made no reply to Mark's last words, nor did she make any now. She lay back in her chair with eyes half closed, feeling, knowing that he was looking at her unceasingly, with that intent, searching gaze of his which she had encountered once or twice before. She felt as if he were trying to reach her very soul—he, the careless ne'er-do-well, the dissolute frequenter of taverns—what did he care for a woman's soul?

And yet it seemed impossible for Lenora at this moment to disguise from that searching gaze all those terrible conflicts which had literally been tearing her heart asunder in the past few hours—nay, more! it seemed as if the very letter which lay inside the folds of her kerchief addressed to her father must be lying open before her husband's eyes and that he was reading it even now.

The feeling became akin to a sweet obsession, and gradually she allowed her senses to yield themselves to its soothing influence. After all had she not been sure that sooner or later God would make His will manifest to her? had she not prayed for guidance? had she not hoped all the morning that something would prevent her journey to Brussels? Content to leave everything in God's hands she had yet hoped that God would point the way to which her own heart was tending.

And now, circumstances had suddenly occurred which did impede the journey—the horse had cast a shoe, the provost at the gate had proved officious, the hour had slipped by and no horse was forthcoming.

Given the absolute simplicity of the girl's religious thoughts, her upbringing, the superstition which underlay all beliefs in the old tenets of the Church during this period of stress and struggle through which she was groping her way through darkness into light: given Lenora's pure nature and the proud humility which accepted unquestioningly all the commands of those whom she had been taught to reverence, was it

111

to be wondered at that while she was quite ready to do her duty, she should nevertheless hope and think that she had at last received a distinct, supernatural sign that her journey to Brussels was not one of those decrees of God before which everything on earth must bow and every obstacle be removed?

But even then—in spite of her wishes and her hopes—she fought on to the last and refused to yield to the sweet, insistent call of peace and of sentiment. What she took to be a sign from God might easily be an insidious machination of the devil. There was a quaint look of gentle amusement in Mark's eyes, which was certainly disquieting, and it was just possible that it was he who had—wittingly or unwittingly—assumed the role of a guiding Providence in the matter.

Therefore she steeled her heart against those subtle whisperings which seemed to lure her on every side to give up the fight, to allow herself to drift on the soothing wave which even now was carrying her to a haven, where all was peace and quietude and where there was neither strife nor intrigue.

"Messire," she said abruptly and as repellently as she could, "I pray you enlighten mine ignorance. How many cowardly deeds of this sort stand to your discredit?"

He smiled quite unperturbed: "You think me an adept?" he asked quietly.

"You are not ashamed?" she retorted.

"Not in the least. What have I done?"

"Insulted me at every turn," she said very calmly. "What is this detention—-here, alone with you, in this strange town, away even from the protection of my own serving wench—what is it but an insult? You have shown me plainly enough, by every means in your power, that you had no liking for me. Even last night..."

She paused because tears of humiliation—which she would have given worlds not to shed—would come to her eyes, and her voice shook in spite of every effort which she made at self-control.

"Madonna," he entreated, and suddenly he was quite close to her, with one knee almost touching the ground, "as you are beautiful, so will you not be merciful to a miserable wretch, who hath been sorely perplexed by all the disdain which you have so generously lavished upon him?"

"Disdain, Messire ... surely I..."

"Surely," he broke in gently, "you have every right to despise a worthless fellow whom an evil Chance hath given you for husband, but have I not been punished enough for daring to accept what the kind goddess did offer me?"

"I had no thought of punishing you, Messire," she said earnestly. "When I stood beside you at the altar, I was a broken-hearted woman to whom Fate in the person of a miserable assassin had dealt a cruel blow. I loved my cousin, Messire ... oh! I know," she broke in quietly, "I

112

ought not to speak of this ... it is unseemly and perhaps unkind ... but I did love him and he was murdered ... foully, abominably, wickedly murdered ... not killed in fair fight–not openly–but in a dark passage–waylaid by a brigand ... killed! he! the only man who had ever spoken tenderly to me! ... and killed by one of your own people ... a friend of the Prince of Orange ... a man whom popular talk hath nicknamed Leatherface.... Oh! I know," she added hastily, seeing that instinctively he had drawn away from her and was now staring straight into the fire, with a hard expression on his face which she could not fathom, "I know that you have no hand in these conspiracies ... that from indifference rather than loyalty, I believe you have never taken up the cause of rebellion against our Sovereign Lord; but tell me, Messire, could I–a young, inexperienced girl–could I dissociate you and yours in my mind from that faction who had sent my kinsman to his death? could I come to you with a whole heart, and a soul freed from all thoughts of hatred and revenge? I meant to do my duty by you and had you but helped me I might have succeeded–instead of which your coldness repelled me. I am of the south, Messire, I am not one of your cold, unemotional Netherlanders who can go through life without one thrill of the heart brought on by a tender word or a caress. I was in your house but a few hours and already my soul was starving–my heart craved for that which you were not able to give."

"God forgive me, Madonna," he murmured, "for a blind, insensate fool!" But he did not look at her as he said this, and there was a curious dreary tone in his voice so unlike his usual light-hearted gaiety. "How you must hate us all!" he added with a sigh.

"I would not hate you, Messire," she said so softly that he scarcely could hear; "your brother Laurence hath been kind to me and I know that you take no part in those miserable plots that have treachery and assassination for their ultimate goal. As for the Prince of Orange and his friends! Yes! I do hate them as I do all pestilential creatures that turn on the hand that feeds them!"

"Madonna," he exclaimed hotly–and suddenly he was quite close to her once again, both her little hands held tightly in his own: his eyes had lost all their merriment: they were full of a glowing ardour which seemed to penetrate into her very soul. "Madonna," he continued, "may God forgive you, for indeed you know not what you say. Child! child! will you think a moment–are we not human creatures like yourself? do we not live and breathe, and eat and love just like you do in Spain? Have we no hearts to feel, no eyes to see the misery which our people suffer through the presence of a stranger in our land? Would you see a Teuton place his iron heel on Spain and on her people? Would you see the Emperor enforce his laws, his faith, his ideals upon your kith and kin? Would you stand by whilst foreign soldiery swaggered about your cities, outraged your women and plundered your homes? Would you rest content if the faith which God hath given you was made akin to

113

treachery and to rebellion? The hand that feeds the Netherlands, Madonna!" he added whilst a bitter, mirthless laugh escaped his lips, "nay! the hand against which the valiant Prince of Orange hath raised his in vengeance, is the hand that hath devastated our land, pillaged our cities and sent our people naked and starving out into the world!"

Gradually while he spoke she had drawn herself away from him, and she would have disengaged her hands too, only that he held them so tightly imprisoned.

"But Ramon was murdered, Messire," she said slowly, "can you expect me to forget that?—and even now—I would dare swear—there are men who would murder the Duke of Alva if they could ... or my father."

He made no answer to that—perhaps had she not mentioned her father he might have tried to tell her that killing was not always murder, but, at times, the work of a justiciary. Ramon—like the noisome brute that he was—deserved death as no mere ordinary criminal ever had deserved it. But how could he tell her that, when in her heart she had evidently kept a picture of the man so totally unlike the vile and execrable reality? So now he only sighed and remained silent.

The time had not yet come when this exquisite, tender-hearted girl must see the riddles of life solved before her one by one—when she would realise that there is a wider horizon in this world than that which she perceived above a convent wall. She had been brought up with ideals, thoughts and aspirations that had nothing to do with the great and bitter truths which were proclaimed in every corner of this downtrodden land. Her ideas of King and country, of duty, of loyalty, must all be shattered by the crude realities of life ere upon their ruins she built for herself a purer, holier edifice of faith and hope and infinite charity.

A tender pity for her innocence and her ignorance filled Mark's heart and soul, A maddening desire seized him to fold her in his arms and carry her away somewhere into a dream-world far away where there were no intrigues and no cruelties, no oppression and misery: and yet again he would have loved to go with her there where sorrow and poverty were keenest, for he knew that her soul—unbeknown even to herself—was full of that gentle compassion which knows how to alleviate pain just by a look from tear-dimmed eyes, or a touch from a gentle hand.

All that and more his look conveyed to her although he remained silent, and she—by a curious intuition—knew just what was in his mind. The impassioned appeal which he had made to her just now, told her that he was not the indifferent ne'er-do-well that every one supposed. He felt deeply and keenly—more deeply and keenly mayhap than those men who plotted murders at dead of night. He was not a blind follower of the Lieutenant-Governor or of her father: he saw the misery under

114

which his people groaned, and his careless, detached air obviously hid intense bitterness and resentment.

But strangely enough, she did not blame him for this. Suddenly she seemed to see the whole aspect of this strange country under a new light: the cause of the Netherlanders had—in one instant—appeared to her from a wholly different point of view. Because Mark was their defender and their champion she felt that they could not be wholly vile. This, mayhap, was not logic, but it was something more potent, more real than logic—the soft insinuating voice of Sentiment which whispered: "Would he champion that cause if it were base? Would that fiery ardour fill his soul for a cause that was unworthy?"

And Lenora suddenly felt an overwhelming desire to confide in this one man; to place before him all the perplexities which were tearing her soul. Somehow she felt that he would help her out of that tangled labyrinth wherein she had been groping all night and all day; but shyness held her back. She did not know how to broach the subject, how to tell him all about her oath, her obedience to her father, what she had done last night, what she thought it her duty to do in the future.

It was all very difficult and Lenora sighed wearily:

"There is so much in what you said just now, Messire," she began timidly, "that I would like to understand more clearly. I am so ignorant ... my life has been so restricted ... I know so little of the world...."

"Will you let me give you a few lessons?" he queried softly. "There are so many mazes in life through which it is only possible to find the way by going hand in hand."

"Hand in hand?" she sighed. "I am a stranger in this strange land, Messire ... all that I know of it hath been taught me by those who have no love for it...."

"You are a stranger in this whole world, dear heart," he said with a smile. "This little bit of Netherlands is but a tiny corner of it: its sorrows, its joys, its pain and happiness are but the sorrows and happiness of the rest of the world. One day perhaps you will let me take your little hand in mine, and then we would go and explore the whole of this strange world together."

"I wonder what we would find?" she mused.

"We would find that despite intrigues and cruelty and hatred there is much in it that is still beautiful and pure. If we went hand in hand, you and I, we would not wander with eyes downcast and seeking in the mud for the noxious things which foul God's creation by their presence—we would look upwards, sweet, and see the soft blue of our northern skies, veiled as it so often is with silvery mists that hold the entire gamut of exquisite colours in their fairy bosoms; we would see the green leaves of the trees turn to russet and gold in the autumn, we would see the linnets nesting in the bay trees in the spring. There are many beautiful things in this dreary world of ours, dear heart, but they

115

can only be seen if two pairs of eyes look on them at one and the same time and two pairs of lips whisper together in thankfulness to God."

How strange it was to hear him talking like this—Mark van Rycke, the haunter of taverns and careless profligate. Lenora's eyes, dark, luminous, enquiring, were fixed upon him—and gradually as he spoke his arm stole closer and closer round her shoulders as it had done two nights ago in Ghent when she had so wantonly turned on him in hatred. Now she felt as if she could go on listening to him for hours and hours—thus alone in this semi-darkness with the glow of dying embers upon his face, showing the strong outline of cheek and jaw, and the fine sweep of the forehead with the straight brows above those kind, grey eyes. She could have listened because she loved the sound of his voice, and the quaint, foreign intonation wherewith he spoke the Spanish tongue.

No! of a truth she did not dislike him: certainly she had no cause for hatred against him, for what had he to do with traitors or with assassins, he who spoke so gently of birds and skies and trees?

"If you will still let me hold this little hand, dear heart," he whispered now, speaking so low that in order to hear she had to lower her head until his lips were quite close to her ear, "we could learn one lesson together which God only teaches to His elect."

"And what lesson is that?" she asked, feigning not to understand, though she knew quite well what the answer would be.

"That which the nightingale teaches its mate when in May the hawthorn is in bloom and the west wind whispers among its leaves. The lesson of love."

"Love?" she said with a strange tremour in her voice, "the world no longer contains love for me...."

"The world perhaps not, dear sweet," he said more gaily, "but there is a heart beating close to yours now which holds I swear an infinity of love for you."

And once more as he spoke, the same magic spell of a while ago descended upon Lenora. It seemed as if for the moment life—the dreary, wretched life of the past few days—had ceased, and a kind of dream-existence had begun. And in this dream-existence she—Lenora—was all alone with this stranger—this man whom but a few days ago she had not even seen—who had had no part in her life in the peaceful past when she knew nothing of the world beyond the old convent walls at Segovia; yet now—in the dream-existence—she was alone with him and she was content. Ramon was not there—he had become the past—all the future for her seemed suddenly to be bound up with Mark, and she was content. He had spoken of beauty, of skies, of birds and of the gifts of God, and he still held her hand, and his arm now was right round her, so that she could feel him drawing her closer and closer to him, the while the magic spell worked upon her senses and she felt a delicious languor pervading her entire being.

"Give me your lips, sweetheart," he whispered in her ear, "and I'll give you your first lesson even now."

And verily I do believe that Lenora would have yielded here and now—content to leave the great solution of her life's riddle in the omnipotent hands of love—forgetting her oath to her father, the death of Ramon, the danger which threatened the Duke of Alva, conspiracies, treacheries, rebellion ... everything! What did it all matter? what did the world and its intrigues and its politics count beside the insistent, the wonderful call of Love?—the call of man to woman, of bird to bird, to mate and to nest and to be happy, to forget the universe in one embrace, to renounce the kingdoms of the world in the first blissful kiss.

For a few seconds Lenora remained quite still, while Happiness—the strange and mysterious elf—fluttered softly about the room. It hovered for awhile above that ingle-nook where two young hearts were mutely calling one to another, and it looked down on the beautiful girl with the glowing eyes and parted lips who with every fibre of her ardent being and the insistence of her youth was ready to capture it....

And Chance, Fate or its own elusive nature drove it relentlessly away.

III

How peaceful was the sleepy little town at this moment when dusk finally faded into night!

The tower bells of the Cloth Hall chimed the sixth hour: outside on the Grand' Place all had been still save for the occasional footstep of a passer-by or the measured tramp of a company of halberdiers on duty.

And now suddenly that peace was broken, the quietude of the town disturbed by piercing woman's shrieks, followed by shouts and curses uttered loudly by a rough, masculine voice.

Mark instinctively jumped to his feet; the cries had become pitiable and were multiplied by others which seemed to come from children's throats, and the shouts and curses became more peremptory and more rough.

"What is it?" asked Lenora, not a little frightened.

"Oh! the usual thing," replied Mark hastily, "a woman insulted in the streets, vain protests, rough usage, outrage and probably murder. We are used to such incidents in Flanders," he added quietly.

Already he was half way across the tapperij.

"You are going?" she queried anxiously, "whither?"

"Out into the street," he said, "can you not hear that a woman is in distress?"

117

"But what can you do?" she urged, "the soldiers are there ... you cannot interfere ... you, a Netherlander...."

"Yes! I, a Netherlander," he said. "It is a Flemish woman who is calling for help now."

He turned to go, and she—with the same instinct that was moving him—rose too and followed him:—the same instinct of protection: his—the man's for the woman who was in distress: hers—the woman's for the man who would pit his strength alone against superior numbers. She overtook him just as he reached the threshold of the tapperij. Beyond it was only the porch, the door of which stood wide open, and beyond that the Grand' Place; the shrieks and the ever-increasing noise of a scuffle came from an adjacent street close by.

"You must not go, Messire," she said insistently, as with both hands she clung to his arms, "what can you do? there is a crowd there ... and the soldiers...."

He smiled and tried very gently to disengage his arm from her clinging, insistent grasp.

"It will not be the first time, Madonna," he said with a light laugh, "that I have had a scuffle with a posse of soldiery ... they sometimes mean no harm," he added reassuringly seeing the look of anxious terror in her eyes, "many a time has a scuffle ended in jollity at a few words of common sense."

"Yes, yes, in Ghent," she urged, "where you are known. But here! ... where no one knows you ... spies of the Inquisition might be about ... if they see you interfering in favour of a heretic or a rebel ... or ... Oh! men have been hanged and burned for lesser crimes than that."

"Ah!" he said looking down with a whimsical smile into her flushed and eager face, "that is part of the benevolent rule which our Sovereign Lord the King exercises over the Low Countries!"

Then seeing that at his flippant words—through which there rang a note of intense bitterness—her eyes had suddenly filled with tears, he murmured tenderly:

"God bless you, Madonna, for your sweet thoughts of me! I pray you let me go! I'll come back soon," he added while a look of triumph flashed up in his eyes, "never fear!"

He ran out quickly into the street.

She hesitated, but only for a second: the next she had followed him, without thought that she had neither hood nor mantle, nor that the unseemliness of her conduct would surely have shocked all the great ladies of Spain.

IV

The Grand' Place was deserted and dark, only here and there in the windows of the Cloth Hall there was a glimmer of light. For a moment Lenora paused in the porch peering out into the gloom, trying to trace whence came the noise of the scuffle, for Mark had already disappeared: then she ran out swiftly, turning to her right from the porch till she reached the corner of a narrow street. Here an oil lamp fixed into a wall by an iron bracket threw a dim circle of light, beyond which the shadows appeared almost impenetrable. It was somewhere in amongst those shadows that a mêlée between shouting soldiers and shrieking women was taking place.

Up to this moment Lenora had never stopped to reflect as to what she meant or wanted to do. Blind instinct had driven her in the wake of Mark, feeling that he was in danger—as indeed he was: a Netherlander these days was in himself always an object of suspicion, and interference with Spanish soldiery under any circumstances was indeed likely to lead him into very grave trouble. If the soldiers were arresting or merely molesting a heretic or a rebel, any one who interfered with them would at once fall under the searching eye of the Inquisition—and there was never a lack of spies on such occasions: the seven stiver people—who for that paltry daily sum spent their lives in reporting treason, listening for it in every tavern, and in every back street of every city.

But now that she stood here at the street corner, hearing the ever-increasing noise of the scuffle close by, hearing the shouts, the cries, the pitiable appeals followed by peremptory commands, she realised how miserably impotent and helpless she was. Yet she could hear Mark's voice—speaking now in Spanish and now in Flemish, as he tried—obviously—to understand the situation and to plead for those who were in distress. At first his voice had sounded rough and peremptory: indeed Lenora could not help but marvel at its commanding quality, then gradually it became cheerful, and its tone turned to one of merry banter. The incident indeed was evidently one of those which, alas! were so usual in the cities and villages of the Low Countries these days: two young women coming home down the dark, back streets from some farm or silk-weaving shop where they had been at work, and a posse of half-drunken soldiers to whom a Flemish peasant was an acknowledged prey for ribald sport.

The women had resisted and tried to flee: they were pursued and rough horse-play had ensued: then they had screamed and the men had sworn, and presently other women and children joined in the scuffle while those who were wise stayed quietly indoors.

Horse-play had become a matter of blows followed by threats of arrest and dark hints at heresy, rebellion and the Inquisition: the mêlée was at its height when Mark interfered. Several blows were still

119

exchanged after that, and there was a good deal of swearing and mutual objurgation. Lenora, listening, wondered with what skill Mark gradually made those curses turn to facetious remarks–ill-natured at first and uncouth–then more light-hearted, and finally grudgingly pleasant. Within five minutes the tumult began to subside: Lenora could hear the women weeping and the soldiers laughing quite good-humouredly. How it had all been done she did not know: presently from the tramping of feet she gathered that the mêlée had broken up: a woman's voice said loudly: "Gott vergelte!" and Lenora thought that indeed God would repay the light-hearted man of the world who had by sheer good-humour and compelling personality turned a drama into pleasing farce.

"Well, friend!" she heard a man's voice saying in Spanish, "I don't know who you are, but a right good fellow; an I'm not mistaken. Perhaps it was wisest to leave those women alone."

"I am sure of it, friend," quoth Mark gaily, "the commandant oft makes a to-do about street-brawling, and you might have been blamed and got two days' guard-room arrest just for kissing a pair of Flemish wenches. The game was not worth the candle. Even the devil would have no profit in it."

"Well said, mate," retorted the other lustily, "come and have a mug of ale on it with me and my men at the 'Duke's Head' down yonder."

"Thank you, friend, but I put up at the 'Merry Beggars' and must return thither now. A little later perhaps."

"At your service, comrade."

There was a pause during which Lenora made up her mind–since all tumult and all danger had passed–to go back to that ingle-nook beside the fire and there to wait till Mark returned ... to wait so that she might resume with him that conversation of awhile ago which had interested her so much. But on the point of turning she halted. Three words–spoken by one of the soldiers–had come to her out of the gloom, and caused her heart to stop its beating.

"You are hurt?" one man had said–in a kind, gruff way–evidently in deep concern.

"No! no! it's nothing," Mark replied, "a small scratch ... in the scuffle just now...."

"But you are bleeding...."

"And if I am, friend, it won't be the first time in my life. I tell you it's nothing," added Mark with obvious impatience. "Good-night!"

"Good-night!" came in chorus from the men.

V

The measured tramp of booted feet slowly dying away in the distance down the narrow street, told Lenora that at last the men had gone.

But Mark was hurt and she stood waiting at the street corner for she heard his step coming slowly toward her.

He was hurt and had made light of it, but one of the soldiers had remarked that he was bleeding and she waited now for him, dreading yet vaguely hoping that he was really wounded—oh! only slightly!—but still wounded so that she might wait on him.

So strange is a woman's heart when first it wakes from the dreams, the unrealities, the fairy-worlds of childhood! With beating heart Lenora listened to that slowly-advancing footstep—how slow it seemed! as if it had lost that elasticity which but a few moments ago had carried Mark bounding down this same street. Now it dragged and finally came to a halt, just as Mark's figure emerged into the shaft of light thrown along the wall by the street lamp close to which Lenora was standing.

She smothered a little cry and ran forward to meet him, for she had seen his figure sway, and halt, then lean heavily against the wall.

"You are hurt!" she exclaimed, even before she reached him.

At sound of her voice, he pulled himself together, and in a moment had straightened out his shoulders and was walking quite steadily toward her.

"Madonna!" he cried in astonishment, "what are you doing here?"

"Oh! I ... I..." she murmured, a little ashamed now that she met his pleasant, grey eyes fixed so kindly upon her, "I heard the noise ... I became anxious...."

"It was only a street-brawl," he said, "not fit for you to witness."

Even now, though he spoke quite firmly, his voice sounded weary and weak.

"You are hurt!" she reiterated.

"Hurt? No!" He laughed, but the laughter died on his lips: he had to steady himself against the wall, for a sudden dizziness had seized him.

"I pray you take my arm," she insisted. "Can you walk as far as the tavern?"

"Indeed I can," he retorted, "on my honour 'tis a mere scratch."

"An you'll not take my arm," she said peremptorily, "I'll call for help."

"Heaven forbid!" he exclaimed gaily. "I should be laughed at for a malingerer. Shall we return to the tavern, Madonna? and will you not take mine arm?"

121

He held his right arm out to her, but as he did so she noticed that he kept the other behind his back.

She did take his arm, however. It was obviously best—since he was more severely hurt than he cared to admit—to go at once back to the tavern, and dress the wound there with water and clean linen.

They walked in silence side by side. It was only a matter of an hundred yards or so, and after a very few moments they reached the porch of the "Merry Beggars," and as the buxom hostess was standing there, vaguely wondering what had happened to her guests, Lenora at once despatched her off for a basin of clean warm water and her very softest linen towels.

Then she went into the tapperij, and Mark followed her.

The room was as peaceful, as deserted as it had been awhile ago. The host himself had in the interval made up the fire, and it was blazing brightly, lighting up the little ingle-nook, with the high-backed chair wherein Lenora had sat and the low one drawn so close to it.

Turning to Mark, she noticed that he still kept his left arm resolutely behind his back.

"Our good hostess won't be long with the water," she said, "in the meanwhile, I pray you let me tend to your wound."

"It was nothing, Madonna, I entreat you," he said with marked impatience, "a blow from a halberd caught me on the arm. I scarcely feel it now."

"Let me see," she commanded.

Then as he made no movement to obey, she—half crying with anxiety, and half-laughing with excitement—ran swiftly round him, and in an instant she had hold, of his left hand, and with gentle pressure compelled him to yield it to her. He tried to struggle, but the pain in his arm rendered it somewhat helpless.

"I insist!" she said gently, and clung to his hand supporting the fore-arm as she did so.

"Your sleeve is covered with blood!" she exclaimed.

"It is nothing!" he persisted obstinately.

But for the moment she was the stronger of the two. Short of doing her violence he could not prevent her from holding his hand with one of hers, and with the other undoing the buttons at his wrist; then with utmost gentleness she detached the shirt which was sticking to a deep, gaping wound, that stretched from the wrist right up to the elbow.

"Oh! but this is terrible!" she cried. "No blow from a halberd could have inflicted such a wound! ... Oh! why does not that woman hurry?" she added, whilst tears of vexation and impatience rose to her eyes. There was nothing to hand wherewith she could staunch the wound, even momentarily—every second was precious!...

"I have a knowledge of such matters," she said gently. "At the convent we tended on many wounded soldiers, when they came to us hurt from the wars. This is no fresh wound, Messire," she added slowly, "but an old and very severe one, dealt not so very long ago ... by a dagger probably, which tore the flesh and muscle right deeply to the bone ... it had not healed completely ... the blow from the halberd caused it to reopen ... and..."

But the next words remained frozen on her lips: even whilst she spoke she had gradually felt a deathlike feeling–like an icy hand gripping her heart and tearing at its strings. An awful dizziness seized her. She looked up–still holding Mark's hand–and gazed straight into his face. He too was as pale as the dead ashes in the grate–his whole face had become wax-like in its rigidity, only his eyes remained alive and glowing, fixed into her own now with a look which held a world of emotion in its depths: passionate tenderness and mute appeal, an avowal and a yearning and with it all an infinity of despair.

And she, thus looking into that face which only lived through the eyes, saw all around her the narrow white-washed walls of the tapperij fading away into darkness. In their stead she saw a narrow passage, dark and gloomy, and in its remotest and darkest corner a figure cowered, clad in dark clothes from head to foot and wearing a mask of leather upon its face–the assassin waiting for his prey. And she saw Ramon–handsome, light-hearted, debonnaire Ramon–her kinsman and her lover, standing unsuspecting by. She saw it all–the picture as her father had painted it for her edification. The assassin lying in wait– Ramon unsuspecting. She saw the murder committed there in the dark, the stealthy, surreptitious blow. She saw Ramon totter and fall–but before falling turn on the dastardly murderer, and with hand already half paralysed by oncoming death, deal him a deep and gashing wound ... in the left fore-arm ... with his dagger which tore flesh and muscle between elbow and wrist right through to the bone.

And while she looked straight into his eyes and yet saw nothing but the vision of that awful deed, her lips murmured automatically the four accusing words:

"Then it was you!"

He had not for one second lost his hold upon himself, since that awful moment when he realised that she guessed. He had no idea that don Ramon, at the point of death, had spoken of the wound which he had inflicted on the man who had meted out summary justice to him for his crimes. But now he knew that the secret which he would have buried with him in a bottomless grave was known to her–to the woman whom he had learned to love with his whole soul. She knew now, and henceforth they must be not only strangers but bitter enemies. Nothing–not even perhaps his own death–would ever wipe away the sense of utter abhorrence wherewith she regarded him now. He took his last look of her as one does of one infinitely dear, who sinks into the arms of Death.

He drank in every line of her exquisite face, the child-like contour of chin and throat, her alabaster-like skin, the exquisite mouth which he was destined now never to touch with his yearning lips. In this supreme moment, his love for her–only just in its infancy–rose to its full effulgence; he knew now that he worshipped her, and knew that never while the shadow of her dead kinsman stood between them would he hold her in his arms.

"Then it was you!" she murmured again, and with those fateful words pronounced his condemnation and her own indomitable hate.

"Madonna," he entreated, speaking with the infinite tenderness and pity which filled his heart, "will you deign to listen, if I try to plead mine own cause?"

But no look of softness came into her eyes: they were glowing and dry and unseeing: she did not see him–not Mark, her husband as he stood there now before her–she saw him cowering in a dark corner, clad in sombre clothes and wearing a leather mask–she saw him with an assassin's dagger in his hand and she saw Ramon lying dead at his feet.

"Then it was you!" she said for the third time.

And he bent his head in mute avowal.

For a few seconds longer she stood there, rigid and silent: slowly her fingers opened and his hand which she had held dropped away to his side. A shudder went right through her, she tottered and nearly fell, only saving herself by holding on to the corner of the table. He made a movement as if he would try and support her, as if he would put his arms around her and pillow her against his breast, but with an exclamation of supreme loathing, she drew away from him, and with a pitiable cry half of hatred and wholly of misery, she turned and fled from the room.

CHAPTER XI

UTTER LONELINESS

I

What happened directly after that, Lenora did not know. Consciousness mercifully left her, and when she woke once more she found herself sitting in a small room which smelt of lavender and warm linen, beside a fire which burned low in a wide-open hearth.

She opened her eyes and looked enquiringly around her. The

room was dark—only faintly lighted by the lamp which hung from a beam in the ceiling. A young girl was busy in a corner of the room bending over an ironing board.

"Does the noble lady feel better?" she asked kindly but with all the deference which those of the subject race were expected to show to their superiors.

She spoke in broken French—most women and men who served in the inns and taverns in the cities of the Low Countries were obliged to know some other language besides their own, seeing that the tapperijen were frequented by Spanish, French and German soldiery.

"I am quite well, I thank thee," replied Lenora gently, "but wilt thou tell me where I am and how I came to be sitting here when..."

She paused; for with a rush the recollection of the past terrible moments came sweeping back upon her, and it seemed as if consciousness would flee from her once again.

"The noble lady must have felt dizzy," said the girl quietly. "Aunt sent me in with the warm water for the noble seigneur's wound, and I saw the noble lady just running out of the tapperij to the porch and then fall—in a swoon. I was frightened, but the noble seigneur ordered me quickly to tie a towel around his wounded arm and then he carried the noble lady up here to a nice warm room, where he told me that mayhap she should deign to pass the night. Oh! the noble seigneur is grievously wounded, he..."

"Silence, girl," cried Lenora suddenly, for indeed with every word the child seemed to be touching an aching place in her heart. "No, no," she added more gently, seeing that the girl, abashed and not a little frightened, had gone back in silence to her ironing-board, "I did not mean to be unkind ... but ... as thou seest, I am not well. Come! tell me what happened after ... after the noble seigneur carried me up here."

"Aunt waited on him, noble lady," said the girl, "for the wound in his arm bled grievously ... but he was impatient and soon ordered her to leave him alone ... then I came up here, and did all I could to bring the noble lady round.... I tried vinegar and burned feathers under the noble lady's nose ... but I was not frightened ... I knew the noble lady would revive ... and the leech lives but two doors off.... We were all of us anxious about the noble seigneur ... because of his wound ... and he looked so pale and haggard ... so aunt and I soon ran down to him again.... We found him sitting by the table ... just sealing down a letter which he had been writing. 'I am going, mevrouw,' he says to aunt quite curtly. 'Take thine orders from the noble lady. She will tell thee her own wishes.' He gave her some money and a letter which he ordered her to give to the noble lady as soon as she deigned to wake. And then he took his hat and mantle and went out by the porch ... just like that ... all alone ... into the darkness ... whither he did not deign to say.... We are just poor people and we did not dare to ask, but the wind has sprung up and it hath begun to rain ... the night will be rough ... and the noble seigneur is not fit to hold a horse with his arm in such a grievous state."

"Where is the letter?" asked Lenora curtly.

From the pocket of her apron the girl produced a letter folded into four and sealed down with wax which she handed to the noble Spanish lady with a respectful curtsey.

"Aunt told me to give it to the noble lady," she said, "as soon as she deigned to wake."

"Is thine aunt the hostess of this inn?" queried Lenora. She was fingering the letter, feeling a curious hesitancy and reluctance to read its contents, and asked a few idle questions whilst she made an effort to control her nerves.

"Yes! at the noble lady's service," replied the girl.

"Art of this city, then?"

"No, so please you. I come from Ghent."

"From Ghent? What is thy name, then?"

"Grete, so please the noble lady," whispered the girl.

Then, as the noble lady said nothing more, but sat just quite still with the unopened letter in her hand, Grete went back to her ironing-board. Lenora watched her mechanical movements for awhile—a mist was before her eyes, and she could not see very clearly, but somehow she liked the look of Grete—Grete who was from Ghent—whom she would have liked to question further, only that when she tried to speak, the words seemed to get choked in her throat.

All of a sudden, she broke the seal upon the letter and swept away the mist before her eyes with an impatient movement of the hand.

"Madonna," he had written, "I would not leave You thus all alone in this ftrange place, to which an act of folly on My part did bring You, but that I read My difmifsal in Your eyes. The fight of me is hateful to You—alas! this I can underftand! By the time You read this, I fhall be far away. But anon upon the road I fhall meet the ox-wagon with Your effects and Your ferving-woman; it cannot be far from here, as the driver had orders to put up in this town for the night. I will fpeed him on as faft as He can, and then to-morrow You can continue Your journey in peace, for the driver will arrange for an efcort to accompany You as far as Brufsels. He will have His orders. In the meanwhile I have ventured to flip a sealed packet containing money into the pocket of Your gown: (it was done while you lay unconfcious in My arms.) I pray You do not fcruple to take it. The money is Yours: a part of Your dowry, an account of which My Father will render unto Yours as foon as may be. In the meanwhile You are free to come and go or ftay in this town, juft as You were in Brufsels or in Ghent. Your pafs and permit as well as Mine were in perfect order; the difpute with the Provoft at the gate, the difficulty about the permits, was but a rufe on My part fo that I might fpend a time in Your company, under the pretence that We were not allowed to continue Our journey to Brufsels. To afk Your forgivenefs for

126

this as well as for other graver matters were ufelefs, I know. To afk You to erafe the events of the paft two weeks from Your memory were perhaps an infult. As for Me I fhall look upon it as a facred duty never to offend You with My prefence as long as I live. But I lay Mine undying homage at Your feet.

"MARK VAN RYCKE."

The letter dropped into her lap, for awhile she sat, staring straight into the fire.

The girl was putting away her ironing-board and folding away the linen, ranging it carefully in the press. Having made the room quite tidy, she asked timidly:

"Will the noble lady deign to take supper?"

But she had to repeat her question three times at intervals before Lenora gave answer.

"What?" she said vaguely, like one waking from a dream. "Yes!– No!–What didst say, girl?"

"Will the noble lady deign to take supper?"

"Bring me some milk and bread," replied Lenora, "and ... can I sleep here to-night?"

"In this bed," said the girl: and she pointed to the recess in the wall, where snow-white sheets and pillows seemed literally to invite repose, "if the noble lady will deign to be satisfied."

"I shall be glad to rest here," said Lenora with a woe-begone little sigh, "for I am very tired. Anon a wagon will be here with my effects and my serving woman. Send her to me directly she arrives."

Her voice was absolutely toneless and dull: she spoke like one who is infinitely weary, or in utter hopelessness: but the girl, whose kind heart ached for the beautiful lady, did not dare to offer comfort. She prepared to leave the room in order to fetch the frugal supper. Lenora turned her head once more toward the fire: her eyes caught sight of the letter which still lay in her lap. With a sudden fierce gesture she picked it up, crushed it between her fingers and threw it into the flames.

II

A few minutes later Grete came back carrying a tray with fine wheaten bread, a jar of milk, and some fresh cheese, her round young face beaming with benevolence and compassion.

"If the noble lady will deign to eat," she said, as she put the tray down upon the table, "the noble lady will feel less weary ... and then, as soon as the ox-wagon arrives with the serving woman, the noble lady could go to bed."

"Wait one moment," said Lenora, as the girl once more prepared

127

to go, "I want a courier—now at once—to take an urgent message as far as Brussels. Can you find me one?"

"There are four butchers in the town, noble lady, who deliver all the messages for three or four leagues round. Uncle can go and see if one of them is inclined to go.... But the night is very rough...."

"I will give the man who will take my message to Brussels this night five golden ducats," said Lenora peremptorily.

Grete opened her eyes wide with astonishment.

"Five golden ducats!" she exclaimed ecstatically. Of a truth the poor trading folk of Dendermonde had never seen quite so much money all at once and in the same hand.

"I doubt not but that Michel Daens, the butcher, at the sign of the 'Calf's Head' in the Meerhem, will be glad to earn the money. And he hath a very strong horse."

"Then tell your uncle, child, to go at once to him: and to give him this letter, which he is to deliver without fail before ten o'clock this night." From the bosom of her gown she drew the letter which she had written during the previous night, and handed it to the young girl.

"The letter," she added slowly, "is for Messire don Juan de Vargas, chief of the Council of His Highness the Lieutenant-Governor. He lodges in Brussels at the sign of the 'Blue Firmament,' over against the Broodhuis. Let your uncle explain to Michel Daens, the butcher, that if this letter is not delivered before ten o'clock this evening, he will be made to suffer the severe penalty imposed by the law on all those who neglect to do their duty to the State. Take the letter, child!"

Indeed, this last peremptory order was necessary, for Grete, hearing to whom the letter was addressed, hardly dared to touch it. Indeed there would be no fear that Michel Daens would fail to execute the noble lady's commands with punctuality and utmost speed. The name of don Juan de Vargas was one that would make any man fly to the ends of the earth if ordered so to do. A message or letter to or from him would of a surety be delivered punctually, even if the heavens were on the point of falling or the earth about to open.

To Grete the name meant something more than that: it was the dreaded symbol of an awful reality—a reality which for her had meant the terrors of that awful night, when the Spanish officer threatened and insulted her and Katrine, when death or outrage stared them both in the face, and the awful catastrophe was only averted by the interference of the mysterious Leatherface.

So she took the letter which was addressed to one who was even greater, even more to be feared than the Spanish officer; she took it with a trembling hand as she would some sacred symbol: then she curtseyed and went out of the room.

Lenora rose and followed her into the passage, where she stood listening until she heard Grete calling to her uncle and aunt. The three of them then spoke together in Flemish which Lenora hardly

128

understood; but she caught the names Michel Daens and Messire don Juan de Vargas, and then the words spoken very emphatically by Grete: "Before ten o'clock this night." Then she went back to her room, and closed the door softly behind her.

III

So, then, the die was cast. There was an end to all the irresolution, the heart-achings, the tearing of soul and nerves upon the rack of doubt and indecision. Hopeless misery and deathly bitterness filled Lenora's heart now.

She had been fooled and deceived! Fooled by soft words and cajoling ways, by lies and treachery: and she had very nearly succumbed to the monstrous deceit.

Fool! fool! that she was! She reiterated the word aloud over and over again, for there was a weird pleasure in lashing her pride with the searing thongs of that humiliating memory. Had not God Himself intervened and torn the mask from the traitor's face she might even now be lying in his arms, with the kiss of an assassin upon her lips! A shudder of loathing went right through her. She shivered as if stricken with ague, and all the while a blush of intense shame was scorching her cheeks.

Fool! Fool!

She had stood with her father beside the dead body of her lover—her lover and kinsman—and there she had registered an oath which a few cajoling words had well-nigh caused her to break. Surely the dull, aching misery which she was enduring at this moment was but a very mild punishment for her perjury.

She had allowed Ramon's murderer to cajole her with gentle words, to lull her into apathy in the face of her obvious duty to her King and to the State. He had played the part of indifference when all the while he—above all others—was steeped to the neck in treason and in rebellion! He! the spy of the Prince of Orange! the hired assassin! the miserable cowardly criminal! And she had listened to him, had sat close beside him by the hearth and allowed his arm to creep around her shoulders ... the arm which had struck Ramon down in the dark ... the arm—she no longer doubted it now—which would be hired to strike the Duke of Alva, or her own father with the same abominable treachery.

Oh! the shame of it! the hideous, abominable shame! He had guessed last night that she was on the watch, that she had seen and heard the odious plotting against the life of the Lieutenant-Governor: he had guessed, and then—by tortuous means and lying tongue—had sought to circumvent her—had lured her into this city—and then, by dint

129

of lies and more lies and lies again, had hoped to subdue her to his will by false kisses and sacrilegious love.

And she had been on the point of sacrificing her country's needs and the life of the Duke of Alva to the blandishments of a traitor!

Oh! the shame of it! The terrible, burning shame!

But God had intervened! ... At least of this she could have no doubt. All day she had prayed for an indication from above—she had prayed for guidance, she had prayed for a sign, and it had come! Awesome, terrible and absolutely convincing. God, in unmasking the one traitor who had well-nigh touched her heart, had shown her plainly that her duty lay in unmasking them all! Traitors! traitors! every one of them! and God had given her an unmistakable sign that He desired to punish them all.

Did she neglect those signs now she would be the vilest traitor that ever defiled the earth.... It had all been so clear.... The mêlée in the streets ... Mark's interference—the blow from the halberd which had reopened the half-healed wound ... his momentary weakness and her sudden vision of the truth! ... Thank God it was not too late! The meeting was to be held this night at the house of Messire Deynoot the Procurator-General ... the Prince of Orange and all the other rebels would make the final arrangements for taking up arms against the King and murdering or capturing the Lieutenant-Governor.

This meeting, at any rate, she—Lenora—had frustrated. Mark of a surety had already warned the conspirators, before he started on the journey—and Laurence too after he received her letter.... The meeting of a certainty would be postponed. But even so, and despite all warnings, the band of assassins could not escape justice. Her letter would be in her father's hands this night: in a few hours he—and through him the Lieutenant-Governor—would know every phase of the infamous plot which had the murder of His Highness for its first aim—they would know the names of the two thousand traitors who were waiting to take up arms against the King—they would know of William of Orange's presence in Ghent, of his recruiting campaign there, of the places where he kept stores of arms and ammunition.

All that she had set forth clearly and succinctly—omitting nothing. Oh! her father would know how to act! He would know how to crush the conspiracy and punish the traitors!

Would he also know how to lay his powerful hand on the mysterious Leatherface ... the man of dark deeds and cruel, treacherous blows ... the murderer of Ramon de Linea—the one whom others paid to do the foul deeds which shunned the light of day...?

Lenora leaned back against the cushions of her chair. Physical nausea had overcome her at the thought of all that she had done. She had served the King and had served the State! She had undoubtedly saved the life of the Duke of Alva, and therefore rendered incalculable service to her country ... she was the means whereby a band of pestilential traitors and rebels would be unmasked ... and punished ... and among these she must reckon Mark van Rycke ... her husband.... Oh! him she hated with a real, personal hatred far stronger and more implacable than that wherewith she regarded—impersonally—all the enemies of the King. He seemed to her more cruel, more cowardly, more despicable than any man could be! ... Yes! she had done all that, and now her one hope was that she might die this night—having done her duty and kept her oath, and then been left unutterably lonely and wretched—in hopeless desolation.

IV

The night was rough, as Grete had foretold. Gusts of wind blew against the window-frames and made them rattle and creak with a weird and eerie sound. The rain beat against the panes and down the chimney making the fire sizzle and splutter, and putting out the merry little tongues of flame. Lenora drank some milk and tried to eat the bread, but every morsel seemed to choke her. She went to the window and drew aside the thick curtains and sat in the seat in the embrasure— for she felt restless and stifled. Anon she threw open one of the casements.

The rain beat in against her face and bare neck, but this she did not mind; she was glad to cool her head and face a little. The Grand' Place looked gloomy and dark; most of the lights in the Cloth Hall opposite were extinguished—only in a few windows they still glimmered feebly. Lenora caught herself counting those lights: there were two small ones in the dormer windows at the top, and one in a tall window in the floor below, and right down on a level with the street the main door stood wide open and showed a long, shallow streak of light. One! two! up above! they looked like eyes! Then one in the middle that was the nose—all awry and out of the centre!—and below the long mouth— like a huge grin! And the roof looked like a huge hat with the tower like a feather! The more Lenora looked into those lights opposite, the more like a grinning face did they seem, until the whole thing got on her nerves, and she started laughing! laughing! ... She laughed until her sides ached, and her eyes were full of tears! she laughed though her head was splitting with pain, and the nerves of her face ached with intolerable agony. She laughed until her laughter broke into a sob, and she fell forward with her hands upon the window sill, her burning forehead upon her hands, the rain and wind beating upon her head, her neck, her back; her hair was soon wet through; its heavy strands fell away from the pins and combs that confined them and streamed down like a golden cascade all about her shoulders, the while she sobbed out her heart in misery and wretchedness.

V

The clock of the Cloth-Hall tower chimed the ninth hour. Lenora raised her head and once more peered out into the night.

Nine o'clock! If Michel Daens had done his duty, he must be more than half-way to Brussels by now. It almost seemed to Lenora's supersensitive nerves at this moment that she could hear the tramp of his horse's hoofs upon the muddy road–Hammer! Hammer! Hammer! Surely, surely she could hear it, or was it her own heart-beats that she was counting?

Hammer! Hammer! Hammer! Two horses, each with a rider, were speeding along the road: one to Brussels–Michel Daens the butcher-messenger, bearing the letter for don Juan de Vargas which would raise in its trail a harvest of death for traitors ... and along the road to Ghent Mark speeding too, to warn those traitors to remain in hiding–or to flee while there was yet time–for justice Was on their track. Mark had gone to Ghent, of this Lenora was sure; she had burned his letter, but she remembered its every word. He spoke of meeting the ox-wagon which was on its way from Ghent! besides which, of course, he was bound to go back. Was he not the paid spy of the Prince of Orange–his mentor and his friend?

And mentally Lenora strained her ears to listen ... to hear which of those two riders would first reach his destination. And as she listened it seemed as if that monotonous hammer! hammer! was beating against her heart, and with every blow was crushing to death more of her life, more of her youth ... and all her hopes of happiness.

VI

Inez–tired out with the jolting of the wagon, wet to the skin, fagged and cold–found her mistress still sitting by the open window, with streaming hair and eyes glowing as with inward fever. The devoted soul very quickly forgot her own discomfort in view of her young mistress' sorry plight. She chafed the ice-cold hands and combed the dripping hair; she took off the heavy gown, and the leather shoes and silk stockings. She bathed the hot brow and little cold feet, and finally got Lenora into bed and had the satisfaction of seeing her smile.

"There now, my saint," she said cheerily, "you feel better, do you not? I tell you when I met Messire van Rycke and he told me that you were here and that we were to get to you at once, I nearly swooned with fright ... I wanted to ask him a dozen questions ... but he had ridden away out into the darkness before I could speak a single word...."

The pillow was fresh and smelt sweetly of lavender. Lenora had

132

closed her eyes and a sense of physical well-being was—despite heart-ache and mental agony—gradually creeping into her bones.

"Where did you meet Messire van Rycke, Inez?" she asked quietly.

"Oh! a long way from here, my saint. We did not start from Ghent till four o'clock in the afternoon, and have been jogging along at foot-pace ever since. Oh! these interminable roads, and horrible, jolting wagons! It was about two hours ago that we came on Messire van Rycke riding like one possessed."

"He was riding toward Ghent?"

"Toward Ghent, my saint. And as I told you—as soon as he had given Jan his orders, he flew by like the wind. The roads were quite lonely after that. I tell you, my saint, I was passing glad that we had a good escort—two mounted men you know rode beside the wagon—or I should have been mightily afraid of malefactors."

"You gave the sealed packet to Messire Laurence van Rycke," asked Lenora, "as I had directed?"

"I gave him the packet two hours after you had started."

"And what did he say?"

"He said nothing, my saint."

With a weary sigh, Lenora turned her head away. She kept her eyes closed resolutely, and after a while Inez thought that she slept. So she tip-toed quietly out of the room, having drawn the coverlet well over her mistress' form. She left the lamp in the room, for she had enough understanding to know that Lenora was perturbed and anxious, and in times of anxiety darkness is oft an evil counsellor.

BOOK THREE

GHENT

CHAPTER XII

REPRISALS

I

It is to the seigneur de Vaernewyck—that excellent and faithful chronicler—that we are indebted for the most detailed account of all the events which occurred in the city of Ghent during those few memorable days in October.

The weather, he tells us, had been perpetually rainy, and the days were drawing in rapidly, for it was then the 19th of the month, and what with the sky so perpetually overcast it was nearly dark when close upon five o'clock in the afternoon the ensigns of the companies of Walloon soldiery first entered the city by the Waalpoort. They demanded admittance in the name of the King, the Regent and the Lieutenant-Governor, and the guard at the gate would certes never have ventured to refuse what they asked.

At first the townsfolk were vastly entertained at seeing so many troops; nothing was further from their mind than the thought that these had been sent into the city with evil intent. So the gaffers and gossips stood about in the streets and open places staring at the fine pageant, and the women and children gaped at the soldiers from the windows of their houses, all in perfect good humour and little dreaming of the terrible misery which these soldiers were bringing in their train into the beautiful city of Ghent.

No one thought of civil strife then.

In the forefront marched men and young boys who carried javelins in their hands and had round shields swung upon their arm; these shields were bordered with a rich fringe of crimson silk and they glittered like steel in the damp atmosphere. After these men came a company of halberdiers from the garrisons of Mechlin and Alost, and they looked splendid in their striped doublets, their plumed bonnets slung behind their backs, their enormous boots reaching half-way up

134

their thighs. In the midst of them rode the Master of the Camp on his cream charger; the ends of his crimson and yellow scarf, soaked through with the rain and driven by the wind, flapped unremittingly against his steel cuirass, whilst the plumes on his felt hat hung—bedraggled—into his face.

Then came the arquebusiers, marching five abreast, and there were several thousands of them, for it took half an hour for them all to cross the bridge. These were followed by a vast number of elegant foot-soldiers carrying their huge lances upon their shoulders, well-armed, magnificently accoutred, their armour highly polished and richly engraved and wearing gauntlets and steel bonnets. Finally came three companies of artillery with culverines and falconets and with five wagons, and behind them the massed drummers and fifers who brought up the rear playing gay music as they marched.

The troops assembled on the Kouter which was thronged to overflowing with gaffers and idlers. Everyone was talking and jesting then, no one had a thought of what was to come, no one looked upon these gaily-decked troops with any sinister prescience of coming evil. They were nearly all Walloons, from the provinces of Antwerp and Brabant, and many of them spoke the Flemish tongue in addition to their own—and when after inspection they stood or walked at ease on the Kouter, the girls exchanged jests and merry sallies with them.

II

Two hours later the Duke of Alva entered the city. It was a very dark night, but the rain had left off. The Lieutenant-Governor had a company of lancers with him, and these were Spanish, every man of them. One hundred torch-bearers accompanied the Duke and his escort and they had much difficulty in keeping their torches alight in the damp night air; the flames spluttered and sizzled and the men waved the torches about so that sparks flew about in every direction to the grave danger of the peaceable citizens who were in the foremost ranks of the crowd.

It was to be supposed that the High-Bailiff and Sheriffs of the city had been warned of the arrival of His Highness, for they met him at the Waalpoort, attired despite the threatening weather in their magnificent civic robes. The Duke who rode a black charger paused just inside the gates and listened in silence to the loyal address which these dignitaries presented to him. The sizzling torches threw a weird, unsteady light upon the scene, distorting every form into a grotesque shape, half-concealing, half-illumining the stern face of the Lieutenant-Governor draped in his velvet robe.

135

When the loyal address had been duly presented, and further speeches of welcome delivered by the senior sheriff and by the Schout, the Lieutenant-Governor demanded that the keys of the city be within the hour brought to him on the Kouter where he would be inspecting the troops. This demand greatly astonished the sheriffs and aldermen, but they did not dare to raise any objections and promised that they would most dutifully comply with His Highness' request.

"With my commands," the Duke corrected them curtly.

Nor would he dismiss the grave seigneurs, but kept them kneeling there before him in the mud, until they had humbly assured him that they would execute his commands.

Whereupon the Duke proceeded to the Kouter.

The troops had been aligned for his inspection, and a very gay and gaudy throng they looked in the flickering torch-light. All the houses round the Place were lighted up from within by now, and crowds thronged in from all the side streets. It was many years since Ghent had seen so gay a sight. There were three hundred torch-bearers on the parade ground by now, each with huge resin torches, and so brightly illumined was the Place that you could have deciphered a letter out in the open just as easily as you would in daylight. Lances and halberds held erect formed a shimmering background to the picture like a forest of straight tall stems, and their metal heads glimmered like little tongues of fire, throwing out strange and unexpected flashes of light as the men moved who held them.

In the centre of the picture the Duke of Alva on horseback. The endurance of the man was absolutely wonderful! He had ridden all the way from Brussels that day–starting at daybreak–a matter of nine leagues and more. He had tired two horses out, but not himself–and he was a man of sixty. The chronicler goes on to tell us that the Duke's face looked grim and determined, but not fatigued, and in his prominent eyes under their drooping lids was a glitter like steel–hard and cruel and triumphant too.

He held the reins of his charger with one hand, the other was on his hip. He wore a felt hat which he had pulled down upon his brow, and a huge cape of dark woollen stuff lined with purple silk which covered his shoulders and fell right round him over his saddle-bow. A group of cavaliers surrounded him in fantastic multi-coloured doublets and hose, all slashed and pinked, and enormous bonnets covered with gigantic plumes, and behind these stood the standard bearers. The autumn wind had caught the folds of the huge ensigns which were grouped in half dozens close together, so that the great folds interlocked from time to time and spread themselves out like a monster moving, waving mass of crimson and yellow with the devices of the companies embroidered thereon in black and silver.

It was indeed a fine and picturesque spectacle, arranged with a view to making it impressive and to strike awe into the hearts of the

136

citizens. The civic dignitaries had returned by now, and the High-Bailiff had brought the keys of the town upon a velvet cushion. He and the ten sheriffs and the Schout, the fifteen Vroedschappen who were the city councillors and the Schepens who were the aldermen all approached the Lieutenant-Governor with back nearly bent double in their loyalty and humility.

But when they were within speaking distance of the Duke they all had to kneel—just as before—in the mud and the dirt. The Master of the Camp was there to direct them and they had not the pluck to resist. Then the High-Bailiff was made to advance alone with the cushion in both his hands and upon the cushion the keys of the city, and he was made to kneel close to the Duke's stirrup and humbly present him with the keys.

The Lieutenant-Governor said curtly: "'Tis well!" and ordered the chief gentleman of his body-guard to take possession of the keys. Then he said in a loud voice so that every one could hear:

"The gates of this city shall be closed this night, and will so remain until such time as the order which I am about to give to the inhabitants is complied with."

There was a prolonged roll of drums; and the gentleman of the bodyguard rode away from the Place with a company of halberdiers, and he carried the keys of the city with him. He was going to close the gates of the city as the Lieutenant-Governor directed.

When the roll of the drums had died away there was a moment's silence on the huge overcrowded Kouter through which you might have heard a thousand hearts beating in sudden deathly anxiety. Here then was no ordinary pageant, no mere display of soldiery and of arms such as the Spaniards were overfond of. Something momentous was about to happen which in these days of perpetual strife and continuous oppression could but mean sorrow and humiliation to this proud city and to her freedom-loving children. The High-Bailiff and the Schout and the town councillors were all kept kneeling, though they were elderly men most of them, and the ground was very damp; and the people crowded in all round the soldiers, as near as they could, in order to hear what His Highness wished to say.

"Citizens of Ghent," he began in his harsh and strident voice which could be heard from end to end of the Kouter. "It has come to my knowledge that William of Nassau Prince of Orange is dwelling in this city, and that, contrary to the ordinance of our Sovereign Lord the King, he hath attempted to levy troops within these gates for an unlawful purpose. Those who have thus in defiance of all law and order enrolled themselves under a standard of rebellion and have taken up arms against our Sovereign Lord and King will be dealt with summarily. But in the meanwhile understand that any one who henceforth harbours under his roof the said William of Nassau Prince of Orange, or assists or aids him to leave this city, is guilty of rebellion,

137

and will be punished with death. Understand also that it is my desire that the person of the Prince of Orange be delivered unto me within forty-eight hours at the Kasteel where I shall be lodging, and that I have ordered that the gates of the city be closed until the expiration of that time. And finally understand that if within forty-eight hours the person of William of Nassau Prince of Orange is not delivered unto me, then will the whole city of Ghent be guilty of treason and rebellion, and every man, woman and child in it will be punishable with death; and the town itself will be dealt with as summarily as were Mons and Valenciennes and Mechlin. God bless our gracious and merciful King!"

He raised his hat and lifted his face up to heaven, and his lips were seen to move as if in prayer. The Master of the Camp gave the signal for a huge and prolonged roll of drums which echoed from end to end of the Kouter and into every corner of the city, and all the soldiers set up a lusty shout of "God bless our Sovereign Lord and King!" But the people were silent. No one uttered a word, no one joined in the shouting. Men looked at one another with scared, wide-open eyes; the boldest had become as pale as death. Some of the women swooned with terror, others broke into terrified sobs; even the children realised that something very terrible had occurred; they clung weeping to their mothers' skirts.

The Lieutenant-Governor, having spoken, wheeled round his horse and rode slowly across the Kouter closely surrounded by his bodyguard and his torch-bearers. Just then, so Messire de Vaernewyck assures us, the wind, which had been very boisterous all the evening, suddenly dropped, and the air became very still and strangely oppressive. A few huge drops of rain fell making a loud patter upon the steel bonnets and cuirasses of the soldiers, and then a streak of vivid lightning rent the black clouds right out over the Leye and a terrific clap of thunder shook the very houses of the city upon their foundation. The Duke of Alva's horse reared and nearly threw him; there was momentary confusion, too, among the bodyguard. Those who were devout Catholics promptly crossed themselves; those who were superstitious at once saw in that curious and unexpected phenomenon a warning from God Himself.

Then the rain came down in torrents and speedily dispersed the crowd. The civic magistrates and councillors were at last able to struggle to their feet—most of them felt cramped from the lengthy kneeling. They assembled in groups and whispered with one another; the townsfolk looked on them with eyes full of anxiety; it was to them that the poorer people must look for help in this awful calamity which threatened them all.

138

III

After the Lieutenant-Governor and his cortège had left the Kouter the soldiers broke ground and ran wild throughout the city. No special lodgings had been allotted to them, but apparently they had been told that they could quarter themselves where they listed. They began by taking possession of the covered markets—and this could easily have been tolerated; but many of them raided the houses of peaceful citizens in a manner most unseemly and often brutal, making terrible noise and confusion throughout the city. They treated the owners of the houses as if the latter were nought but menials and they themselves the masters of the place; so much so indeed that several families left their homes in the possession of these soldiery, and took refuge with relations who had not been thus inflicted.

Terror and misery had rapidly spread throughout the city. There were many who had not heard the proclamation of the Lieutenant-Governor, and when the rumour reached them that numbers of soldiers were billeted in the town they made preparations for immediate flight. Some even went so far as to load all their furniture and effects upon wagons, ready to go out of the city this very night—for they remembered how five years ago when first the Duke of Alva's troops were quartered in Ghent, how abominably they had behaved toward all the citizens—robbing, looting, and pillaging, for all the world as if they were bands of brigands, rather than disciplined soldiers.

Great was the terror and consternation of those who wanted to flee now when they understood that all the city gates were closed and that no one would be allowed to go through them until the Prince of Orange, who was said to be in Ghent, was delivered over to the Lieutenant-Governor.

This was indeed a terrible state of things and one destined to strike hopeless terror in the hearts of most, seeing that hardly any one inside the city knew aught of the Prince of Orange or of his comings and goings, and yet they were liable to be punished for treason in which they had had no share.

And in the meanwhile the soldiers ran riot throughout the city—even though, with much ostentation, a great deal of to-do and much beating of drums, their provosts read out at the four corners of the city a proclamation forbidding all looting and marauding, and enjoining the men under pain of hanging to take anything from the citizens without paying for it.

This proclamation was of course a mere farce, for the soldiers, despite the lateness of the hour, had at once raided the butchers', bakers', and other provision shops, and though they professed to pay for everything they took, they refused to give more than one sou for a pound of meat, and then they cut out all the bone, and threw it back in the face of the wretched butcher who tried to argue with them.

And all the while remember that these men were not Spaniards; they were Walloons of the provinces immediately adjacent to the two Flanders, and their kith and kin had also grievously suffered from Spanish arrogance and oppression. But what will men not do for money or under compulsion—or mayhap under that abject fear which the very name of Alva had brought forth into the heart of people who had once been so proud and so independent? The Seigneur de Vaernewyck puts it on record that in his opinion the employing of Walloon troops to check the so-called revolt of Ghent was an act of refined cruelty on the part of the Duke. He liked to pit brother against brother, kinsman against his own kind. He had cowed the Flemings and the Walloons to such an extent that now at last he could use one against the other, and could rely on each side being more cruel and relentless through that extraordinary perversion of human nature which makes civil strife so much more brutal and horrible than any war between the nations.

CHAPTER XIII

MY FAITHFUL WATCH-DOG

I

Some two hours later—in a long, low, vaulted room which was the refectory of the convent of the Sisters of St. Agneten—some two thousand men were assembled. They sat on wooden benches all round the two huge, horseshoe-shaped tables at which the Sisters were wont to take their meals. The room was situate on the ground floor of the convent building, and a row of low, groined windows ran the whole length of one of the walls; heavy curtains hung before all the windows, and portières were drawn over the doors at either end, both in order to deaden all sound and to prevent all light from showing without. Tallow candles burned in tall pewter candelabra at intervals upon the tables.

The bulk of the men who were there were young—or at any rate still in the prime of life, strong and well-knit in figure—the sort of men whom any leader would be glad to enrol as soldiers under his banner; but there were others among them who were grave and elderly—like Messire Deynoot, the Procurator-General, and the Baron van Grobbendock, chief financial adviser on the Town Council. Messire Pierre van Overbeque, Vice-Bailiff of Ghent, was also there, as well as Messires Lievin van Deynse, the wealthy brewer at the sign of the "Star of the North" in the Nieuwpoort, Laurence van Rycke, son of the High-Bailiff, and Frédéric van Beveren, wardmaster of the Guild of Armourers; and there were a good many others—gentlemen of substance and consideration in the town.

At this moment every one of those two thousand men were keeping their eyes fixed upon one who alone was standing under the dais at the end of the refectory where the abbess of the convent usually had her place. This portion of the room was raised two steps above the rest, and standing there, the man who thus held the attention of all the others looked abnormally tall, for he was dressed in doublet and hose of some dark stuff which clung to him like a skin. His high boots reached well over his thighs, his head was closely shrouded in a hood, and his face was hidden by a mask, made of untanned leather—which left the mouth only quite free.

"His Highness the Prince of Orange, whom may God protect," he was saying in a loud, clear voice which rang out from end to end of the room, "was fortunately able to furnish me with all your names and places of abode. With the help of Messire van Deynse, who lent us his horses, and Messire Laurence van Rycke and Frédéric van Beveren, who gave me their assistance, we were able to communicate with you all during the night and warn you of the imminent danger which hung over your heads."

"It was well done, friend Leatherface," said Messire Deynoot, "so well, indeed, that we are all ready and willing to place ourselves under your guidance and to accept you as our leader, for of a truth we know not what we must do."

"Would to God," said the man whom they called Leatherface, "that I could do more for you than the little which I have done. To each of you last night I gave the same warning: 'Danger is nigh! terrible! imminent! for our plans are discovered and the presence of the Prince of Orange in Ghent known to the Duke of Alva! Let all those who wish to do so leave the city at once with their wives and children, for death and torture threatens those who remain!'"

"As you see, my dear friend," said Lievin van Deynse, the wealthy brewer, quietly, "not one of us hath followed this portion of your advice."

"You are all brave men and noble sons of Flanders," quoth Leatherface earnestly. "His Highness is proud of you, he believes in you, he trusts you. A cause which has such men as you for its champions and defenders is assured of victory."

A murmur of satisfaction went round the room, and Leatherface resumed after a little while:

"In the meanwhile, with the help of God, the precious person of the Prince of Orange is safe."

A hearty cheer—quickly suppressed—greeted this announcement from every side. "Unfortunately," continued Leatherface, "I could not persuade His Highness to leave the city early this morning. He would not believe in the danger which was threatening him.... He would not believe that his plans and his presence here had been betrayed."

"Yes! betrayed!" now said one of the younger men vehemently, "and by whom? Dost know by whom, friend Leatherface?"

And all around the tables, grimly set lips murmured:

"By whom? My God! by whom were we betrayed?"

And Laurence van Rycke's glowing eyes were fixed upon the man under the canopy as if he would have torn the mask from off his face and read in those mysterious eyes the confirmation of his own horrible fears.

And Leatherface, looking straight into Laurence's pale and haggard face, said slowly:

"By one who hath already paid the full price for all the misery which that betrayal will bring in its wake."

"Dead?" came in awed yet eager query from most of them there.

Leatherface bent his head, but gave no direct reply, and all of them there were satisfied, for they believed that the faithful and wary watch-dog—justiciary as well as guardian angel—had discovered the betrayer, and had killed him, making him pay the "full price" for all the misery which he had brought about. Only Laurence hung his head and dared not ask any more.

II

"And now tell us about the Prince," urged Messire van Overbeque, the Vice-Bailiff. "Where is he now?"

"Well on his way to Brügge, please God," replied the man with the leather mask. "All day I had entreated him to go, but he refused to listen. 'You dream of treachery,' he said to me, 'and see it where none exists!' I spent the day scouting as far as Melle and Wetteren, for I felt that nothing would convince him but actual facts. At four o'clock in the afternoon the advance courier arrived from Alost. Luckily, his horse was less swift than mine. I managed to gain on him and brought in the news of the Duke of Alva's arrival to His Highness half an hour before the commandant of the garrison knew of it."

"Even then it might have been too late," quoth one of the listeners.

"It very nearly was," retorted Leatherface light-heartedly. "Had the Lieutenant-Governor sent advance orders that his arrival be kept a secret until his troops passed through the city gates, the Prince of Orange would still be in Ghent at this hour."

"Holy Virgin!" exclaimed Laurence van Rycke, "and what did you do?"

"His Highness donned doublet and hose of common buffle and pulled a tattered felt hat well over his eyes, as did also the Count of Hoogstraaten and young Count Mansfeld. I made myself look as like a draper's assistant as I could, and then the four of us joined the crowd. The rumour of the Duke's coming had spread all over the city; there were plenty of gaffers about. All round by the Waalpoort they abounded, and as the twilight slowly faded into dusk the approaches to the gate were densely packed. No one was allowed to loiter round the guard-house or upon the bridge, but there were many who, with overwhelming loyalty, desired to greet the Duke of Alva even before he reached the confines of the city. That was our opportunity. The commandant at the Waalpoort happened to be in rare good humour; he thought the idea of meeting the Lieutenant-Governor and his troops some way outside the city an excellent one. He allowed those who wished, to go across the bridge. The Prince of Orange, his two friends and I were merged in that crowd, and no one took notice of us. Directly we reached Meirelbeke we struck across the fields. In ten minutes we left the crowd a long way behind us, and had skirted the town as far as Wondelghem. We were in no danger then, but His Highness was greatly fatigued. There was a difficulty too about getting horses; young Count Mansfeld was footsore and the Count of Hoogstraaten perished with thirst. In short, it was six o'clock before we had the horses ready, and I had the satisfaction of seeing the Prince safely started on his way. When I returned it was close on eight, and the city gates had all been locked."

He gave a light, good-humoured laugh, and one of the men asked: "Then how did you get in?"

"I swam and I scaled the walls," he replied simply.

"But ... how?" asked another.

"Oh! I swim like a fish and climb like an ape...."

"But were you not seen?"

"Oh, yes! and shot at ... but the Spaniards are bad shots and ... I am here."

Again he laughed gaily, light-heartedly like a 'prentice after an escapade, and the two men who sat nearest him—the Procurator-General and the Baron van Groobendock—surreptitiously took hold of his hand and pressed it warmly.

III

"So much for the past, seigniors," resumed Leatherface, after awhile: "my duty is done. I leave the planning of the future to wiser heads than mine."

"No! no!" quoth the Vice-Bailiff emphatically. "Have we not said that we want you to lead us?"

"I?" retorted the other gaily. "What do I know of leadership? I am only His Highness' watch-dog. Let me follow a leader and bear my share in the present trouble. I am not fit to command...."

A murmur went round the room, and the Procurator-General rejoined earnestly: "The men will obey no one but you. Take off your mask, friend, and let us all look upon the face of a man."

"You have all despised me too much in the past to heed my counsels now."

"There you spoke a lie, man," said Messire van Deynse, the brewer. "We have all honoured the man whom we called Leatherface, as the bravest amongst us all. We do not know who you are—we only know you as a gallant gentleman to whom next to William of Orange himself we owe every triumph which our cause hath gained over our execrated tyrants. Therefore I pray you to unmask and let us know at least to whom—next to God Himself—we owe the life of the noble Prince of Orange, and also to whom we must look in future for guidance and leadership."

Once more the murmur went round the room: words of warm approval came from every side, whilst among the younger men the cry was raised and repeated insistently: "Unmask!"

"Unmask!" cried Laurence van Rycke. "Be you criminal or ne'er-do-well in the eyes of others, you are a hero in our sight."

"Unmask! unmask!" they reiterated unanimously.

The man with the leather mask then advanced to the very edge of the platform, and, putting up his hand, he asked for silence.

"Seigniors," he began, "I am your servant and will do as you wish. I have told you that I am no leader and am not fit to command ... yet you choose to honour me, and this is no time for false humility and the diffidence which is the attribute of cowards. But—despite your gracious choice of me as your leader in this terrible emergency—will you ere you finally decide to follow me hear from me what plan I should pursue, and to what heights of self-sacrifice I would ask you to rise in the face of the awful calamity which threatens our city. Seigniors," he continued, and indeed now save for the ring of that deep-toned voice, so great was the silence in the vast refectory that every heart-beat might have been heard, "you have heard the decree of our tyrant. Unless we deliver to him the precious person of our noble Prince, the whole city will be delivered over to the brutal soldiery, who will pillage our houses, desecrate our churches, murder and outrage our wives, our mothers and our children—just as they did in Mons, in Valenciennes and in Mechlin. Seigniors, we are men—all of us here—and at thought of what awaits us and our fellow-citizens our very heart blood seems to freeze with horror. It is of our women that we must think and of our children! Thank God that the Prince knows nothing of this decree—

which hath been framed by the most inhuman monster the world hath ever known—or of a certainty he would have gone straight to the Kasteel and given up his precious life to save our fellow-citizens. Seigniors, what the Prince would have done, we know; and as he would have acted, so must we be prepared to act. But before I parted from him, I had his advice on the plan which I now beg leave to place before you. On my word of honour, seigniors, he approved of it in its entirety, and much that I will submit to you anon hath been framed under his guidance."

He paused awhile and through the holes in the mask his glowing eyes searched the faces of his listeners with a masterful glance that was both challenging and appealing.

"Every one of us here," he said abruptly, "is, I know, ready to sacrifice his life for faith, for freedom and country, and ere we give in to the monstrous tyranny which hath planned the destruction of our city we must fight, seigniors, fight to the death, fight for every inch of our ground, fight for every homestead which we would save from outrage. Death awaits us all anyhow, then at any rate with God's help let us die fighting to the end."

Once more he paused in order to draw breath, even whilst from every side there came emphatic words of enthusiasm and of approval. He held his hearers now in the hollow of his hand; they were unemotional, stolid men for the most part, these Flemish burghers and patricians—men who throughout the terrible oppression under which they had groaned for over fifty years had grimly set their teeth and endured where others had fought—because reason and common sense had shown the futility, the irreparableness of the conflict—but they were men, too, who, once roused to action, would never give in until they had won their fight or had been destroyed to the last man of them; and with that inspiring prophet standing there before them, stirring their sluggish blood with his ringing voice, some of that same determination began to creep into their bones which had animated valiant Orange and his brothers and his Dutch followers to carry on the struggle for freedom at all costs and with the last drop of their blood.

"We'll fight with you and under your standard, friend," said the Procurator-General who was the spokesman of the others. "We are well armed...."

"Aye! ye are well armed," rejoined Leatherface triumphantly. "The guild of armourers are with us to a man; and we have been able to supplement our secret stores with all the treasure in the magnificent armoury which Messire van Beveren has placed at our disposal in the name of his guild. Aye! we are well armed and well manned! There are two thousand of us, seigniors, and our numbers will be doubled before noon to-morrow. The Duke hath brought ten thousand soldiers with him! well! it will be a three-to-one fight; but if we were still more completely outnumbered we would still carry on the struggle, seeing

145

that the lives of our children and the honour of our women are at stake."

"We can fight," murmured one of the older men, "but we cannot conquer."

"No! we cannot conquer," said Leatherface earnestly. "We must perish, because might is greater than right, unless God chooseth to perform a miracle—and I, for one, still believe that He will. But we must not weaken our determination by reckoning childishly on divine interference. If we fight, we fight because we refuse to die like cowards, because we refuse to go before our Maker shamed at having allowed our homes to be devastated, our women outraged, our children massacred without striking a blow—however futile—in their defence. We fight then, seigniors?" he added exultantly. "Is that your decision?"

There was not one dissentient voice. Old and young, grave and gay, prudent and hot-headed, every man there was ready to follow the leader of their choice.

"For freedom, faith and country!" cried Leatherface loudly.

"For freedom, faith and country," came from two thousand panting throats.

"As to our plan of campaign," now resumed the man with the mask as soon as silence and calm was restored once more, "I have not yet had the time to think on all the details soberly. But the main outline of it was dictated to me by the Prince of Orange even whilst we halted at Wondelghem, waiting for horses. He is the finest military strategist the world hath ever known, misfortune hath pursued him, but hath not impaired his marvellous powers of command. I will ask some of you, seigniors, to aid me with your counsels, and with the directions which His Highness hath given me we may yet give such a fine account of ourselves as will force our tyrants to treat with us for peace. There are only two thousand of us now; by to-morrow we can reckon on several thousands more; but of a certainty at the first clash of arms all our young and able-bodied fellow-citizens will take heart and join us in our desperate struggle, and may God help us all!"

There is no doubt that he had enflamed the blood of his hearers; by the dim light of the tallow candles every face now looked flushed, every pair of eyes glowed with the noble fire of patriotism and of courage. Leatherface waited for a time in silence while whispered conversation and discussion became general. He did not join in it himself, but stood somewhat apart from the others, the cynosure of all eyes, a strange, almost mysterious figure in his tightly-fitting clothes which gave full play to the powerful muscles of arms and thighs and displayed the great breadth of shoulder and depth of chest. Many there were who still eyed him curiously; Laurence van Rycke in particular did not take his eyes off him, but no one thought of challenging him again to unmask. What mattered what the face was like, when the heart was so great and fine?

IV

After a few minutes the man with the mask once more advanced to the edge of the platform. There was still something that he wished to say.

"We must not forget, seigniors," he began very quietly, "that the tyrant hath given us a respite of forty-eight hours before he will embark on his hellish work of destruction. He hath demanded the person of the Prince of Orange as the price of his mercy. Well, seigniors, the Prince, thank God, is no longer here; but it is just possible that we may bribe the wild beast yet into satisfaction by giving him some of the blood for which he thirsts, and thus save our beautiful city from all the horrors which he hath in contemplation against her."

"And how wilt do that, friend?" sighed, Messire van Overbeque despondently.

"With your permission I will explain," rejoined the other. "I propose that anon in the early morning a certain number of you seek out the Duke of Alva in Het Spanjaard's Kasteel and tell him that the Prince of Orange–aided by his humble watchdog–did succeed in evading once again the trap which had been set for him; but," he continued with slow and deliberate emphasis, "that you are prepared to deliver into his hands the person of the man Leatherface, since you happen to know his whereabouts in the city."

For a moment he could not continue, loud and vehement protestations against this monstrous proposal arose from every side.

"I entreat you, seigniors, to remember," he continued with deep earnestness as soon as the tumult had subsided, "that a certain amount of mystery hath hung–not through mine own seeking, believe me–around my person. Next to our Prince himself, there are few in this unfortunate country whose death would be more welcome to our Spanish tyrants than that of the miscreant Leatherface; and my belief is that if you offered to give him up to the Lieutenant-Governor you might obtain from that cruel despot a small measure of mercy for our city."

He had long since finished speaking, but now there were no longer any protestations or murmurs; an awesome silence hung about the vaulted room. No one had stirred; no one spoke; not one man dared to look his neighbour in the face. Every man stared straight before him at that slim figure, which suddenly appeared to them all, to be unearthly as it stood there, beneath the canopy, like the very personification of simple self-sacrifice, offering up his life so willingly, and above all, so cheerfully to save his fellow-men.

In these days of cruel oppression and of sublime virtues, such an act of abnegation was probably not rare; men were accustomed to suffer death and worse for an ideal, and for the sake of others who were weaker than themselves; but there was something so engaging, so light-hearted in that stranger there that every man who heard him felt that by sacrificing such a man he would be sending a brother, a son, or dear friend to the gallows.

"Well, seigniors," said Leatherface, "I still await your decision."

"You speak glibly, friend," murmured the Procurator-General sombrely, "but if the tyrant hath you in his power, it will not only mean death for you, remember, it will not mean the axe or the gallows, it will mean the torture-chamber of the Inquisition first and the stake afterwards."

"I know that," retorted the other simply. "Better men than I have gone through it all for faith and freedom. I am young, 'tis true—but I have no ties of interest or affection that bind me to this earth. Few men will go to their Maker so little regretted by kith or kin as I shall be. So I pray you do not think of me. Rather turn your thoughts, I entreat, to the details of the plan, the composition of the deputation that would be prepared to meet the Duke of Alva to-morrow. Those posts, too, will be full of danger, and the negotiations, too, might fail—what is the life of one man worth when weighed in the balance with an entire city?"

"And which of us would you entrust with the abominable errand?" queried Laurence van Rycke abruptly.

"Not you, of a certainty," said the other. "Your mother will have need of comfort and protection, since she refused to place herself in safety. Messire the Procurator-General should, I think, lead the deputation, he hath never been suspected of heresy or rebellion, and the proposal would thus come quite naturally from him; if Messire van Overbeque will join him and you, Seigneur van Groobendock, meseems that we could not choose better."

"Nay! I cannot do it," interposed the Vice-Bailiff vehemently. "I would sooner cut off my right hand now."

"Would you sooner sacrifice this city, all the women and children, your own wife, Messire, and daughters, rather than one man whose identity you need never know?"

It was indeed a terrible puzzle, one which even these brave men found it hard to solve.

"I entreat you, seigniors," continued Leatherface earnestly, "to do what I ask. Nay!" he added resolutely, "I'll do more. Just now you chose me as your leader. Then I command you to act in accordance with my will."

"You are quite determined, then?" asked the Vice-Bailiff.

"Would you counsel me to waver?" retorted the other. "Ah, seigniors!" he added, with that ringing note in his voice which was so inspiring to them all, "I entreat you do not grieve for me. Rather grieve for yourselves and gather courage for your errand. So help me God, yours will be no easy task. You will have to fawn and to cringe before the tyrant whom you hate. You will have to bear his arrogance and the insolence of his menials. You will have to swallow your wrath and to bend your pride. Your sacrifice indeed will be far harder to make than

148

mine. I only offer mine own unworthy life; you will offer up to-morrow your dignity, your manhood, all that you and your fathers hold so dear. Nay! I would not change places with you for ten such worthless lives as mine. See, what a coward I am—I send you to do this abominable errand, while I sit at home in comfort and dream of the happiness of giving my life for Ghent and for her children!"

"God help us all!" murmured Messire Deynoot, the Procurator-General.

"Indeed, He alone can do that," rejoined Leatherface, "for grave fears assail me that our proposal will be rejected; is it likely that it would appeal to such a blood-thirsty tyrant as the Duke of Alva? My one hope—and that alas! is a slender one—is that he hath it not in his mind to destroy our beautiful city, and might be glad of an excuse of exercising mercy."

A groan of execration greeted this suggestion. Was it likely that any thought of mercy could ever enter the mind of such a man?—more cruel than any beast of prey, for he killed for the mere sake of killing, inflicted inhuman tortures on innocent victims for the sake of gloating over their sufferings, and rejoiced in bloodshed and outrage and desecration for their own sakes, without any thought of benefiting himself.

"Then if these negotiations fail, seigniors," concluded Leatherface finally, "nothing will be left for us but a bitter struggle which may end in defeat, but which will leave us proud and unconquered still."

"Amen to that," said the Procurator-General fervently.

"Then let us go quietly to our homes to-night. Let us keep from those who are weak and anxious all knowledge of that which we have resolved; let our women pray while we prepare to act. Flemish women have hearts of steel; they will not waver when the hour comes. They will help us with their prayers now, and load our arquebuses for us when we need them. For them we will fight and for our children, and if defeat stares us in the face at the last, then will we save them by one supreme act from falling into the hands of the tyrant. Until then and after, seigniors, allow me to keep this mask upon my face. When you go to meet the Duke of Alva to-morrow, you will offer him a paltry chattel, a man whom you do not know, who hath no name, no identity, the spy of the Prince of Orange—just him whom you call Leatherface."

"God reward you," they murmured fervently.

"Perhaps He will," whispered the man with the mask, under his breath, "and with a speedy death!"

"And now," he added, "as the hour is late, let us disperse. To-morrow, here, and at this hour, we meet again. Messire Deynoot will give you a report of his audience with the tyrant, and I may be lucky enough to be allowed to give my life for this city which I love. Farewell, seigniors, may God guard you until then. If Alva will have none of me, then I will have the honour of leading you–to victory, I hope–to death if God wills!"

One by one they rose from the benches where they had been sitting, and all took what they believed to be a last farewell of that strange man whose identity was still unknown to them, yet whom they had all learned to love as a leader and as a friend. Indeed, their noble hearts were torn asunder by the awful alternative which he himself had placed for them. It was a case of grim determination, of smothering every call of Sentiment which might prove insistent against thus sacrificing a brave man to the cruel lust of an abominable tyrant. It had to be, and these men were fine and great enough in themselves to understand that in offering up his life to save his fellow-citizens, Leatherface had certainly chosen the better part.

And having looked their last on him, they went out through the postern gate of the convent of St. Agneten in groups of twos and threes. They crossed the two bridges that span the Leye at this point. The night was dark, and this was an isolated part of the city, situate far from the Stadthuis and the Kouter. From the St. Baafs and St. Nikolas quarters of the city came faintly echoing across the river the sound of riotous merriment proceeding from those buildings and houses wherein the Walloon soldiery had installed themselves. But the men who had just pledged themselves to fight a losing battle against overwhelming odds paid no heed to what went on around them. They glided noiselessly through the dark and narrow streets; some went to right, some to left, some to north and others to south, and quietly regained their homes.

V

But in the vast refectory two men had remained behind after every one else had gone: they were the man with the mask, and Laurence van Rycke.

The latter had waited in silence whilst the whole of the assembly filed out by the door, but when Leatherface in his turn prepared to go, Laurence threw him such a look of appeal, that after an instant's hesitation, he too decided to wait.

Then when the last of the assembly had gone, Laurence tried to speak, but the words died in his throat ere they reached his quivering lips. There was still that look of mute appeal in his eyes, and of well-nigh unendurable mental torment in every line of his haggard face, and suddenly he gave a cry like some wounded creature in mortal pain; he fell on his knees against the table, and burying his face in his hands, he sobbed like a child. The other waited patiently and silently until the paroxysm was over: his mouth beneath the mask looked set but kindly, and his eyes through the holes in the leather were fixed upon the stricken man.

"She is safe from the vengeance of our people," he said, as soon as he saw that Laurence had momentarily regained his self-control. "Is that what troubles you, Messire?"

Laurence—already ashamed of his tears—had struggled to his feet. He passed his hand across his moist forehead and through his unruly hair, and tried to look Leatherface valiantly between the eyes.

"Partly that," he said resolutely. "But I'll not speak of her. It was she then who betrayed us all?" he added with another heartbroken cry.

To this Leatherface made no answer, and Laurence continued more calmly:

"It was of the lists I wish to speak. The papers which His Highness entrusted to my care."

"Yes?"

"I went to look for them after ... after she left the house, and found that they had gone."

"Then what did you do?"

"I knew that we were betrayed ... then ... there ... at once ... and by her ... an exquisite woman, Messire, whom I ... Oh! it was horrible!" he exclaimed, and even now a look that was almost like death came over his wan cheeks and hollow eyes.

Then once more he resumed quietly: "For a few moments the blow of this awful discovery completely stunned me. I could neither think nor act. My first coherent thought was to consult with my mother as to what had best be done. How to find His Highness until evening I knew not, or how to obtain duplicate lists, so that I could run round the town and warn all our followers of the terrible danger that threatened them."

"You did not think of flight? ... for your mother, I mean?..."

"I entreated my mother to leave the city at once, but she refused to go, and we were standing face to face with one another and the terrible calamity that had befallen us all when Pierre came in with a letter, which—he said—was given to him in the open street by a man whom he did not know. The letter, I take it, came from you."

"Yes," replied the other, "I was afraid that you might do something rash, and raise the alarm before it was necessary. The lists," he added, "are quite safe. I was able after His Highness left the High-Bailiff's house last night to extract them from the bureau, where I did not feel that they were over safe; in their place I put a packet containing fictitious lists of men who do not exist, and places of abode which are not to be found in this city. It is these which have been sent to señor de Vargas. I had just time to scribble these and to place them in a conspicuous place in the bureau."

"You used a false key then?" queried Laurence in bewilderment.

"Am I not a spy of the Prince of Orange?" retorted the other with

151

a quaint little laugh, "and are not all spies provided with means of forcing secret locks? Here are the lists," he added, as from inside his doublet he half drew the packets of papers. "When you are called to account for them, you can return them without fear. No one will know that they ever left your care ... that is, if you have not spoken of it before now...."

"No. I had not the heart. We all knew that we were betrayed. You warned us all and took measures to convene us here to-night; but until the hour when your letter warned me that for the moment all was well, I endured mental torments such as surely the lost souls in hell have never suffered. I saw those lists in the hands of our tyrants–placed there by the instrumentality of a woman who is to me the embodiment of all that is pure and good; I saw–in my mind–the spies of Alva going the round, this very night, and arresting our brave followers one by one ... Oh God! you do not know what I suffered...."

"Do not think of that any more, Messire," rejoined Leatherface quietly. "As you see, the lists are now safe in my care. Alas! it is too late to beg you to take your mother out of the city. Guard and protect her well and God help us all."

He once more now prepared to go, and Laurence was ready to follow him, but just at the last an impulse caused the latter to detain the mysterious stranger once more. There was still one question which hovered on his lips, the answer to which would perhaps ease that awful burden of sorrow which Lenora's betrayal had placed upon his soul:

"Messire," he said appealingly, "what of her?"

"Pray for her, Messire," replied Leatherface quietly, "she suffers more than you do."

"Must we all curse her then? or else be traitors to our own people."

"Nay! you can pity her! What she did, she did from her own sense of patriotism and of justice. She hates us all, Messire, as the enemies of her people. She hates and despises me as the assassin of the man she loved. Pray for her, Messire, but in pity pray also for the man who whilst striving to win her heart, only succeeded in breaking his own."

VI

An hour later in the house in the Nieuwstraat, Clémence van Rycke was still awake. She sat in her favourite tall chair beside the hearth, and Laurence her son was kneeling beside her.

"It is too late now, mother," he was saying gloomily. "No power on earth can save you. Would to God you had let me take you to Brügge this afternoon."

"And desert my post like a coward," retorted Clémence hotly. "I

152

can do little, 'tis true; but when the hour comes I can tend the sick and the dying, and pray for the dead; and if you are taken from me, Laurence, I can be laid beside you.... But," she added, with such an intensity of bitterness and hatred that her voice nearly choked her as she spoke, "I would not owe my safety to that execrable traitress..."

"Hush, mother, in the name of Heaven..." broke in Laurence with a heart-broken sob.

"Are you, too, going to defend her?" retorted the mother fiercely.

"She was compelled to act as she did," murmured Laurence; "she acted in ignorance and innocence. I'd stake my life that she is pure and good."

"Pure and good!" exclaimed Clémence with a strident laugh. "A spawn of the devil, without virtue and without mercy. Oh! that my lips should ever have touched her lying face–that white forehead which concealed thoughts of falsehood and treachery! Do not defend her, Laurence, or you will break my heart. Leave her defence to your brother Mark, who cares nothing for his country and for his kindred, who will smile and drink whilst the walls of Ghent fall about his ears, who hath allowed his weak and cowardly heart to be captured by that murderess! Leave him to defend her, I say. Lenora de Vargas is worthy of Mark van Rycke!"

"Mother!" cried Laurence with uncontrolled vehemence as he threw his arms round his mother's shoulders. "In the name of God stop, for you almost blaspheme. Speak not of Mark save with a blessing on your lips. Pray for him this night, as you have never prayed before."

"Laurence," cried the mother, "are you mad? What do you mean? What has happened to Mark? Where is he?"

"In his bed, no doubt, at this moment, mother."

"Sleeping whilst we all weep and pray!"

"Sleeping in peace whilst giving up life, and more than life, to try and save us all!" retorted Laurence, as he slowly rose to his feet.

"Laurence! you are mad! Mark is..."

"Mark is the friend and saviour of the Prince of Orange, mother dear," said the young man quietly, "and we have all known him hitherto as Leatherface."

"It is false!" cried Clémence vehemently.

"I swear by God that it is true," proclaimed Laurence, fervently.

The exclamation which she would have uttered froze upon Clémence van Rycke's lips; for a moment she remained quite still, leaning slightly forward with hands resting upon the arms of the chair. Then a pitiable moan escaped her, and slowly she rose and then fell upon her knees.

"Oh God! forgive me," she cried, "if this be true."

"It is true, mother," said Laurence firmly. "For close on two hours to-night I sat close to him whilst he spoke. In the absence of the Prince of Orange we have chosen him as our leader; if the Duke of Alva refuses the proposals which we are going to put before him, Mark will lead us to fight or to death."

"The proposal! What proposal?"

"That Leatherface be given up to the tyrant as the price of the safety of the city."

"And you—his brother—agreed to this infamous suggestion?" murmured Clémence hoarsely.

"We must not leave a stone unturned or a man alive to save the women and children," replied Laurence sombrely.

"Then may God have mercy on us all!" cried Clémence, and she fell back heart-broken against the cushions of her chair.

CHAPTER XIV

THE TYRANTS

I

The next morning, at the tenth hour, five reverend seigniors presented themselves before the Duke of Alva, Lieutenant-Governor of the Low Countries and Captain-General of the Forces, in the apartments which he occupied in Het Spanjaards Kasteel.

They were Messire Pierre van Overbeque, Vice-Bailiff of Ghent; Messire Deynoot, Procurator-General, and Messire Jan van Migrode, Chief Sheriff of the Keure; then there was Messire Lievin van Deynse, the brewer at the sign of the "Star of the North," and Baron van Groobendock, chief financial adviser on the Town Council.

They had waited on His Highness at a very early hour, but had been kept waiting in the guard-room for two hours, without a chair to sit on, and with a crowd of rough soldiers around them, some of whom were lounging about on the benches, others playing at cards or dice, whilst all of them improved the occasion and whiled away the time by indulging in insolent jests at the expense of the reverend burghers, who—humiliated beyond forbearance and vainly endeavouring to swallow their wrath—did not dare to complain to the officer in command, lest worse insults be heaped upon them.

At one hour before noon the seigniors were at last told very peremptorily that they might present themselves before His Highness. They were marched between a detachment of soldiers through the castle yard to the magnificent apartments in the Meeste-Toren, which at one time were occupied by the Counts of Flanders. Now the Duke of Alva's soldiery and his attendants were in every corridor and every ante-room. They stared with undisguised insolence at the grave seigniors who belonged to the despised race.

The Lieutenant-Governor was graciously pleased to receive the burghers in his council-chamber where, seated upon a velvet-covered chair upon an elevated platform and beneath a crimson dais, he looked down upon these free citizens of an independent State as if he were indeed possessed of divine rights over them all. The officer in command of the small detachment which had escorted the deputation into the dreaded presence, now ordered the five seigniors to kneel, and they, who had a petition to present and an act of mercy to entreat, obeyed with that proud humility wherewith their fathers had knelt thirty-two years ago in sackcloth and ashes before the throne of the Emperor Charles.

"Your desire, seigniors?" queried the Duke curtly.

Some of the members of his abominable Grand Council sat around him, on benches placed well below the level of the platform. Alberic del Rio was there—bland and submissive; President Viglius, General de Noircarmes, and President Hessels—men who were as bitter against Orange and his followers as was Alva himself—and, sitting a little apart from the others, don Juan de Vargas, but recently arrived from Brussels.

"Your desire, seigniors?" the Duke had questioned peremptorily, and after a few moments Messire Deynoot, the Procurator-General, who was spokesman of the deputation, began timidly at first—then gradually more resolutely.

"It is with profound grief," he said, "that we became aware last night that your Highness' visit to our city was not one of goodwill and amity. Your Highness' severe restrictions upon our citizens and stern measures taken against them hath filled our hearts with sorrow."

"Your abominable treachery hath filled our heart with wrath," retorted the Duke roughly, "and nothing but the clemency enjoined upon us by our suzerain Lord and King prevented us from reducing this accursed city to ashes and putting every one of her citizens to the sword, without giving them a single chance of retrieving their hellish conduct by surrendering themselves unconditionally to our will."

"It is with the utmost confidence," rejoined the Procurator-General humbly, "that we rely upon the well-known clemency of our suzerain Lord the King, and place the future of our beautiful city unconditionally in your Highness' hands."

"The future of the city is in my hands, Messire," said the Duke dryly, "by the power of our suzerain Lord and with the help of the troops at my command. I told you last night under what condition I will spare your town from total destruction. I am not in the habit of changing my mind during the course of one night."

"Alas, your Highness! but the city is quite unable to fulfil the one condition which would appease the wrath of our suzerain Lord and your own."

"Then," retorted Alva haughtily, "why waste my time and your own in bandying words which must remain purposeless? Either William of Orange is delivered into my hands, or my soldiers burn your city down at sunset to-morrow. By our Lady! is that not clear enough?"

"Clear enough, alas!" rejoined the Procurator-General, and suddenly in his mind there rose a picture of the tall man last night beneath the dais, of his inspiring words, his whole-hearted sacrifice: his ringing voice seemed to echo through this narrow room, and some of the words which he spoke knocked at the gates of the grave seignior's memory.

"Yours will be the harder task," he had said gaily; "you will have to fawn and to cringe, to swallow your wrath and to bend your pride!" Well! God knew that they had done all that: they had swallowed their wrath and bent their pride before an insolent soldiery, and now they were fawning and cringing to a tyrant whom they abhorred.

Ghent! beloved city! once the home of the free! what must thy citizens endure for thy sake?

And the Procurator-General—the descendant of an hundred free men—had to lick the dust before Alva's throne. He forced his voice to tones of humility, he looked up at the tyrant with eyes full of unspoken devotion.

"What can we do?" he said timidly, "to prove our loyalty? I entreat your Magnificence to look down on our helplessness. Orange is no longer in Ghent, and we do not know where to find him."

"A pretty tale, indeed," interposed de Vargas suddenly, with a strident laugh which was echoed obsequiously by the other members round the council board, "a pretty, likely tale, which I trust your Highness will not think to believe."

"I neither believe nor disbelieve any tale which these grave seigniors choose to tell me," rejoined the Duke. "I want Orange—or we burn this city down till not a stone in it be left upon stone."

And Messire Deynoot, whose entire soul rose in revolt against that rough dictate of a hellish tyrant, had perforce to subdue his passionate wrath and to speak with affected humility and unconcern.

"We had hoped," he said quietly, "that we might offer to your Highness such a proof of our loyalty that you would no longer wish to cast aside a city that hath always hitherto proved staunch and true."

"What mean you, sirrah? What proofs can you give me now of this accursed city's loyalty, when you harbour a veritable army of traitors within your walls?"

"We would wish to prove to your Magnificence that the city itself takes no part in the vagaries and plottings of a few hot-headed malcontents."

156

"Hot-headed malcontents, forsooth!" exclaimed the Duke fiercely. "Two thousand men prepared to take up arms against our Suzerain Lord the King! ... arms concealed in churches and cemeteries! money poured into the lap of Orange and all his rebels!"

"There are more than two thousand men who are prepared to fight and die for their country and their King," said the Fleming suavely, "and who are equally ready to pour money into the coffers of their Liege Lord, as represented by His Highness Ferdinand Alvarez de Toledo, Duke of Alva, and by the reverend members of his Council."

This he had said very slowly and with marked emphasis, and even while he spoke he had the satisfaction of seeing more than one pair of eyes round that Council board gloating with delight at the vision of treasure and wealth which his words had called forth. He and his colleagues had long after the assembly of last night discussed between them this one proposal, which might, they hoped, tempt the cupidity of the Spaniards, which they knew to be boundless. They were wealthy men all of them—the town was wealthy beyond the dreams of Alva's avarice, and the five men who had been deputed to offer up a brave man's life as the price of a city's safety, had resolved to sacrifice their last stiver, and keep the hero in their midst.

But Alva, with a sneer, had already destroyed all the fond hopes which had been built upon that resolve.

"If you offered me every treasure—to the last gulden—contained in your city," he said, with emphasis no less strongly marked than had been the other man's offer, "I would not deny myself the pleasure of razing this abominable nest of rebels to the ground. Why should I," he added with a cynical shrug of the shoulders, "take from you as a bribe what my soldiers can get for me by the might of fire and sword? Orange alone would tempt me, for I would wish to have him alive—we might kill him by accident when we destroy the town."

"We can collect two million gulden in gold," said Messire Deynoot insinuatingly, "and lay that sum at the feet of your Magnificence to-morrow."

"Ah?" said the Duke blandly, "then I am greatly relieved that so much money can be got voluntarily out of this city. Your words, Messire, are honey to mine ears; they prove, beyond a doubt, that if you can raise two million gulden in forty-eight hours my soldiers can put up ten times that amount in a two days' sacking of this town."

"The money voluntarily offered, Monseigneur," here interposed the Vice-Bailiff, "would shame neither the giver nor the receiver. The destruction of a free and loyal city would be an eternal disgrace upon the might of Spain."

"Spare me thy heroics, sirrah!" quoth Alva fiercely, "or I'll have that impudent tongue of thine cut out before nightfall."

And once more the burghers had to bend their pride before the appalling arrogance of their tyrant.

157

"Begone now!" added the Lieutenant-Governor peremptorily, seeing that the Flemings were silent for the moment. "The business of the State cannot be held up by such profitless talk. And if you have nothing better to offer to our Gracious King than money which is already his, why, then, you are wasting my time, and had best go back to those who sent you."

"No one sent us, Monseigneur," resumed the Procurator-General, with as much dignity as he could command, even though his back ached and his knees were painfully cramped. "We are free burghers of the city of Ghent, which, alas! hath earned your Highness' displeasure. We have offered of our treasure so as to testify to our loyalty ... but this offer your Magnificence hath thought fit to refuse. At the same time we are not at the end of our resources or of our protestations of loyalty. We have yet another offer to place before your Highness which, perhaps, may be more agreeable in your sight."

"And what is that offer, sirrah? Be quick about it, as my patience, of a truth, is at the end of its resources."

The Procurator-General did not make immediate reply. Truly he was screwing up his determination for the terrible ordeal which was before him. He hung his head, and, despite his fortitude—probably because of weakness following on fatigue—he felt that tears gathered in his eyes, and he feared that his voice now as he spoke would become unsteady. The others, too, kept their eyes fixed to the ground. They could not bear to look on one another, at this moment when they were about to offer up so brave and gallant a life in sacrifice for their city and for all the townsfolk. Indeed, Messire Deynoot ere he spoke forced his mind to dwell upon all the horrors of Mons and Valenciennes and Mechlin, upon all the women and children, the feeble and the old, his own wife, his daughters and his mother, so as to gather courage for the task which had been imposed upon him.

Thus there was silence for a minute or so in this narrow room, wherein the close velvet draperies made the air heavy, so that the number of men here assembled—Spaniards and Flemings and soldiers—felt as if an awful load was weighing their senses down. Councillor Hessels, as was his wont, had fallen asleep. He woke up in the oppressive silence in order to murmur drowsily: "To the gallows with them all!" Alva sat sullen and wrathful, looking down with contempt and scorn on the kneeling burghers before him. De Vargas, now and again, turned anxious, furtive eyes to where a rich portière of damask-velvet hid a door in the panelling of the wall. Even now it seemed as if that portiere stirred—as if an unseen hand was grasping it with a febrile nervous clutch—it seemed, in fact, as if some one lived and breathed there behind the curtain, and as if all that was said and would be said in the room would find its echo in a palpitating heart.

Anon the Duke of Alva's impatience broke its bounds: "An you'll not speak, sirrah," he cried, "get you gone! Get you gone, I say, ere I order my lacqueys to throw you out of my house."

"Your pardon, Monseigneur," said Messire Deynoot with sudden resolution, "I but paused in order to choose the words which might best please your ears. The offer which I am about to make to your Highness is in the name of all the citizens of Ghent, and I feel confident that your Highness will gladly acknowledge that no greater mark of loyalty could be offered by any town to our suzerain Lord the King."

"Speak!" commanded Alva.

"Next to the Prince of Orange himself," said the Procurator-General timidly, "is there not a man who hath gravely incurred your Highness' displeasure, but who hath hitherto evaded the punishment which your Highness would no doubt mete out to him?"

"Yes; there is!" replied the Duke curtly. "A man who chooses to wrap himself up in a mantle of mystery; a spy of Orange–a rebel and traitor to the King. There is such a man, sirrah! He hath several times thwarted my projects with regard to Orange. If, as you say, Orange is not in Ghent then hath that man had a hand in helping him to get away. Well! what of that man, sirrah? I want him. He is called Leatherface by my soldiers. What of him, I say?"

"Leatherface is in Ghent, Monseigneur," murmured Deynoot, scarce above his breath.

"Come! that's good! Then will our booty be even richer than we thought."

"Leatherface is in Ghent, Monseigneur," continued Deynoot, more steadily. "But he is an elusive creature. Mysterious agencies are at work, so they say, to enable him to escape the many traps that are set for him. He swims like a fish, and climbs like an ape. He entered the city last night, an hour after all the gates had been closed. In the terrible confusion which will attend the destruction of our city, he would escape again.... But just now he is in Ghent, and..."

"And you will deliver him over to me," broke in Alva with a harsh laugh, "if I will spare your city?"

The Procurator-General nodded his head in reply. His lips refused him service for that awful, that irreparable "Yes!" The five men now no longer hung their heads. White as the linen ruffles round their throats, they were gazing straight into the face of the tyrant, trying to read the innermost thoughts of that inhuman devil, who held the destiny of their city–or of a brave man–in the hollow of his claw-like hands.

Alva pondered; and while he did so his prominent, heavy-lidded eyes sought those of his colleagues no less inhuman, more devilish mayhap, than himself. And from behind the heavy portière there seemed to come a long drawn-out sigh, like some poor creature in pain. De Vargas frowned, and a muttered curse escaped his lips.

"How long has she been there?" asked Alva quickly, in a whisper.

"All the time," replied de Vargas, also under his breath.

"But this is not for women's ears."

"Nay! your Highness does not know my daughter. It was the man Leatherface who killed her first lover. She would be happy to see him hang."

"And she shall, too. She hath deserved well of us. We owe our present triumph to her."

Then he turned once more to the burghers.

"I like your offer," he said coldly, "and, in a measure, I accept it.... Nay!" he added with that cruel and strident laugh of his, seeing that at his words a certain look of relief overspread the five pale faces before him, "do not rejoice too soon. I would not give up the delight of punishing an entire city for the mere pleasure of seeing one man hang. True! I would like to hold him. Next to Orange himself, I would sooner see that mysterious Leatherface dangling on a gibbet than any other heretic or rebel in this abominable country. But to give up my purpose over Ghent, that is another matter! Once and for all, seigniors," he added with fierce and irrevocable determination, "Ghent shall burn, since Orange has escaped again. But I have said that I accept your offer, and I do. I take it as an expression of tardy loyalty, and will reward you in accordance with its value. We will burn your city, seigniors; but if when your flaming walls begin to crumble about your ears; when my soldiery have taken their fill of your money and your treasures, and human lives begin to pay the toll of your rebellion and treachery, then, if you deliver to me the person of Leatherface alive, I will, in return, stay my soldiers' hands, and order that in every homestead one son and one daughter, aye, and the head of the house, too, be spared. Otherwise—and remember that this is my last word—not one stone shall remain upon stone within the city—not one inhabitant, man, woman, or child, shall be left to perpetuate rebellion inside these walls. I have spoken, and now go—go and tell Leatherface that I await him. He hath not aided Orange's escape in vain."

He rose, and with a peremptory gesture pointed to the door. The five burghers were silent. What could they say? To beg, to implore, to remonstrate would, indeed, have been in vain. As well implore the fierce torrent not to uproot the tree that impedes its course, or beg the wolf not to devour its prey. Painfully they struggled to their feet, roughly urged along by the soldiers. They were indeed cramped and stiff, as well mentally as physically; they had done their heart-breaking errand—they had swallowed their wrath and humbled their pride—they had cringed, and they had fawned and licked the dust beneath the feet of the tyrant who was in sheer, lustful wantonness sending them and their kith and kin—guilty and innocent alike—to an abominable death....

160

And they had failed—miserably failed either to bribe, to cajole, or to shame that human fiend into some semblance of mercy. Now a deathlike sorrow weighed upon their souls. They were like five very old men sent tottering to their own graves.

Some could hardly see because of the veil of tears before their eyes.

But, even as one by one they filed out of the presence of the tyrant, they still prayed ... prayed to God to help them and their fellow-citizens in this the darkest hour of their lives. Truly, if these valiant people of Flanders had lost their faith and trust in God then they would have gone absolutely and irretrievably under into the awful vortex of oppression which threatened to crush the very existence of their nation, and would have hurled them into the bottomless abyss of self-destruction.

CHAPTER XV

TWO PICTURES

I

These stand out clearly among the mass of documents, details, dissertations and chronicles of the time—so clearly indeed that only a brief mention of them will suffice here.

First: Lenora in the small room which adjoined the council chamber within Het Spanjaard's Kasteel in Ghent. She had stood for close upon an hour under the lintel of the open door, her hand clinging to the heavy velvet portière; not one sound which came from the council chamber failed to strike her ear: every phase of that awesome interview between the supplicants and their vengeful tyrant struck at her heart, until at last unable to keep still, she uttered a moan of pain.

All this was his work! Not hers! Before God and her own conscience she felt that she could not have acted differently; that if it had all to be done again, she would again obey the still, insistent voice which had prompted her to keep her oath and to serve her King and country in the only way that lay in her power.

It was his work! not hers! His, whose whole life seemed to be given over to murder, to rebellion and to secret plottings, and who had tried to throw dust in her eyes and to cajole her into becoming a traitor too to all that she held dear.

161

It was his work, and the terrible reprisals which the Duke of Alva's retributive justice would mete out to this rebellious city lay at the door of those who had conspired against the State, and not at hers who had only been an humble tool in Almighty hands.

But in spite of her inner conviction that she had done right, in spite of her father's praise and approval which he had lavished on her all the way from Dendermonde to Ghent, she could not rid herself of a terrible sense of utter desolation and utter misery, and of a feeling of pity for all these poor people which caused her unendurable—almost physically unendurable—agony.

When anon the Lieutenant-Governor dismissed the burghers and after a few words with her father and señor del Rio left the council chamber, Lenora had a feeling as if the ground was opening before her, as if an awful chasm yawned at her feet into which she must inevitably fall if she dared look into it. And yet she looked and looked, as if fascinated by the hideousness of what she saw—pictures of cruelty and of evil far more horrible than any which had ever been limned of hell. And in the overwhelming horror which faced her now, she felt herself screaming aloud, with appealing defiance: "It is his work! not mine! Let the blood of his kinsfolk fall upon him—not me!" ere she tottered and fell back.

When full consciousness returned to her, her father was by her side. He looked pale and sullen and instinctively she drew away from him, whereat he smiled, showing his large teeth which looked like the fangs of a wolf.

"I ought never to have allowed you to come here, Lenora," he said roughly. "As His Highness said, it was not at all fit for women's ears."

"His Highness," she retorted coldly, "also said that to be here was my right ... your triumph to-day being all due to me."

"Well!" he added lightly, "'tis you wanted to come, remember."

"Yes," she said, "I wanted to come."

"I would have sent you to Brussels with Inez and a good escort. It is not too late. You can still go. Ghent will not be a fitting place for women during the next few days," he added, whilst a glow of evil satisfaction suddenly lit up his sallow face. "Would you prefer to go?"

"No, father, I thank you," she replied. "I would wish to stay."

"Ah! that's a brave daughter, and a true Spaniard," he cried, "and I promise you that you shall be satisfied with what you see. Ramon, your cousin, will be avenged more completely than even you could have dared to hope, and that assassin Leatherface will suffer: you shall see him dangling on a gibbet, never fear."

A slight shudder went right through her. Her face was as white as her gown; and as she made no reply, her father continued blandly:

"You little thought that your marriage would bring such a magnificent harvest of reprisals quite so soon! The city of Ghent and

162

the man Leatherface! The destruction of the one and the death of the other are your work, my daughter."

She closed her eyes; for she saw that awful chasm once more yawning at her feet, and once more she felt herself falling ... falling ... with no one to cling to but her father who kept asking her whether she was satisfied with what she had done.... His voice came to her as through a shroud ... he talked and talked incessantly ... of Ghent ... of rebels ... of murder and pillage and gibbets and torture-chambers ... of women and children and fathers of families ... of sons and of daughters ... and of one—Leatherface ... of the High-Bailiff of Ghent ... of Laurence and of Mark ... her husband.

"I wonder where that fool is now," she could hear her father saying through a muffler which seemed to envelop his mouth. "On the high road to Brussels mayhap with a message from you to me ... did you say you had sent him on from Dendermonde or straight away from Ghent? I am half sorry I gave in to your whim and brought you here with me ... but 'tis you wanted to come ... eh, my girl? ... you were so obstinate ... I was weak enough to give in ... but I ought not to have let you listen to those mealy-mouthed Flemings! ... ah! you are my true daughter ... you wanted to see these traitors punished, what? and Ramon's murder avenged! Well! you shall see it all, my dear, I promise you.... But I wish you could tell me what has become of that fool of a husband of yours ... we shall have to know presently if you are still wife or widow...."

He said this quite gaily and laughed at his own jest, and Lenora, pale and wild-eyed, echoed his laugh. She laughed as she had done two nights ago at Dendermonde when a face made up of lighted windows grinned at and mocked her across the Grand' Place. She laughed until the whole room began to dance a wild galliarde around her, until her father's face appeared like one huge, mocking grin.

Then she just glided from the couch down on to the floor. And there she lay, white and inert, whilst señor de Vargas, cursing the megrims of women, went calmly in search of help.

II

The second picture has for background the refectory in the convent of St. Agneten at the same hour as when last night the newly chosen, mysterious leader had roused boundless enthusiasm in the hearts of all his hearers. There is no lack of enthusiasm now either, but tempers are more subdued—gloom hangs over the assembly, for Messire the Procurator-General has just given a graphic account of his mission to the Lieutenant-Governor.

163

When he has finished speaking, the man with the mask who sits at the head of the table at the top of the long, low room, asks quietly:

"Then he refused?"

All the five men who this morning had knelt humbly before the tyrant, exchange silent glances, after which Messire Deynoot says firmly:

"He refused."

"Nothing will save our city," insisted Leatherface solemnly, "except if we track the Prince of Orange and bring him bound and a prisoner to the feet of Alva?"

"Nothing! save Orange's person will move Alva from his resolve."

Leatherface sits for a moment quite still, with his head buried in his hands: and the vast crowd now assembled in the room waits in breathless silence for his next word. There are far more than two thousand men here this night; the number has indeed been more than doubled. The deadly danger which threatens the city has already brought over three thousand new recruits to the standard.

Suddenly with a resolute gesture Leatherface draws his mask away and rises to his feet in full view of all the crowd.

"Mark van Rycke!" comes as one cry from several hundred throats.

"Aye!" he says with a light laugh, "your ne'er-do-well and frequenter of taverns was just the watch-dog of our noble Prince. Unknown I was able to render him some small service. Now that you are no longer called upon to throw me as a bait to the snarling lion, I'll resume mine own identity, and hereby ask you, if—knowing me for what I am—you still trust me to lead you to victory or to death?"

"To victory!" shout the younger men enthusiastically.

"To die like men," murmur the older ones.

"To-morrow we fight, seigniors!" says Mark earnestly, "to-morrow we defend our homes, our wives, our daughters, with scarce a hope of success. To-morrow we show to the rulers of the world how those of the down-trodden race can die whilst fighting for God and liberty."

"To-morrow!" they all assent with unbounded enthusiasm.

The ardour of a noble cause is in their veins. Not one of them here hesitates for one second in order to count the cost. And yet every one of them know that theirs is a forlorn cause. How can a handful of burghers and apprentices stand up before the might of Spain? But they are men at bay! they—the sober burghers of a fog-ridden land, steady, wise of counsel, without an ounce of impetuosity or hot-headedness in their blood; and yet they are ready to go into this desperate adventure without another thought save that of selling their lives and the honour of their women folk as dearly as they can.

For leader they have a man! for help they have only God! For incentive they have their own dignity, their pride, their valour ... for weapon they have the justice of their cause, and the right to die like men.

CHAPTER XVI

THE RIGHT TO DIE

I

And after the lapse of three hundred and more years the imagination projects itself into that past so full of heroic deeds, so full of valour and of glory, and stands still wondering before the glowing pictures which the insurrection of Ghent reveals.

Memory—the stern handmaiden of unruly imagination—goes back to that 21st day in October 1572 and recalls the sounds and sights which from early dawn filled the beautiful city with a presage of desolation to come; the church bells' melancholy appeal, the deserted streets, the barred and shuttered houses, the crowds of women and children and old men sitting at prayer in their own halls, the peaceful folk of a prosperous city quietly preparing for death.

At four o'clock in the afternoon the Duke of Alva rides out of the Kasteel with his staff and his bodyguard, which consists of three squadrons of cavalry, one bandera of Spanish infantry—halberdiers and pikemen—and five companies of harquebusiers, The Bandes d'Ordonnance—the local mounted gendarmerie—are on duty in the Vridachmart, and thither the Duke repairs in slow and stately majesty through silent streets, in which every window is shuttered, and where not one idler or gaffer stands to see him pass by. A cruel, ironical smile curls his thin lips beneath the drooping moustache as he notes the deserted aspect of the place.

"Terror," he mutters to himself, "or sulkiness. But they cannot eat their money or their treasures: and there must be a vast deal of it behind those walls!"

On the Vridachmart he halts with his armed escort grouped around him, the Bandes d'Ordonnance lining the market place, his standard unfurled behind him, his drummers in the front. Not a soul out upon the mart—not a head at any of the windows in the houses round! It seems as if Don Frederic Alvarez de Toledo, Duke of Alva, Lieutenant-Governor of the Netherlands and Captain-General of the Forces, was about to read a proclamation to a city of the dead.

165

A prolonged roll of drums commands silence for His Highness—silence which already is absolute—and then the Duke, in his usual loud and peremptory voice, demands the immediate surrender of the Prince of Orange now an outlaw in the town. And suddenly from every house around the huge market comes the answering cry: "Come and take him!" And from every doorway, from every adjoining street men come rushing along—with pikes and halberds and muskets, and from end to end of the town the defiant cry arises: "Come and take him!"

The Bandes d'Ordonnance, hastily summoned by the Duke to keep back the rabble, turn their arms against the Spanish halberdiers. Taking up the cry of "Come and take him!" they go over in a body to the side of the insurgents.

At once the Walloon arquebusiers are ordered to fire. The rebels respond this time with their own battle cry of "Orange and Liberty!" and a death-dealing volley of musketry. Whereupon the mêlée becomes general; the cavalry charges into the now serried ranks of the Orangists who are forced momentarily to retreat. They are pushed back across the mart as far as the cemetery of St. Jakab. Here they unfurl their standard, and their musketeers hold their ground with unshakable valour, firing from behind the low encircling wall with marvellous precision and quickness whilst two bodies of halbertmen and pikemen pour out in numbers from inside the church, and their artillerymen with five culverins and three falconets emerge out of the Guild House of the Tanners which is close by, and take up a position in front of the cemetery.

Alva's troops soon begin to lose their nerve. They were wholly unprepared for attack, and suddenly they feel themselves both outnumbered and hard-pressed. The Duke himself had been unprepared and had appeared upon the Vridachmart with less than two thousand men, whilst the other companies stationed in different portions of the city had not even been warned to hold themselves in readiness.

And just when the Spanish cavalry upon the Market Square is beginning to give ground the cry of "Sauve qui peut" is raised somewhere in the distance.

The Spanish and Walloon soldiery quartered in the various guild-houses, the open markets or private homesteads were just as unprepared for attack as was the garrison of the Kasteel. They had been promised that as soon as the evening Angelus had ceased to ring they could run wild throughout the city, loot and pillage as much as they desired, and that until that hour they could do no better than fill their heads with ale so as to be ready for the glorious sacking and destruction of the richest town in the Netherlands. Therefore, a goodly number of them—fresh from Mechlin—have spent the afternoon in recalling some of the pleasurable adventures there—the trophies gained, the treasure, the money, the jewels all lying ready to their hand. Others have listened

166

open-mouthed and agape, longing to get to work on the rich city and its wealthy burghers, and all have imbibed a great quantity of very heady ale which has fuddled their brain and made them more and more drowsy as the afternoon wears on. Their captains too have spent most of the day in the taverns, drinking and playing hazard in anticipation of loot, and thus the men are not at the moment in touch with their commanders or with their comrades, and all have laid aside their arms.

And simultaneously with the mêlée in the Vridachmart, the insurgents have made a general attack upon every guild-house, every market, every tavern where soldiers are quartered and congregated. With much shouting and to-do so as to give an exaggerated idea of their numbers they fall upon the unsuspecting soldiers—Walloons for the most part—and overpower and capture them before these have fully roused themselves from their afternoon torpor; their provosts and captains oft surrender without striking a blow. In almost every instance—so the chroniclers of the time aver—fifty and sixty men were captured by a dozen or twenty, and within half an hour all the guild-houses are in the hands of the Orangists, and close on fifteen hundred Walloons are prisoners in the cellars below; whilst all the arms stowed in the open markets go to swell the stores of the brave Orange men.

But some of the Walloons and Spaniards contrive to escape this general rounding up and it was they who first raised the cry of "Sauve qui peut!"

Now it is repeated and repeated again and again: it echoes from street to street; it gains in volume and in power until from end to end of the city it seems to converge toward the Vridachmart in one huge, all dominating wave of sound: "Sauve qui peut!" and the tramp of running feet, the calls and cries drown the clash of lance and pike.

Suddenly the bowmen of the Orangists scale the low cemetery wall as one man and their defence is turned into a vigorous onslaught: the cavalry is forced back upon the market square, they catch up the cry: "Sauve qui peut! They are on us! Sauve qui peut!" They break their ranks—a panic hath seized them—their retreat becomes a rout. The Orangists are all over the cemetery wall now: they charge with halberd and pike and force the Spaniards and Walloons back and back into the narrow streets which debouch upon the Schelde. Some are able to escape over the Ketel Brüghe, but two entire companies of Spanish infantry and a whole squadron of cavalry are—so Messire Vaernewyck avers—pushed into the river where they perish to the last man.

II

At this hour all is confusion. The picture which the mind conjures up of the stricken city is a blurred mass of pikes and lances, of

167

muskets and crossbows, of Spaniards and Walloons and Flemings, of ragged doublets and plumed hats–a medley of sounds: of arrows whizzing with a long whistling sound through the air, of the crash of muskets and clash of lance against lance, the appeal of those who are afraid and the groans of those who are dying–of falling timber and sizzling woodwork, and crumbling masonry, and through it all the awful cry of "Sauve qui peut!" and the sound of the tocsin weirdly calling through the fast gathering night.

And amidst this helter-skelter and confusion, the Duke of Alva upon his black charger–untiring, grim, terrible–tries by commands, cajoleries, threats, to rally those who flee. But the voice which erstwhile had the power to make the stoutest heart quake had none over the poltroon. He shouts and admonishes and threatens in vain. They run and run–cavalry, infantry, halbertmen and lancers–the flower of the Spanish force sent to subdue the Netherlands–they run; and in the general vortex of fleeing cavalry the Duke is engulfed too, and he is carried along as far as the Ketel Brüghe, where he tries to make a stand.

His doublet and hose are covered with mud and grime; his mantle is torn, his hat has fallen off his head and his white hair floats around his face which is as pale as death.

"Cowards!" he cries with fierce and maddened rage: "would you fly before such rabble?" But his voice has lost its magic; they do not heed him–they fly–past him and over the bridge to the safety of Het Spanjaard's Kasteel.

Then prudence dictates the only possible course, or capture might become inevitable. Cursing savagely and vowing more bitter revenge than ever before, the Duke at last wheels his horse round and he too hastens back to the stronghold–there to work out a plan of campaign against the desperate resistance of that handful of Flemish louts whom His Highness and all Spanish grandees and officials so heartily despise.

III

Half an hour later, and we see courier after courier sent flying from Het Spanjaard's Kasteel to every corner of the city.

The city gates–thank the God of the Spaniards!–have been well garrisoned and well supplied with culverins and balls, it is from there that help must come, for–strange to tell–those louts have actually invested the Kasteel and have the pretension to lay a regular siege to the stronghold.

Was there ever such a farce? A couple of thousand of an undisciplined rabble–they surely cannot be more–daring to pit themselves against a picked guard! Courier to the Waalpoort where

Lodrono is in command! courier to the Braepoort!—Serbelloni is there with two culverins of the newest pattern and two hundred musketeers, the like of whom are not known outside the Spanish army!

The only pity is that the bulk of the forces inside the city are Walloons! such poltroons as they have already proved themselves, surrendering in their hundreds to those confounded rebels! they have been scattered like flies out of a honey-pot, and the entire centre of the city is in the hands of the Orangists. But, anyway, the whole affair is only a question of time; for the moment the evening is closing in fast and the position cannot therefore be improved before nightfall; but in the morning a general closing-in movement, from the gates toward the centre would hold the rebels as in a claw and break their resistance within an hour. In the meanwhile the morale of the troops must be restored. Attend to that, ye captains at the city gates!

Courier follows courier out of the gate-house of the Kasteel: naked men, ready to crawl, to swim, or to dive, to escape the vigilance of the Orangist lines. Impossible! Not one is able to cross the open ground beyond the castle moat; the houses on the further bank of the Schelde are filled with Orangists; bows and muskets are levelled from every window. The culverins are down below, covered by the angles of the cross-streets; the messengers either fall ere they reach the Schelde or are sent back the way they came.

Attend to the morale of your men, ye captains at the city gates! The Duke of Alva, with some three or four thousand men, is inside the Kasteel, and no orders or communication can be got from him now before morning. And just like the flies when driven out of the honey, fly, scared, to the edges of the pot, so the Walloon soldiers, those who have escaped from the guild-houses, go and seek refuge in the shadow of the guard-houses at the gates. But the tactics of the Orangists have worked upon their nerves. At first there had appeared but a rabble upon the Vridachmart, but since then the numbers are swelling visibly; insurgents seem to be issuing out of every doorway, from under every arch in the city ... they rush out with muskets and crossbows, with pikes and halberds; and to the Walloons—already unnerved and fatigued—their numbers appear to be endless and their arms of a wonderful precision. Their muskets are of the newest pattern such as are made in Germany, and these they use with marvellous skill, discharging as many as ten shots in one quarter of an hour, and none but the picked French musketeers have ever been known to do that.

And they are led by a man who seems to know neither fatigue nor fear. Here, there and everywhere he appears to the Walloon and Spanish soldiers like a mysterious being from another world. He wears no armour, but just a suit of leather which envelopes him from head to foot, and his face is hidden by a leather mask. His voice rings from end to end of the market place one moment; the next he appears inside the enclosure of the cemetery. Now he is at St. Pharaïlde and anon back at

St. Jakab. Three of Alva's couriers hastily despatched to the commandants at the various gate-houses fall to his pistol, which is the only weapon he carries, and it is he who leads the last attack on the Ketel Brüghe which results in the flight of Alva and all his cavalry to the safe precincts of the Kasteel.

Before the evening Angelus has ceased to ring, the whole of the centre of the city is swept clear of Alva's troops, and the insurgents have completely surrounded the Kasteel. Darkness finds the Orangists bivouacking in the open markets and along the banks of the Schelde and the Leye with their artillery still thundering against Alva's stronghold and the gate-houses of the city, like bursts of thunder-clouds in a storm. The mantle of night has fallen over a vast hecatomb of dead and dying, of Walloons and Flemings and Spaniards, of brothers who have died side by side, with muskets raised in fratricide one against the other, and of women and children who have died of terror and of grief.

IV

And memory conjures up the vision of the tyrant, the author of all this desolation, riding slowly through the portal of the gate-house into the yard of Het Spanjaard's Kasteel a quarter of an hour or so ere the darkness of the night will finally cover all the abomination and the crimes, the murder, the misery and the bloodshed which the insatiable tyranny of this one man has called down upon a peaceable and liberty-loving people.

He rides with head erect, although fatigue and care are writ plainly on his ashen cheeks and the wearied stoop of his shoulders. His horse has received a wound in the flank from which the blood oozes and stains its rider's boots. Here in the castle-yard, some semblance of order has been brought about through the activity of the captains. The horses have been stabled in the vaulted cellars, the men have found quarters in different parts of the Kasteel; the musketeers and arquebusiers are up on the walls, the artillery well-screened behind the parapets.

The night has called a halt to men, even in the midst of barren victories and of unlooked-for defeat, and their sorrow and their hurts, their last sigh of agony or cry of triumph have all been equally silenced in her embrace; but over the city the sky is lurid and glowing crimson through a veil of smoke; the artillery and musketry have ceased their thundering; but still from out the gloom there come weird and hideous noises of hoarse shouts and cries of "Mercy" and of "Help," and from time to time the sudden crash of crumbling masonry or of charred beams falling in.

But Alva pays no heed to what goes on around him. He swings himself wearily out of the saddle and gives a few brief orders to the captains who press close beside his stirrup, anxious for a word or a look of encouragement or of praise. Then he curtly asks for water.

Don Sancho de Avila, captain of the castle guard, hands him the leather bottle and he drinks greedily.

"We are in a tight corner, Monseigneur," whispers de Avila under his breath.

"Hold thy tongue, fool!" is Alva's rough retort.

Whereupon the captain stands aside more convinced than before that disaster is in the air.

The Duke had been the last to turn his back on the Ketel Brüghe and to retire into the stronghold of the Kasteel. The banks of the Schelde by now are lined with the ranks of the insurgents, and it was a musket shot fired from the Vleeshhuis that wounded his horse—close to the saddle-bow. His quivering lips, and the ashen hue of his face testify to his consciousness of danger.

But his brow clears perceptibly when he sees Juan de Vargas coming out to meet him.

"Where is thy daughter?" he asks as soon as the other is within earshot.

"In chapel, I imagine," replies de Vargas.

"No woman should be abroad this night," says Alva dryly. "Send for her and order her to remain within her apartments."

"She has been tending the wounded, and will wish to do so again."

"Well! let her keep to the castle-yard then."

"You are not anxious, Monseigneur?"

"No. Not anxious," replies Alva with a fierce oath, "we can subdue these rebels of course. But I would I had brought Spanish soldiers with me, rather than these Walloon louts. They let themselves be massacred like sheep or else run like poltroons. Vitelli declares he has lost over a thousand men and at least a thousand more are prisoners in the various guild-houses—probably more. We ought never to have lost ground as we did," he adds sullenly, "but who would have thought that these louts meant to fight?"

"Who, indeed?" retorts de Vargas with a sneer, "and yet here we are besieged in our own citadel, and by a handful of undisciplined peasants."

"Nay! their triumph will be short-lived," exclaims Alva savagely. "We have over two thousand men inside the Kasteel and surely they cannot be more than three thousand all told unless..." He broke off abruptly, then continued more calmly: "Darkness closed in on us ere reprisals could commence ... if I had more Spaniards with me, I would try a sortie in the night and catch these oafs in their sleep ... but these

171

Walloons are such damnable fools and such abominable cowards.... But we'll fight our way through in the morning, never fear!"

"In the meanwhile cannot we send to Dendermonde for reinforcements? The garrison there is all Spanish and..."

"How can we send?" Alva breaks in savagely. "The way is barred by the artillery of those bandits—save upon the north and north-east, where that awful morass nearly half a league in length and width is quite impassable in autumn. No! we cannot get reinforcements unless we fight our way through first—unless one of the commandants at the gates has realised the gravity of the situation. Lodrono at the Waalpoort has intelligence," he continues more calmly, "and Serbelloni hath initiative—and by the Mass! if one of them doth not get us quickly out of this sorry place, I will have them all hanged at dawn upon their gates!"

The Duke of Alva's fierce wrath is but a result of his anxiety. He holds the Netherlanders in bitter contempt 'tis true! He knows that tomorrow perhaps he can send to Dendermonde for reinforcements and can then crush that handful of rebels as he would a fly beneath his iron heel. He would have his revenge—he knew that—but he also knew that that revenge would cost him dear. He has fought those Flemish louts, as he calls them, too often and too long not to know that when the day breaks once more he will have to encounter stubborn resistance, dogged determination and incalculable losses ere he can subdue and punish these men who have nothing now to lose but their lives—and those lives his own tyranny has anyhow made forfeit.

V

De Vargas makes no further comment on his chief's last tirade: remembering his daughter, he goes to transmit to her the order formulated by the Duke. Lenora is in the chapel, and, obedient to her father's commands, she rises from her knees and returns, silent and heavy-footed, to her apartments.

The hours drag on like unto centuries; she has even lost count of time; it is forty-eight hours now since she held Mark's wounded arm in her hand and discovered the awful, the hideous truth. Since then she has not really lived, she has just glided through the utter desolation of life, hoping and praying that it might finish soon and put an end to her misery.

She had acted, as she believed, in accordance with God's will! but she felt that her heart within her was broken, that nothing ever again would bring solace to her soul. That long, miserable day yesterday in Dendermonde whilst she was waiting for a reply from her father had been like an eternity of torment, and she had then thought that nothing on earth or in hell could be more terrible to bear. And then to-day she realised that there was yet more misery to endure, and more and more each day until the end of time, for of a truth there would be no rest or surcease from sorrow for her, even in her grave.

The one little crumb of comfort in her misery has been the companionship of Grete; the child was silent and self-contained, and had obviously suffered much in her young life, and therefore understood the sorrows of others—knew how to sympathise, when to offer words of comfort, and when to be silent.

Though Inez was a pattern of devotion, her chattering soon grated on Lenora's nerves; and anon when don Juan de Vargas agreed to allow his daughter to come with him to Ghent, Lenora arranged that Grete be made to accompany her and that Inez be sent straight on to Brussels. The girl—with the blind submission peculiar to the ignorant and the down-trodden—had consented; she had already learned to love the beautiful and noble lady, whose pale face bore such terrible lines of sorrow, and her sister Katrine and her aunt both believed that the child would be quite safe under the immediate protection of don Juan de Vargas. Inez was sent off to Brussels, and Lenora and Grete are now the only two women inside the Kasteel.

Together they flit like sweet, pale ghosts amongst the litters of straw whereon men lie groaning, wounded, often cursing—they bandage the wounds, bring water to parched lips, pass tender, soothing hands across feverish foreheads. Then, at times, Lenora takes Grete's rough little hand in hers, and together the women wander out upon the ramparts. The sentries and the guard know them and they are not challenged, and they go slowly along the edge of the walls, close to the parapets and look down upon the waters of the moat. Here the dead lie in their hundreds, cradled upon the turgid waters, washed hither through the narrow canals by the more turbulent Schelde—their pale, still faces turned upwards to the grey evening light. And Lenora wonders if anon she will perceive a pair of grey eyes—that were wont to be so merry—turning sightless orbs to the dull, bleak sky. She scans each pale face, with eyes seared and tearless, and not finding him whom she seeks, she goes back with Grete to her work of mercy among the wounded only to return again and seek again with her heart torn between the desire to know whether the one man whom she hates with a bitter passion that fills her entire soul hath indeed paid the blood-toll for the dastardly murder of Ramon, or whether God will punish her for that irresistible longing which possesses her to hold that same cowardly enemy—wounded or dying—assassin though he be—for one unforgettable moment in her arms.

VI

But it is not desolation that reigns in the refectory of the convent of St. Agneten, for here the leaders of the rebellion have assembled, as soon as the guns have ceased to roar. The numbers of their followers since last night have increased by hundreds, and still the recruits come pouring in. Those men who but four days ago had received the Prince of Orange's overtures with vague promises and obvious indifference, rushed to arms after the first musket shot had been fired. Ever since the attack in the Vridachmart men have loudly clamoured for halberts or pikes or muskets, and the captains at the various secret depots, as well as the guild of armourers, had much ado to satisfy all those who longed to shed their blood with glory rather than be massacred like insentient cattle. They are men who have fought at Gravelines and St. Quentin, and have not forgotten how to shoulder musket or crossbow or how to handle a culverin. Since then, fifteen years of oppression, of brow-beating, of terrorising, fifteen years under the yoke of the Inquisition and of Spanish tyranny have worn down the edge of their enthusiasm.

When Orange begged for money and men that he might continue the fight for liberty, the goodly burghers of Ghent forgot their glorious traditions and preferred to bend their neck to the yoke rather than risk the fate of Mons and of Mechlin. But now that danger is within their doors, now that they and their wives and daughters are at the mercy of the same brutal soldiery whom Alva and de Vargas take pleasure in driving to bestial excesses and inhuman cruelties, now that they realise that the fate of Mechlin is already inevitably theirs—their dormant courage rises once more to its most sublime altitude. Die they must—that they know!—how can they, within the enclosure of their own city walls, stand up against the armies of Spain, which can at any moment be brought up in their thousands to reinforce the tyrant's troops? But at least they will die with muskets or pikes in their hands, and their wives and daughters will be spared the supreme outrage which they count worse than death.

Thus close on five thousand volunteers file past their leaders this night in the refectory of St. Agneten and tender their oath of allegiance to fight to the last man for Orange and liberty. On the faces of those leaders—of Messire van Beveren, of Lievin van Deynse, of Laurence van Rycke and Jan van Migrode, there is plainly writ the determination to keep up the fight to the end, and the knowledge that the end can only be death for them all.

But in Mark van Rycke's deep-set eyes there is something more than mere determination. There is a latent belief that God will intervene—there is a curious exultation in their merry depths—a kind of triumphant hope: and those who stand before him and swear that they will fight for Orange and liberty with the last drop of their blood look him straight in the face for a moment and then turn away feeling less grim and more courageous with a courage not altogether born of despair.

The angel of liberty has unsheathed his sword and infused his holy breath into these men—easy-going burghers for the most part, untrained soldiers or even undisciplined rabble—who have dared to defy the might of Alva.

VII

And when the first streak of dawn folds the night in its embrace and lifts from off the stricken city the veil of oblivion and of sleep, we see some five thousand Orangists prepared to stand up before Alva's forces which still number close on eight. The streets are littered with dead, with pikes and lances hastily cast aside, with muskets and plumed bonnets, with broken rubbish and wheelless wagons, and scraps of cloth or shoes or leather belts.

And in the cemetery of St. Jakab the flag of liberty still flaunts its blazing orange in the pale morning light and around it men still rally, defiant and unconquered. The Guild House of the Tanners close by is in flames, and the tower of St. Jakab a crumbling ruin; the hostel of St. Juan ten Dullen is a charred mass of debris, and the houses that front on the Vridachmart a fast crumbling heap of masonry and glass.

The situation of the insurgents is more desperate than even Alva knows. Of their three captains, Pierre van Overbeque is dead, Jan van Migrode severely wounded, and Laurence van Rycke exhausted. Of their company of halberdiers, all the provosts except two have fallen. The investing lines around the Kasteel have five officers killed and twenty of their artillerymen have fallen. Six hundred of their wounded encumber the Vridachmart. The narrow streets which debouch upon the gates are deserted save by the dead.

But as soon as the rising day hath touched the ruined tower of St. Jakab with its pale silvery light, Mark van Rycke, their commander, intrepid and undaunted, wakes the sleeping echoes with his cry: "Burghers of Ghent! to arms! we are not vanquished yet!"

A volley of arrows from the crossbowmen upon the Waalpoort answers the defiant cry: one arrow pierces a loose corner of Mark's doublet.

"Van Rycke!" cries the provost who stands nearest to him, "spare thyself in the name of God! What shall we do if you fall?"

And Mark, unmoved, the fire of enthusiasm unquenched in his eyes, cries loudly in response:

"Do? What alone can burghers of Ghent do in face of what lies before them if they give in? Do? Why, die like heroes—to the last man."

His doublet hangs from him in rags, his hose is torn, his head bare, his face black with powder. He grasps musket or crossbow, halberd, lance or pike, whichever is readiest to his hand, whichever company hath need of a leader; a beam from the burning building has fallen within a yard of him and singed his hair: "Heroes of Ghent!" he cries, "which of you will think of giving in?"

The morning Angelus begins to ring. For a few minutes while the pure clear tones of the church bells reverberate above the din of waking men and clash of arms, Spaniards and Walloons and Flemings pause in their hate and their fight in order to pray.

Up in the council chamber of the Kasteel, Alva and de Vargas and del Rio on their knees mock the very God whom they invoke, and when the last "Amen!" has left their lips, Alva struggles to his feet and murmurs fiercely:

"And now for revenge!"

Through the wide open windows, he gazes upon the spires and roofs of the beautiful city which he hath sworn to destroy. Already many of these are crumbling ruins, and from far away near the church of St. Jakab a column of black smoke rises upwards to the sky. The windows give upon an iron balcony which runs along the entire width of the Meeste-Toren: from this balcony an open staircase leads down into the castle-yard. The yard and vaulted cellars opposite are filled with horses, and the corridors of the palace swarm with men. And as the Duke, anon, steps out upon the balcony he sees before him the five breaches in the castle-walls which testify to the power of the insurgents' culverins. He hears the groans of the wounded who lie all round the walls upon the litters of straw, he sees the faces of innumerable dead, floating wide-eyed upon the waters of the moat, and the carcasses of horses in the yard which add to the horror of the scene by their pathetic hideousness.

And seeing all this, he hath not a thought of pity for all the innocent whom he vows to punish along with the guilty.

"Now for revenge!" he reiterates fiercely and shakes a clenched fist toward the tower of St. Jakab, "and if only I had my Spaniards with me, we would have burned the town down before now."

VIII

The day drags on in the weary monotony of incessant firing, incessant fighting—constant attacks to be repulsed, numbers of wounded to be added to those who already encumber the yard—numbers of dead to be added to those who encumber the waters of the moat.

The finest general the victorious Spanish armies have ever

known is besieged in his stronghold by a few hundred undisciplined, untaught, unseasoned rebel troops. What is happening beyond the wide tract of open ground which lies all round the Kasteel the Duke cannot get to know. The Orangist lines are all round him screened by the buildings which face the further bank of the Schelde; and though his culverins have turned the magnificent Vleeshhuis into a smoking ruin, those of the Orangists have made serious havoc in the castle walls.

The last onslaught delivered a couple of hours after noonday resulted in the crumbling together of three of the widest breaches already existing, making one huge yawning cavity, which has to be strongly and persistently defended–a defence which exacts an enormous toll of wounded and dead every time the Orangist artillery and musketry return to the attack.

"We cannot hold out till nightfall!" Captain de Avila cries despairingly. "We have lost two hundred men in less than two hundred minutes. If we get no help we are undone!"

"Help!" cries Alva fiercely, "where are we to get help from if those oafs at the city gates do not find us some?"

On the north-east side of the Kasteel lies the open way to Dendermonde–where Captain Gonzalo de Bracamonte is quartered with a garrison of five thousand men, and between that open way of salvation, and those who hold the Kasteel, there lies a league of spongy morass. The way through it is free from the Orangist musketry. Nature alone bars it, and does so effectually.

Three times to-day has Alva tried to send runners through that way. Stripped to the skin they are lowered by ropes from the parapet, and at first find firm foothold at the base of the walls. From up above Alva and his captains watch the naked men who walk on boldly, proud of their achievement; their skins shine like metal beneath the grey, autumnal sky on which the smouldering ruins of a devastated city have painted a crimson tint. Alva watches them until they appear as mere black dots upon the low horizon–tiny black specks that move for a while, slowly along, with arms swinging as the mud gets deeper and walking heavier. Then suddenly the speck ceases to move ... the arms are thrown up with frantic wheelings and beatings of the air ... sometimes the speck will turn and move back slowly toward the castle, but more often than not it grows shorter and shorter still, till even the tall arms disappear–engulfed in the morass.

Three times have men been sent out on this errand of death ... three or four at a time ... twice has one man come back from those hideous, yawning jaws of a loathsome death–livid, covered with green slime, trembling in every limb as if stricken with ague. After that, men refuse to go ... Alva commands and threatens ... another batch go off ... another spectre returns from the shores of another world.... Then the men are obstinate ... to insist, to command, to threaten further would provoke mutiny, and the stronghold once more lapses into utter isolation.

The din of musketry from end to end of the city drowns every other sound, smoke from smouldering ruins obscures the view beyond the Schelde. What has happened in the centre of the city during all these hours, whilst the high and mighty Lieutenant-Governor and Captain-General of the Force of Occupation is a virtual prisoner in the hands of the rebels, he himself cannot possibly tell.

"The rebels have lost more heavily than we have," says de Avila, whilst he snatches a brief rest during the afternoon, "and they must be getting short of powder."

"So are we," says Alva grimly.

"Surely Captain Lodrono has come in touch with Captain Serbelloni by now. It is inconceivable that the garrisons at the gate-houses can do nothing."

"Those Netherlanders are fighting like devils," says de Vargas with his evil sneer, "they have nothing to lose ... they know that they are doomed, every man, woman and child of them ... aye! if I had my way, every man who speaks the Flemish tongue."

"Aye!" retorts Alva with a curse, "but in the meanwhile, if Serbelloni or Lodrono have not sent a runner to Dendermonde, those Flemish louts will carry this castle by storm, and when I am a prisoner in their hands, they'll either slaughter us all or dictate their own terms."

"Ah!" says Avila quietly, "they have not got the Kasteel yet."

"How long can we hold out?" queries de Vargas, who at Alva's grimly prophetic words, had become livid with fear.

"Unless those rebels have lost more heavily than we hope, we cannot hold out more than another few hours. We still have three thousand men and a goodly stock of powder.... The breach we can defend with stones of which there is a large store; we killed or wounded over a hundred of those louts at their last assault ... we can go on like this until nightfall. But if at dawn they attack us again in full force—and we lose many more men to-day ... why..."

"Hold thy tongue," cried Alva fiercely, for at the senior captain's words, many of the younger ones have exchanged quick, significant glances. "Shall I have to hang some of my captains so as to discourage the men from playing the coward too?"

IX

The evening Angelus has just ceased to ring, and a man is ushered into the presence of the Captain-General; he is naked, and his body is covered with sticky mud and dripping with slime; his face is hardly recognisable through a thick mask of sweat and grime.

"I come from Braepoort, Magnificence," he says in a low, quaking voice, for obviously he is all but exhausted. "I ran round the town, and struck into the morass ... I am a man of Ghent ... I know a track ... that's why Captain Serbelloni sent me."

"With what news?" queries Alva impatiently.

"None too good, Magnificence," replies the man. "The commandants at the gates are sorely pressed ... I hailed the guard at the Brügge and Waalpoorts as I passed ... they are isolated ... every one of them ... and each separately attacked by bands of rebels who fight desperately.... The Braepoort cannot hold out much longer ... Captain Serbelloni asks for help even before nightfall."

"Help?" vociferates Alva savagely, "how can I send them help? We are besieged in this accursed place; we cannot fight our way through the rabble, unless some of those oafs at the city gates come to our assistance. Help? 'Tis I want help here."

"The gates are being bravely defended, Magnificence. But the rebels still hold the centre of the city. They have seized 'Sgravensteen. Two thousand Walloons have surrendered to them..."

"Two thousand!" exclaims Alva with a fierce oath, "the miserable poltroons."

"At least three thousand rebels threaten the Kasteel."

"I know that well enough," retorts Alva roughly. "They have made five breaches in our wall! ... the bandits! Help! 'tis I want help!" he reiterates with a loud curse.

"Captain Serbelloni bade me tell your Highness that he hath sent to Dendermonde for immediate reinforcements. He hoped your Highness would forgive him if he hath done wrong."

Alva's eyes flash a look of satisfaction, but he makes no immediate comment. Not even his colleagues—not even de Vargas his intimate—should see how immense is his relief.

"Did he send a mounted man," he asks after a while, "or two? Two would be better in case a man gets hurt on the way."

"The Captain sent three men, Magnificence. But they had to go on foot. We have no horses at the gates. The insurgents rounded them all in long before nightfall. But the men hope to pick up one or more on their way."

Alva, as is his wont, smothers a savage curse. The small body of Spanish cavalry which he had with him in the town had been the first to run helter-skelter over the Ketel Brüghe into the Kasteel, whilst a whole squadron perished in the Schelde. One of those horses down there in the yard would mean reinforcements within a few hours.

"When did the messenger start for Dendermonde?" he asks again.

"When the Angelus began to ring at noon, Magnificence."

"Why not before?"

"The captain was undecided. He thought that every moment

would bring help or orders from your Highness. He also tried to send messengers to Captain Lodrono at the Waalpoort, but the messengers must all have been intercepted and killed, for no help came from anywhere."

"Dost know if the message which thy captain sent to Dendermonde was couched in urgent terms?"

"I believe so, Magnificence. The señor captain was growing very anxious."

Once more the Duke is silent; his brows contract in an anxious frown. His active brain is busy in making a mental calculation as to how soon those reinforcements can arrive. "The men will have to walk to Dendermonde," he muses, "and cannot get there before nightfall.... the commandant may start at night ... but he may tarry till the morrow.... It will be the end of the day before he and his men are here ... and in the meanwhile..."

"At the Braepoort?" he queries curtly, "how many of the guard have been killed?"

"We had a hundred and twenty killed when I left, Magnificence, and over three hundred lay wounded on the bridge. We have suffered heavily," adds the man after a slight moment of hesitation—the hesitation of the bearer of evil tidings who dreads his listener's wrath.

Alva remains silent for a moment or two, then he says abruptly: "Dost know that I have half a mind to kill thee, for all the evil news which thou hast brought?"

Then he laughs loudly and long because the man, with a quick cry of terror has made a sudden dash for the open window, and is brought back by the lance of the provost on guard upon the balcony. The pleasure of striking terror into the hearts of people has not yet palled upon his Magnificence.

"If I had a whole mind to kill thee," he continues, "thou wouldst have no chance of escape. So cease thy trembling and ask the provost there to give thee water to cleanse thyself, food to put inside thy belly and clothing wherewith to hide thy nakedness. Then come back before me. I'll give thee a chance to save thy life by doing a service to thy King."

He makes a sign to one of the provosts, who seizes the man roughly by the shoulders and incontinently bundles him out of the room.

In the council chamber no one dares to speak. His Highness has become moody, and has sunk upon his high-backed chair where he remains inert and silent, wrapped in gloomy meditations, and when he is in one of those sullen moods no one dares to break in on his thoughts—no one except señor de Vargas, and he too is as preoccupied as his chief.

180

X

"De Vargas!" says Alva abruptly after a while, "dost mind that to-morrow is not only Sunday, but the feast of the Blessed Redeemer and a holy day of obligation?"

"Aye, Monseigneur," replied de Vargas unctuously, "I am minded that if we do not go to Mass to-morrow, those of us who die unabsolved of the sin will go to hell."

"The men are grumbling already," breaks in don Sancho de Avila, captain of the bodyguard. "They say they will not fight to-morrow if they cannot go to Mass."

"Those Walloons..."

"Not only the Walloons, Monseigneur," rejoins de Avila, "the Spaniards are better Catholics than all these Netherlanders. They fear to die with a mortal sin upon their soul."

Nothing more is said just then; the grey day is already yielding to dusk; the fire of artillery and musketry is less incessant, the clash of pike and halberd can be heard more distinctly, and also the cries of the women and the groans of the wounded and the dying.

A few moments later a tall, lean man in the borrowed dress of a Spanish halberdier is ushered into the presence of the council. Water, food and clothes have effected a transformation which Alva surveys critically, and not without approval. The man—lean of visage and clean of limb—looks intelligent and capable; the Duke orders him to advance.

"'Tis good for thee," he says dryly, "that thy death is more unprofitable to me than thy life. I want a messenger ... art afraid to go to the miserable wretch who dares to lead a rebel horde against our Sovereign King?"

"I am afraid of nothing, Magnificence," replies the man quietly, "save your Highness's wrath."

"Dost know where to find the rebel?"

"Where musket-balls fly thickest, your Highness."

"Then tell him," says Alva curtly, "that as soon as the night has fallen and the fire of culverins and muskets has ceased, I will have the drawbridge at the south-east of this castle lowered, and I will come forward to meet him, accompanied by my captains and the members of my council. Tell him to walk forward and meet me until we are within earshot of one another: and to order his torch-bearers to throw the light of their torches upon his face: then will I put forward a proposal which hath regard to the eternal salvation of every man, woman and child inside this city. Tell him to guard his person as he thinks fit, but tell him also that from the ramparts of this Kasteel three hundred muskets will be aimed at his head, and at the slightest suspicion of treachery the order will be given to fire. Dost understand?"

"Every word, your Highness," says the man simply.

"Then go in peace," concludes Alva, and the man is dismissed.

181

XI

An hour later the drawbridge at the south-east gate of the Kasteel was lowered. Twilight had now faded into night; the dull, grey day had yielded to black, impenetrable night. Here and there far away in the heart of the city lurid lights shot through the darkness, and every now and then a column of vivid flame would strike up to the dense black sky, and for a while illumine the ruined towers, the shattered roofs and broken chimneys around ere it fell again, sizzling in the damp atmosphere.

The Duke of Alva rode out in the gloom; he was seated upon his black charger, and was preceded by his torch-bearers and by his bodyguard of archers. Behind him walked his captains and the members of his council. The procession slowly wended its way under the portal of the gate-house and then over the bridge. At the farthest end of the bridge the Duke reined in his horse, and his bodyguard, his captains and the members of his council all stood behind him so that he immediately faced the tract of open ground beyond which were the Orangist lines.

The flickering light of resin torches illumined the commanding figure of the Duke, dressed in sombre clothes and silk-lined mantle, and wearing breast and back plates of armour, with huge tassets over his wide breeches and open steel morion on his head. To right and left far away, toward the open country, the bivouac fires of the insurgents gleamed weirdly in the night.

All noise of fighting had ceased, and a strange silence had fallen over the city–a silence which hid many secrets of horror and of despair.

Suddenly something began to move, something that at first appeared darker than the darkness of the night; a few moments later it appeared as a speck of ruddy light which moved quickly–now toward the castle bridge; anon it was distinguishable as a group of men–a dozen or so–with a couple of torchbearers on in front, the light from whose torches fell full upon a tall figure which stood out boldly amongst the others. Now the group came to a halt less than fifty paces away, and those upon the bridge could see that tall figure quite clearly; a man in ragged doublet and hose, with grimy hands and face blackened with powder; he held his head very erect and wore neither helmet nor armour.

At sight of him, de Vargas gave a cry of rage and surprise.

"Mark van Rycke!" he exclaimed. "What hath he to do with it all?"

"Thy daughter's husband," said Alva coolly. "Nay, then we'll soon make her a widow."

But to the Orangists he called peremptorily: "'Tis with the rebel whom ye call Leatherface that I wish to speak."

182

"I have been known as Leatherface hitherto," retorts Mark van Rycke coolly. "Speak without fear. I listen."

Vargas' cry of rage was echoed by more than one Spanish captain present. They remembered Mark van Rycke, the ne'er-do-well with whom they had oft drunk and jested in the taverns of Ghent and Brussels, aye! and before whom they had oft talked openly of their plans.

"Spy as well as rebel!" they cried out to him wrathfully.

"Pity he cannot hang more than once," added de Vargas with bitter spite.

But to Alva the personality of the rebel was of no consequence. What cared he if the man was called van Rycke and was the husband of his friend's daughter? There stood an abominable rebel who had gained by treachery and stealth a momentary advantage over the forces of his suzerain Lord the King, and who would presently suffer along with the whole of this insurgent city the utmost rigour of Alva's laws! In the meanwhile he deigned to parley with the lout, for he was sore pressed inside the Kasteel, and the messengers who were speeding to Dendermonde for reinforcements could not possibly bring help for at least another four-and-twenty hours.

Therefore, now he–the Lieutenant-Governor of the Netherlands and Captain-General of His Majesty's forces–demanded attention in the name of the King.

"Do ye come as traitors?" he asked in a loud voice, "or as loyal men? If as traitors ye shall die ere ye advance another step. But if ye are loyal men, then listen, for I will speak with you in amity and peace."

"Thou knowest best, Magnificence," came Mark's clear voice out of the group, "if we are loyal men or no. Thou didst send an emissary to us; he goeth back to thee unhurt: thou standest before our bowmen even now and not an arrow hath touched thine armour. We are loyal men and are prepared to listen to what ye have to say."

"Listen then," resumed the Duke curtly, "but let no false hopes lure ye the while. Ye are rebels and are under the ban of the law. Nothing but unconditional surrender can win mercy for your city."

"Nothing but humility can save thee from the wrath of God," retorted Mark boldly. "We are unconquered, Magnificence! and 'tis thou who askest to parley–not we."

"I do not ask," retorted Alva loudly, "I demand."

"Then since 'tis the vanquished who demand, let us hear what they wish to say."

"To-morrow is Sunday, rebel, hadst forgotten that?"

"No, tyrant, I had not. God hath forbidden us to work on that day, but not to fight against oppression."

"He hath also enjoined us to attend Mass on His day. Are ye heretics that ye care naught for that?"

"We care for the Lord's Day as much as Spaniards do."

"Yet will ye prevent His people from praying in peace!"

"We'll pray for those whom thy tyranny keeps locked up within thy castle walls."

"Not so," exclaims Alva, "my men are free to go: they will attend Mass in the churches of this city. Will you butcher them whilst they are at prayer?"

There was no immediate reply to this taunt, but from the insurgents' ranks there came a loud, warning call:

"Do not heed him, van Rycke! Remember Egmont and Horne! Do not fall into the tyrant's trap! There's treachery in every word he says."

Alva waited in silence until the tumult had subsided. He knew what he wanted and why he wanted it. A few hours' respite would mean salvation for him ... a few hours! ... and the garrison of Dendermonde would be on its way to Ghent. He wanted to stay the hand of time for those few hours and had invented this treacherous means to gain that end.

"'Tis no wonder," he said quietly as soon as the clamour on the Orangist side was stilled, "that ye who are traitors should seek treachery everywhere. What I propose is loyal and just and in accordance with God's own decrees. If ye refuse, ye do so at the peril of thousands of immortal souls."

"We know not yet what it is ye ask," said van Rycke quietly.

"We demand a truce until the evening Angelus to-morrow–the Lord's Day which is also the feast of the Holy Redeemer. We demand the right to attend Mass in peace ... and in exchange we'll agree not to molest you whilst ye pray and whilst ye bury your dead."

"A truce until the evening Angelus," broke in Mark hotly, "so that ye may send for reinforcements to the nearest garrison town. We refuse!"

"You refuse?" retorted Alva. "For two days and a night ye have raised your arms against your lawful King. If you fight to-morrow you will add sacrilege to your other crimes."

"And thou, treachery to thine!" said van Rycke boldly. "Whence this desire to keep holy the Sabbath day, tyrant? Wouldst thou have ceased to destroy, to pillage or to outrage this day if we had not raised our arms in our own defence?"

"Well said, van Rycke!" cried the Orangists.

"The immortal souls which your obstinacy would send to hell," said the Duke of Alva, "will return and haunt you till they drag you back with them."

"Can you not pray in your Kasteel?" retorted Mark.

"We have no priest to say Mass for us."

"We will send you one."

"We have no consecrated chapel."

"The priest will say Mass in your castle-yard, beneath the

consecrated dome of heaven. The Walloon prisoners whom we have taken are receiving the ministry of our priests in the guild-houses where they are held."

"Nay! but such makeshift would not satisfy the children of Spain who are also the chosen children of the Church. But," continued Alva with a sudden assumption of indifference, "I have made my proposal. Take it or not as ye list. But remember this: the dead who lie unburied in your streets will have their revenge. Pestilence and disease will sweep your city of your children, as soon as we have vanquished your men."

"Treachery!" cried some of the Orangists, "do not heed him, van Rycke."

But of a truth the cry was not repeated quite so insistently this time. Alva's last argument was an unanswerable one. Pestilence these days was a more formidable foe than the finest artillery wielded by a powerful enemy: there were over two thousand dead lying unburied in the city at this hour: as the tyrant said very truly, these would take a terrible revenge. And there was something too in the sanctity of the Lord's Day which touched the hearts of these men who were deeply religious and devout and had a profound respect for the dictates of the Church. Most of them were Catholics—the importance of attending Mass on the Lord's Day on pain of committing a deadly sin weighed hard upon their conscience. Alva was quick to note the advantage which he had already gained, and when the first dissentient voice among the Orangists was heard to say: "A truce can do no harm and 'twere sacrilege to fight on the Lord's Day," he broke in quickly:

"Nay! 'tis not fighting ye would do, but murder. Aye! murder on the Day of the Holy Redeemer who died that ye should live.... My men are Catholic to a man! not one of them but would far rather let himself be butchered than commit a deadly sin. Rebels, who have outraged your King, to-morrow morning the church bells will be calling the faithful to the Holy Sacrifice: the truce which you refuse to hold with us we will grant you of our own free will. We will not fight you on the day of the feast of the Holy Redeemer. But to-morrow every Spaniard and every Walloon in our armies will go unarmed and present himself at your church doors. I—even I—with my captains and the members of the King's Council will attend Mass at the church of St. Baafs and we will be unarmed, for we shall have placed ourselves under the care of the Holy Redeemer Himself. And now tell thy soldiers, rebel, tell them that Spaniards and Walloons will be in the churches of Ghent in their thousands and that they will be defenceless save for the armour of prayer which will encompass them as they kneel before the altar of God!"

"And in the meanwhile," retorted van Rycke, "ye will be sending to Dendermonde and Alost and Antwerpen: and when after the evening

185

Angelus we take up arms once more against your tyranny, there will be five thousand more Spaniards at our gates."

"By the Holy Redeemer whom I herewith invoke," said Alva solemnly and raised his hand above his head with a gesture of invocation, "I swear that no messenger of mine shall leave the city before ye once more take up arms against your King. I swear that no messenger of mine hath left this city for the purpose of getting help from any garrison town, and may my soul be eternally damned if I do not speak the truth."

Those who were present at this memorable interview declare that when Alva registered this false and blasphemous oath a curious crimson light suddenly appeared in the East—so strong and lurid was it that the perjurer himself put up his hand for a second or two as if blinded by the light. Philip de Lannoy, seigneur de Beauvoir, assures us that the light was absolutely dazzling and of the colour of blood, but that he took it as a warning from God against the sacrilege of fighting on this holy day, and that it caused him to add the weight of his influence with Mark van Rycke to grant the truce which the Spaniards desired.

Undoubtedly, the solemn oath spoken by the tyrant who was such a devout and bigoted Catholic greatly worked upon the feelings of the Orangists: never for a moment did the suspicion of the oath being a false one enter their loyal heads: nor must they be blamed for their childish confidence in a man who had lied to them and deceived them so continuously for the past five years. They were so loyal themselves, such a trap as Alva was setting for them now was so far from their ken, that it was impossible for them to imagine such appalling treachery: as for the sanctity of an oath, they would as soon have thought of doubting the evidence of their own eyes.

Mark van Rycke, it is true, held out to the last. He knew these Spaniards better than those simple burghers did: not in vain had he spent his best years in the uncongenial task of worming out their secret plans—their treacherous devices—over tankards of ale and games of hazard in Flemish taverns. He mistrusted them all, he mistrusted Alva above all! he had no belief in that execrable monster's oath.

"God is on our side!" he said quietly, "we'll bury our dead when we can, and pray when God wills. He'll forgive the breaking of His Sabbath for the justice of our cause.

"They are weary of the fight," he added obstinately, "we are not."

But already every one of his friends was urging him to grant the truce:

"For the sake of our women and children," said van Deynse who voiced the majority, "let there be no fighting to-morrow. The tyrant has pledged his immortal soul that he will not play us false. No man would dare to do that unless he meant to be true."

"Rebel!" now shouted Alva impatiently, "I await thine answer."

186

"Accept, van Rycke, accept," cried the Orangists unanimously now, "it is God's will that we accept."

"I await thine answer, rebel," reiterated Alva.

"What answer can I give?" retorted van Rycke. "You say your men will go to our churches unarmed. We are not butchers as ye would have been."

"You will let them pray in peace?"

"As thou desirest. You who were prepared to destroy our city and to murder our women and our children will have nothing to fear from us while ye are unarmed and at prayer."

"Until the evening Angelus ceases to ring?"

"Until then."

"And until that hour we remain as we are. Our guard at the gates...."

"Our prisoners in our hands."

"And may God guard thee," concluded Alva unctuously.

"May God have mercy on thy soul if thou hast lied to us," said Mark van Rycke quietly.

To this Alva made no reply, but his grim face looked in no way troubled. Special absolution even for speaking a false oath could easily be obtained, alas! these days by any Duke of Alva or other tyrant powerful enough to demand it; and no doubt the Lieutenant-Governor, sent to subdue the rebellious Low Countries, was well provided with every kind of dispensation which embodied the principle that "the end justifies the means!"

He wheeled his horse round and, wholly callous and unconcerned, he rode back slowly over the bridge.

As soon as the last of the Spaniards had filed under the gate-house of the Kasteel and the drawbridge was once more raised, Mark van Rycke turned with unwonted peremptoriness to his friends who were crowding round him, eagerly approving of what he had done.

"Van Deynse," he said curtly, "to-morrow at dawn, see that your musketeers are massed inside the ruins of the Tanners' Guild House, and you, Laurence, place three hundred of your picked archers under the cover of the Vish Mart. Lannoy, your pikemen beneath the arcades of the Abbey opposite St. Baafs, and you, Groobendock, yours in the doorways of the houses opposite St. Pharaïlde, and every one of you under arms. Let the Spaniards pray in peace if they have not lied. But at the first sign of treachery, remember your wives and your daughters and do not spare the murderers of your children or the desecrators of your homes."

CHAPTER XVII

TRUTH AND PERFIDY

I

The cathedral bells of St. Baafs were the first to ring on that unforgettable 23rd day of October which was the feast of the Holy Redeemer: the appealing, sweet, melancholy sound came clearly through the humid air. Lenora, who was in her room with Grete, stood quite still for a moment and listened. The bells of St. Pharaïlde took up the call, then those of St. Jakab and St. Agneten until the clang of bells echoed from end to end of the city and drowned every other sound—of strife or of misery. The roar of the artillery now was mute, the clash of pikes and lances was no longer heard—only that curious medley of weird and terrible sounds still lingered in the air—a medley made up of sighs and groans, of men falling down exhausted with pain, of masonry still crumbling and woodwork still sizzling—a medley to which now was added the roll of drums which on either side called to the men to lay aside their strife and to go and pray in peace.

On the walls of the castle-yard the Duke's proclamation of the Lord's Day truce was posted up and he himself was giving a few brief orders to his captains:

"Let the men understand," he said, "that they are free to go to Mass in the various churches of the city, and that they can do so without the slightest fear. But they must all be back inside the Kasteel precincts by two hours after noon. Let the couriers go to the gate-houses at the six Poorts and issue the same orders there, and have the proclamation posted up. Make it known here as well as at the Poorts that if any man fails to respect the truce, if there is any brawling in the streets or in the taverns, I shall proceed with merciless severity against the culprits."

Then he turned to the captain of the castle-guard, don Sancho de Avila: "Yours will be the duty to see that runners are sent out in secret on the Dendermonde road with orders that any troops which may be on the way, make all possible speed. You had best remain in command here while I go to Mass: keep your picked guard and the musketeers under arms, for, the moment that the Dendermonde banderas are in sight, we must be ready to co-operate with them by a sortie en masse."

"I quite understand, Magnificence," replied the captain.

A few moments later the bridge was lowered and some three thousand men filed out across it in orderly lines as for parade—but unarmed. The Spanish halberdiers formed the van and the rear-guard, the Walloon pikemen and archers were massed in the centre, and in the midst of them walked the Duke of Alva with his immediate cortège: de Vargas who had his daughter on his arm and Grete close beside her, don Alberic del Rio, Councillor Hessels and two or three other members of the Council. Behind them came the standard-bearers with standards unfurled and the drummers.

In silence they reached the lines of the Orangists, which they had to cross in a double file, each man holding up his hands to show that he was unarmed. The Orangist leaders stood by in a group, and when the Duke and the members of the Council had to file through the lines in their turn, they stepped forward in order to greet them in amity.

"God guard ye!" they said as the Duke walked by.

"We'll aid Him in that," retorted the Spaniards cynically.

Mark van Rycke was in the forefront of the group at the moment that Lenora went by leaning on her father's arm. She looked up just then and saw him. He held his head erect as he always did, but she could not fail to see how completely he had changed in those few hours since last she saw him at Dendermonde. The hours seemed to have gone over him like years: gone was that quaint, gentle, appealing way to which she had so nearly yielded. His attitude now was one of lofty defiance, sublime in its unshakable determination and in its pride. Well! perhaps it was better so! Was he not the embodiment of everything that Lenora had been taught to hate and despise since her tenderest childhood–the despised race that dared to assert itself, the beneficiary who turned on the hand that loaded him with gifts and, above all, the assassin who cowered in the dark, the slave who struck his master whom he dared not defy? Yes! Mark van Rycke, her husband, the murderer of Ramon, stood for all that, and Lenora despised herself for every tender feeling which had gripped her soul in the past two days whenever she thought of him as wounded, helpless, or mayhap dead.

And yet now when his eyes met hers, they suddenly took on a wonderful softness, that quaint look–half-whimsical, half appealing– came back to them and with it too a look of infinite pity and of unswerving love; and as she caught the glance–she who felt so lonely and so desolate–there came to her mind the remembrance of the sweet and pathetic story of the primeval woman who was driven forth by God's angel from the gates of Paradise. Somehow she felt that once–not so very long ago–she too had wandered for a brief while within the peaceful glades of a Paradise of her own, and that now an angel with a flaming sword stood at its gates and would not allow her to return, but forced her to wander out through life in utter loneliness and with the unbearable load of agonising remorse.

II

Of all the episodes which the historical records of the time present to the imagination, not one perhaps is quite so moving and so inspiring as that of the solemn Mass which was offered up in every church of the stricken city on this Sunday morning—the feast of the Holy Redeemer—when the Duke of Alva and the members of his odious Blood Council knelt side by side with the heroic men who were making their last desperate stand for justice, for liberty and the sanctity of their homes.

The Lieutenant-Governor and the Spanish high dignitaries, both civil and military, are present in the Cathedral of St. Baafs, as are also the Orangist leaders. The Spaniards occupy one side of the aisle, the Flemings, with the women and children, are on the other, and crowd every corner of the stately edifice. Up at the high altar, Father van der Schlicht is officiating with others of the cathedral clergy, and the pure voices of the choir boys resound through the building like the call of the angels of peace.

The fabric of the exquisite building bears traces of that awful fate which an abominable tyranny was reserving for the entire city. The walls themselves stand, but in places they are torn by large fissures, which look like gaping wounds in the flesh of a giant. Reverend hands have hastily swept aside the debris of glass and masonry, the fragments of stone statues and scraps of iron and wood; but here and there the head of an angel, the clasped hands of a saint or palm of a martyr, still litter the floor; the slender columns of the aisle have taken on a curious rusty tint, and over the screen the apostles of carved wood are black with smoke.

There are two large holes in the roof, through which the bleak October breeze comes sighing in, and the sweet smell of stale incense which usually hangs about the place of worship has yielded to the pungent odour of charred wood and of singed draperies.

On the Flemish side a dull tone of colour prevails, browns and russets and dull reds—many women have wrapped black hoods over their heads, and long, black mantles hang from their shoulders; but on the other side the fantastic garb of the Spanish halberdiers throws a note of trenchant yellow right through the sombre tint of the picture: and the white ruffs round the men's necks gleam like pale stars upon the canvas. And over it all the light through the broken window falls crude and grey. Only the chancel glows with a warm light, and Father van der Schlicht's vestments of crimson silk, the gilt candlesticks upon the high altar, the flickering yellow flames of the candles, the red cassocks of the young servers, all form a kaleidoscope of brilliant colours which is almost dazzling, whilst up above, the banners and coats-of-arms of the Knights of the Golden Fleece still flaunt their rich heraldic tints against the dark vaulting of the roof, and above the high

190

altar the figure of the Redeemer with arms stretched out to bless, seems to mock by its exquisite pathos and peace the hideous strifes of men.

The church is crowded from end to end: Flemings and Walloons and Spaniards, the tyrants and the oppressed, all kneel together, while Father van der Schlicht up at the altar softly murmurs the Confiteor: some have rough linen bandages round their head or arm; some have ugly stains upon their doublet or hose; others—unable to stand or lean—lie half prone upon the ground, supported by their comrades. The Duke of Alva holds his head erect, and señor de Vargas bows his down until it well-nigh touches the ground: most of the women are crying, some of them faint and have to be carried away. The Spaniards are more demonstrative in their devotions than are the Netherlanders, they strike their breasts at the Confiteor, with wide, ostentatious gestures, and need much elbow room when they make the sign of the Cross.

At the reading of the Gospel every one stands, and men, women and children solemnly make profession of that Faith of Love and Goodwill which the events of the past two days have so wantonly outraged.

Lenora from where she stands can see her husband's head—with its closely-cropped brown hair—towering above the rest of the crowd. He does not look to right or left of him, but gazes fixedly upon the altar; Lenora can see his lips moving as he recites the Creed, and to her straining senses it seems as if right through the murmurings of all these people she can distinguish his voice amongst all the others, and that it strikes against her heart with sweet persistence of unforgettable memories.

And suddenly the high altar with the figure of the Redeemer fades from her sight; the crowds vanish, the priest disappears, the voices of the choir boys are stilled. She is back once more in the small tapperij of the inn at Dendermonde, sitting beside the hearth with Mark—her husband—half kneeling, half sitting close to her—she lives again those few moments of dreamlike peace and joy when he lulled her with gentle words and tender glances which had shown her the first glimpse of what human happiness might be—and she lives again the moment when she stood in that same room with his wounded arm in her hand, and realised that he was the cowardly assassin who had struck Ramon down in the dark.

God in Heaven! was not her hatred of him justified? Even at the foot of this altar, where all should be peace and goodwill, had she not the right to hate this one man who had murdered Ramon, who had fooled and cajoled her, and used her as an insentient tool for his own ends, his own amusement? Her father had told her that she would see him hanged, and that his death would be her work under the guidance of God. Not one moment of the past would she undo, and she regretted nothing save the moments of weakness which came over her whenever she met his glance. He was the leader of these abominable rebels—a leader every inch of him, that she could see—but yet a murderer for all that, and the deadly enemy of her country and her King.

God had had His will with her, and now He was dealing punishment with equal justice to all; and Lenora standing there, shivering under the cold draught which came on her from the shattered roof, yet inwardly burning with a fever of regret and of longing, marvelled, if among the thousands that would suffer through God's retributive justice, any one would endure the martyrdom which she was suffering now.

III

Later on, during the noonday rest, Lenora sat in her room in the Meeste-Toren and tried to visualise once more all that she had lived through in the past hour—her meeting with Mark when she went through the Orangist lines with her father—the crowded church, the sombre colours, the pathetic aspect of broken statuary and holy images charred and shattered—the return to the Kasteel in silence—the outline of Mark's profile above the crowd—Mark! always Mark! If only she could forget!

The air in the narrow room felt stuffy and oppressive: she ordered Grete to open the window. It gave on the same iron balcony to which the council chamber and the apartments of the Duke of Alva had access; but as it was high up in the wall and very small, she could sit quite close beside it and yet not be seen by any one who might be walking on the balcony. Lenora's head ached intolerably, and Grete, always kind and anxious, took down the wavy masses of fair hair and brushed them gently, so as to soothe the quivering nerves.

A strange hush hung in the air—the hush of a Sunday afternoon when a big and peaceful city is at rest—a hush in strange and almost weird contrast to the din which had shaken up the very atmosphere during the past two days. Only from the castle-yard down below there comes the sad sound of groans and sighs of pain, and an occasional call for "donna Lenora!" with the cool, soft hands and the gentle voice, the ministering angel of goodness and consolation.

"Grete," queried Lenora abruptly, "dost love me truly?"

"With my whole heart, noble lady," replied the child simply.

"Then, if thou lovest me, didst pray at Mass this morning for the success of our cause and the confusion of those abominable rebels?"

Grete made no reply, and anon a low, suppressed sob caused Lenora to say, not unkindly:

"Thy heart is with the rebels, Grete."

"I know most of their leaders, noble lady," murmured the girl, through her tears. "They are brave, fine men. When I think of those

192

who surely must die after this, I feel as if my heart must break with sorrow and with pity."

"Didst know them well?"

"Aye, noble lady. They used to come to the 'Three Weavers.'"

"The 'Three Weavers,' Grete?"

"Aye! my father kept the tavern, here in Ghent.... The noble seigniors of the city and the Spanish officers of the garrison all used to come to us in the afternoons.... Messire Jan van Migrode, the Chief Sheriff, Messire Lievin van Deynse and the seigneur de Beauvoir, they all came regularly. And ... and Messire Mark van Rycke," she added under her breath, "him they call Leatherface."

"My husband, Grete," murmured Lenora.

"I know it, noble lady."

"Didst know then that Messire Mark van Rycke was Leatherface?"

"Not till yesterday, noble lady ... not till the men spoke of it and said that the mysterious Leatherface was the leader of the rebels ... and that he was the son of the High-Bailiff of Ghent, Messire Mark van Rycke...."

"Thou didst know him, too, then as Leatherface?"

"Aye, noble lady," said Grete quietly, "he saved my life and my sister's. I would give mine to save him now."

"Saved thy life? How? When?"

"Only a few days ago, noble lady," murmured the child, speaking with a great effort at self-control. The recollection of that awful night brought fresh terror to her heart.

But Lenora's brows contracted now in puzzlement. A few days ago? Mark was courting her then....

"I do not understand," she said impatiently, "a few days ago Leatherface ... Messire Mark van Rycke ... was in Ghent ... I was betrothed to him on the seventh day of this month...."

"And 'tis on that night he saved my life ... and Katrine's ... aye! and saved us from worse than death...."

She paused abruptly; her round, young cheeks lost their last vestige of colour, her eyes their clear, childlike look. She cast a quick, furtive glance on Lenora as if she were, afraid. But Lenora was unconscious of this change in the girl's manner, her very senses seemed to be on the alert, hanging upon the peasant girl's lips.... The night of her betrothal was the night on which Ramon was murdered ... the tavern of the "Three Weavers" was the place where he was found. This girl then knew something of that awesome occurrence, which, despite outside assurances, had remained vaguely puzzling to Lenora's mind. Now she would hear and know, and her very heart seemed to stand still as her mind appeared to be waiting upon the threshold of a mystery which was interwoven with her whole life, and with her every hope of peace.

193

"But what?" she queried with agonised impatience. "Speak, girl! Canst not see that I only live to hear?"

"Our father was taken," said Grete quietly, "he was hanged eight days ago."

"Hanged?" exclaimed Lenora, horror-struck. "Why? What had he done?"

"He was of the Protestant faith ... and..."

Lenora made no comment, and the girl wiped her eyes, which had filled with tears.

"Thou and Katrine were spared?" asked Lenora, after awhile.

"We were spared at the time," said Grete, "but I suppose," she added with quaint philosophy, "we remained objects of suspicion. The soldiers would often be very rough with us, and upon the seventh day of October the commanding Spanish officer in Ghent..."

Once more she paused timidly, fear of having said too much, fighting with the childish love to retail her woes, and pour her interesting story into sympathetic ears.

"Well?" queried Lenora, more impatiently, "go on, child. What did the commanding Spanish officer in Ghent do to thee on the seventh day of October?"

But at this Grete burst into a flood of tears. The events were so recent, and the shock of horror and of fear had been so terrible at the time, that the recollection of it all still had the power to unnerve her. Lenora, whose own nerves were cruelly on the rack at this moment, had much ado to keep her impatience in check. After a few moments Grete became more calm, and dried her eyes.

"There was a big to-do at the Town House," she said more quietly, "and the whole city was gaily decorated. The apprentices had a holiday in the evening. They were very hilarious, and so were the soldiers."

"Well? And—"

"The soldiers came to the 'Three Weavers.' They had been drinking heavily, and were very rough. The commanding Spanish officer came in late in the evening.... He encouraged the soldiers to drink, and to ... to make fun of us ... of Katrine and of me.... We were all alone in the house, and we were very frightened. The Spanish officer ordered Katrine to wait on the soldiers, then he made me go with him to a private room...."

The tears were once more very near the surface, and a hot blush of shame for all that she had had to endure overspread Grete's face and neck.

"Go on, child," queried Lenora. "What happened after that?"

"The Spanish officer was very cruel to me, noble lady. I think he would have killed me, and I am sure the soldiers were very cruel to Katrine.... Oh! it was horrible! horrible!" she cried, "and we were quite alone and helpless...."

"Yes. I know that," said Lenora, and even to herself her own voice sounded curiously dull and toneless; "but tell me what happened."

"I was crouching in a corner of the room, noble lady. My back ached terribly, for I had been thrown across the table, and I thought my spine must be broken—my wrists, too, were very painful where the noble officer had held them so tightly. I was half wild with terror, for I did not know what would become of me. Then the door opened, and a man came in. Oh! I was dreadfully frightened. He was very tall and very thin, like a dark wraith, and over his face he had a mask. And he spoke kindly to me—and after awhile I was less frightened—and then he told me just what to do, how to find Katrine, to take some money and run away to our kinswoman who lives in Dendermonde. I thought then that he was no wraith..." continued Grete in an awestruck whisper, "but just one of the archangels. For they do appear in curious disguises sometimes ... he saved my life and Katrine's, and more than life, noble lady," added the girl with a note of dignity in her tone, which sat quaintly upon her timid little person, "do you not think that it was God who sent him to protect two innocent girls from the cruelty of those wicked men?"

"Yes; I think so, child," said Lenora quietly. "But, tell me, dost know what happened after that?"

"No, lady, I do not. I went to look for Katrine, just as the stranger ordered me to do. But," she added under her breath, and still under the spell of past terrors, "we heard afterwards through Pierre Beauters, the butcher, that the noble seignior commandant was found killed that same night in the tavern of the 'Three Weavers.' The provost found him lying dead in the same room where the archangel had appeared."

"Stabbed, child, didst thou say?"

"No, noble lady. The provost told Pierre Beauters that the noble Spanish commandant had been felled by mighty hands in a hand-to-hand fight; he had no wound on him, only the marks of powerful fingers round his throat. But his own dagger, they say, was covered in blood. Pierre Beauters helped to place the body in the coffin, and he said that the noble Spanish commandant had been killed in fair fight—a fight with fists, and not with swords. He also said that the stranger who killed him was the mysterious Leatherface, of whom we hear so much, and that, mayhap, we should never hear of him again, for the Spanish commandant must have wounded him to death ... the dagger was covered with blood almost to the hilt. But," concluded Grete, with a knowing little nod of the head, "this I did not believe at the time, and now I know that it was not so; the stranger may not have been one of the archangels, but truly he was a messenger of God. When the noble lady brought me back with her to Ghent I heard the men talking about the mysterious Leatherface. Then the day before yesterday when the cavalrymen flew helter-skelter into the castle-yard, they still talked loudly of Leatherface; but I guessed then that he was not a real archangel, but just a brave man who protects the weak, and fights for justice, and..."

She paused, terrified at what she had said. Ignorant as she was, she knew well enough that the few last words which she had uttered had caused men and women to be burned at the stake before now. Wide-eyed and full of fear she looked on the noble Spanish lady, expecting every moment to see a commanding finger pointed on her, and orders given for her immediate arrest.

Instead of which she saw before her a pale, slim girl scarce older than herself, and infinitely more pathetic, just a young and beautiful woman with pale face and eyes swimming in tears, whose whole attitude just expressed an immense and overwhelming grief.

The veil of mystery which had hung over Ramon's death had indeed been lifted at last by the rough, uncouth hands of the innkeeper's daughter. Lenora as yet hardly dared to look into the vista which it opened up before her: boundless remorse, utter hopelessness, the dreary sense of the irreparable—all that lay beyond the present stunning blow of this terrible revelation.

God in Heaven! she cried out mutely in her misery, how could she ever have thought—even for a moment—that those grey eyes, so merry and yet so tender—could mask a treacherous and cowardly soul? How could she think that those lips which so earnestly pleaded for a kiss could ever have been framed to hide a lying tongue? Would to God that she could still persuade herself that all this new revelation was a dream; that Grete—the unsophisticated child—had lied and concocted the whole story to further some hidden schemes of her own! Would to God she could still believe that Mark was vile and false—an assassin and a perjurer—and that she could hate him still!

She met Grete's eyes fixed so fearfully upon hers—she met them at the moment when she was about to give herself over to the transient happiness of a brief day-dream ... dreams of two unforgettable hours when he sat beside her with his hand shading his face ... his eyes resting upon her ... dreams of his voice when he said: "When I look at you, Madonna, I invariably think of happiness."

IV

But Grete recalled her to herself, and to the awful present. Despite her great respect for the noble Spanish lady, she suddenly put her arms round her shoulders, and tried to draw her away from the open window.

"His Highness!" she whispered hurriedly, "he will see us."

"What matters, child," murmured Lenora, "he will not harm us."

Instinctively, however, she did yield to Grete's insistence and

196

drew back slightly from the window. From the balcony down below there came the sound of measured tramping. Two or three men were walking there slowly up and down and talking confidentially together while they walked. Whenever they were close to the window their voices came up quite distinctly, but it was impossible to hear all that they said, but one or two disjointed sentences gave a faint clue to the subject of their conversation. Lenora now leaned closer to the window-frame trying to hear, for she had recognised her father's voice as well as that of the Duke of Alva, and they were speaking of their future plans against the rebels and against the city, and Lenora felt that she would give her life to know what those plans were.

After a moment or two she heard the voice of Captain de Avila; he was apparently coming up the iron stairs from the yard and was speaking hurriedly:

"A runner, your Highness," he said, "straight from Dendermonde."

"What news?" queried the Duke, and his voice sounded almost choked as if with fierce impatience.

"One of Captain Lodrono's messengers reached Dendermonde last night," replied de Avila, "he was lucky enough to get a horse almost at once."

"Well...? and...?"

"This man came running straight back to bring us the news! Captain Bracamonte started at break of day: he should be well on his way with the reinforcements by now."

There was a hoarse exclamation of satisfaction and a confused murmur of voices for a moment or two. Then de Vargas spoke:

"It was a bold venture, Monseigneur," he said.

"This truce, you mean?" retorted Alva. "Well! not quite so bold as it appeared. Those Netherlanders are such mighty fools that it is always easy to make them believe anything that we choose to tell them: do they not always fall into our traps? I had only to swear by my immortal soul that we had not sent for reinforcements and the last of their resistance was overcome."

Lenora could hear her father's harsh laugh after this and then del Rio said blandly:

"Van Rycke did not believe in that oath."

"Perhaps not at first," Alva said, "but it was so finely worded and spoken with such solemnity, it was bound to carry conviction in the end."

"You were not afraid, Monseigneur," queried de Vargas, "this morning ... in the crowd ... after Mass ... that the rebels would break the truce and fall upon our men?"

"No," replied the Duke curtly, "were you?"

There came no answer from de Vargas, and to the listeners it seemed as if by his silence he was admitting that he did not believe the

197

Orangists capable of such abominable treachery. A fine tribute that—Lenora thought—from her father who hated and despised the Netherlanders! But he and Alva would even now call such loyalty and truth the mere stupidity of uncultured clowns.

"Anyhow it was worth the risk," de Vargas resumed after awhile, with that cold cynicism which will sacrifice friends, adherents, kindred for the furtherance of political aims.

"Well worth the risk," asserted Alva, "we have gained the whole of to-day. If these rebels had rushed the Kasteel this morning, I verily believe that we could not have held it: I might have fallen into their hands and—with me as their hostage—they would by now have been in a position to dictate their own terms before reinforcements reached us—always supposing that they did not murder us all. Yes," he reiterated with obvious satisfaction, "even if treachery had been in the air it was still well worth the risk."

"And in the meanwhile..." suggested del Rio.

"In the meanwhile Bracamonte is on his way here.... He must have started well before noon ... he might be here before nightfall...."

"With at least five thousand men, I hope," added de Vargas.

"Night may see us masters of this city once more, seigniors," rejoined Alva, "and by God we'll punish those rebels for the fright they have given us. Ghent will be envying Mons and Mechlin...."

The three men walked slowly away after that, and their voices were lost in the distance. The listeners could no longer distinguish what was said, but anon a harsh laugh struck their ear, and leaning out of the window Lenora could see the Duke and her father standing just outside the council-chamber. The Duke had thrown back his head and was laughing heartily, de Vargas too looked highly amused. Not one single word of remorse or regret had been spoken by either of them for the blasphemous oath which had finally overcome the resistance of the Orangists: of a truth it did not weigh on the conscience of the man who had so wantonly outraged his Maker less than an hour before he knelt at the foot of His Altar, and de Vargas and his kind were only too ready to benefit by the perjury.

The sack of Ghent—jeopardised for a few hours—was once more looming ahead as a coveted prize. What was a false oath or so—one crime the more—when weighed in the balance with all the money and treasure which the unexpected resistance of a few Flemish clowns had so nearly wrenched from these noble Spaniards' grasp?

V

"Didst hear?" came in a smothered whisper from Lenora. She had turned suddenly and now faced Grete, who stood wide-eyed and terrified in the centre of the room. Her arms were behind her, and she clung to the window-ledge: her fair hair—all loose—streamed round her shoulders; pale, with glowing eyes and quivering lips, she looked like some beautiful feline creature at bay.

"Didst hear?" she reiterated hoarsely.

"Every word, most noble lady," came the whispered response.

"What didst make of it?"

"That His Highness sent to Dendermonde for help, and that troops are on their way."

"But His Highness swore most solemnly that he would respect the truce which he himself asked for, and that both sides would resume the fight ... this evening ... just as they were before ... without fresh help or reinforcements."

"I heard the men say last night, noble lady, that reinforcements had already been sent for from Dendermonde ... the Duke feared that the Netherlanders were getting the upper hand ... he asked for the truce only to gain time...."

"Then ... if Captain Bracamonte arrives from Dendermonde with fresh troops the Netherlanders are lost!"

"God guard them," said Grete fervently. "He alone can save them now."

"Oh!" cried Lenora with sudden passionate bitterness, "how can men conceive such abominable treachery? How can God allow them to triumph?"

Grete said nothing. Her eyes were full of tears. Lenora stared straight out before her into the dark corner of the room: there was a frown of deep thought between her brows, and her fresh young mouth became hard and set.

"Grete," she said abruptly, "is it not horrible to think that those we care for are liars and traitors?"

Then, as Grete made no reply, she continued with the same passionate vehemence: "Is it not horrible to think that brave men must be butchered like cattle, because they trusted in the oath of a perjurer? ... Oh! that all the baseness, all the lying should be on one side and all the heroism on the other! and that God should allow those monsters to triumph!..."

She paused and suddenly her whole expression changed—the vehemence, the passion went out of it ... her lips ceased to quiver, a curious pallor overspread her cheeks and the lines of her mouth became hard and set.

"Grete," she said abruptly, "art afraid?"

"Of what, noble lady?" asked the child.

"Oh! of everything ... of insults and violence and death?"

"No, noble lady," said Grete simply. "I trust to God to protect me."

"Then wilt come with me?"

199

"Whither, noble lady?"

"Into the city ... alone with me ... we'll pretend that we go to Benediction...."

"Into the city...?" exclaimed the girl. "Alone?"

"Art afraid?"

"No."

"Then put up my hair and get hood and cloak and give me mine...."

Grete did as she was ordered. She pinned up Lenora's fair hair and brought her a mantle and hood and wrapped them round her: then she fastened on her own.

"Come!" said Lenora curtly.

She took the girl by the hand and together the two women went out of the room. Their way led them through endless corridors and down a long, winding staircase; hand in hand they ran like furtive little animals on the watch for the human enemy. Down below the big flagged hall was full of soldiers: the two women only realised this when they reached the last landing.

"Will they let us pass?" murmured Grete.

"Walk beside me and hold thy head boldly," said Lenora, "they must not think that we are afraid of being challenged."

She walked down the last flight of the stairs with slow majestic steps: her arms folded beneath her cloak, looking straight ahead of her with that air of calm detachment and contempt of others which the Spanish noblesse knew so well how to assume.

Captain de Avila was below: at sight of donna Lenora he came forward and said with absolute respect:

"La señora desires to go out?"

"As you see," she replied haughtily.

"Not further than the precincts of the Kasteel, I hope."

"What is that to you, whither I go?" she queried.

"My orders..." he stammered, somewhat taken aback by this grand manner on the part of the señora who had always been so meek and silent hitherto.

"What orders have you had, seigneur capitaine?" she queried, "which warrant your interference with my movements?"

"I ... truly..." he murmured, "señor de Vargas..."

"My father, I presume, has not given you the right to question my freedom to go and come as I please," she retorted, still with the same uncompromising hauteur.

"No ... but..."

"Then I pray you let me pass.... I hear the bells of St. Pharaïlde ... I shall be late for Benediction...."

She swept past him, leaving him not a little bewildered and completely abashed. He watched her tall, graceful figure as she sailed through the portico and thence across the castle-yard, then he shrugged his shoulders as if to cast aside any feeling of responsibility which threatened to worry him, and returned to the guard-room and to his game of hazard. It was only then that he recollected that it lacked another two hours to Benediction yet.

In the yard Lenora had more serious misgivings.

"There's the guard at the gate-house," she murmured. "Keep up thy look of unconcern, Grete. We can only win if we are bold."

As she anticipated the provost at the gate-house challenged her.

"I go to St. Pharaïlde," she said calmly, "my father is with me. He hath stopped to speak with Captain de Avila. Lower the bridge, provost, and let us pass. We are late enough for Benediction as it is."

The provost hesitated for a moment.

"The seigneur capitaine sent me orders just now that no one was to leave the Kasteel," he said.

"Am I under the seigneur capitaine's orders," she retorted, "or the daughter of señor de Vargas, who will punish thee, sirrah, for thine insolence?"

The provost, much disturbed in his mind, had not the courage to run counter to the noble lady's wish. He had had no orders with regard to her, and as she very rightly said, she was not under the orders of the seigneur capitaine.

He ordered the bridge to be lowered for her, vaguely intending not to let her pass until he assured himself that señor de Vargas was nigh: but Lenora gave him no time for reflection: she waited until the bridge was down, then suddenly she seized Grete's hand and quick as a young hare she darted past the provost and the guard before they thought of laying hands on her, and she was across the bridge before they had recovered from their surprise.

Once on the open ground Lenora drew breath. The provost and the guard could not very well run after her, and for the moment she was safe from pursuit. On ahead lay the sharp bend of the Lower Schelde, beyond it the ruined mass of the Vleeshhuis, and the row of houses, now all shattered to pieces, where the Orangists held their watch. Her heart was beating furiously, and she felt Grete's rough little hand quivering in hers. She felt such a tiny atom, a mere speck in this wide open space. In front of her was the city, which seemed even in the silence of this Sunday afternoon to be quivering in the throes of oncoming death: to right and left of her the great tract of flat country, this land of Belgium which she had not yet learned to love but for which she now felt a wonderful pity.

It was a rude lesson which she had been made to learn within the last hour: the lesson that the idols of her childhood and girlhood had not only feet of clay but that they were steeped to the neck in the mire of falsehoods and treachery: she had also learned that the man whom she had once hated with such passionate bitterness was worthy of a pure woman's love: that happiness had knocked at the gateway of her own heart and been refused admittance: and that God was not wont to give very obvious guidance in the terrible perplexities which at times beset His creatures.

Therefore now she no longer lured herself with the belief that she was acting at this moment under the direct will of God, she knew that she was guided by an overmastering and blind instinct which told her that she must see Mark—at once—and warn him that the perfidy of the Duke of Alva had set a deathly trap for him and for his friends.

A few more minutes and she and Grete were over the Ketel Brüghe and under the shadow of the tall houses on the river embankment beyond.

"Take me!" she said to Grete peremptorily, "to the house of the High-Bailiff of Ghent."

CHAPTER XVIII

THE LAST STAND

I

The word has gone round, we must all assemble in the cathedral church—every burgher, every artisan, every apprentice who belongs by blood to Ghent must for the nonce cast aside pick and shovel: the dead can wait! the living claim attention.

Quite a different crowd from that which knelt at prayer this morning! It is just two o'clock and the sacred edifice is thronged: up in the galleries, the aisles, the chancel, the organ loft, the pulpit, everywhere there are men—young and old—men who for two days now have been face to face with death and who wear on their grim faces the traces of the past fierce struggle and of the coming cataclysm. There are no women present. They have nobly taken on the task of the men, and the dainty burghers' wives who used to spend their time at music or needlework, wield the spade to-day with as much power as their strength allows.

Perfect order reigns despite the magnitude of the crowd: those who found no place inside the building, throng the cemetery and the precincts. Behind the high altar the Orangist standard is unfurled, and in front of the altar rails stand the men who have fought in the forefront of the insurgents' ranks, who have led every assault, affronted every danger, braved musket fire and arrow-shot and burning buildings and crumbling ruins, the men who have endured and encouraged and cheered: Mark van Rycke the popular leader, Laurence his brother, Pierre Deynoot, Lievin van Deynse, Frédéric van Beveren and Jan van Migrode, who is seriously wounded but who has risen from his sick bed and crawled hither in order to add the weight of his counsel and of his enthusiasm to what he knows van Rycke will propose.

Yes! they are there, all those that are left! and with them are the older burghers, the civic dignitaries of their city, the Sheriffs of the Keure, the aldermen, the vroedschappen, the magistrates, and the High-Bailiff himself–he who is known to be such a hot adherent of Alva.

It is he who has convened this meeting–a general rally of the citizens of Ghent. He called them together by roll of drums and by word of mouth transmitted by volunteer messengers who have flown all over the town. This morning we spent in prayer–to-day is a day of peace–let us meet and talk things over, for if wisdom waits upon enthusiasm, all is not lost yet. The proposal has come from the High-Bailiff, at the hour of noon when men only thought of the grim work of burying the dead, and women wandered through the streets to search for the loved one who has been missing since yesterday.

But at the word of the High-Bailiff the men laid aside their picks and spades. If all is not lost, why then there's something still to do and–the dead must wait.

And every man goes to the cathedral church to hear what the High-Bailiff has to say: the church and precincts are crowded. In silence every one listens whilst he speaks. He has always been a faithful subject of King Philip, an obedient servant of the Regent and the Lieutenant-Governor: his influence and well-known adherence to the King has saved the city many a time from serious reprisals against incipient revolt and from many of the horrors of the Inquisition. Now, while up there in the Kasteel Alva impatiently awaits the arrival of fresh troops which will help to crush the rebellious city, the High-Bailiff pleads for submission.

He has faith in the human tiger.

"Let us throw ourselves at his feet," he urges, "he is a brave soldier, a great warrior. He will respect your valorous resistance if he sees that in the hour when you have the advantage over him you are prepared to give in, and to throw yourselves upon his mercy. Let us go– we who are older and wiser–let those who have led this unfortunate revolt keep out of the way–I will find the right words I know to melt the heart of our Lieutenant-Governor now turned in wrath against us–let us go and cry for mercy and, by God, I believe that we shall get it."

Like the waves upon the sea, the crowd in the church moves and oscillates: murmurs of assent and dissent mingle from end to end, from side to side: "No!–Yes!–'Twere shameful!–'Twere wise!–There are the women to think of!—And the children!—He will not listen!—Why this purposeless abasement?"

Van Rycke and the other leaders make no comment upon the High-Bailiff's appeal—even though their whole soul revolts at the thought of this fresh humiliation to be endured by the burghers of Ghent, once so proud and so independent! But they won't speak! Mark knows that with one word he can sway the whole of this crowd. They are heroes all—every one of these men. At one word from him they will cast aside every thought save that of the renewed fight—the final fight to the death—they are seething with enthusiasm, their blood is up and prudence and wisdom have to be drilled into them now that they have tasted of the martyr's cup.

You can hear Father van der Schlicht's voice now. He too is for humility and an appeal for mercy on this the festival day of the Holy Redeemer. The Lieutenant-Governor is a pious man and a good Catholic. The appeal is sure to please his ears. Oh! the virtues that adorn the Duke of Alva in the estimation of his adherents! He is pious and he is brave! a good Catholic and a fine soldier! mercy in him is allied to wisdom! he will easily perceive that to gain the gratitude of the citizens of Ghent would be more profitable to him than the destruction of a prosperous city. See this truce which he himself suggested: was it not the product of a merciful and a religious mind? To pray in peace, to obey the dictates of the Church, to give the enemy the chance of burying the dead!—were these not the sentiments of a good and pious man?

Messire Henri de Buck, senior Schepen and Judge of the High Court, has many tales to tell of the kindness and generosity of the Duke. Oh! they are very eloquent, these wealthy burghers who have so much more to lose by this revolt than mere honour and mere life!

And the others listen! Oh yes! they listen! need a stone be left unturned? and since Messire the High-Bailiff hath belief in his own eloquence, why! let him exercise it of course. Not that there is one whit less determination in any single man in the crowd! If the High-Bailiff fails in his mission, they will fight to the last man still, but ... oh! who can shut his heart altogether against hope? And there are the women and the children ... and all those who are old and feeble.

God speed to you then, my Lord High-Bailiff—Charles van Rycke, the pusillanimous father of a gallant son! God speed to all of you who go to plead with a tiger to spare the prey which he already holds between his claws! The High-Bailiff will go and with him Father van der Schlicht and Father Laurent Toch from St. Agneten, and Messire de Buck and François de Wetteren: all the men who two days ago were kneeling in the mud at the tyrant's feet, and presented him so humbly with the gates of the city which he had sworn to destroy. There is no cheering as they detach themselves from the group of the rebel leaders who still stand somewhat apart, leaving the crowd to have its will.

204

No cheering, it is all done in silence! Men do not cheer on the eve of being butchered; they only look on their standard up above the high altar behind the carved figure of the Redeemer, and though they have given silent consent for this deputation to the tyrant they still murmur in their hearts: "For Orange and Liberty!"

Jan van Migrode, weak and ill from his wound, has had the last word. He begs that every one should wait–here–just as they are ... in silence and patience ... until the High-Bailiff and his friends come back with the news ... good or bad! peace or renewed fighting–life or death!– whichever it is they must all be together in order to decide.

Just at the last the High-Bailiff turns to his son.

"You do not approve of our going, Mark?" he asks with some diffidence.

"I think that it is purposeless," replies Mark; "you cannot extract blood out of a stone, or mercy out of the heart of a brute!"

II

They go, the once proud burghers of the city of Ghent, they go to throw themselves for the last time at the feet of that monster of tyranny and cruelty who even at this hour is gloating over the thought of the most deadly reprisals he hath ever dealt to these down-trodden people.

They go with grave yet hopeful faces, in their dark robes which are the outward sign of the humility, the loyalty which dwell in their hearts. The crowd have wished them God speed! and as they file out of the stately cathedral and through the close, the men stand respectfully aside and eye them with a trustful regard which is infinitely pathetic. Their leaders have remained beside the altar rails, grouped together, talking quietly among themselves: Mark van Rycke, however, goes to mingle with the crowd, to speak with all those who desire a word with him, with the men whose heart is sore at the humiliation which they are forced to swallow, who would sooner have died than see the dignitaries of their city go once again as suppliants before that execrable tyrant whom they loathe.

"What is thine idea, van Rycke?" most of the men ask him as they crowd around him, anxious to hear one word of encouragement or of hope. "Dost think the tyrant will relent?"

"Not unless we hold him as he holds us–not unless we have him at our mercy."

"Then what can we do? what can we do?"

"Do?" he reiterates for the hundredth time to-day, "do? Fight to the last man, die to the last man, until God, wearied of the tyrant's obstinacy, will crush him and give us grace."

"But we cannot win in the end."

"No! but we can die as we have lived, clean, undaunted, unconquered."

"But our wives, our daughters?"

"Ask them," he retorts boldly. "It is not the women who would lick the tyrant's shoes."

The hour drags wearily on. In imagination every one inside and around the cathedral follows the burghers on their weary pilgrimage. Half an hour to walk to the Kasteel, half an hour for the audience with the Duke, half an hour to return ... unforeseen delay in obtaining admittance ... it may be two hours before they return. Great many of the men have returned to the gloomy task of burying the dead, others to that of clearing the streets from the litter which encumbers them: but even those who work the hardest keep their attention fixed upon the cathedral and its approach.

Van Rycke had suggested that the great bell be rung when the burghers came back with the Duke's answer, so that all who wished could come and hear.

III

And now the answer has come.

The High-Bailiff has returned with Fathers van der Schlicht and Laurent Toch, with Aldermen de Buck and de Wetteren and with the others. They have walked back from the Kasteel bareheaded and shoeless with their hands tied behind their back, and a rope around their neck.

That was the Duke of Alva's answer to the deputation of Flemish patricians and burghers who had presented themselves before him in order to sue for his mercy. They had not even been admitted into his presence. The provost at the gate-house had curtly demanded their business, had then taken their message to the Duke, and returned five minutes later with orders to "send back the beggars whence they came, bareheaded and shoeless and with a rope around their necks in token of the only mercy which they might expect from him!"

The bridge had been lowered for them when they arrived, but they were kept parleying with a provost at the gate-house: not a single officer—even of lower rank—deigned to come out to speak with them; the yard was filled with soldiers who insulted and jeered at them: the High-Bailiff was hit on the cheek by a stone which had been aimed at him, and Father Laurent Toch's soutane was almost torn off his back. Every one of them had suffered violence at the hands of the soldiery whilst the Duke's abominable orders were being carried out with appalling brutality: every one of them was bleeding from a cut or a

206

blow dealt by that infamous crowd who were not ashamed thus to maltreat defenceless and elderly men.

When they crossed the open tract of country between the castle moat and the Schelde a shower of caked mud was hurled after them from the ramparts; not a single insult was spared them, not a sting to their pride, not a crown to their humiliation. It was only when they reached the shelter of the streets that they found some peace. In silence they made their way toward the cathedral. The crowds of men and women at work amongst the dead and the wounded made way for them to allow them to pass, but no one questioned them: the abject condition in which they returned told its own pitiable tale.

The cathedral bell had tolled, and from everywhere the men came back to hear the full account of the miserable mission. The crowd was dense and not every one had a view of the burghers as they stood beside the altar rail in all their humiliation, but those who were nearest told their neighbours and soon every one knew what had happened.

The younger leaders ground their heels into the floor, and Jan van Migrode, sick and weak as he was, was the first to stand up and to ask the citizens of Ghent if the events of to-day had shaken them in their resolve.

"You know now what to expect from that fiend. Will you still die like heroes, or be slaughtered like cattle?" he called out loudly ere he fell back exhausted and faint.

Horror had kept every one dumb until then, and grim resolve did not break into loud enthusiasm now, but on the fringe of the crowd there were a number of young men—artisans and apprentices—who at first sight of the returned messengers had loudly murmured and cursed. Now one of them lifted up his voice. It raised strange echoes in the mutilated church.

"We are ready enough to die," he said, "and we'll fight to the end, never fear. But before the last of us is killed, before that execrable tyrant has his triumph over us, lads of Ghent, I ask you are we not to have our revenge?"

"Yes! yes!" came from a number of voices, still from the fringe of the crowd where the young artisans were massed together, "well spoken, Peter Balde! let us have revenge first!"

"Revenge! Revenge!" echoed from those same ranks.

Every word echoed from pillar to pillar in the great, bare, crowded church; and now it was from the altar rails that Mark van Rycke's voice rang out clear and firm:

"What revenge dost propose to take, Peter Balde?" he asked.

The other, thus directly challenged by the man whose influence was paramount in Ghent just now, looked round at his friends for approval. Seeing nothing but eager, flushed faces and eyes that glowed in response to his suggestion, the pride of leadership entered his soul. He was a fine, tall lad who yesterday had done prodigies of valour against the Spanish cavalry. Now he had been gesticulating with both arms above his head so that he was easily distinguishable in the crowd by those who had a clear view, and in order to emphasize his spokesmanship his friends hoisted him upon their shoulders and bearing him aloft they forged their way through the throng until they reached the centre of the main aisle. Here they paused, and Peter Balde could sweep the entire crowd with his enthusiastic glance.

"What I revenge would take?" he said boldly. "Nay! let me rather ask: what revenge must we take, citizens of Ghent? The tyrant even now has abused the most sacred laws of humanity which bid every man to respect the messengers of peace. He is disloyal and ignoble and false. Why should we be honourable and just? He neither appreciates our loyalty nor respects our valour—let us then act in the only way which he can understand. Citizens, we have two thousand prisoners in the cellars of our guildhouses—two thousand Walloons who under the banner of our common tyrant have fought against us ... their nearest kindred. I propose that we kill those two thousand prisoners and send their heads to the tyrant as a direct answer to this last outrage."

"Yes! yes! Well said!" came from every side, from the younger artisans and the apprentices, the hot-headed faction amongst all these brave men—brave themselves but writhing under the terrible humiliation which they had just endured and thirsting for anything that savoured of revenge.

"Yes! yes! the axe for them! send their heads to the tyrant! Well spoken, Peter Balde," they cried.

The others remained silent. Many even amongst the older men perhaps would have echoed the younger ones' call: cruelty breeds cruelty and oppression breeds callous thoughts of revenge. Individually there was hardly a man there who was capable of such an act of atrocious barbarism as the murder of a defenceless prisoner, but for years now these people had groaned under such abominable tyranny, had seen such acts of wanton outrage perpetrated against them and all those they held dear, that—collectively—their sense of rightful retribution had been warped and they had imbibed some of the lessons of reprisals from their execrable masters.

At the foot of the altar rails the group of leaders who stood as a phalanx around Mark van Rycke their chief, waited quietly whilst the wave of enthusiasm for Balde's proposal rose and swelled and mounted higher and higher until it seemed to pervade the whole of the sacred edifice, and then gradually subsided into more restrained if not less enthusiastic determination.

"We will do it," said one of Balde's most fervent adherents. "It is only justice, and it is the only law which the tyrant understands—the law of might."

"It is the law which he himself has taught us," said another, "the law of retributive justice."

"The law of treachery, of rapine, and of outrage," now broke in Mark's firm, clear voice once more; it rose above the tumult, above the hubbub which centred round the person of Peter Balde; it rang against the pillars and echoed from end to end of the aisle. "Are we miserable rabble that we even dream of murder?"

"Not of murder," cried Balde in challenge, "only of vengeance!"

"Your vengeance!" thundered Mark, "do you dare speak of it in the house of Him who says 'I will repay!'"

"God is on our side, He will forgive!" cried some of them.

"Everything, except outrage! ... what you propose is a deed worthy only of hell!"

"No! no! Balde is right! Magnanimity has had its day! But for this truce to-day who knows? we might have been masters of the Kasteel!"

"Will the murdering of helpless prisoners aid your cause, then?"

"It will at least satisfy our craving for revenge!"

"Right, right, Balde!" they all exclaimed, "do not heed what van Rycke says."

"We will fight to-morrow!"

"Die to-morrow!" they cried.

"And blacken your souls to-day!" retorted Mark.

The tumult grew more wild. Dissension had begun to sow its ugly seed among these men whom a common danger, united heroism, and courage had knit so closely together. The grim, silent, majestic determination of a while ago was giving place slowly to rabid, frenzied calls of hatred, to ugly oaths, glowing eyes and faces heated with passion. The presence of the dozen elderly patricians and burghers still bare-headed and shoeless, still with the rope around their necks, helped to fan up the passions which their misfortunes had aroused. For the moment, however, the hot-headed malcontents were still greatly in the minority, but the danger of dissent, of mutiny was there, and the set expression on the faces of the leaders, the stern look in Mark van Rycke's eyes testified that they were conscious of its presence.

IV

Then it was that right through this tumult which had spread from the building itself to the precincts and even beyond, a woman's cry rang out with appalling clearness. It was not a cry of terror, rather one of command, but so piercing was it that for the moment every other cry was stilled: Peter Balde's adherents were silenced, and suddenly over this vast assembly, wherein but a few seconds ago passions ran riot, there fell a hush—a tension of every nerve, a momentary lull of every heart-beat as with the prescience of something momentous to which that woman's cry was only the presage.

209

And in the midst of that sudden hush the cry was heard again—more clearly this time and closer to the cathedral porch, so that the words came quite distinctly:

"Let me get to him ... take me to your leader ... I must speak with him at once!"

And like distant thunder, the clamour rose again: men and women shouted and called; the words: "Spaniard!" and "Spy!" were easily distinguishable: the crowd could be seen to sway, to be moving like a huge wave, all in one direction toward the porch: hundreds of faces showed plainly in the dull grey light as necks were craned to catch a glimpse of the woman who had screamed.

But evidently with but rare exceptions the crowd was not hostile: those who had cried out the word "Spy!" were obviously in the minority. With death looming so near, with deadly danger to every woman in the city within sight, every instinct of chivalry toward the weak was at its greatest height. Those inside the cathedral could see that the crowd was parting in order to let two women move along, and that the men in the forefront elbowed a way for them so that they should not be hindered on their way. It was the taller of the two women who had uttered the piteous yet commanding appeal: "Let me go to him!—take me to your leader!—I must speak with him!"

She reiterated that appeal now—at the south porch to which she had been literally carried by the crowd outside: and here suddenly three stalwart men belonging to one of the city guilds took, as it were, possession of her and her companion and with vigorous play of elbows and of staves forged a way for them both right up to the altar rails. Even whilst in the west end of the church the enthusiastic tumult around Peter Balde which this fresh incident had momentarily stilled, arose with renewed vigour, and the young artisans and apprentices once more took up their cry: "Revenge! Death to all the prisoners!" the woman, who was wrapped up in a long black mantle and hood, fell—panting, exhausted, breathless—almost at Mark van Rycke's feet and murmured hoarsely:

"Five thousand troops are on their way to Ghent ... they will be here within two hours ... save yourselves if you can."

Her voice hardly rose above a whisper. Mark alone heard every word she said; he stooped and placing two fingers under her chin, with a quick and firm gesture he lifted up the woman's head, so that her hood fell back and the light from the east window struck full upon her face and her golden hair.

"I come straight from the Kasteel," she said, more clearly now, for she was gradually recovering her breath, "let your friends kill me if they will ... the Duke of Alva swore a false oath ... a messenger left even last night for Dendermonde...."

"How do you know this?" queried Mark quietly.

"Grete and I heard the Duke speak of it all with my father just now," she replied. "He asked for the truce in order to gain time.... He hopes that the troops from Dendermonde will be here before nightfall ... the guards at the gate-houses are under arms, and three thousand men are inside the Kasteel ready to rush out the moment the troops are in sight."

It was impossible to doubt her story. Those who stood nearest to her passed it on to their neighbours, and the news travelled like wild-fire from end to end of the church: "They are on us! Five thousand Spaniards from Dendermonde to annihilate us all!"

"God have mercy on our souls!"

"God have mercy on our women and children!"

Panic seized a great many there; they pushed and scrambled out of the building, running blindly like sheep, and spread the terrible news through the streets, calling loudly to God to save them all: the panic very naturally spread to the women and children who thronged the streets at this hour, and to the silent workers who had quietly continued their work of burial. Soon all the market squares were filled with shrieking men, women and children who ran about aimlessly with wild gestures and cries of lamentation. Those who had kept indoors all to-day—either fearing the crowds or piously preparing for death—came rushing out to see what new calamity was threatening them, or whether the supreme hour had indeed struck for them all.

Inside the cathedral the cries of revenge were stilled; dulled was the lust to kill. The immense danger which had been forgotten for a moment in that frantic thirst for revenge made its deathly presence felt once more. Pallid faces and wide-open, terror-filled eyes were turned toward the one man whose personality seemed still to radiate the one great ray of hope.

But just for a moment Mark van Rycke seemed quite oblivious of that wave of sighs and fears which tended toward him now and swept all thought of mutiny away.

He was supporting Lenora who was gradually regaining strength and consciousness: just for a few seconds he allowed tumult and terror to seethe unheeded around him: just for those few seconds he forgot death and danger, his friends, the world, everything save that Lenora had come to him at the hour when his heart yearned for her more passionately than ever before, and that she was looking up into his face with eyes that told so plainly the whole extent of her love for him.

Only a few seconds, then he handed her over to the gentle care of Father van der Schlicht, but as with infinite gentleness he finally released himself from her clinging arms he murmured in her ear: "God reward you, Madonna! With your love as my shield, I feel that I could conquer the universe."

Then he faced the terror-stricken crowd once more.

211

V

"Burghers and artisans of Ghent," he called loudly, "we have two hours before us. The perjured tyrant is bringing five thousand fresh troops against us. If by nightfall we have not conquered, our city is doomed and all of us who have survived, and all our women and children will be slaughtered like sheep."

"To arms!" cried the leaders: Jan van Migrode and Lievin van Deynse, Pierre Deynoot and the others.

"To arms!" was echoed by a goodly number of the crowd.

But a great many were silent—despair had gripped them with its icy talon—the hopelessness of it all had damped their enthusiasm.

"Five thousand fresh troops," they murmured, "and there are less than four thousand of us all told."

"We cannot conquer," came from Peter Balde's friends at the west end of the church, "let us at least take our revenge!"

"Yes! Revenge! Death to the Walloons!" they cried.

"Revenge! yes!" exclaimed Mark van Rycke. "Let us be revenged on the liar, the tyrant, the perjurer, let us show him no mercy and extort from him by brute force that which he has refused us all these years—civil and religious freedom."

"Van Rycke, thou art raving!" broke in the men who stood nearest to him—some of them his most ardent supporters. "Alva by nightfall will have three times the numbers we have. The gates will be opened to his fresh troops."

"We must seize the Kasteel and the gates before then!" he retorted.

"How can we? We made several assaults yesterday. We have not enough men."

"We have half an hour wherein to increase their numbers."

"Thou art raving," they cried.

"Not one able-bodied man but was fighting yesterday—not half their number knew how to handle pike or lance, musket or crossbow."

"Then we must find two thousand men who are trained soldiers and know all that there is to know about fighting. That would make it a two to one fight. Burghers of Ghent, which one of you cannot account for two Spaniards when the lives of your women and your children depend on the strength of your arm?"

"Two thousand men?" The cry came from everywhere—cry of doubt, of hope, of irony or of defiance.

"How are we to get them? Where can we get them from?"

"Come with me and I'll show you!" retorts Mark and he immediately makes for the door.

The other leaders stick close to him as one man, as do all those who have been standing near the altar rails and those who saw him even when first he turned to them all, with eyes glowing with the fire of

212

the most ardent patriotism, with the determination to die if need be, but by God! to try and conquer first!

It was only those who were in the rear of the crowd or in the side aisles who did not come immediately under the spell of that magnetic personality, of that burning enthusiasm which from its lexicon had erased the word "Failure!" but even they were carried off their feet by the human wave which now swept out of the cathedral–by the south door–bearing upon it the group of rebel leaders with Mark's broad shoulders and closely cropped head towering above the others.

The throng was soon swelled to huge proportions by all those who had been hanging about in the precincts all the afternoon unable to push their way into the crowded edifice. The tumult and the clamour which they made–added to the cries of those who were running in terror through the streets–made a pandemonium of sounds which was almost hellish in its awful suggestion of terror, of confusion and of misery.

But those who still believed in the help of God, those in whom faith in the justice of their cause was allied with the sublime determination of martyrs were content to follow their hero blindly–vaguely marvelling what his purpose could be–whilst the malcontents in the rear, rallying round Peter Balde once more began to murmur of death and of revenge!

Mark led the crowd across the wide cathedral square to the guild-house of the armourers–the fine building with the tall, crow-step gables and the magnificent carved portico to which a double flight of fifteen stone steps and wrought-iron balustrade gave access. He ran up the steps and stood with his back to the portico fronting the crowd. Every one could see him now, from the remotest corners of the square–many had invaded the houses round, and heads appeared at all the windows.

"Burghers of Ghent," he called aloud, "we have to conquer or we must die. There are less than four thousand of us at this moment fit to bear arms against Alva's hordes which still number seven. Five thousand more of them are on their way to complete the destruction of our city, to murder our wives and our children, and to desecrate our homes. We want two thousand well-trained soldiers to oppose them and inflict on the tyrant such a defeat as will force him to grant us all that we fight for: Liberty!"

"How wilt do that, friend of the leather mask?" queried some of the men ironically.

"How wilt find two thousand well-trained soldiers?"

"Follow me, and I will show you."

He turned and went into the building, the whole crowd following him as one man. The huge vaulted hall of the guild-house was filled in every corner with Walloon prisoners–the fruit of the first day's victory. They were lying or sitting about the floor, some of them playing hazard with scraps of leather cut from their belts; others watched them, or merely stared straight in front of them, with a sullen look of hopelessness: they were the ones who had wives and children at home, or merely who had served some time under Alva's banner and had learned from him how prisoners should be treated. When the leaders of the insurrection with Mark van Rycke at their head made irruption into the hall followed by a tumultuous throng, the Walloons, as if moved by a blind instinct, threw aside their games and all retreated to the furthest end of the hall, like a phalanx of frightened men who have not even the power to sell their lives. Many of those who had rushed in, in Mark's wake, were the malcontents whose temper Peter Balde's hot-headed words had inflamed. Awed by the presence of their leaders they still held themselves in check, but the Walloons, from their place of retreat, crowded together and terrified, saw many a glowing face, distorted by the passion to kill, many an eye fixed upon them with glowering hatred and an obvious longing for revenge.

Then Mark called out:

"Now then, friends: in two hours' time the tyrant will have twelve thousand troops massed against us. We have two thousand well-trained soldiers within our guild-houses who are idle at this moment. Here are five hundred of them–the others are close by! with their help we can crush the tyrant–fight him till we conquer, and treat him as he would have treated us. Here is your revenge for his insults! Get your brothers to forswear their allegiance and to fight by your side!"

A gasp went right through the hall which now was packed closely with men–the five hundred Walloon prisoners huddled together at one end, and some four thousand men of Ghent filling every corner of the vast arcaded hall. In the very midst of them all Mark van Rycke hoisted up on the shoulders of his friends–with gleaming eyes and quivering voice–awaited their reply.

The malcontents were the first to make their voices heard:

"These traitors," they shouted, "the paid mercenaries of Alva! Art crazy, van Rycke?"

"The Spanish woman hath cajoled thee!" some of them exclaimed with a curse.

"Or offered thee a bribe from the tyrant," cried others.

"We'll hang thee along with the prisoners if thou darest to turn against us," added Peter Balde spitefully.

"Hang me then, friends, an ye list," he said with a loud laugh, "but let me speak while ye get the gallows ready. Walloons," he added, turning to the prisoners who were regarding him with utter bewilderment, in which past terror still held sway, "ye are our kith and kin. Together we have groaned under the most execrable tyrant the world has even known. To-day I offer you the power to strike one blow at the tyrant–a blow from which he will never recover–a blow which will help you to win that which every Netherlander craves for: Liberty! Will ye help us to strike that blow and cover yourselves with glory?"

"Aye! aye!" came from the Walloons with one stupendous cry of hope and of relief.

"Will you fight with us?"

"Yes!"

"Die with us?"

"Yes!"

"For the freedom of the Netherlands?"

"For Liberty!" they cried.

But all the while murmurings were going on among the Flemings. Their hatred of the Walloons who had borne arms against their own native land and for its subjugation under the heel of an alien master was greater almost than their hatred against the Spaniards.

"The Walloons? Horror!" they shouted, even whilst Mark was infusing some of his own ardent enthusiasm into the veins of those five hundred prisoners. "Shame on thee, van Rycke!" whilst one man who has remained nameless to history cried out loudly: "Traitor!"

"Aye! traitor thou!" retorted van Rycke, "who wouldst prefer the lust of killing to that of victory!"

"Burghers of Ghent," he continued, "in the name of our sacred Motherland, I entreat you release these men; let me have them as soldiers under our banner ... let me have them as brothers to fight by our side ... you would shed their blood and steep your souls in crime, let them shed theirs for Liberty, and cover themselves with glory!"

"Yes! yes!" came from the leaders and from the phalanx of fighting men who stood closest to their hero.

"Yes! yes! release them! Let them fight for us!"

The call was taken back and echoed and re-echoed until the high-vaulted roof rang with the enthusiastic shouts.

"Walloons, will you fight with us?" they asked.

"To the death!" replied the prisoners.

"One country, one people, one kindred," rejoined Mark with solemn earnestness, "henceforth there will be neither Flemings nor Walloons, just Netherlanders standing shoulder to shoulder to crush the tyrant of us all!"

"Netherlanders! Orange and Liberty!" cried Walloons and Flemings in unison.

"Give them back their own arms, provosts," commanded Mark, "our untrained men have not known how to use them! and follow me, friends! We have not gathered our reinforcements together yet. In half an hour we shall have two thousand brothers under our flag!"

"Long live Leatherface! To arms, brothers!" were the last shouts which rang through the hall, ere Mark van Rycke led his followers away to the nearest guild-house and then to the next, where two thousand

Walloon prisoners were by the magic of his patriotism and his enthusiasm transformed into two thousand friends.

VI

Once more the roar of artillery and of musketry fills the air. It is long before the evening Angelus has begun to ring, but from far away the news has come to every captain at the city gates that reinforcements are on the way from Dendermonde. No one can respect a truce which hid the blackest perfidy ever perpetrated by a tyrannical master against a brave people. As soon as the news has filtrated into the heart of the city the Orangists rush to their arms, reinforced by two thousand trained troops; their battle cry becomes triumphant.

"Netherlands! Orange! and Liberty!" resounds defiantly from end to end of the city.

The besieging force rush the Kasteel! they sow the open tract of ground around the moat with their heroic dead; again and again they rush for the breach: culverins and falconets upon the ramparts are useless after a while: and a shower of heavy stones falls upon the plucky assailants. There are five hundred Walloon bowmen now who know how to shoot straight, and some musketeers who vie with the Spaniards for precision. They cover the advance of the halberdiers and the pikemen, who return to the charge with the enthusiasm born of renewed hope.

The Brügge gate has fallen, the Waalpoort is in the insurgents' hands: Captain Serbelloni at the Braepoort is hard pressed, and up in the Meeste Toren of the Kasteel Alva paces up and down like a caged tiger.

"Bracamonte or nightfall!" he cries with desperate rage, for he cannot understand why the Dendermonde troops are detained.

"Surely that rabble has not seized all the gates!" Twice he has ordered a sortie! twice the moat has received a fresh shower of dead. The breach has become wider: the Orangist halberdiers are fighting foot by foot up the walls. They have succeeded in throwing their bridge made of pikes and lances across the moat, and soon they are crossing in their hundreds.

"Heavens above, how come they to be so numerous?"

Captain de Avila has been severely wounded: three younger captains have been killed. The Orangist falconets—a light piece of artillery and not easy to use—works incessantly upon the breach. Alva himself is everywhere. His doublet and hose are torn, too, his breast-plate and tassets are riddled with arrow-shot; he bleeds profusely from

216

the hand. His face is unrecognisable beneath a covering of smoke and grime. Rage and fear have made him hideous—not fear of personal danger, for to this he is wholly indifferent, but fear of defeat, of humiliation, of the heavy reprisals which that contemptible rabble will exact.

He insults his soldiers and threatens them in turn; he snatches musket or crossbow, directs, leads, commands ... and sees his wildest hopes shattered one by one.

The din and confusion from the city itself is hardly heard above the awful pandemonium which reigns in and around the besieged Kasteel. The Vleeshhuis on the Schelde is a mass of flames; the roof suddenly falls in with a terrific crash which seems to shake the very earth to its depths: there is not a single window left in the Meeste-Toren, and the rooms, as well as the yard below, are littered with broken glass.

"We have no more balls left, Magnificence," reports the captain in charge of the artillery. "What must we do?"

"Do?" cries the Duke of Alva fiercely. "Throw yourselves into the moat or get the musketeers to turn their muskets against you; for of a certainty you will be massacred within the hour."

Inside the city it is hell let loose. Fighting—hand to hand, pike to pike—goes on in every street, on every bridge, under every doorway, aye! even beneath the cathedral porch. The doors of the houses have all been broken open and men who are wounded and exhausted crawl under them for shelter and safety. The women and children had all been ordered to go inside their own homes before the first battle cry of the Orangists rang out; a goodly number of them, however, took refuge in the churches, and there were defended by companies of Walloons posted at the doors.

The bridges are fought for inch by inch; when at last they fell into the hands of the Orangists they are destroyed one by one.

Hell let loose indeed! Desperate men fighting for freedom against a tyrant who has never known defeat. The evening Angelus was never rung on that Lord's Day—the feast of the Holy Redeemer—but at the hour when day first fades into evening Mark van Rycke—superb, undaunted and glowing now with the ardour of victory—leads the final assault on the Kasteel.

"Netherlanders! For Liberty!" he cries.

A stone has hit his shoulder, there is a huge cut across his face, the sleeve has been torn right out of his doublet, his bare arm and the hand which wields an unconquered sword gleam like metal in the fast gathering twilight.

"To the breach!" he calls, and is the first to scramble down the declivity of the moat and on to the heap of masonry which fills the moat here to the top of the bank.

An arrow aimed at his head pierces his right arm, a stone hurled from above falls at his feet and raises a cloud of dust which blinds him, a heavy fragment hits him on the head; he stumbles and falls backwards, down to the brink of the moat.

"Never mind me," he calls, "for Liberty, Netherlanders! The Kasteel is yours! hold on!"

He has managed to hold on for dear life to the rough stones on the declivity, crawling along the top of the bank to escape being trampled on by the pikemen. The latter have a hot time at the breach: the Spanish musketeers, under the Duke of Alva's own eyes, are firing with remarkable accuracy and extraordinary rapidity, whilst from the ramparts the shower of heavy stones makes deadly havoc: twice the Walloons have given ground—they are led by Laurence van Rycke now—who twice returns to the charge.

Mark struggles to his feet: "Hold on, Walloons! the Kasteel is ours," he cries.

And while the Walloons continue the desperate fighting at the breach, he gathers together a company of Flemish swordsmen, the pick of his little army, those who have stuck closely to him throughout the past two days, who have fought every minute, who have been decimated, lost their provosts and their captains, but have never once cried "Halt!" and never thought of giving in.

A hundred or so of them are all that is left: they carry their sword in their right hand and a pistol in their left. They follow Mark round the walls to where the moat melts into the wide tract of morass which surrounds the north-east side of the Kasteel.

The shadow from the high walls falls across the marshy ground, the men move round silently whilst behind them at the breach and on the bridge the noise of musketry and falling masonry drowns every other sound.

Now the men halt, and still in silence they strip to their skins; then with their pistols in their right hand and their sword between their teeth they plunge ankle deep into the mud. They are men of Ghent every one of them—men of the Low Countries who know their morasses as mariners know the sea: they know how to keep their foothold in these slimy tracks, where strangers would inevitably be sucked into a hideous grave.

They make their way to the foot of the wall, they move like ghosts now, and are well-nigh waist deep in the mud. Night closes in rapidly round them: behind them the sky is suffused with the crimson reflection of an autumnal sunset. Their arms, chests and backs are shiny with sweat, their hot breath comes and goes rapidly with excitement and the scent of danger which hovers behind them in that yawning morass and ahead of them on the parapet of those walls.

"Victory waits for you, my men," says Mark in a commanding

voice, "up on yonder wall. Whoever is for Orange and for Liberty, follow me!"

Then he starts to climb, and one by one the men follow. What atoms they look up on those high walls, crawling, creeping, scrambling, with hands and knees and feet clinging to the unevenness in the masonry, or scraps of coarse grass that give them foothold: like ants crawling up a heap–on they go–their bare backs reflect the crimson glow of the sun. Mark, their hero, leads the way, his torn arm and lacerated shoulder leave a trail of blood upon the stones.

At the breach the Walloons must be hard pressed, for cries of triumph follow each volley from the Spanish musketry.

"On, on, Netherlanders! for Orange and Liberty!"

Now Mark has reached the top: his arm is over the parapet, then his knee. The look-out man has seen him: he shoulders his musket to give the alarm, but before he can fire Mark is on him, and three more Flemings now have scrambled over the wall. This portion of the Kasteel is never seriously guarded: the morass is thought to be impassable, and forms the only guard on the northeast wall; but these men of Ghent have conquered the morass and they are on the walls, and have overpowered the look-out men ere these have had time to scream.

Naked, sweating, bleeding at hands and knees, they look like wraiths from some inferno down below. They rush down helter-skelter into the castle yard. The Spanish musketeers caught in their rear whence they never expected attack, down their weapons and run with a mad Sauve qui peut to the shelter of the Meeste-Toren. The Walloons– not understanding what has happened–see the Spaniards running and seize the lucky moment. Laurence van Rycke leads them through the breach, and they rush into the yard with pikes and halberds fixed and fill it suddenly with their cry of triumph: then they fight their way round to the gatehouse and lower the bridge, and the Flemings in their turn come pouring into the Kasteel.

Within ten minutes every Spaniard inside the Kasteel has laid down his arms: the stronghold is in the hands of the Orangists, and Mark van Rycke up on the iron balcony outside the Duke of Alva's council chamber, surrounded by his naked stalwarts, demands the surrender of the Lieutenant-Governor of the Netherlands in the name of Orange and of Liberty.

Then without a sigh or a groan he throws up his arms, and those who are nearest to him are only just in time to catch him ere he falls.

CHAPTER XIX

THE HOUR OF VICTORY

I

To the women and children shut up in the different churches and in the houses throughout the city, during those terrible hours whilst their husbands, brothers, sons were making their last desperate stand, it was indeed hell let loose; for while the men were doing, they could only wait and pray. It was impossible for them even to wander out to try and help the wounded or to seek amongst the dead for the one dear face, the mirror of all joy and happiness. They all sat or knelt huddled up together, their children closely held in their arms, murmuring those vague words of comfort, of surmise, of hope and of fear which come mechanically to the lips when every sense is lulled into a kind of torpor with the terrible imminence of the danger and the overwhelming power of grief.

The danger in the houses was greater than in the churches, for everywhere the horrible concussion of artillery and the crash of falling masonry broke the windows and shook the floors. But many women have that same instinct which causes the beasts of the forests to hide within their lair; they feel that they would rather see their home fall in about their heads, than watch its destruction from a safer distance. Clémence van Rycke refused to leave her house when first Laurence received Lenora's warning of the impending catastrophe; she refused to leave it now when her sons were face to face with death and any moment a stray cannon ball might bring the walls down with a crash.

She sat in the high-backed chair in the small withdrawing-room where, less than a week ago, the first card was played in that desperate game for human lives which was finding its climax at this hour; she sat quite still—staring into the empty hearth with that stolidity peculiar to these women of the North—and which is only another, calmer, form of courage. The High-Bailiff, sullen and silent, sat close to the table with his head buried in his hands. Since his return from his humiliating errand this afternoon he had not spoken a word to anyone—he believed that the Orangist cause was doomed, and both his sons certain of death. What happened to him after that he really did not care.

Pierre and Jeanne sat in the hall together, quietly telling their beads. The din outside was deafening, and the evening hour was slowly creeping on—day yielded to twilight; a brilliant sunset lit up for a while the desolation of an entire city, then sank into a blood-hued horizon, adding its own lurid light to the crimson glow of burning buildings.

And as the veils of night fell more heavily over the city, gradually

220

the dismal sounds of cannon and musketry were stilled. Pierre came in after a while carrying a lamp.

"Firing has ceased," he said, "men are running down the streets shouting that the Kasteel is in our hands and that the Duke of Alva has surrendered to Leatherface!"

He put the lamp down and prepared to go, for Clémence and the High-Bailiff have made no comment on the joyful news—perhaps it has failed to reach their dulled senses, perhaps they do not believe it. At any rate, what is victory to them if two brave sons have fallen for its sake?

But already the cries through the streets become more insistent and more sure; men and women run hither and thither up and down the Nieuwe Straat, and as Pierre stands by the open door, peering curiously out into the gloom, people shout to him as they rush by:

"Van Rycke has seized the Kasteel! The Duke of Alva is a prisoner in our hands."

Clémence hears the cries. She can no longer doubt her ears. "Mark? Laurence?" she calls out. "Where are they?"

The High-Bailiff rouses himself from his apathy. "I will go to the Town House," he says, "and will be back with news."

"News of Mark—and of Laurence," cries the mother.

The High-Bailiff goes, and she remains alone in the narrow room, with just the feeble light of the lamp upon her pale face and trembling hands. Now and then still, right through the night, a terrific crash shakes the house to its foundations, or a sudden lurid light flares upwards to the sky—roofs are still falling in, crumbling ruins still burst into flames, but firing and clash of steel have ceased, and from the various churches the peals of bells send their triumphant call through the night.

The hours go by. It is nigh on ten o'clock now. The High-Bailiff has not yet returned, but Laurence has just come back—wounded and exhausted but full of the glorious victory.

"Where is Mark?" queries the mother.

"Mark is hurt ... but he will be here anon," says the boy, "the men have made a stretcher for him—he would not be tended at the Kasteel—he begged to be brought home—oh! mother dear, how we must love him after this!"

Clémence hastily gives orders that Messire Mark's room be made ready for him at once. Jeanne, buxom and capable, is rendered supremely happy by this task.

"Mother dear," whispers Laurence, "next to Mark himself, we all owe our salvation to Lenora."

He has no time to say more, even though Clémence's face has hardened at mention of that name which she abhors; for Pierre has just come running in breathless and trembling with excitement.

221

"Mevrouw," he stammers, "it is the noble lady ... the Spanish lady ... it is..."

Before Laurence could further question him, he has uttered a cry of surprise, which is echoed by one of horror from Clémence. Lenora was standing under the lintel of the door. Clémence rose from her chair as if moved by a spring and stood up, rigid, and with arm raised, pointing straight to the door:

"Go!" she commanded sternly.

But Lenora advanced slowly into the room. She was whiter than the ruff at her throat, her black mantle hung round her in heavy folds, but the hood had fallen back from her head, and her golden hair with the yellow light of the lamp falling full upon it looked like a gleaming aureole which made her eyes appear wonderfully dark by contrast and her beauty more ethereal than it had been before. Laurence gazed on her in speechless wonder, but Clémence, full of hatred for the woman whom she believed to be the author of all the misery of the past few days, still pointed to the door, and sternly, relentlessly, in a voice which quivered with the passion of intense hatred, she reiterated her command:

"Go!"

"They are bringing Mark home," said Lenora quietly; "he is wounded ... perhaps to death ... I could not get to hear ... but when he opens his eyes he will ask for me. I cannot go unless he sends me away."

"They are bringing Mark home," assented the mother, "and 'tis I who will tend him. Never shall thy treacherous hand touch my son..."

"Mother," broke in Laurence firmly, "she is Mark's wife and she has saved us all."

Clémence gave a loud sob and fell back in her chair. Laurence tried in vain to comfort her. But Lenora waited quietly until the worst of Clémence's paroxysm of tears had passed away, then she said with the same patience and gentleness:

"I know, mevrouw, that from the first I was an intruder in your house. I, too, have oft in the last few miserable days longed in vain that Mark and I had never met. But do you not think, mevrouw, that our destinies are beyond our ken? that God ordains our Fate, and merely chooses His tools where He desires?"

"And Satan, too, chooses his tools," murmured Clémence through her tears. "Oh go! go! I beg of you to go," she added with sudden passionate appeal; "cannot you see that the sight of you must be torture to us all?"

"Will you let me stay until I have seen Mark?" said Lenora calmly, "and then I will go."

"I will not let you see him," protested Clémence with the obstinacy of the weak. "I would not allow a spy like you to come near him ... aye! a spy ... an assassin mayhap ... how do I know that you are

222

not an emissary of our tyrants? how do I know that beneath your cloak you do not hold a dagger?..."

Laurence was trying his best to pacify his mother and throwing pathetic looks of appeal to Lenora the while, whilst the girl herself was bravely trying to hold herself in check. But at this last cruel taunt she uttered a cry of pain, like a poor wild creature that has been hurt to death. In a moment she was across the room, down on her knees beside the old woman and holding Clémence's trembling hands imprisoned in her own.

"Hush! Hush!" she implored wildly, "you must not say that ... you must not ... Heavens above, have you not realised that when I acted as I did, I did so because I believed God Himself had shown me the way? You call me base and vile ... I swear to you by all that I hold most sacred that I would gladly die a thousand deaths to undo the work of the past few days ... you speak of an assassin's dagger ... I believed that my cousin Ramon was murdered ... foully and in the dark ... by the man who was known as Leatherface ... my father made me swear that I would avenge Ramon's death ... what could I do? what could I do? I believed that God was guiding me ... I spied upon you, I know ... I found out your secrets and gave them to my father ... but he had commanded me and I had no one else in the world ... no one ... only my father ... and I believed in him as I believe in God...."

Her voice broke in a sob, her head fell forward upon her hands and those of the older woman, and a pitiable moan of pain came from her overburdened heart. Laurence, with his head buried in his hands, would have given his life to spare her all this misery. But Clémence said nothing—she did not repulse the girl nor did she draw her to her heart; whether she still mistrusted her or not it were impossible to say, certain it is that she listened, and that words of hatred no longer rose to her lips.

"You will not let me see Mark," continued Lenora, trying to speak more calmly, "you are afraid that I would go to him as an enemy ... a spy ... an assassin.... Ah! you have chosen the weapon well wherewith to punish me! An enemy, ye gods!—I who would give the last drop of blood in my veins to help him at this hour, I who love him with every fibre of my heart, with every aspiration of my soul! ... Don't you understand? cannot you understand that he has forced his way right into my very being, that I have left my people, my father, to come to him ... to warn him, to help him ... to be with him in the hour of danger.... Let me stay.... Let me be with him! ... Cannot you see that Love for him is all that I live for now?..."

She had ceased speaking, and over the high, oak-panelled room there fell a silence which soon became oppressive. A few moments ago while Lenora was pouring out her heart in wild words of passionate longing, Clémence and Laurence had suddenly uttered a cry—half of horror and half of joy—a cry which was quickly suppressed and which the girl did not hear. Now the tension on her nerves was suddenly relaxed and she broke down utterly–physically and mentally she felt like one who has received a blow with a pole-axe and is only just alive–no longer sentient, hardly suffering. She was crouching on the ground with her head on the older woman's knee, a pathetic picture of hopelessness. She felt indeed as if this earth could hold no greater suffering than what she endured now–to have dreamed for one brief while that she had helped the man she loved in the hour of his greatest danger, and then to be made to feel that she was still an enemy in the sight of all his people.

She lost count of time, it might have been but a few seconds that she knelt there broken-hearted; it might have been a cycle of years; the din from the streets outside, the bustle inside the house only reached her ears like sounds that come in a dream. A kind of torpor had fallen over the broken-hearted girl's senses and mercifully saved her from further pain. She closed her eyes and semi-consciousness wrapped her in a kindly embrace. Semi-consciousness or a happy dream. She could not tell. All that she knew was that suddenly all misery and all suffering fell away from her; that an invisible presence was in the room which was like that of the angel of peace, and that strong, kind arms held her closely, so that she no longer felt that an awful chasm yawned before her and that she was falling into a hideous abyss where there was neither hope nor pardon. Of course it must have been a dream–such dreams as come to the dying who have suffered much and see the end of all their woe in a prescient glimpse of heaven–for it seemed to her that the kind grey eyes which she loved were looking on her now, that they smiled on her with infinite tenderness and infinite understanding, and that the lips which she had longed to kiss whispered gentle, endearing words in her ear.

"It is your love, Madonna, which led me to victory. Did I not say that with it as my shield I could conquer the universe?"

"Mark," she murmured, "you are hurt?"

"Not much, dear heart," he replied with that quaint laugh of his which suddenly turned this delicious dream into exquisite reality, "kind hands have tended me and gave me some clean clothing. I would have had you in my arms ere now, but was too dirty an object to appear before you."

Then the laughter died out from his eyes, they became intent, searching, desperately anxious.

"Madonna," he whispered–and he who for three days had faced every kind of danger, trembled now with apprehension–"what you said to my mother–a moment ago–did you mean it?"

"Your love, Mark," she murmured in reply, "is all that I live for now."

Then he folded her in his arms once more.

"Mother, dear," he said, "you must love her too. My whole happiness hangs upon her kiss."

EPILOGUE

Many there are who hold to the belief that the death of Alva would have saved the unfortunate Netherlanders many more months of woe and oppression at his hands, and that mayhap it would have deterred the royal despot over in Madrid from further acts of perfidious tyranny.

Therefore Mark van Rycke–the responsible leader of the successful insurrection of Ghent–has often been blamed for his leniency to a man who–if he had been victorious–would not have spared a single woman or child in the city.

With the right and wrongs of that contention this chronicle hath no concern. Mark van Rycke led the men of Ghent to victory, and having done that he fell sick from wounds and exhaustion, and after being hastily tended by his friends, he was taken home where for many days he hovered between life and death.

It was the civic dignitaries–the High-Bailiff, the Aldermen and Sheriffs of the Keure who assumed the responsibility of dealing with the tyrant, and they remained true apparently to their principles of conciliation and of loyalty, for within two days of their heroic and desperate stand for liberty and while the ruins of their beautiful city were still smouldering, the men of Ghent had the mortification of seeing the Duke of Alva ride–humiliated but unscathed–out of the town.

Just as fifty years ago the town of Brüges held the Archduke Maximilian, King of the Romans, a prisoner till he ordered the withdrawal of all foreign troops from their gates, so did the men of Ghent now exact the same undertaking from the Duke of Alva.

For the moment Ghent was freed from the immediate danger of annihilation, and the departure of Alva from Belgium less than a year later saved her perhaps altogether from the fate of many of her sister cities; certain it is that the High-Bailiff and the older burghers extracted from their prisoners–among whom was señor de Vargas and several members of the Blood Council–concessions and privileges for which they had clamoured in vain for half a century; but beyond that the tyrant was allowed to go free, and against this decision of their magistrates and their Griet Mannen the heroes of the insurrection did not raise a protest. Perhaps they had suffered too much to thirst for active revenge.

END